The explosion . . .

Mahan slammed forward, pitching twenty-eight degrees down at the bow. The CDC sailors who had neglected to strap themselves in were flung away from their consoles. The screams of the injured, the harsh snap of electronics sparking as negative and positive leads met in ways the designers never intended, the all-encompassing boom of the explosion. The lights went out, along with the green glow from the radar screens and the large-screen display.

Also by C. A. Mobley

RITES OF WAR
RULES OF COMMAND

CODE
OF
CONFLICT

C. A. MOBLEY

BERKLEY BOOKS, NEW YORK

CODE OF CONFLICT

A Berkley Book / published by arrangement with the author

PRINTING HISTORY
Berkley edition / October 1999

The Penguin Putnam Inc. World Wide Web site address is
http://www.penguinputnam.com

ISBN: 0-425-17108-6

BERKLEY®
Berkley Books are published by The Berkley Publishing Group,
a division of Penguin Putnam Inc.,
375 Hudson Street, New York, New York 10014.
BERKLEY and the "B" logo
are trademarks belonging to Penguin Putnam Inc.

PRINTED IN THE UNITED STATES OF AMERICA

10 9 8 7 6 5 4 3 2 1

ANALYSIS

I

USS *MAHAN*, FIFTEEN MILES OFF THE COAST OF BANGLADESH

He slept with his ship more often than with his wife, but he knew well the sounds that each made at night. Emily: the gentle rhythm of her breathing, murmurs born of nightmares, the occasional snort or cough. USS *Mahan:* the sea against her hull, water running through pipes, the faint hard hammer of pumps kicking in, the ever-present whine of gas turbines, the cyclic rhythm of the shaft. Predictable sounds, even the ones that were intermittent, as familiar as his own heartbeat and just as reassuring.

Navy Commander Jack Lockridge lay curled on his side with eyes still closed, and listened. His hand clutched a corner of the scratchy gray blanket, holding it and the stiff cotton sheets immobile and snug against his neck as protection against the air-conditioning. He held his breath, trying to hear if the sound of the ship had changed.

Change was dangerous. As commanding officer of USS *Mahan,* he was responsible for every action onboard the cruiser, whether or not he was physically present, whether or not he approved of the action.

Engineering? No. I'd know that by now.

4 C. A. MOBLEY

The background hum of the twin jet turbines radiated throughout the steel hull, reverberating up the steel frame of his bed. A bilge pump was on line somewhere below, contributing an awkward *thump-thump* counterpoint. He classified the rest of the intermittent groans, hisses, and whines, identifying each source, then finally opened his eyes. Nothing, other than the normal sounds of a healthy ship at sea.

Combat? Maybe. But why?

Mahan was steaming—and an odd word, that, he reflected, since gas turbines and jet fuel had replaced boilers and superheated steam—fifteen miles off the coast of India and Bangladesh conducting Freedom of Navigation operations, exercising international rights of free transit through the territorial waters of a sovereign nation. In the last two decades, the swath of land just north of the Tropic of Cancer, the stretch that began in Iraq and ran east through Iran, Pakistan, India, and Bangladesh had been the source of most of the world's problems. FON operations were a convenient label for establishing a continuing presence in any part of the world without having to provide an explanation. While there was little hard evidence to support it, the theory was that an American presence might prevent hostilities from erupting into war. Whether or not the American forces stretched thin across the globe would be in the right place at the right time was more problematic.

The growler, his direct connection with both the bridge and the combat direction center, hung mute on the bulkhead directly over his head. If the officer of the deck or the tactical action officer had had the slightest doubts about something—*anything*—they would have called.

Maybe the weather. There was a deep tropical depression to the south, but even if it formed into a typhoon, it wouldn't be in their area for days. Besides, his standing night orders required the officer of the deck to notify him if the barometer changed by more than two-tenths of an inch or the wind by fifteen knots.

He rolled over, tried to slip back into sleep. It evaded him, chased away by the inchoate warning that had woken him up five minutes earlier. Finally, he gave up.

He reached for the khaki shirt and pants draped over the chair. No point in ruining his dark-adapted eyes, although he hadn't yet decided whether to visit the bridge, Combat, or Engineering first. How many times had he gotten dressed in the dark, waking while under way for some reason that his consciousness refused to recognize?

Most of the time for no reason.

Most of the time.

He retrieved the reading glasses from the table next to his bed, hesitated, then tucked them into his pants pocket. In the last year, message traffic had become damned near unreadable without holding it away from his face. Presbyopia, the ophthalmologist had said, a normal, expected sign of aging.

Well, damned if he had to like it. Not the glasses, or the vanity—*denial*—that made him avoid using them. Refusing to wear them was as oddly vain as the balding man combing thin strands of hair across a shining pate, hoping that the illusion would be sufficient.

He debated stopping by the wardroom for a cup of coffee, then decided against it. Caffeine wouldn't help. Walking the ship would. He'd go back to bed after reassuring his subconscious that nothing was wrong.

By the time he was dressed, he'd decided to sacrifice his dark-adapted eyes to habit. He started his rounds just as he had when he was a junior officer, beginning with Engineering. Two decks down, aft past the wardroom, the clean white hatch entrance into Main Control was dogged shut. He undogged it, jerked it back to overcome the slight negative pressure differential, and stepped over the watertight combing.

Lieutenant (junior grade) Teddy Threlkeld, *Mahan*'s damage control Assistant was EOOW—engineering officer of the watch—looked up and came to his feet immediately. "Good morning, sir. Something I can help you with?" A sailor with a sound-powered phone slung around his neck watched for a moment then keyed the button and quietly reported to his counterpart on the bridge that the captain was in Main Control.

Lockridge felt the young officer reach out mentally to the rest of the watch section, prodding them into alertness. Of course, they were all awake. Not at their sharpest, not at this hour of the night, caught between the demands of their normal daily routines and the dog watch from 0200 to 0400 in the morning.

Lockridge waved him back into his seat. "Just taking a look around. How's everything going?"

"Everything's fine, sir." Threlkeld ran quickly through the engineering configuration of the ship, detailing which turbine was on line, which emergency diesel in standby, the electrical switch boxes and fuel pumps, and the other myriad details that constitute a standard oncoming watch brief.

Lockridge could hear the uneasiness in Threlkeld's voice. When you were a junior officer, if you weren't on watch or eating or answering the CHENG's—chief engineer's—questions or catching up on engineering logs or periodic maintenance schedules or enlisted evaluations or studying for surface warfare officer qualification or eating—you slept. You didn't get up and roam around the ship, not unless something was wrong. To Threlkeld, that meant that the captain's presence in Engineering at this time of the night meant that Threlkeld or someone in his division had fucked something up.

At least that's what it would have meant with *Mahan*'s last captain. Commander Steve Naves, Lockridge's predecessor, had been of the "eat your young" school of surface warfare training. Lockridge winced, remembering the tedious week of turnover time he'd had with Naves.

Threlkeld had been onboard *Mahan* for eighteen months. No doubt that Naves had hunted Threlkeld down for a serious ass chewing more than once on a midwatch. A hell of a waste, if the asshole had permanently screwed up this young officer. There was more to command at sea than throwing your weight around and looking good to your type commander—there was the deadly serious job of training the men and women that would someday stand in your shoes.

And there were better ways to do it than holding public executions like Naves did. You had to teach them the skills you'd expect them to have later as more senior officers. Let them make mistakes under your watchful eyes, where you could correct them before they endangered the ship, coach them into sound habits of independent thinking and decision-making. That was the way you grew the kind of leaders the Navy wanted.

Lockridge let his eyes roam over the compartment, checking the green lights and reading gauges, his eyes confirming what his ears and instincts already knew. "Everything looks good. Anything I need to know?" There wouldn't be, at least nothing major.

Threlkeld shook his head. "No, sir."

The hatch to Engineering slammed back against the bulkhead. A fireman apprentice, the second most junior rate on the ship, vaulted over the combing and landed in main control.

"Heeee's back!" Alarm and embarrassment immediately replaced the exuberant expression on the sailor's face. "Sorry—Captain, I didn't know—I mean—"

"Fireman Irving likes the midwatch, Captain," Threlkeld observed. "He volunteers for the sounding and security watch every chance he gets."

Lockridge studied the pale, thin face, black hair clipped Marine short, trying to recall the details of his standard welcome-aboard interview with Irving. Decent test scores, some civilian experience in auto mechanics, an interest in seeing the world outside of—Kentucky, that was it. He'd grown up in a small mining town, gone into the Navy like his dad had. "Why is that? The midwatches, I mean."

Irving stared down at the deck. Lockridge felt a flash of annoyance—did the entire crew have to act like whipped dogs every time he talked to one of them? He'd been onboard for two months now, long enough for them to begin to recover from the Naves syndrome.

"It's quiet, sir," Irving said as the silence lengthened.

"You ever get bored?" Lockridge asked. The sounding and security rover moved continually around the ship's lower levels, checking with lead plumbs attached to chains that the water level had not risen in the bilges and other unoccupied spaces. He was also on alert to anything out of the ordinary, the smell of fuel where it shouldn't be, other changes that might presage danger.

"Sometimes. But it's like you're doing something important. You get so's you know where everything is, what it sounds like." Irving glanced up, a momentary flash of pride on his face. "Caught an air compressor starting to go bad last night. It started making this weird sound, you know?"

Lockridge nodded. "That happens. You get so that stuff will wake you up at night. That's why I'm up right now—thought I heard something out of the ordinary."

Fireman Irving looked up from the deck and shook his head. "Wasn't down here, Captain. I'd know it by now."

The certainty and man-to-man tone in Irving's voice both amused and gratified Lockridge. It just took time, that was all. It was already his ship—and soon it'd be his crew, too. "That's what I think, too." He clapped Irving lightly on the shoulder. "Must be something topside I heard. You keep up the good work."

The sense of foreboding still nagged him. Lockridge headed back up the ladder toward CDC.

The combat direction center was the dark, cold heart of the ship. It was located below the waterline, protected by the exterior layers of honeycombed compartments and the Kevlar coating on the weatherdecks of the ship. Red overhead lights lit the space and reduced the glare off radar repeaters and status boards.

Lieutenant Commander Greg Mallard stood as Lockridge entered the compartment, clearly forewarned by Engineering that the captain was on the prowl. One ear of his headset was shoved back so that he could hear the compartment noises, most particularly the sound of the security door opening. "G' morning, Captain."

"Morning, Ops. Couldn't sleep." Lockridge felt a momentary flash of irritation at his own need to offer up an excuse for the unannounced visit, at the damage Naves had done to this crew. *Mahan* was *his* ship—if he wanted to tour CCD every thirty minutes, he would. "Anything going on?"

Mallard was *Mahan*'s operations officer and stood watch as tactical action officer, the TAO. A big, corn-fed raw-boned ex–Naval Academy linebacker, Mallard was on his fourth sea tour, his second rotation as a department head. He'd reported onboard *Mahan* only two weeks before they'd deployed and had already qualified as TAO. Fast, but not extraordinary—not for an officer who'd done his first division officer tour as an ensign onboard *Mahan* as combat systems officer. Mallard was from Iowa, and retained the blond-haired, blue-eyed innocent look that always reminded Lockridge of Dennis the Menace.

"Everything's quiet." Mallard reached down, rolled the trackball around to circle a cluster of contacts with his cursor on the large-screen tactical display dominating the front of the compartment. "There've been a few ghost contacts, but nothing as bad as it was yesterday. I turned to check a couple of them out, and it was classic—nothing there, the radar contact maintaining constant distance and bearing from us. It's just the inversion playing hell with the radar. Bunch of merchants, fishing boats, and two Indian destroyers. The *Boganddiya* is still headed south and the intell summaries say she's probably redeploying to the Indian Ocean. There's supposed to be a submarine in company with her, but nobody's seen it. We're making sure the lookouts keep an eye out for it."

Lockridge nodded. More than half of the submarine intelligence reports they routinely received turned out later to be erroneous. Until someone got a Mark I Mod O eyeball on a periscope, it was nothing to disrupt their freedom of navigation operations.

While FON operations were tolerated by most seagoing

nations, the presence of India's premier aircraft carrier had made each evolution additionally worrisome. Even exercising FON rights didn't mean forgoing normal rules of navigation, and an aircraft carrier conducting flight operations still had the right-of-way over a smaller ship. "They still sending their fighters over for a look-see?"

"No, sir, not for the last five hours. She's reaching the edge of her unrefueled flight range. We did have a P-3C come out to take a look at us, but she stayed well clear. Looked like just a normal surveillance flight. We're well outside the twelve-mile limit."

Lockridge turned back to study the tactical display. The LINK picture combined with the Joint Maritime Combat Information System, or JMCIS, displayed the location, course, and speed of every military unit deployed in every part of the world. Had he zoomed the picture out, he could have reviewed the disposition of forces off the coast of Argentina in as much detail as the Indian destroyers off his quarter.

Most of India's naval forces were bunched up along her western coast, supposedly for a routine naval operation. U.S. intelligence sources indicated it was probably in preparation for one of their biannual conflicts with Pakistan. The two nations had been beating each other bloody every two years for decades. The rest of the battle group heading for the Gulf would have to watch out for it, but as long as *Mahan* was on India's east coast conducting FON operations, it wouldn't be a problem for them.

"Who else is in our LINK?" The LINK was the information web that served all units in a given area, usually by high-frequency or satellite communications. Even aircraft, submarines, and shore establishments could enter the LINK, contributing their contact data to a common tactical picture. Net Control—*Mahan*, in this case—evaluated the reliability of each individual contact detection, whether from sonar, radar, or other sensors, correlating and merging all sensors into a single display that was then retransmitted to the rest of the participating units, or PU's. Everyone fought off the same picture.

Mallard's fingers tapped out a command on his keyboard. A screen of figures and letters flashed up on an auxiliary display. "The usual lurkers, sir, in receive-only mode. Seventh Fleet, PACFLEET, the War College. That's all that's showing up on our data rolls."

Computer technology and satellite connectivity made the LINK picture from *Mahan* accessible to anyone with a desktop computer, a modem, and the right crypto gear to monitor the classified circuit. Seventh Fleet and PACFLEET would be integrating his LINK broadcast with other nets, displaying a worldwide, virtually real-time picture of all their areas of responsibility. The War College monitored some nets to extract lessons learned, shortening the learning curve on new technology and tactics for their students returning to the fleet. Various other players drifted in and out of the net, dipping in for a quick look at *Mahan*'s LINK, but those were the big three for now. Rumor had it that the CIA and NSA could also tap into any LINK picture covertly without their PU showing up on Net Control's screen.

Lockridge nodded, studying the contacts on the screen as he listen to the TAO. Nothing to worry about, nothing at all. And with Seventh Fleet watching, too, it was doubtful he was overlooking anything in the big picture. He waited for whatever it was that had driven him from his rack to subside.

In varying degrees, a subtle sense of uneasiness had been with him since the moment they pulled away from the pier in San Diego. It had bothered Lockridge at first, as though there were some hidden incompetence lurking inside him, some weakness he had yet to discover that made him unfit. In reality, he hadn't slept well since he'd taken command of *Mahan*.

Finally, he'd chalked it up to a feeling of being constantly watched, courtesy of the new LINK upgrades. Command nerves, maybe, coupled with the nature of *Mahan*'s mission.

And what was *that,* exactly? Lockridge knew what he'd been told, but that did little to clarify the scenario. Reassuring the Bangladeshi government? Great, but it wasn't Bangladesh that was threatened—it was Pakistan. Reminding India that for all her land mass and new aircraft carriers, the U.S. ruled the oceans? True ten years ago, but not now. Keeping the Middle East guessing about U.S. intentions in this area of the world? Maybe, but how well had that worked in the last several decades? With an election year just starting, it was difficult for a mere Navy Commander to decipher the intricately overlapping rationales, political and strategic, tactical and immediate.

Not that it mattered. *Mahan* was here, and would be for the next two weeks, skirting the twelve-mile limit from India's coast for a few days, then cruising northeast to do the same to Bangladesh. No favoritism.

As though that would defuse the situation. It was like making delicate microcircuit adjustments with a sledgehammer. With all the awesome firepower that the cruiser possessed, she could still only destroy targets, not reach into the hearts and minds of the people that made war a continuing necessity in the world.

Mallard was staring off at a corner, ignoring his captain for a moment. Lockridge recognize the expression—the TAO was listening to the voices talking on the ship's interior circuit, hearing something out of place, something small and troublesome that was most probably just someone screwing up and passing the buck up the chain of command. Mallard rolled his eyes up. "Sonar, can you be a little more specific than 'something weird'? That's not much—"

The Electronic Warfare corner started chirping. Mallard turned and frowned at the corner that held the Slick-32, the AN/SLQ-32 EW gear. "Hey! What the hell are you—?" Mallard pulled his headset off and started toward the EW console. Lockridge grabbed his arm and stopped him. Another Naves legacy—a quiet Combat is a good Combat. But Mallard's place was in the center of the room at his own console. If anything was going wrong, he needed to be in a position to do something about it.

Lockridge kept his own eyes fixed on the large-screen display, the uneasiness that had roused him now solidifying into cold, clear dread. An arc of pixels in the display shimmered, flashed brilliantly in white, then resolved into a blood-red inverted V. A long speed leader protruded out from the point of the V—too long for commercial air traffic—aimed directly at *Mahan.*

The sailor manning the EW console screamed then, his warning audible even without an interior communications circuit headset on. "Missile—*Silkworm!*" The Slick-32 erupted into a high-pitched staccato warning.

"Who the hell is—*General Quarters!*" Lockridge slammed the alarm lever over to the GQ setting then slid into the seat next to Mallard's. He reached for an ICS headset, his eyes still fixed on the incoming missile symbol. "Where did it come from? Anybody see it?"

Mallard had taken half a step toward the EW when the first hard electronic gong of GQ joined the cacophony. He pivoted in mid-step, stumbled off balance, and turned to stare at the screen.

"*TAO, get your ass in gear,*" Lockridge snapped. "*All stations, standby for antiair action to starboard!*"

Mallard flinched, then brushed by him to reach his own console. Without sitting down, he reached out and twisted the close-in-weapons system key into the full automatic position, simultaneously slipping his headset back on. "All stations, TAO. CIWS in full auto, stand by for missile launch." His fingers flew over the keyboard, calling up the information on the inbound missile. *No data, no data*—he turned to say something to Lockridge then simply pointed at the screen.

One second: The weapons coordinator spewed the coffee he'd been about to swallow onto the control screen in front of him. His fingers skidded over the trackball, assigning a weapon to the incoming targets as he barked a sharp hoarse demand for release authority. He assigned two launches to the incoming missiles, while he started demanding information on the attacking platform.

Two seconds: As TAO, Mallard had full authority to launch missiles without asking permission of the CO, but the Naves legacy persisted. With his hand resting on the key that unlocked the firing circuits, Mallard hesitated.

Three seconds: Lockridge swore and reached past Mallard. The bitch box spouted demands for information from the bridge but there was no time for explanations or discussion. Or incompetence. Lockridge turned the launch authorization key, felt it click past the détente position and snap into the lock.

Four seconds: The shrill, nails-on-chalkboard squeal of a vertical-launch-tube cover popping open, followed by the high-pitched missile launch warning bell signaling personnel on the forecastle to stand clear. Thunder started deep in the belly of the cruiser, rattling consoles in CDC.

Five seconds: The ship shivered. The forward video camera showed the missile surging up, spouting flame and noxious fumes over the bow of the ship. The air track supervisor and the weapons coordinator rapped out terse launch reports.

Six seconds: The missile streaked out of sight, leaving behind only a hanging fog of exhaust and a blackened scorch mark on the weatherdecks. Another launch tube popped open.

Seven seconds: Again the shuddering boom of missile launch.

Another set? If the first two don't catch it—no, it's closing too fast. Wait two seconds, the system got it, there was enough time, there had to be, the missiles are—

The speed leader and missile symbol blinked out. "We got it, we got—!" a voice shouted, stopping abruptly as the buzzsaw whine of the close-in-weapons system sounded.

We didn't. Too late. It went sea-skimmer, down below our radar threshold. Another few seconds and we might have. Lockridge turned to stare at Mallard.

Silence.

Emily.

Lockridge clamped his hands down on the hard, smooth plastic of the chair's arms to brace himself. The radio speaker directly over his head keyed up, the odd characteristic burble of a secure transmission beginning. "*Mahan,* this is Seventh—"

Then noise, more noise than he'd ever heard inside a ship. Steel bulkheads flexed, screaming in protest. Wave after wave of it rolled over him, obliterating every other reality, a vast undifferentiated wave of power and destruction. The ship gyrated around all three axes simultaneously.

Mahan slammed forward, pitching twenty-eight degrees down at the bow. The CDC sailors who had neglected to strap themselves in were flung away from their consoles. The screams of the injured, the harsh snap of electronics sparking as negative and positive leads met in ways the designers never intended, the all-encompassing boom of the explosion. The lights went out, along with the green glow from the radar screens and the large-screen display.

That they had been hit had barely begun to penetrate. Lockridge felt himself shift into automatic, running through well-rehearsed actions and reactions to the attack without even having to give it conscious thought.

Secondary explosions now, more felt than heard, the forces slamming through the ship like cherry bombs in a garbage can.

Chaos, more complete and all encompassing than before. Lockridge howled, felt his mouth and vocal cords stretching and straining inside his throat, but no sound issued. Something in his neck snapped, and pain slashed through his throat.

The explosion. Dimly, he realized that he was deaf, but had no time to wonder whether or not it would be permanent.

Acrid smoke ate at raw tissue, filled his nostrils with the scent of scorched metal, burning electronics, and dead and dying men. It was thicker now, billowing in from all sides. He could see through it vaguely, see men and women moving like ghosts, hauling their shipmates to safety, breaking out damage control gear, frantically moving to secure power to consoles and radar components. There was no time for finesse, for the finer points of damage control. This was sheer, brute force, hacking through power cables when the switches weren't accessible, hauling burnt flesh and bleeding sailors to safety, funneling torrents of CO_2 and seawater onto equipment the moment the power was off.

Lockridge moved by reflex to the center, seeking the point from which he could control them. Hand gestures, arms flailing—they must be as deaf as he was—trying to find ways to coordinate the damage control efforts.

A hand on Lockridge's shoulder jerked him back from the center of the wrecked compartment. Lockridge twisted away, but the hand followed, clamping back down around his biceps, pulling him back from the conflagration. Lockridge turned, ready to fight his way free.

Lieutenant Commander Mallard, his face grimy and smoke-blotted, pointed toward the hatch. His mouth was moving, but it was clear that he could no more hear his own words than Lockridge could.

Too little and too late. Mallard was right. With CDC hard down, Lockridge's place was on the bridge. There was nothing he could do in CDC itself that couldn't be done by others.

Lockridge nodded his understanding and turned toward the bridge.

The watchstanders there were badly injured as well. A quartermaster lay sprawled across the chart table, blood still gouting out of his neck and onto the chart. The junior quartermaster knelt on the deck, administering CPR to a boatswain's mate. The officer of the Deck, Lieutenant Tom Groves, stood in the middle of the bridge, his eyes dull and slack. Blood coated the left side of his head, masking his eye, but he appeared to be in no immediate danger. It took Lockridge just a few seconds of watching Groves's mouth to determine that he was operating with some semblance of organization.

Lockridge grabbed a plastic board and a grease pencil, scribbled, "Keep her into the wind. Stay calm," and shoved it at the OOD. He mouthed: *I can't hear.* Groves appeared to understand him, nodded, and said something.

"What?" Lockridge shook his head.

"Who fired?" Groves was shouting now, his face red and strained.

Lockridge shook his head, pointed at the board, then darted to the bridge wing. The question of who had attacked was not as critical as two others: how badly were they hit and would there be a follow-up attack? He could answer the first question, given enough time. But with CDC gutted, he had no way of knowing what could be even now heading their way.

He stared aft at the ship. Warm air ripped past him, peeling sheets of black smoke away from the stricken ship. Smoke still guttered up from gaping holes at the waterline, pumping with a rhythm indicating that the damage control team was making some effort to desmoke.

Lockridge laid his hands flat on the skin of the ship, felt the wrongness of her heartbeat. The reassuring *thrum* of her massive gas turbines was gone, replaced by the hammering discordance of the backup emergency diesel engines. Pumps, fans, the faint background hum of electronics, the rhythmic sweeping of the radars—all silent, all wrong.

How bad is it? Is she going to stay afloat? A spasm of sick horror at that—no, not abandon ship. *Bad enough that we took a hit, maybe totaled her, but just don't let it*—He stared back aft at the ship, bile choking him. He had to get a better look at the extent of the damage. There might be a way—if anyone could find it, he could. Maybe if he climbed up to the next level, on top of the bridge. He grabbed the rungs of the ladder mounted to the side of the bridge and started to haul himself up.

A sound finally. Not a separate sound, merely dull roar at the edge of consciousness. A few separate beats, barely discernible through the static in his ears. Enough to attract his attention. He turned from a position halfway up the access ladder to the next deck and stared down at Groves.

The lieutenant's lips were moving, and there was a correlation between the movements and breaks in the static. Lockridge watched the young man's mouth move, the exaggerated

effort to form words. The conflagration aft drew his eyes back
to it. The lieutenant's fingers clutched at Lockridge's pants
leg, scrabbling to find purchase on the ironed cotton.

Lockridge kicked. Groves dodged, but Lockridge's safety
boot grazed one cheek and made him stumble back. Lockridge
scrambled on up the ladder, and turned to get a better view.

Steel twisted and Kevlar smoldered under the raging heat
of the fire. The center of the ship was a gutted, smoking hole.
Damage control crews attacked it from the stern and the bow,
forcing it back and containing the flames and toxic fumes.

Defeated, he climbed back down the ladder and stumbled
back onto the bridge.

". . . ship, sir?"

Lockridge stared at Groves, trying to puzzle out what he'd
said. In the sound coming back now, not enough to let them
understand conversation, but enough to help them make sense
of the emergency lip reading. Something about—now he had
it. His understanding was confirmed by the scribbled words
on the plastic board Groves thrust at him: *Prep for abandon
ship?*

"No. Not yet." It was odd, to feel the words leaving his
mouth, the lips shaping the sounds, vocal cords grating. Was
he understandable? Lockridge shook his head, adding emphasis to his decision. He could see the doubt on the lieutenant's
face, fear raging with panic. He reached out, grabbed the
younger officer by his shoulder, and shouted, "She's not going
to sink. Not now, not *ever.*" The doubt in the other man's
face dimmed slightly, crawled off his skin and hid behind his
eyes.

"You understand me?" Lockridge asked. Groves nodded.
"Good. In a couple of hours, you can fall apart. It won't
matter then. But for now, the crew is counting on you. *I'm*
counting on you."

Groves's shoulders and chest heaved. "I'm okay."

Lockridge barely heard the words. "I know you are. Now,
keep her heading into the wind. I'll let you know when to
change course. We may need to come right, depending on how

bad damage is below. I'm going down her to take a look."

"The XO—"

"Is dead. His stateroom is amidships." Lockridge pointed toward the sound-powered phones. "Do you have communications with the damage control team?"

Groves shook his head.

"I'm going aft. To see for myself."

Lockridge sprinted back onto the bridge, then out the hatch and down two ladders. Smoke filled the passageway, eddying and curling around the ventilation grills. Too much for the normal environmental system to handle.

He could feel the heat when he reached the wardroom, hellish and unnatural, radiating up from the deck, carried along by a strong draft. The stench of burning fuel, scorched steel, other noxious smells he couldn't identify immediately. He pushed himself on through it, coughing now as the combustion by-products replaced oxygen.

Around the first turn, he met the damage control party. They were clustered immediately outside the heavy Kevlar curtains hung from the girders overhead as smoke boundaries. They were dressed out in damage control suits equipped with independent breathing apparatuses. The clear faceplates set in the shiny asbestos hoods were partially fogged and masked their features.

Lockridge stepped forward, grabbed the largest by his arm, and squinted into the faceplate. "Johnson?"

"Captain, what the hell . . . ?" The voice was muffled but understandable.

Now Lockridge could make out the strong black face of Damage Control Petty Officer First Class Darryl Johnson, the team leader. Rivens, a second class, was handling the communications handset. A recorder held a plastic board with a damage control diagram of the ship on it, grease pencil scribbling down the details as Johnson directed. Two backup fire party members stood against one bulkhead.

"How bad is it?" Lockridge shouted, unable to tell whether Johnson could hear him or not. Lockridge could barely hear his own voice, whether from residual deafness or the noise, he wasn't certain.

"You can't stay down here," Johnson said, motioning to Rivens. The petty officer produced an EEBD, an emergency breathing device, and shoved it into Lockridge's hands. "Not without gear, sir."

Lockridge popped open the case, pulled the plastic hood over his head, and jerked the tab on the emergency package. There was a small puff of smoke that stunk, then a trickle of fresh oxygen produced by the chemical reaction. He took a deep breath and started coughing.

"Go back, Captain," Johnson urged. "We're trying to set smoke and fire boundaries. I'll know more in a few minutes. Kirkland is the primary investigator—he's in there, and we're trying to establish communications with anyone in the aft of the ship."

A silver-suited hand slid through the curtains, wrenched apart the Velcro that held them together, and the messenger from the fire party slid through. He staggered and was caught by one of the relief firefighters while Rivens reattached the smoke boundary curtains.

"Kirkland says he's not getting you on the sound-powered phone. It's bad—we can't get through to the other side, no way. Got fuel secured, halogen activated. For all the good it's going to do. We've lost airtight integrity completely. Halogen's not going to do much good without it. The port loop of the fire main is fucked up and we've lost two fire pumps."

"What about smoke boundaries?" Johnson demanded.

The messenger slumped down against the bulkhead. "On-scene leader doesn't think we can contain it. He said look for survivors aft and get ready to get out."

"*No.*" Lockridge grabbed the messenger by the shoulders. "Tell him to set boundaries wherever he can. We can move them in later, try to contain it, cross-connect the fire mains. For now, just stop it from spreading."

The entire diagram of the ship leaped into his mind, in full color with all the watertight hatches throbbing at him. If it had hit at frame 83, if they could contain it between 62 and 107—maybe they had a chance. The secondary cross-connect valve was located somewhere just aft of here—the team would know.

"Captain, it's not going to work." The team leader's face shone with sweat and tears. "We have to get these people out of here. *Now.*"

A low shuddering sound, then a blast of sound and super-heated air blew through the curtained barrier. It sent them staggering down the passageway, fleeing as much from survival instincts as because the blast bowled them over with its force. Lockridge felt the fire-resistant plastic of the hood soften, heated beyond its endurance, then mold itself, scorching, onto the back of his neck. He flailed at it and pulled off melted patches of plastic fused to skin. "The fire pumps—can they be lit off from a remote?"

Johnson shook his head. "Tried it from the secondary panel, Captain. They're not kicking off. I don't even know if they're still operational." He gestured back toward the charred passageway. "No way to tell."

Lockridge led the way as the damage control team members staggered behind with their communications equipment and the damage control status board on which they tracked the progress—or lack of it—in containing the fire.

The messenger pulled away, started back toward the conflagration. "I know what's wrong. Number three fire pump, it's always hard to start. It's okay—it's got to be. I just got to get to it and I know I can get the fire pumps cross connected if you can get the valve open. I *know* I can."

Johnson grabbed him. "Dammit, Irving, you're not qualified as anything except a messenger, and you're sure as hell not heading back into Engineering until we get the flames knocked down. Get your ass out of the way while I get the team together."

Fireman Irving. Lockridge saw him then, the blur behind the messenger's faceplate resolving into the gaunt features of the midwatch Sounding and Security rover.

"I *know* what's wrong with it," Irving shouted, pulling free. "Besides, Kirkland is still back there. If I can't get through, I'll get back up to Combat."

"They couldn't have survived that last secondary. No, you're coming with us." The team leader motioned to the backup firefighters. "Bring him along."

"*No*." Irving broke away from them, slamming one against the scorched bulkhead in the process. He trotted back down the passageway and disappeared around the corner.

Lockridge stared after him, oddly heartened. At least one other person didn't think it was hopeless.

"Go after him," the team leader said, motioning to Riven. "Damn it, tell them to get the hell out of there, get up to Combat."

Fury surged through Lockridge. *Mahan* was his ship, *his*. And this was his crew. No one was going to take them without a fight.

Lockridge grabbed Johnson by one silver shoulder and tried to jerk him around, but the massive petty officer barely moved. "He's right. We've got to get to the cross-connect valve. Follow me." He shoved his way past Johnson and headed toward the conflagration. He felt hands clawing at him as the rest of the men tried to stop him. The cross-connect valve should be down this passageway somewhere, maybe fifteen feet or so. He swore silently, trying to remember the exact position.

Lockridge's right foot hit something hard. He stumbled, caught himself against the smoldering bulkhead. The skin on his palm flashed into charred flesh immediately. He screamed, jerked his hand off the bulkhead, and left a patch of skin behind. Pain, hard and immediate, threatened to overwhelm him.

"Captain," someone behind him cried. "Sir, you can't—"

Lockridge looked down and saw a curled, blackened body lying crosswise across the passageway. He'd tripped on it—*on her,* he amended as he saw the face. The sailor's eyes were shriveled and black. Dirty white bone shone poked out from her right cheek, short black hair singed off that side of her skull. He recognized her as one of the junior radiomen.

Lockridge started forward again, slower now, not wanting to risk another fall over an obstruction. The pain in his hand was duller, becoming a familiar sensation too quickly.

It had to be here somewhere. How far down the passageway was he? Halfway? That should be about right, shouldn't it? He stretched and started pawing at the overhead, trying to feel for it through the miasma of smoke. He could see the valve, the shape of it, almost feel it waiting for him. Black smoke roiled around him, reducing visibility to less than two feet, but he had the mental picture now, felt that invisible connection with the ship that made it an extension of his own body.

His injured hand knocked hard against a rounded metallic object. He grabbed it and felt the heat shoot back up his arm again. The skin on his hand sizzled, pulling away from the underlying flesh as it cooked. He wrenched the valve hard to the left, trying to open it, but his hand couldn't get traction. Skin mixed with blood and serum was too slippery.

"I've got it!" he shouted, not knowing whether they'd followed him or not.

A massive white-gloved hand appeared out of the smoke and slid over his. Lockridge moved his hand away and felt the last remnants of skin pull off his palm. He heard the shouted words, heard the sound at least, but couldn't make out the words themselves.

Two asbestos gloves were now clamped down on the valve, then three, then four. Lockridge stumbled back to give them room. Clad in their firefighting ensembles and protected from the scorching heat, they could do what he couldn't. All he could do now was get out of the way.

It was darker now than it had been a few minutes before. Darker, and getting harder to breath. Lockridge reeled back away from them, eyes streaming from the toxic gases and lungs heaving.

Hard plastic clamped down over his face and metallic air flooded over his blistered lips. He felt hands under his armpits, and the realization that he was lying on the deck finally dawned. He was being dragged backward, back down the way he'd come. His butt and his heels thumped over the dead sailor he'd tripped over, and he said a silent apology to her.

Water fog suddenly cascaded over him, cooling him for just a second before it flashed into steam. Somewhere behind him, someone was wielding a fire hose. The fog solidified into a solid stream of water. Two sailors holding the nozzle charged forward toward the valve team.

Then the second missile hit.

The deck lifted up underneath Lockridge, flinging him against a scalding hot bulkhead. Irving landed heavily on top of him, then they both slid back down to the deck. Or onto a bulkhead—*down* had ceased to have any real meaning, not with the interior passageway of the ship rolling and flexing around them. Flames leaped out from the gap in the Kevlar curtains, licking at Johnson and the others.

Johnson's face appeared in front of him, now almost completely obscured within the hood. A heavy, red haze coated everything Lockridge saw. Lockridge tried to speak, was aware that his lips were moving, but the little bit of hearing he'd regained was lost.

Johnson shook his head. He reached down, lofted Lockridge over his shoulder, and staggered down the passageway toward the bow. Lockridge lay limp for a few steps then started struggling. Johnson put him down. Lockridge held himself up against the bulkhead, the hot metal burning into his flesh, and pointed back toward the silver-suited body on the deck. Irving was lying motionless where he'd fallen.

Johnson turned Lockridge away from the fire and gave him a gentle shove. Lockridge started walking, leaning against the bulkhead for stability, glancing back over his shoulder to watch.

Johnson retreated back down to Irving and hoisted him up as he'd done Lockridge. Lockridge nodded and started back toward the ladder up to the bridge.

The next thirty minutes were oddly disjointed. The panic and anger that had taken possession of him earlier evaporated,

replaced by an almost calm acceptance of what had happened.
Urgency beat under the surface, but now it was aimed solely
at determining who was still alive and which life rafts and
boats were still operational. He saw it happen in flashes:

Smoke, fire, flames gouting up from the deck.

Shoving away the plastic board with the Abandon Ship
checklist on it.

Chief Ford, the senior radioman, reporting all classified material was destroyed except for the crypto gear on one last
SATCOM circuit rigged to the forward dish.

The hurried voice report to Seventh Fleet, telling them that
Mahan had been hit, no indication of the attacking platform,
then ordering Chief Ford to disconnect the circuit as the questions began to interfere with damage control operations.

The Indian destroyers on ship-to-ship commercial radio circuits, offering to take off the crew.

His refusal, hard and angry.

The Indian aircraft carrier *Boganddiya* radioing her intention to return to the area and render assistance as needed.
Lockridge didn't answer her queries.

The procession of dead, dying, and wounded carried down
to the mess decks for triage. Fireman Irving among them, still
wearing his firefighting ensemble but with the hood removed.
His eyes barely open, dull and unseeing, blood trickling down
one corner of his face. His face oddly unmarked but the back
of his ensemble seared off, blackened flesh exposed.

The fire guttered out shortly before dawn, their damage control efforts aided by an ugly, spitting rain spawned at the edges
of a southern tropical depression. It was another two hours
before Lockridge was sure *Mahan* would stay afloat.

2

TWO HUNDRED KILOMETERS NORTHEAST OF THE BANGLADESH-INDIA BORDER

If he poked his head up over the edge of the ditch, Bengali scout Kabir Khan could see a ship burning on the horizon. It glowed orange, reflecting off the low clouds over the night water, the hard edges of the flames diffused by light fog. Every so often—less often now than half an hour before—it shot streams of sparks far into the overcast, lighting up the clouds with a hellish glow for a few moments.

Low, scudding clouds reached from horizon to horizon. The southeastern breeze stiffened, heavy and moisture laden. Kahn recognized the signs. Soon, within days, the killer winds would come. The wind would eat every man-made structure in the countryside, whipping the flimsy huts from the ground, and stripping every sign of human habitation from the landscape. Scouting was often dirty, difficult work, but never more so than during the rainy season in Bangladesh.

Khan plucked a leech off his wrist and smashed it between two fingers. Blood dripped into the muddy waters of the ditch, both from his wrist and from the crushed leech. He tossed the deflated body away in disgust. While Khan's Islam beliefs prevented him from swearing at the leech on his wrist, a Hindu in India would not even have killed it. Khan snorted at the idiocy of that particular religious belief.

Certainly the man crouched down in the ditch beside him had no such compunctions. In fact, Khan had come to suspect that Master Sergeant Billy Elwell, United States Army, had few compunctions about anything having to do with this war. Not about eating. The Bengali had seen Elwell pop a leech into his mouth after plucking it from his skin, swallowing it in one gulp with an almost absentminded look on his usually impassive face. And despite his fastidious personal habits, Elwell was not overly concerned with cleanliness. For the past two weeks, the American noncom had led Khan on a series of nighttime forays into that most challenging of tactical objectives: the garbage dump.

At least they'd made a little progress in their relationship during that time. At first, Khan had had a difficult time getting Elwell to explain anything at all to him. Not the reason for the way Elwell moved through the night, silent as a dark cloud. Not the odd pattern of surveillance the Army noncom set up for Khan's platoon of scouts. And not until two days ago, the reason for the search missions into the Indian platoon's trash. The leeches—that, Khan had never been able to squelch his revulsion sufficiently to ask about.

All in all, Khan was beginning to suspect that Billy "call me Sarge" Elwell was something quite more than the Army technical advisor that he'd been billed as. Something quite a lot more indeed. Even without hard evidence to refute what Khan suspected was Elwell's cover story, Khan knew it as well as he knew that the attack on the American ship was just the beginning.

No, not the real beginning, he amended. That had been two months ago, when the small, silent detachment of Americans had arrived in their camp and offered their assistance. Khan's commander, a bare-faced young lieutenant barely older than Khan himself, had accepted gratefully. The Americans brought with them food, supplies, and an interesting array of weapons. So tempting—but none in the camp had dared to touch the foreigners' belongings. Elwell's ineffable air of menace was sufficient deterrent.

Not that the Americans were unpleasant on an individual basis, no. Elwell had been a quiet presence at Khan's side since the day the Americans had arrived, taking the first month of patrols on his own, disappearing for hours without warning and returning with complete situation reports pinpointing the locations of the Indian forces. When he was actually in the camp, Elwell was always ready to lend a hand with any of the innumerable unpleasant tasks that went along with life in the field, a congenial, helpful fellow that got along with everyone.

But out on patrol, Elwell was a different man entirely. When India started moving toward the Bengali border, Elwell's quiet suggestions became abrupt commands, pleasant comments about the weather harsh admonitions when Khan's field craft fell short of Elwell's expectations.

And the leeches. Dear Allah, the leeches.

Khan had spent enough time with UN peacekeeping forces to be able to read American Army insignia. If the Americans had worn patches on their uniforms, Khan would have also known which unit they were formally attached to and what their specialties were.

But none of them wore any sort of insignia on their camouflage field uniforms, not even rank insignia on the collars. Indeed it was sometimes difficult to remember which of them were in charge. Khan suspected that the chain of command varied with the mission.

And what was their mission? Maybe the lieutenant knew the details. If so, he had not seen fit to share them with the rest of the camp. The Americans had simply arrived, pitched a field tent, and integrated themselves into the daily routine.

Like now. Two hours ago, a lookout messenger had run into company headquarters, shouting the report and waking the camp. Khan had made the mistake of being the first to emerge from his tent fully dressed, and had been sent to investigate. Elwell was already there.

It had to be the American ship that was burning. It had been prowling up and down the coast for days, sometimes out of view over the horizon, occasionally venturing into visual range of the decrepit fishing vessels that plied the waters around the Ganges outlet. An annoyance to the fishermen perhaps, but its presence held the Indian tanks at bay. The tanks would come eventually, storming across the fragile border between the two countries—but not until the Americans tired of patrolling the coast.

Khan sunk lower into the flooded ditch, letting the water lap almost to his neck. His fingers dug into the viscous mud, and he tried not to think about the leeches. He crept forward silently another three hundred meters. Finally, a clear view.

Six Soviet-made T-84 tanks were assembled in a circle, turrets facing out. A tarpaulin was lashed overhead between them, providing some shelter from the drenching rains. It would go quickly when the winds came. The garbage dump, Elwell's favorite patrol destination, lay two hundred meters away, just past the rude field privy the Indian troops had erected. But there was no sign of a missile launcher, or of any vehicle capable of towing one. If the Indians had indeed taken a shot at the American ship, it had come from farther inland.

It was surprising that the tanks had made it so close to the border under these conditions. The day before, five others had bogged down in the flooded farm land ten kilometers to the east.

A new tread design, some magic that would let them cross flooded fields? A cold shudder ran up Khan's spine. If that were true, then blood and carnage would soon mix with the mud.

Not that they weren't starving anyway. The Bengali nation, severed from India in 1947 as a Muslim nation when Britain granted the continent independence, had never really mastered the art of self-governance.

Part of the problem was in the insane idea that Pakistan and what was then called East Pakistan, separated by one thousand miles of Indian territory, could form one nation. The two Pakistanis had nothing in common, other than their Muslim religion. In 1971, East Pakistan had rectified that problem, declaring its independence and forming a provisional government. With the change in political structure came another name change—Bangladesh. But even after the fact, the illiterate pagan Indians refused to acknowledge the inevitability of Bangladesh's independence. The same foolish obstinance that kept them driving their tanks through the ever-deepening mud.

Elwell shifted his weight slightly in the trench next to Khan and then made an almost imperceptible gesture toward the rear of the Indian camp. The garbage again. But why? And most particularly, why now? The enemy soldiers were awake, moving in agitation throughout their small encampment, voices raised and orders shouted. Even without the lack of evidence of a missile launched, Khan would have surmised from their evident surprise that they'd had nothing to do with the attack on the Americans.

Khan glanced back at the Indians, making sure Elwell saw the gesture, then shook his head from side to side. Elwell frowned, then shrugged. Without a sound, the American slid past his Bengali counterpart and started down the trench toward the circuitous path they usually took to the dump.

Khan sighed, then fell in behind him, although he moved with considerably less skill than Elwell. It was a bad idea, never more so than now. Besides, what was to be learned from the Indian refuse, other than the appalling personal habits of its men?

Half an hour later, he knew. Knew without Elwell even having to break the silence he'd maintain since they'd left camp, knew without any further explanation. Not as immediately as Elwell had, of course. The American had come here expecting something of this sort, Khan now understood. Maybe not this exactly, but something of the sort.

And how had Elwell known? Had he suspected even before he'd shown up in the Bengali camp, been searching for confirmation since that time? And how was it related to the attack on the American ship?

Elwell handed him the prize, then led the way back into the safety of deep cover. Khan tucked it carefully into a blouse pocket, almost afraid to touch it even then. Not so much to look at, not if you were a civilian.

A glove. Dark leather, aged beyond any color. The inside liner was a raspy material, heavily soiled and stained with an Indian soldier's sweat. Khan felt as though he could smell the stench even now, the odd, vegetarian stink he always associated with the Indians. And the flaw, the defect that had led one of the soldiers to discard the glove—a rip in the inner fabric near the base of the thumb.

Khan followed Elwell, retracing his steps, staying semisubmerged in the water and mud until the Indian camp was out of sight.

India's decision to mass troops on the West Bengal/Bangladesh border puzzled Khan. Relationships between India and Bangladesh had been mostly civil for the last year and a half. With the help of the United States, the democratic and moderate government had been restored to Bangladesh, replacing the military junta that had seized power three years ago. The Bengali Muslim and Indian Hindu religious leaders had worked together to create relief societies that emphasized the traditions of aid to the poor in both religions. If he had been a betting man—and he wasn't, the Koran forbade it—he would have bet that India would be attacking Pakistan to her west, not her eastern neighbor, Bangladesh.

Particularly with American ships off the coast. When the Americans did decide to intervene in the internecine warfare of the continent, they usually had an effect.

But killing the American ship would lead to killing Bengalis. He stared at the tanks, trying to summon up hatred, a desire for vengeance, to keep him company on the long walk back to camp. But alone on the flooded plains, dirty and hungry, aching at the numerous small spots the leeches had raised on his skin, all he felt was bone-deep exhaustion.

"Go on. I'll meet you back at camp." Elwell spoke for the first time since they'd left camp.

Khan shot him a grateful look and took one last look at the ship burning in the water before he slid back into the tree line. He had time for a detour before he reported back in to his company.

The path back to his small hut was familiar under Khan's boots. He slipped through the humid jungle, covering the fifteen miles back to his village in a ground-eating stride. Just as the light started to fade, early in the surly sky, he reached his hut. He stood outside for a moment, caught his breath, and forced a cheerful expression onto his face. Then, after one last anxious glance at the sky, now shot full of purples and oranges, he slipped into the darkness of the hut.

Kahn stood inside for a moment, letting his eyes adapt to the gloom, then crossed the dirt floor covered with woven mats and knelt down next to the cot. The figure on the ragged wooden frame did not stir.

He put his hand on his wife's forehead. No change—the fever still ate at her like a snake. If she didn't regain enough strength to move inland before the rains came, she had no chance to survive. He reached down with his free hand and picked up a flat metal bowl, a relic from the field kit he'd been issued during his last United Nations assignment. A thin gruel coated the inside of the field messing plate, a small amount of rice moistened with water and warmed in the hot sun. He scooped out a little on his finger and brought it to his wife's mouth.

Eat. You must eat, he said softly. Her eyes fluttered open, and a bare trace of recognition crossed her face. Then the fever glazed her eyes over again, pulling her eyelids down as it tried to consume her from within. Kahn smeared a little of the paste on her lips, hoping she'd lick it off. The small hut flexed, as the wind shifted more southerly. A bad sign. It meant the winds were approaching. Kahn went outside the hut and glanced up at the sky again.

Sometimes the storms were almost survivable, even on the flat plains of the jute fields, but not this one, not if his experience was any guide. So little time to get away, maybe no more than one day.

For a moment, hot anger flared in his soul. *Allah, the compassionate, the merciful*—the phrase began each book of the Koran. But Allah was also the one responsible for the monsoons, the winds, the floods. The words of Surah VII ran through his mind, mocking and laughing: "And He, it is who sendeth forth the winds as the heralds of his compassion, until they bring up the laden clouds, which we drive along to some dead land and send down water thereon, by which would cause an upgrowth of all kinds of fruit. Thus we will bring forth the dead. Happily you will reflect."

But what kind of Allah sent winds as heralds to destroy his own people? Allah, the compassionate—hah! Allah today in Bangladesh was no better than Siva, the god of death and destruction, was to the Hindu pagans in India. Why had Allah brought them out, given them their own country and a divine role in the world, just to destroy them with His own winds? It had never made sense to Khan, and made even less now as his wife lay dying. He turned to face the wind, and almost swore.

The wind pushed his hair out of his eyes, streaming it behind him in lank strands. He could see again and—suddenly, he realized what he'd almost done. To swear at Allah, to protest and complain of one's lot on the earth. Heresy, risking eternal damnation. Perhaps it was not Allah who was no better than Siva, but Khan himself who was no better than the Indians. Horrified, he fell to his knees, prostrated himself in the mud and begged Allah's forgiveness.

Master Sergeant Billy Elwell watched Khan go with a sense of relief. A good kid, but still raw. Time in the field would cure that, but Elwell didn't have time right now. None of them did, not if what he suspected was going on was actually happening.

One of the advantages of operating as part of covert intelligence operations was that the chain of command was some-

what more flexible than it would be in an organized regular
Army unit. Officers, especially junior ones, were sticklers for
going by the book. Elwell's report from the field would have
to be transcribed into the proper formatted message, released
by someone in authority, and shuffled through the channels
until it eventually reached the people that might be able to
integrate his little bit of information into the rest of the intelligence picture. National imagery, satellite visuals, and electronic wizardry would be correlated, cross-checked.
Eventually, someone in one of the myriad intelligence agencies in the U.S. would understand what Elwell knew right
now—that things were about to go to shit on the Bengali-India
border, and go to shit in a big way.

He didn't have time for that. Neither did Khan or the rest
of the small cadre of Bengali troops stationed just along the
border. Neither did, Elwell suspected, the United States.

He made his way back to camp and sought out the soldier
who had possession of the keys to the rickety truck they'd
commandeered. An hour into town, a little more time to make
sure he was alone. The telephone—then, maybe if there was
time, a real shower.

But first the telephone.

Elwell had been given a good deal of discretion in how he
made his reports back to his parent unit, but perhaps not as
much as he was about to exercise. There were some times,
though, that you just had to go with your gut and cut a few
corners off the ponderous behemoth of the Army.

There was one person he thought might be able to make
immediate use of his information, or at least make sure it got
to the right people. Not Army, not even an Army spook, but
someone in the right spot. And, almost as importantly, someone he trusted to understand what he was going to say.

A glove. One battered, ripped, discarded glove. One battered, ripped discarded heavily insulated glove. In the sweat-
box that was Bangladesh in the summer, there was only one
reason for a soldier to have insulated gloves. Certainly not the
weather. And the few odd fittings and scraps of nozzles he'd

found in the garbage dumps merely reinforced his theory.

Elwell had used this sort of glove before, even owned a couple of pairs that were in his kit somewhere back in Germany. He hadn't brought them with him, hadn't thought he'd need them. After all, his top secret mission briefing had said that he would not be handling the dangerous liquid coolants used to propel tactical missiles. They could have been tipped with biological, chemical, or nuclear warheads.

One person—now if he could just find her. Elwell pulled out a small dog-eared green notebook and thumbed through the pages. There she was, both her home and work telephone numbers. It would be the middle of the night in D.C., but this was worth waking her up for.

Jerusha Bailey. She'd understand about gloves and soldiers in Bangladesh.

Later that night, Khan's wife died, slipping easily out of this world while asleep. He buried her the next morning, piling the plentiful rocks over the top of her grave and praying for her soul. He spent the rest of the night in prayer, begging Allah to forgive him for his earlier sin, and fighting not to recognize the peace that his wife's death had brought him. There was no more choice between staying with her and fleeing the winds. With her death, he was free to go with his company when they deployed inland to safety.

As free as any Bengali would ever be, with tanks massed at their southern border.

3

NATIONAL SECURITY AGENCY, WASHINGTON, D.C.

Jerusha Bailey signed in with the night watch and headed up to her office. She'd called Terry Intanglio, the director of the NSA, as soon as she'd hung up from talking to Master Sergeant Elwell. She couldn't go into details, not over an unencrypted telephone line, but this late at night, it wouldn't take him that long to drive in from his home in Burke, Virginia. If what Elwell had told her proved out, it would be worth a lost night's sleep.

Master Sergeant Billy Elwell—now how the hell had he know how to find her? It had been six months since she'd met him in Panama, but the memories came flooding back as though it were yesterday. When she'd returned to the States, she'd done a little quiet research into his past. Was it really possible that most of the United States Army had run across the man they knew as Uncle Billy at one time or another? Most of his service record was fairly straightforward, at least to her untrained eyes. If he'd been a sailor, she'd have known how to read between the lines of the official reports, but she hadn't broken the code on Army service records. A couple of phone calls to other reserve officers, though, had earned her an expert opinion from one Army intelligence officer. Billy Elwell had led a very interesting career in the Army—interesting, and highly classified.

The cipher-locked front door to her section spaces clicked and the heavy steel vault door swung out. Intanglio stepped in her anteroom. His suit unwrinkled, his eyes bright and alert, an inquisitive spark in his dark brown eyes. Did he ever sleep? Perhaps not.

"Morning," Jerusha said. "I think you're going to find this interesting." She briefed him on Elwell's spot report, and finished with, "The question is, how does that tie in with what happened to *Mahan*?"

"I heard the news on CNN on the way in. India is denying responsibility, of course." Intanglio walked over to the coffeepot and started fussing with it. Bailey watched him with a bit of relief. If Terry felt coffee was in order, then he probably though she wasn't wasting his time. "India is accusing the Bengalis of the attack, and Bangladesh swears it was India. Both sides have privately hinted that they'd be willing to consider the Chinese as the possible source as well, but they can't say that in public. Not with China as an uneasy neighbor. But if Elwell's right, this throws some more pieces into the puzzle."

"India is the more reasonable candidate of the two." Bailey frowned. "Although I wouldn't put it past China to be involved."

"They've been walking carefully since the Canal," Intaglio said. "Seizing control of Panama didn't sit well with the rest of the world."

"At least it wasn't Pakistan."

"At least it wasn't nuclear."

Bailey shuddered. "Not yet."

"India is having problems with the Bengalis," Intanglio continued. "Of course, the fact that they've massed a brigade of tanks on the Bengali border doesn't have anything to do with it. Not from their point of view."

"Which makes it entirely unreasonable that the Bengalis

would attack a U.S. ship," Bailey said. "As long as we're off the coast, India's going to think twice about invading Bangladesh. Besides, where would the Bengalis get the weapons? It's not as though they're major players on the world's arms market."

"They've got some cash," Intanglio pointed out. "Every UN peacekeeping force around has a ton of Bengali officers in it, and most of the money the UN pays to Bangladesh stays in the government's pocket. It's like the North Koreans—people starving to death, and they buy submarines. Makes no sense at all."

"Not much does in this part of the world," Bailey agreed. "Least of all why either of them would attack *Mahan*. They've never given any indication that they objected to FON operations, at least nothing beyond the usual protests."

Intanglio sighed and leaned back in his chair. "So we're headed into a theater of operations, maybe for the beginning of a major India-Bangladeshi war, maybe as the start of a show of force by the U.S., and you can't even tell me who took a shot at *Mahan*?"

It wasn't a particularly fair question. India and Bangladesh were well outside her area of responsibility. But Intanglio seemed to think that if a ship was involved, she was supposed to have at least a working theory about what had happened, no matter what part of the world was involved.

Besides, she wasn't the only one who had no answers. Still, when the primary function of NSA was to provide intelligence estimates, particularly as they related to the adversary's electronic capabilities and intentions, it didn't look good if you had no answers. No matter that the rest of the world had none. The hard questions being asked along Embassy Row, the angry accusations hurtled across the rows of seats at the United Nations, even the confidential, very-off-the-record discussions held at D.C.'s most exclusive meetings would net no clear consensus of opinion, much less a national security formal assessment of the attack on *Mahan*. Somebody would speculate that *Mahan* had suffered some sort of accident in her munitions locker, and that the U.S. was trying to cover up its own ineptitude by blaming India or Bangladesh. There would even be a few takers for that theory, but it wouldn't make it much beyond the usual scandal rags.

After a year at NSA, Bailey knew that Intanglio preferred the truth to tap dancing. When he asked a question, he expected an answer. "That's correct, sir. I don't know who fired on *Mahan*. But based on what Master Sergeant Elwell said, I do believe India's staging NBC weapons along the Bengali border. I don't believe in coincidences. There's a connection."

"Well." Intanglio fell silent for a moment, his eyes unfocused and distant. Bailey waited. Terry's lessons were often subtly taught, unlike those of her immediate boss, Atchinson. Now, there was another bridge she'd have to cross later today, the question of why she'd gone directly to Terry rather than following her own chain of command and calling Atchinson.

It only made sense. Calling Atchinson would have resulted in delay, and that's the least thing we can afford right now. Billy Elwell was right—we've got to move quickly on this if there are nuclear weapons on the border. Atchinson wouldn't have understood that the way that Terry did.

Why the director of the National Security Agency had taken her under his wing was something she'd yet to understand. He'd hired her straight out of the Navy, made some fairly extravagant promises about the level of responsibility she'd be given, and had promptly appeared to forget about her.

Until Germany. Until Panama. Coincidence the first time, that she'd been on her two weeks of active duty in England just as Germany made her latest bid for continental dominance? Maybe, but Intanglio had made sure she was on scene while the rest of the world was focused on what looked like a war starting in Korea.

Then what about Panama? At least that had been a bit more clear-cut. Intanglio had made some sort of deal with the Navy to have her unit mobilized for duty there just as the Chinese seized control of the Panama Canal.

But he couldn't just keep doing that, having her unit mo-

bilized every time he wanted a covert set of eyes and ears on
a conflict. Even if the Navy would put up with it, the two
back-to-back tours in combat would have a major impact on
the civilian careers of the other reserve unit members. While
she appreciated the opportunity he'd given her to be on scene
during both the European war and Panama, there was something vaguely distasteful about the conflict between her duty
to the Navy and her obligations to NSA.

It wasn't fair to the Navy, or to her unit. In the last twelve
months, they'd see more active duty than any twenty units
combined.

"What Master Sergeant Elwell says makes sense," Intanglio said thoughtfully. "Pakistan's been claiming India had
nukes forward deployed along the border, albeit on the other
coast. But there are some holes in the picture, big holes. And
that worries me." He leaned forward at his desk. "Too much
is getting filtered before it gets to us. I don't like the data
we're getting from the Navy. It's askew in some way I can't
really pinpoint."

"How do you mean?" she asked.

He shook his head. "I'm not entirely sure. But you've read
the after-action report on *Mahan,* haven't you? Didn't it strike
you as a bit incomplete in some spots?"

Of course she'd read the report. Studied every paragraph,
fleshing out the stark official phrases with her own experience,
understanding the human cost behind the dry recitation of the
damage. "The record traffic in a situation like that doesn't
always give the details, of course. Sure, it bothers me that they
don't know who fired the missile. It bothers me that *Mahan*
had no clue and neither does anyone else. Apart from that, is
there something else?"

Intanglio nodded. "For starters, the captain—Lockridge. He
just *happened* to wake up in the middle of the night and knew
something was wrong? That doesn't make sense."

"It does to me," Jerusha answered. "Just like you can tell
me something's wrong with the data from the Navy, but you

can't tell me why you have that feeling." She saw by his expression that he didn't buy the analogy.

How could she tell a civilian that a ship or unit you commanded became an extension of your own body? That you could feel it when sentries were in position, when the engineering department was alert and on top of things, that you develop a sixth sense of the whole ship as a living, breathing entity.

She remembered her own early tours on board ships. After the first two or three weeks, the constant low-level noise became part of the background, something you never even noticed. Even when a loud air blower kicked off in the compartment next to your stateroom, you didn't really hear it. Not as long as it sounded like a healthy air blower lighting off on its usual schedule.

But let the air blower go off early or cut out too soon, and you woke up. Immediately. You might not know exactly what it was that woke you up, but the absence of a familiar noise, one supposed to be in the background, was just as noticeable as the General Quarters alarm going off. Officers who didn't develop that sense of the ship didn't last long. They were constantly being surprised by the events that everyone else knew about, by malfunctions and breakdowns and inefficiencies that they should have caught before they became problems.

While Intanglio was far too senior to dabble in raw electronic intercepts anymore, he might remember how it felt when you saw the data patterns change, the twitch in your gut when you saw a drastic change in intercept volume, how your skin crawled when a new frequency popped up between two foreign military commands.

Intanglio looked away for a moment. "I need better answers," he said finally. "First *Mahan,* now this. Something feels real wrong about the whole situation and we're not getting enough information. We need our own asset in the loop."

"You want me to pay *Mahan* a visit, see what I can find out?" she asked.

"No, that won't be necessary. You're going to the Naval War College."

"Newport?" She laughed. "Now, that's a nice change of pace."

"They've got *Mahan's* tapes along with their own data from that night," he answered. "And they've got the experience to look at the whole picture. This whole conflict—or the possibility of it—is being played out at the Maritime Battle Center there." He shook his head, as though amused. "And I thought the political maneuvering among the civilian agencies was bad. The Navy really ruffled some feathers getting MBC set up, but it may pay off. God knows how they're going to have to juggle the aircraft carriers."

She turned to stare at the small-scale briefing map that dominated one end of the room. The disposition of American forces around the world was updated only once a day, but accurate enough for her purpose.

The bulk of America's at-sea strength was concentrated in the Middle East. Just outside the Gulf, the aircraft carrier USS *Eisenhower* patrolled on "long tether," within two days' steaming of the Gulf. She was nearing the middle of her eight-month deployment, settled in to her routine.

Mahan, originally part of the *Lincoln* battle group en route to the Middle East, was just east of Bangladesh. The USS *Abraham Lincoln* herself was south of *Mahan,* heading for the tip of India, bound for the Indian Ocean and, later, the Gulf. Once *Lincoln* was within range of *Eisenhower,* her onboard aircraft would begin to shuttle the admiral and his staff back and forth to *Eisenhower* for turnover briefings, into Saudi for CENTCOM briefings, and generally trying to minimize the degradation in readiness that always took place when the new carrier reported in to Fifth Fleet. *Mahan* was supposed to conduct three days of FON operations, then catch up with her battle group during the turnover period.

In the Med, the USS *John F. Kennedy* was nearing the end of her deployment. Her relief, the USS *Saratoga,* was still transiting the Atlantic. The shorter distances involved gave the

Atlantic Fleet a good deal more flexibility in responding to operational changes. Everything was closer together.

Of the carriers that remained, two were in SLEP, the service life extension program that kept a carrier in drydock for three years for a complete refit. Another was near the equator off the west coast, conducting counter drug operations. *Nimitz* had limped back into port three days ago following a two-day exercise with fleet landing qualifications, FLQs, that left her with a serious problem on two shafts. There simply wasn't a lot of naval power available to send.

"When they figure out how it happened, *Lincoln* will get tapped for the response," Intanglio said. Uncanny, how he seemed to read her mind. "It's the closest airfield we've got there. The way the Middle East is right now, I wouldn't count on anyone allowing any overflights or basing rights."

"We can reach India from the States with land-based air," Bailey noted, more for completeness than from any real conviction. They both knew that this was a Navy mission, not Air Force. "If *Eisenhower* leaves the Middle East on schedule, that'll leave us with no carrier in the area."

"The Med—still one there," Intanglio pointed out.

"And it's easy enough to block off the big ditch," Bailey answered, referring to the Suez Canal.

"But their aircraft can strike from the Med, even if that happens."

"With refueling. And if we don't worry too much about overflight permission."

And that was a possibility as well, she reflected. While the United States made a point of obtaining permission to overfly Turkey and the Middle Eastern states during most operations, the real point of obtaining that permission was more political than military. Granting basing or refueling rights, even with restrictions on the number of aircraft that could be on the ground at any time, was tantamount to supporting the United States decision. It forced a nation to show some commitment to military actions that were undertaken on their behalf.

After all, it wasn't as though the United States really needed permission. Even one aircraft carrier carried enough firepower in its air wing to escort the land-attack aircraft through most hostile airspace. What wasn't freely given could be taken by force if necessary.

But Intanglio was right. It would probably be *Lincoln,* and it would probably be soon.

"How confident are you in this Elwell's assessment?" Intanglio asked. "One glove—not a lot to base an intelligence estimate on."

"Confident," she said immediately. "After Panama, I know Elwell's not a guy that gets worried without cause. And he's plenty worried right now."

Intanglio tapped absentmindedly on his desk with his pencil. "We put out a report and it turns out he's wrong, we've got serious problems. Not only with our credibility, but with our entire national security posture."

Jerusha leaned over and laid her hand on the pencil, stilling the incessant tapping. "And if he's right?"

Intanglio pulled the pencil out from under her hand and looked at it thoughtfully. "If he's right, we've got even more problems."

4

USS *EISENHOWER,* THE GULF OF OMAN

Trouble almost always starts on the midwatch. Lieutenant Commander Gar Tennant, flag tactical action officer, or TAO, almost missed the first signs of it. He had just settled in for the midwatch and was studying the large-screen display on the bulkhead in front of him. Two F-14F Tomcats were airborne, well into their second ninety-minute cycle already. One SAR helo was airborne, another on Alert 15 on deck.

From her position just outside the Straits of Hormuz, *Eisenhower* had a clear picture of the entire Middle East. The battle group consisted of the one destroyer, two cruisers, two guided missile frigates, and a replenishment ship. The fighter aircraft patrolled the air around *Eisenhower*, while sophisticated arrays of electronic equipment on all of the ships watched the electromagnetic spectrum. Between the battle group's organic sensors and national assets such as satellites, very little that happened in the Middle East went unnoticed.

Eisenhower had been on station in the Middle East for three months so far. The crew hadn't had liberty since Singapore, and that had only been three days. *Eisenhower* had been on long tether to the Gulf, patrolling back and forth from outside

the straits to just off the coast of Pakistan, juggling the possibilities of the always-posturing Middle East against the odds
of a major blowup between India and Pakistan. Translation
into Navy terms: no liberty. Even a few days in Dubai would
have been a welcomed respite from the endless days at sea,
but with two of India's three aircraft carriers headed toward
Pakistan, the situation didn't look like it was going to improve
anytime soon.

Liberty would have also given Gar a badly needed break
from Rear Admiral Alan Monarelli, the battle group admiral
embarked on *Eisenhower*. Two weeks ago, Monarelli had been
notified that he'd been selected for another star. All the admiral had to do right now was survive this deployment, just
not screw the pooch, and he'd put it on as soon as the battle
group returned to homeport.

*Hard to bitch too much about Moanin', though, after what
happened to Jack.* Gar's expression sobered as he thought
about his old Academy roommate. Compared to getting your
ship shot out from under you, putting up with Monarelli for
another four months until he got promoted off the ship seemed
like a piece of cake.

If anyone wanted Moanin' promoted, it was his staff. Anything to get Moanin' off the carrier, away from the fleet, and
most particularly away from the staff officers assigned to this
carrier battle group. After six months of workups, six weeks
of transit, and three months on station, they'd collectively
come to the conclusion that their leader was a merciless asshole.

Monarelli was from Texas, and even after all these years
bouncing around the world with the Navy, he'd retained—or
purposefully cultivated—a twangy drawl that added an edge
to every sarcastic comment and public taunt. He was barely
five feet, eight inches tall, but made up for what he lacked in
height by piling cords of muscles on his upper torso with fa-
natical weightlifting. During his first three months onboard,
whispered discussions debated the validity of the Napoleon
complex as the root of Moanin's leadership style, and a con-

sensus had finally been reached that Moanin' was a poster boy for the disorder.

As impossible as they would have thought it at the time, the staff now viewed those days as halcyon, peaceful times of quiet contemplation and leisure. Ever since the promotion list had hit the street, Monarelli had gone from being a cross they all bore with quiet courage to a raging martinet who pushed them all past their collective better natures.

Gar had spent many quiet hours on watch mentally comparing the monthly retirement check for a two-star admiral to that of a mere commander. With that much money at stake, not to mention the civilian job Moanin' would have after he retired, no wonder their battle group commander sometimes sounded paranoid and overly cautious. It was just that—damn it all, the man ought to at least trust his own staff.

"So, Commander, when did we quit being the lead dog?" Petty Officer Simmons asked. He was manning the JMCIS console, keeping the data link between flag circuits and the tactical net under control. "I mean, you know what they say about the view. And I hear we're going back on short tether tomorrow to support contingency operations in Pakistan. It's about time for them to blow up again."

"Hadn't heard that," Gar answered. He liked Simmons, appreciated the way the petty officer stood a watch and knew how to make the time pass easily. "Might have something to do with *Mahan* instead. Wonder if they'd send us all the way back out just to escort her?"

"Probably not. *Lincoln's* closer. But if they divert to assist *Mahan,* we're going to be on station awhile longer," Simmons said. "Seems like we ought to have done something about whoever took a shot at her by now." The display on the screen dominating the forward half of the compartment shifted slightly in response to Simmons's key strokes.

You're damned right we ought to, Gar thought. *If I were Admiral Fairchild on* Lincoln, *I'd have blown the hell out of someone by now, warning order or no warning order, just on my own order.* But that wasn't the kind of criticism of an admiral you wanted to vent in front of your enlisted guys, no matter how much you thought of them.

"Don't know," Gar said after a moment's thought. "But there's a lot of ocean and not a hell of a lot of surveillance coverage in some areas. I heard earlier today that CNN is saying a sub got *Mahan*."

"Yes, sir, I heard that, too. It'd make sense. That's what I mean about the lead dog."

Gar considered that for a moment. "You mean that nobody picks on the lead dog?"

"No. You've heard that old line before, haven't you, sir? That the view never changes unless you're the—*Shit*, sir, unidentified air contact inside the keep-out range," Simmons interrupted himself. "Speed three-fifty, altitude twenty-five thousand."

"Mode four?" Gar asked, referring to the encrypted signal that military aircraft transmitted when queried by a friendly transponder. It was the only positive form of identification as a friendly at this range.

"Negative, sir, no Mode 4. Squawking Mode 3 as an Air Force tanker, though." Simmons's voice calmed down as he pulled up the rest of the electronic data on the contact.

"Figures." *Why is it so damned hard for the Air Force to accept the fact that they have to talk to us?* "Are they on Tactical?"

"No answer to my call-up, sir."

"You try MAD yet?" Military Air Distress or MAD, a standard worldwide equivalent to the civilian air distress system, was sometimes referred to as "Air Force Common" by the Navy since they had to resort to it so often to reach their light blue brethren. Every ship and aircraft in the American inventory monitored in constantly.

"Was just going to call, sir. You want to take it?"

Gar reached for the handset. "Sure. It's about time somebody chewed their ass about transit routes. Christ, that's all we need, a blue on blue because the damned Air Force doesn't remember to let us know they're in the area."

SENTRY 601

Major Sheila Elam, the AWACS mission commander, reached behind her and chivvied the lumbar support pad into a more comfortable position. The raised portion of the lumbar support slid up to rest against the lat that was starting to protest already. She rubbed up and down against it, trying to coax the muscle to relax. With ten hours of surveillance mission ahead of her, then two hours flight time back to their base, the last thing she needed right now was to start the inevitable backache any earlier than she had to.

The AWACS E-3 Sentry settled into a gentle right-hand turn. Considerate pilots—of which there were a few in the Air Force, although not many—occasionally reversed the direction of the turn just to even the strain on what they thought of as cargo in the back.

The MAD circuit hissed with dead static, carefully turned down to a level that wouldn't distract the crew. When it came to life, the effect was immediate.

"Eager Sentry"—the tanker's JANAP call sign for unclassified circuits—"request you meet me," the voice coming over the MAD circuit said then rattled off the unclassified alphanumeric joint identification for the classified tactical net in the Gulf, finishing with "for coordination purpose."

Elam called up the communications matrix and verified that the tactical net was already dialed in to their crypto. She assigned the circuit to a speaker. She thumbed her circuit selection dial over to MAD. "Monitoring that circuit now, Hard Rocket. Eager Sentry out."

The same voice from the carrier immediately began a call up over tactical. After Elam answered, the voice asked, "Interrogative your scheduled mission. We're in receipt of SPINS and don't see this time frame listed for AWACS support."

"Check with your comm people, then," Elam said. "You've missed a modification."

"And you're almost missing a wing. We get an unidentified aircraft inbound on us, no Mode 4, we put CAP in the air. I have two Tomcats turning on the deck as we speak, another two the TAO just vectored in on you. This is not a good place to be flying around unidentified," the carrier said. "You don't break for mode 4."

"We're not due on station for another fifteen minutes. You might have noticed, we weren't monitoring your tactical. We would have dialed it up to check in, *Ike*."

"Standard procedure calls for—"

"*Your* standard procedure."

"*Fifth Fleet's* standard procedure."

"We haven't chopped to Fifth Fleet yet. I suggest that you'd have been in serious trouble if you even thought about putting a missile on this aircraft."

"Not as serious trouble as you would have been in. And what's going on with your LINK? We're not holding you as a PU."

"Check your crypto," she said, deciding that she knew the reason for the IFF problem, the latest software patch that had tested oh-so satisfactory on the deck but apparently had taken a hit somehow after they'd gotten airborne. "Perhaps you missed a change in that as well."

"We didn't—"

"Anything further, *Ike*?"

Cold silence, then a short "It's the *Eisenhower* to you, fly-boy. Flygirl. Whatever."

From preflight to debrief, this mission was going to run twenty hours and change in the air. Well, there were worse ways to kill the boredom than sniping with the aircraft carrier. "We'll double-check our crypto on this end, *Eisenhower*, if you'll do the same there." Elam glanced down at the display in front of her. "Looks like we're holding your transmissions just fine. The problem could be no receive side."

"Or on your *transmit* side."

"We'll check if you will."

A new voice cut into the circuit. "Young lady, might I also suggest that you resolve whatever problem you have in short order? Both with your crypto and with your attitude." The voice left no doubt that whoever was behind it was senior to an Air Force major, even if she was the mission commander.

Elam stared up at the speaker, mentally swearing at the little demon in her that had thought it'd be fun to fuck with the carrier puke on the other end. The last thing she needed was the carrier supposedly in control of the airspace completely pissed off at her. And most particularly if the standard pissing contest between Air Force and Navy caught the attention of a guy with stars on his collar. No way to retaliate, since the carrier kept its flag officer right handy, while her own Air Force counterpart was nowhere near.

"Roger, *Eisenhower,* copy all. Will advise you immediately once we've located the problem," she said promptly in her most professional voice.

USS *EISENHOWER*

Gar took the handset back from his watch officer. "She bought it."

Lieutenant Commander Harley Kattner grinned. The lanky Chicagoan was the flag watch officer, Gar's assistant in this watch section. "Command presence—just a natural gift, sir. I'm going to make a hell of a flag officer."

Gar slammed the handset down hard enough to satisfy his annoyance but not so hard that he'd have to explain to the electronics division officer how he'd broken it. Why couldn't the Air Force play by the rules? Didn't they realize the problems they caused when an entire ship mobilized to launch fighters because an Air Force aircraft hadn't checked in with them?

The secure phone line on the console between the two men rang. Kattner answered it, listened, then held the phone out. "SCIF, sir."

"Better not be a SPINS mod," Gar muttered as he took the handset. "TAO," he announced into the mouthpiece.

"I think you'd better come over here, sir," the voice of the intelligence watch officer said. "We've got warning and indications."

Gar started to ask just what *kind* of W&I, then realized that if SCIF could have told him on this line, he would have. "On my way." He tossed the receiver back to the lieutenant. "I'll be next door." Kattner lost a touch of his earlier bravado and sat a little straighter in his chair. Gar would be only a few seconds away in the adjoining compartment, but if SCIF was calling for Gar, something was up. Kattner might not *have* a few seconds to wait for Gar's return.

Gar pushed down the lever that dogged the Tactical Flag Command Center, or the TFCC, entrance door shut and stepped over the hatching coming into the vestibule that TFCC and SCIF shared. Another steel door led into the outer flag conference room, and one to his left led into SCIF. Gar keyed in the crypto sequence necessary to unlock the door and then stepped into the black-curtained area just inside the SCIF doorway. A sailor armed with a .45 stood behind a counter.

"Go on in, sir," the sailor said. A formality—Gar was in charge of every watch station onboard the ship—but one that would always be observed. SCIF was one of those places that processed information that was sometimes too sensitive to use. Even the flag TAO waited for clearance to enter SCIF proper.

Gar pushed aside the black curtain. The heart of SCIF was surprisingly mundane. Status boards annotated in grease pencil covered most of the wall space. A tactical console, two signal analyzers, and stacks of message binders tacked to the walls took up the rest of it. The lieutenant commander in charge of the SCIF watch greeted him.

"We've got launch indications just outside the Iraqi no-fly zone," she said, stepping to a wall-mounted chart and tapping her finger just south of the area inside Iraq.

"What's the composition?" Gar asked.

"Fighters, eight of them. There's been some unusual activity on the ground for the last three hours, weapons upload and preflighting." She looked slightly uncomfortable. "It's routine for them to do that, just run some drills. Pretty much the way we would.''

"How long ago did it start?''

"Half an hour.''

"You should have notified me,'' Gar snapped. The fact that if he'd checked the board more often he would have known earlier rankled. But he shouldn't have to—SCIF was supposed to make sure he knew when things were getting hot.

"The assessment was that they were practice loadouts,'' she said, her tone defensive. "Routine, until they went into pre-flight.''

Gar studied the grease-penciled marks on the board for a moment, not staring at that area but trying to look at the bigger picture. "I'm going to vector the two Tomcats airborne over to the AWACS and launch the alert five fighters to take their CAP stations. We'll move another section up to alert five—no, make that two sections. Any indication of their intentions?''

She shook her head.

"Anything at all out of the ordinary?'' Gar pressed. There was a reason that warfare officers rather than Intelligence officers stood TAO. While most of them were damned sharp, sometimes it took actual operational experience to be able to see the nuances of an enemy's intentions.

"Nothing in the air. The surface picture's about the same, too. Two submarines still deployed in the Gulf itself, both Russian-built Kilos. The German 219 diesels are just inside the Straits, we think.''

"I heard that at the morning brief. Anything more definite on their locations? Or on whose they are?'' *Eisenhower* had been flying periodic USW patrols with its S-3B Vikings, but had so far been unable to detect or track any of the German-built submarines now owned by every nation with access to the sea in this region.

"No, sir. Acoustics are still crappy as hell, and we haven't had a visual on them in days. Even with a visual, Intell doesn't think they'll be able to tell whether they belong to India, Pakistan, Iran, or Iraq. A Kilo's Kilo—same boat, same acoustics.'' She shrugged. ''The only difference is what's on the wardroom menu, as far as I can tell.''

Gar could feel the tension trickling back down his spine. Something somewhere, some data point, was screaming for attention, but he was damned if he could pinpoint exactly what it was. Maybe just common sense. An unlocated diesel submarine was a problem, a serious problem. The ship-killer torpedoes they carried could crack the keel of an aircraft carrier if they detonated close enough. Add fighters to that, and— *Mahan.*

''General Quarters,'' he heard himself say, then blinked in surprise as he heard the words. They seemed to come from some distance away rather than from his own mouth.

''Sir?''

''You heard me.'' While he still could not define exactly what it was that bothered him so much, he was certain it was the right decision. He stared at her for a second then nodded as she reached for the toggle that would activate the General Quarters gong. ''I'll brief the admiral when he comes in.''

Gar left, securing the hatch behind him and stepping back into TFCC. His watchstanders were already pulling on the soft cloth flash gear, the gloves and hood that were intended to provide them some additional protection from fire. His own gear was tucked into the pocket of his jacket.

''Sir?'' Kattner asked.

Gar shook his head. ''Not now. Just watch.''

SENTRY 601

''What the hell?'' Major Elam stared at the radar scope. ''I thought we had our differences ironed out, *Ike,* and now you're sending the fighters after me anyway?'' She reached out to toggle her headset to the common tactical circuit just as the reason for the *Eisenhower*'s action became clear. Eight symbols designating hostile aircraft popped onto her screen. Elam swore quietly.

"Sentry 601, I'm vectoring fighters over to you now," the carrier said. The earlier belligerence she'd heard in the voice was gone, replaced by cool competence.

"I'm holding the Iraqis now. Anything on their intentions?" she asked. "It's starting to feel awful lonely up here." The AWACS, capable though it was in electronic warfare, carried no weapons and was dependent on the carrier for air defense.

"Nothing definite. I don't like the way the picture's unfolding, though. The submarine contacts are unlocated and this fight launch could be the start of a coordinated attack," *Eisenhower* said. "Probably no reason to be alarmed, but I'll feel better if you're under fighter escort. Two Tomcats ought to be enough."

She nodded, not nearly as confident as the carrier voice sounded. Two Tomcats wasn't all that much air power when you had a multimillion-dollar electronics aircraft at stake. And one without parachutes at that. "We're closer to the bogies than you are," she said. "Now that we're holding them, if they start to turn, we'll see it first."

Just then, the bogies' speeder leaders jogged south.

USS *EISENHOWER*

Gar swore quietly, watching the pictures on the plat camera as the Tomcats spooled up. Fast, but not fast enough. Not nearly fast enough. It was one thing to be encased in tons of aircraft carrier, protected by a phalanx of escort ships and close-in-weapons systems, another entirely to be airborne over the Persian Gulf without fighter protection. For a moment, he regretted giving the AWACS mission commander a hard time, even though she'd deserved it.

SENTRY 601

"*Eisenhower,* it's getting awful lonely up here," Elam repeated. Her throat felt dry and her pulse was hammering in
her temples. Her harness straps bit into her shoulders. The
AWACS was in a hard turn to starboard, standing nearly on
wingtip in the air. "We're turning south to move inside your
missile protection envelope. Tell the Tomcats to change intercept course."

"They're on their way, Sentry." The carrier TAO's voice
had lost all trace of animosity. "Going buster now. Just hang
in there—suggested you might want to lose some altitude,
Sentry."

"We will, sir. Not right this second." The suggestion
chilled her.

Altitude and speed were interchangeable quantities in aerial
combat. You lost speed gaining altitude but, in the eternal
equation of flying, could trade it back anytime. Making a mad
dash for the deck—in this case, the relatively smooth surface
of the ocean—was one of the few maneuvers an AWACS had
against an incoming missile. The tactic depended on being
able to get low enough fast enough, and confusing an incoming missile by getting lost in the clutter from the sea returns.
It didn't work well against any missile that locked onto the
hot exhaust streaming out of the AWACS engines, nor was it
particularly effective in calm seas. Still, it was better than
nothing.

The times that the tactic worked best were when the missile
was already in the air and the AWACS had enough warning
to head for the deck. That the carrier was already suggesting
it . . . "*Eisenhower,* you know anything we don't know?" she
asked, her mind racing furiously. Not electronic—the AWACS
was more sophisticated than anything the carrier had at her
disposal. No emissions, no radar info. So why—?

"Negative, Sentry," the carrier answered, a peculiar note
of sympathy in the voice. That chilled her more than anything
she saw on her radar scope. "All we've got is what our E-2

is holding. The bogies are veering east a bit. They may not have been on an intercept after all.''

''Roger, copy all.''

Twenty seconds passed in radio silence. The Sentry had already come out of her hard turn to the south and had nothing to report. The carrier had no suggestions. Both settled in to watch the geometry unfold.

''Shit!'' A red missile symbol flashed onto the screen. ''South, dammit—Red, get this bitch on the deck!'' The AWACS was already in a steep dive as she said the words. ''How far out are the Tomcats?''

''Within weapons range in twenty seconds, Sentry,'' the carrier TAO answered. ''Just keep heading for the deck and leave this fight to the big boys. Button three for coordination.''

Fuck coordination. If your fighters had been on top of things, we wouldn't be having this problem at all. Elam fought back a surge of nausea as the AWACS went into a steep descent, her hands clamped down on her armrests and feet planted to hold her weight off of her flight harness. Terror built in her gut and, just as suddenly as it had started, faded away, replaced by icy calm. It was what it was—they knew that every time they climbed into the aircraft. Every aviator knew it.

''Are you an aviator?'' she asked suddenly, forcing the words out against the G-forces. ''What do you fly?''

USS *EISENHOWER*

They're not going to make it. Gar stared at the symbols inching across the light blue background, seeing not simply airframes and sterile designations but the woman behind the voice on the circuit. He clicked his mike on, his gaze still locked on the AWACS aircraft symbol. ''Tomcats, Major. Same kind that are going to save your ass now.''

That major, the mission commander—a smart ass, but what did you expect from the Air Force? She sounded like she knew

what she was doing, even if her transmit end of the LINK was
hosed up. And she'd had the guts to give back as good as she
got.

"You got a G-suit I could borrow?" the Air Force major
asked. "We didn't exactly come prepared for aerobatics, Tomcat."

"Sure thing." Gar heard her grunt and knew what she was
doing—tensing her muscles, forcing the blood to keep circu-
lating up to her brain to avoid graying out. "Hang in there,
Major. We're on our way."

"AWACS at ten thousand feet and descending," the operations specialist reported. Simmons sounded almost bored,
although Gar knew better. It was how you coped with it, that
hard professional exterior that said *I don't give a shit about
that aircrew up there getting ready to buy it.* If you *did* think
about it, if you let them be people instead of designations,
names and faces instead of missions numbers, it all got too
real too fast. Because if they could buy it, you could. If they
could die, you could. And in order to do your job, to climb
into that cockpit or down five ladders to your compartment so
far below the waterline, you had to know for certain that you
weren't going to die. That whatever happened to the AWACS
had happened to a blue carat on a computer display, not to
somebody who probably had the same problems making car
payments that you did.

But that major, she'd screwed it up for him. Gar felt a momentary flash of anger at her, anger coming from the fear. She
had to die a number, dammit. Not a woman.

"Vampire," Simmons said, his voice slightly louder and
higher. For a moment, Gar thought the OS would lose it, but
then the moment passed. Simmons had almost as much time
in the Navy as Gar did, knew that if you panicked you screwed
up. "Inbound on the AWACS, sir. Tomcat 201's going after
it—sir, he hasn't got a chance."

Even with a good angle, with every bit of geometry working
for you, shooting down a missile with another missile wasn't
a high probability game. Imagine throwing spears at each other

from fifteen miles apart and trying to get them to intersect in midair. Even if you were both trying, it wasn't likely to happen.

And this, this was the worst of all the geometries, second only to a true tail chase. The missiles were head-on to each other, the radar cross sections of each barely one foot. You had to be right the first time, dead right.

There were Tomcat pilots almost good enough to pull it off, but not in the air right now. Even for the best, the most seasoned Top Gun graduated, it would have been chancy. This was simply no contest.

The impossibly long speed arc shot out from the symbol, designating that contact as a hostile missile. It was a straight line almost five inches long on the current scaled display, and cut across the speed leader protruding from the first Tomcat. Intercept, maybe—but probably not.

"Tallyho on one bogie," the lead Tomcat announced. "*Eisenhower,* I am weapons free at this time."

"Confirmed, weapons free," Gar said. "Kill it, 201. Hard and fast."

"Roger, weapons free," the pilot answered. "Little bastard's trying to run, but it's not going to do him any good. I got firing position on him."

"Counterfire," Simmons announced. "One AMRAAM off lead. He's at the edge of his weapon's envelope. Doesn't look good." The symbology and speed leaders lagged the announcement by only a few seconds, but their position and speed leaders confirmed what Gar had known in the first seconds.

Not going to make it, not going—they're low, they might get lost in the clutter. Those Iraqi weapons, they're poorly maintained, might lose lock. And the AMRAAM will force the Iraqi's to maneuver, maybe complicate the problem.

Even as he tried not to start hoping, Gar knew it wouldn't be enough. The sea state wasn't high enough to provoke radar into locking onto spurious detections from the waves. Besides, the AWACS wasn't low enough yet to get lost in the clutter, even if there'd been clutter.

"Chaff, flares," the AWACS major announced over tactical. She forgot to unkey the mike as she continued with "Come on, you suckers, go for it. Go for it, go for it . . ." Her voice trailed off.

They waited. The metallic strips of foil splashed across the sky painted bright spats of radar return on their screens. Radar-spooking chaff and the enticingly brilliant heat source of the flares were an AWACS's only defenses. If that didn't work, she had nothing else to rely on.

But the Tomcats would be within shooting range in seconds. The AWACS didn't need a long streak of luck—just one break, just one little three-inch strip of foil or burning flare that enticed one missile.

"Tell my husband I love him." The voice from the AWACS major was calm, professional now. In these last few seconds, she'd decided how she wanted to be remembered. "My crew has done an outstanding job, and each one of them deserves—" Gar could hear the scream of the AWACS engine in the background, the jolt in her voice as the aircraft tried to jink away from the inevitable.

There was one second of incredible, world-shattering noise over the circuit that abruptly cut off. Then silence, as much from the watchstanders inside TFCC as from the now-destroyed AWACS radio transmitter.

"Lost radar contact on the AWACS," Gar said finally.

"SAR already inbound," Simmons said, his voice equally quiet. Unlike most Navy aircraft, the Air Force AWACS had no ejection system. If the missile had downed the AWACS, it had taken her crew with it.

Gar saw that the Iraqi aircraft had turned back to the north and were already inching over the Iranian border. The two *Eisenhower* Tomcats were closing in on them.

"Weapons tight," a voice behind him said. Gar recognized Monarelli's voice. "Jesus, Tennant, what are you doing? They're over *Iran* now."

Gar felt heat creep up the back of his neck, a sour, sick feeling starting in his gut. He started to keep silent, then heard again Simmons's question: *When did we stop being the lead dog?*

"TAO, recall that flight of Tomcats," Admiral Monarelli ordered.

Gar reached for the mike, his hand moving slowly. Not intentionally, no—not on purpose.

"Fox one, Fox one," the oxygen-masked voice said over the speaker.

"Fox two, Fox two," the second Tomcat said. The speed leaders popped into view on the blue screen display.

Gar keyed the mike. "Roger. Tomcat flight, RTB. I say again, return to base."

Stunned silence in TFCC. Finally, Admiral Monarelli said, "I told you to go weapons tight and RTB. They were in Iranian airspace—hell, they were over Iran. What the *hell* were you doing?"

"I heard you order weapons tight, but I didn't have time to react," Gar heard himself say. "By the time I could get to the mike, the weapons were off the rail. Simmons had his headset on—he didn't hear anything. Neither did Kattner. Admiral, *you saw them shoot that AWACS down.*" Gar tried to put as much force behind his words as he could, signaling the operations specialist and his watch officer that *this* was the version of the story he expected them to support, even over the admiral's attempt to shoulder the entire blame.

"I'm not sure— " Kattner began.

"I am." Gar cut him off. "You, too, Simmons. I'm sure. That's exactly what happened."

Simmons shrugged, an exaggerated motion. His back was still to the three officers. "*I'm* not certain, sir. I was watching the screen and coordinating the Tomcats just launching with CDC. I didn't hear anything, and that's the truth."

As opposed to the official story. No matter, even better if it's true.

"I know what they did," Monarelli snapped. "But you

gave them weapons free without consulting me."

"You gave me that authority when you assigned me as
TAO, sir," Gar said. The conversation was taking place on
two levels—first, sorting out what had just happened, and second, deciding who had screwed up.

Monarelli snorted. "I was standing TAO watches when you
were wondering if you'd survive plebe year, mister. Don't
presume to tell *me* what authority you have."

"I'm sorry, sir. I would have called you if there'd been
time, but the engagement was unfolding too quickly." Gar's
hands were moving over his keyboard quickly now, keying in
the results of the action in a standard message form. "OPREP-
3, Admiral—you'll want one, I'm assuming?"

"That's right." The admiral's voice was unusually calm
and even. "We'll make this work."

"Only intermittent contact now on the bogeys," Simmons
said, still watching his own screen. The symbols representing
the Iraqi aircraft flickered in and out of existence, the pixels
glowing faintly even after the symbols disappeared.

"They may have descended on a bombing run," Gar said.
"Without the AWACS up, our over-land detection capability
is seriously degraded." *Not to mention the possibility that the
Tomcats got a couple of them.* "Do you still want me to recall
the Tomcats, Admiral?"

"Have them stand off the coast, well outside the twelve-
mile limit. We'll wait and see if the Iraqis pop back up
when—if—they head home," the admiral said. "Intell will
want to know where they end up." He was standing beside
Gar now, in the space between Gar's seat and that of the watch
officer, close enough that Gar could smell the sour scent of
sleep. Monarelli was humming, a monotone, off-key noise that
he often made just before he exploded.

Gar nodded, concentrating on adhering to the format requi-
rements of the OPREP-3 and watching as the carrier launched
section after section of fighters. Too late to protect the
AWACS, and it looked like the Iraqi knew better than to take
the Tomcats on. A defenseless AWACS was one thing, the

full force of a pissed-off carrier air wing entirely another matter.

The number of aircraft that returned from Iran, if any, might tell them one thing—just how many *Eisenhower* had shot down and whether they'd taken some small step toward avenging the slaughter of the AWACS.

"Zulu Bravo, this is Zulu Alpha." The voice booming out of the loudspeaker overhead startled Gar out of his gloomy assessment of the weapons scenario unfolding.

Fifth Fleet. Gar reached out and flipped the communications switch over to the channel that corresponded to the overhead speaker and answered the call up.

"Warning order on its way, Zulu Bravo. It's being released as I speak. Is Admiral Monarelli there?"

Holy shit, warning orders. It's happened, right now. We're gonna be lead dogs for a change. The Middle East, not Pakistan. For certain now. I'm sorry, Jack—wish I could have had a shot at whoever hit your ship, but I've got my own AWACS to make the Iraqis pay for. Gar tamped down his excitement and held his voice steady. "Sir, this is the TAO. The admiral is right here." He waited as the admiral slid into his own command chair and pulled on his own headset, then Gar turned to Simmons. "Anything on IAD or MAD?" the two international air distress frequencies.

"This is Admiral Monarelli." The admiral's Texas drawl was cool and confident. Like it was all a drill, like his staff didn't know how frantic Monarelli was to find a way to look good out of all this. "What do you have for me, sir?"

"Record traffic is on the way, but we're moving you into the Persian Gulf. I'll want your intentions within the next two hours if you can, Alan." Fifth Fleet *himself,* then, Gar thought. Only he would address a battle group commander by his first name.

"Anything more you can tell me?" Monarelli asked after a moment.

There was a surreal feeling to the conversation, listening to the two most senior admirals in this part of the world discuss

the start of hostilities as though they were catching up on the
latest sports scores. Gar stared at the large-screen display,
heard the whispers from the rest of his people. The warning
order probably meant that they were going to exact a price for
the loss of the AWACS. Simmons would probably be thinking
that they were going to get a shot at being lead dog for a
change, but he'd remember that nobody'd issued a warning
order when *Mahan* was hit. Maybe it was going to be a catch-
up ball game, but at least with the AWACS the U.S. knew
who was responsible. The rest of them would think what Admiral Monarelli told them to think.

"Not on this circuit," Fifth Fleet said. "More data coming
in over Sipranet."

"Roger, copy that. I'll get on it and take a look."

Gar flipped through the emergency action plans, pulled out
the correct laminated checklist, and handed the second page
to his watch officer. "Everybody on the list should be somewhere in flag spaces at their GQ stations. Have the rover round
them up."

Gar checked the time notation clicking off the minutes at
the bottom of the screen. Two minutes had elapsed since he'd
ordered General Quarters and the ship was counting down the
progress over the 1MC. The AWACS crew had been dead for
just over ninety seconds. Just long enough for the wreckage
to be hitting the ocean's surface by now.

They were all dead long before that. They had to be. He
tried to find comfort in the thought.

"The Iraqi strike aircraft," Simmons said. "TAO, lost contact."

"How far over the Iranian border were they when you last
held them?" Gar asked.

"Eight miles, sir."

"Maybe we got a couple," Gar said, then shook his head.
No, it felt wrong. His nerves were jangling, warning him that
whatever he'd thought was happening was a mistake. He cast
his mind around for other possibilities. It wasn't that he had
to know what the Iraqis were doing, not exactly. But if he

didn't know what they *were* doing, then he didn't know what they *weren't* doing.

Like turning inbound on the carrier.

Shit, the two countries could go at it as far as he was concerned, burn each other down into glassy smears on the earth and most of the world would applaud. You could still drill through glass, keep that black gold flowing out into world, and it would be a hell of a lot easier to deal with under the management of businessmen rather than religious ideologues.

Way over his paygrade, the whole issue of oil and international relationships. Right now he'd settle for knowing exactly where the little bastards were and, later, what exactly they'd targeted.

"Give the cruiser a yell. See if they know why they're not holding them," Gar said finally. Not much chance that the cruiser would have any answers—if they'd held contact on the aircraft, the info would be in the data link. "Maybe they've had an equipment casualty."

Gar listened, his gaze glued to the tactical screen, as his watch officer contacted the cruiser on tactical. "Negative, *Eisenhower*. We've lost contact, too." Gar held out his hand for the telephone handset to the circuit.

"*John Paul Jones,* this is the TAO."

"This is *John Paul Jones* proper," the voice answered, using the code word to identify the speaker as the commanding officer of the ship. "If you've got answers, I'm listening."

Gar glanced over his shoulder to see if Admiral Monarelli wanted to speak directly to the CO of the other ship. The admiral was still briefing Fifth Fleet on the loss of the AWACS, and motioned to Gar to continue.

Gar paused for a moment, gathering his thoughts and trying to figure out how to put them in order. Finally, he decided to go with his gut. "Sir, any thoughts on why we've lost them?" he asked *JPJ*'s skipper.

Silence for a few moments, and he had a sense of being closely scrutinized over the radio circuit, could almost feel the captain's penetrating gaze. Finally *JPJ* said, "Assuming that there are no equipment casualties—and I'm having my people double-check that—then I'm going to have to fall back on the Aegis theory of radar. If we don't see it, it's not there.''

''But that doesn't make any sense, does it? Iraqi fighters inbound on a strike on Iran, and they turn off course long enough to take out an AWACS, then head back toward Iraq. Then there's no fur ball, no antiair action, and the aircraft disappear off the screen. Where did they go?'' Gar asked.

''It's possible they could have continued east until they were out of our range,'' *JPJ* answered. ''But I doubt it. When you lose a contact due to range, it fades out. Intermittent contact for a bit, then you lose it. These contacts just disappeared. That means they were either so close to the ground that we lost them in ground clutter or . . .'' *JPJ* stopped, and Gar had the sense that he was trying to decide whether or not to voice his suspicions on this circuit, to be recorded and analyzed down the road. Gar saved *JPJ*'s CO the trouble of deciding.

''Or they landed,'' Gar said, aware as he spoke the words how they sounded.

''Right. They landed.''

And maybe that's what they didn't want the AWACS to see.

Eight minutes later, General Quarters was set throughout the *Eisenhower*. Two SAR helos from the carrier, along with one from *JPJ,* were airborne and searching the wide swath of ocean under the AWACS flight path. The first section of Tomcats were vectored over to assist in SAR efforts and were already querying the carrier about tankers. Both helos and both Tomcats reported seeing debris in the water and an oil slick surrounding it. There were no emergency beacons activated and no trace of the crew. The OPREP-3 message was completed in final draft and spit out over the electronic pathways that connected the ships.

Gar's suggestion that the Iraqi aircraft had landed peacefully in Iran would require confirmation from SCIF, outside intelligence agencies, and the entire chain of command within the military before it was accepted as a working hypothesis on what had happened to the Iraqi fighters. But at the moment he said it, Gar knew that what he and *JPJ* had concluded was the truth. The Iraqi fighters were on the ground of their own free will in Iran. Now all that was left was for the rest of the world to get into the act and come up with the one conclusion neither he nor *JPJ* or even Admiral Monarelli was prepared to offer.

Why?

5

BANGLADESH

Elwell stared across the flat expanse of the field. The tanks were still there, as silent and immobile as they'd been the day before. The camp itself was taking on the look of a long-term stay, with the standard-issue camp structures already extensively modified by the troops. Like any army in the world, the Bengali soldiers had their ways of coping with long-term bivouacs.

The news about the downing of the AWACS was filtering in now, the facts clear to those who could read between the paragraphs of India's political rhetoric attacking the U.S. for once again invading another nation's airspace while simultaneously proclaiming India's innocence in the attack on *Mahan*. Pakistan had been oddly silent—or, Elwell corrected, effectively censored out.

After a few decades of kicking around the world, you came to an understanding of how ground warfare worked. Nothing fancy, just the basics. You expected to see three-to-one superiority in troops to take a lightly defended enemy position, five-to-one if the other side was heavily dug in. You knew that tracer fire works both ways, that no plan survives the first salvo, that you don't want to march to Moscow in the winter. Usually the guys on the other side knew the same things.

But nothing about the current situation made sense, particularly not if you looked at the big picture. Not the timing of India's forward deployment just as the monsoon season was starting, not the composition of forces facing him—tanks and support units, far too few ground troops, no air coordination support—and not the lack of movement from the other side. And particularly not the fact that India seemed to be concentrating her forces on her border with virtually defenseless Bangladesh while the Middle East was going to shit again and, even closer to home, Pakistan was making military forays into India. Nothing since the attack on *Mahan* had followed any principle of ground warfare he knew.

He looked over at Khan. The Bengali paid attention, had gone a long way toward correcting the sloppy habits he'd picked up in the UN peacekeeping forces. Like now—Elwell noted with approval that Khan was crouched back on his heels, one hand on his rifle, the other on his binoculars. The Bengali's head was well below the top of the trench, yet he was poised to move immediately if he had to. In such small virtues are the seeds of survival on the ground.

Elwell no longer worried about the chain of events that had led to his excursion in country. Nor was he concerned about what Jerusha Bailey was doing. He'd done his part, called her like he was calling in mortar shells on a target. One thing about the Army, you learned to trust the rest of the people on your team to know what they were doing, and to let them do it without breathing down their necks.

Except lieutenants. Most dangerous thing in the world to a mud puppy—a junior officer with a good idea.

So he wasn't worried—no, that wasn't the right word at all. Apprehensive, maybe. Unsettled. There was just something a little too hinky about what was going on here. All he knew for certain was that he didn't want to be caught in the middle of it whenever whatever it was blew up.

Elwell shifted slightly, just enough to catch Khan's attention. He made a small motion with his hand, back in the direction from which they'd originally made their approach on the campsite. Khan nodded, ran his hands lightly over his own gear checking for anything loose that might make noise, then started the smooth duck waddle down the trench toward the woods.

Once they reached the small stand of ground cover, Khan straightened up. He pointed in a direction slightly off the one they'd approached from, and Elwell nodded his approval. Never leave exactly the same way you arrive, take a different route whenever you can. Elwell no longer remembered whether that was something he'd been taught in the Army or whether it was a holdover from how his father had taught him to move in the mountain wilderness in Tennessee. Wherever the first lesson had been taught, the rule had saved his ass too many times for him to abandon the practice now. Khan moved out, Elwell following silently twenty yards behind.

Two hours later, they were back inside Bengali borders. Khan motioned for a stop, then leaned up against a tree and uncapped his canteen.

"Any ideas?" Elwell asked as he unscrewed his own.

Khan shook his head. "No. It was as you said. They are staying there for some time, I think." He shrugged, took another slug from his canteen. "Good for us. They stay longer, their tanks will not work as well."

"Don't count on it." Privately, Elwell agreed with him, but complacency was always a bad idea in the field, no matter how well supported by the facts.

"What will happen to the ship, Sarge?" Khan asked.

Elwell shook his head and didn't answer. Another question he didn't have the answer to—and didn't have to worry about right now. The reports coming through on the international news were spotty. According to most of them, the ship was still afloat, although the Indian news media was reporting it a complete loss. He fiddled with the SINCGAARS tablet stuck in his left blouse pocket. If the cruiser had the right crypto, he could just call them up and ask, but that was a low-probability event. SINCGAARS was a ground force comm system, frequency agile and completely secure, and the odds of a Navy ship without embarked Marines having the right equipment or crypto was zero.

"It'll be okay," he answered. "They're still floating, right? And it's American steel. They can take a couple of hits and still keep fighting."

Not like an AWACS. He screwed the cap back on his canteen, reflecting on the survivability of steel ships and steel aircraft, and decided that if given the choice, he'd take the ship. And Bangladesh over the Middle East.

USS *MAHAN*

Fourteen miles offshore Bangladesh, Jack Lockridge was too immersed in the details of keeping his ship afloat to worry about the Middle East and the warning order that had gone out to his former battle group commander onboard the *Eisenhower*. *Mahan* was having serious difficulty maintaining any control at all over her own movement, and Lockridge had ordered the signalmen to fly the two vertical red lights and corresponding day shapes that signified a vessel not under command. After a few forays in close to offer assistance, the Indian ships had settled into position twenty thousand yards away, *Boganddiya* in the center of her protective cluster of destroyers. Lookouts and intelligence observers must have been crammed onto the catwalks and island with cameras and binoculars, judging from the sunlight he saw glinting off the sides of the carrier. The calls over channel eleven had tapered off, and the unclassified commercial frequency had been silent for a little over an hour now. Even the normal chatter between fishing boats had ceased.

"She's stable, at least." Threlkeld rubbed a blistered and grimy hand across his forehead. "That's about the best thing I can tell you, Captain. Goes downhill from there."

"For how long?" Lockridge asked.

Threlkeld shook his head. "The patches are holding for now, but they won't last forever. We've got some mattresses backed with plywood over the larger ones, backstopped with beams to put pressure against the hull. There's some leakage. The pumps are keeping up right now, but it's getting worse. That's our most serious problem right now."

Lockridge ran his good hand down the side of the mattress, felt the sweating hull under his fingertips. His left arm was bandaged close to his chest, the burned hand suspended in a sling. The pain had been building over the last three hours as the medication wore off. It was now a dull red drumbeat that made thinking difficult. "So we can make five knots, maybe. Any more than that and we're going to have problems keeping the patches in place."

Threlkeld shook his head. "Five knots is pushing it. That shaft—Captain, the bearings are shot. The main thrust bearing sounds like a roller coaster and you can see the warping in it at two knots."

"I know. The port shaft looks okay, though."

The only reason he hadn't shut down the starboard shaft completely was that he thought it might freeze up. Sure, maybe it couldn't contribute much to forward speed, but there might be a time when every knot counted.

Lockridge thumped his closed fist against the wooden beam bracing the mattress in place. Solid, well braced. The damage control teams had done a good job.

But even the best repairs were only temporary, a temporary measure to keep them all out of the ocean. They could hold the sea at bay for a while, but not forever.

Will it hold long enough to get to a repair shipyard? Maybe. Probably.

"Any word yet?" Threlkeld asked, his tone of voice showing that he already knew the answer to his question.

Lockridge shook his head. "They'll send us to Singapore. It's the closest repair facility."

But just when exactly would the orders come? Following the shoot down of the AWACS, the entire focus of the U.S.

military had been directed toward the Middle East. It seemed almost as though *Mahan* and her crew had been forgotten, buried under the swarm of mobilization orders, forward deployments, and the rush to position overwhelming force around the oil-rich fields in the Middle East. Lockridge had made his messaged queries and requests for orders increasingly urgent.

One more day. If there were no orders forthcoming, he'd head east as best he could, take his chances on Singapore himself.

Lockridge squatted down on the deck and tapped at the beam placed parallel to the plywood backing. No movement. The deck was coated with a thin veneer of seawater, oil, and soot, noxious under his hand. Still, the braces were holding.

He heard a thump and a muffled curse and glanced over at Threlkeld. The lieutenant was holding onto an overhead stanchion, a pained look on his face. "Sorry, Captain." He pointed at the P250 pump. "Getting clumsy, I guess. I tripped over it."

Lockridge straightened up, heard his knees pop and crackle. The movement sent blinding flashes of pain racing up his arm. For a moment, he considered taking another pain pill. No, it made him too fuzzy. Thinking through pain was easier than thinking through codeine. "How long has it been since you've had any sleep? Or food and water, for that matter?"

Threlkeld tried to paste a stoic expression, but his answer was clear on his face. "I've eaten, sir. Had a nap a while back."

"Uh-huh." Lockridge studied him for a moment. It was tempting to order his DCA to hit the rack immediately, at least for a few hours. Exhaustion shone in the red-rimmed eyes, the slackness in his mouth, the awkwardness that had sent him staggering into the P250. Threlkeld and his people were the most critical parts of the entire equation right now, and *Mahan* couldn't lose him.

But now was not the time. Threlkeld knew his own limitations, and while Lockridge thought he'd probably reached them, the lieutenant showed no signs of giving in to what must have been complete exhaustion.

"A little later today, sir," Threlkeld said as though to forestall any suggestions. "I'm fine—really."

Fine is the last word I'd use to describe any of us right now. For a moment, Lockridge drifted, lost again in the immediate aftermath of the missile attack.

"Sir? What did—I mean, why did it happen, sir? We were just transiting their waters. Who was behind it?" Threlkeld's voice, which had held steady thus far, acquired a tremor.

Jack felt his own weariness and pain threaten to overwhelm him. So many dead, so many injured—and for what? He shut his eyes for a moment, reaching for some inner reservoir of strength that captains were supposed to have. All he felt was a black, aching emptiness.

He opened his eyes and looked at Threlkeld. "We don't know yet, Teddy. But we will. So help me God, we will." He clapped his hand down on the lieutenant's shoulder, dug deep into the other man's muscles to try to convey something Lockridge was no longer sure he possessed himself. "For now, let's just keep her afloat. You do that and I'll take care of the rest."

Threlkeld nodded, his eyes red-rimmed and bleary. "That I can do, sir. At least for now."

As Lockridge headed back up to CDC to take another look at the shattered gear there, he reflected that Threlkeld might have the easier job of it after all.

6

NATIONAL SECURITY AGENCY

"Rental car," Jerusha insisted. "Terry said I'd be in Newport for two weeks, and I'm not going to be stuck on the base eating at the galley the entire time."

"Really, Jerusha," Jim Atchinson, her immediate superior and a continual roadblock between her and Intanglio, demurred. "The expense . . ."

"At my grade, I'm entitled."

"I must insist—" Atchinson began. Jerusha cut him off by shoving the telephone across his desk at him.

"Call Terry. Now. I don't have time to put up with this bullshit, Jim. Call him."

"I'm not going to bother Mr. Intanglio with your temper tantrums every time I disapprove one of your requests. He does have other things to do, you know."

"I know that, you know that. So why are you wasting my time arguing over a rental car when you know he'll approve it? Hell, even the travel section says I'm entitled to it. Sign off on the orders or I'll call Terry myself."

Atchinson leaned back in his chair and regarded her with an annoyed expression on his face. "Someday you're not going to have him to go crying to, you know. You ought to make an effort to get along with the rest of us.''

"I do get along with everyone else," Jerusha said. "Everyone but the one person who ought to be in my corner—you. I don't know what it is, Jim. You've been pissed off at me since the day I reported aboard. I've put up with it for long enough now. I don't know what your problem is with me, but you need to get over it. Now would be a very good time for that to happen.''

"You think you're some sort of power around here, don't you?" Atchinson sneered. "The golden girl, the one on the spot in all the world's problems. Have a war and need a solution? Hey, just call Jerusha Bailey in. Let her dress up in her spiffy little khaki uniform and play Navy for a while, and *poof!* The problem's solved. Is that it?''

"I never asked to go to Germany. Not for that reason. Or to Panama. Terry sent me. You know that.''

" 'Terry sent me,' " he mocked. "Terry this, Terry that. Pretty frequent phrase in our conversations, isn't it?''

"Look, I didn't ask—''

"*Mister* Intanglio from now on. You got that? It's *Mister*. He's your boss, my boss, four grades senior to me and in the SES—the Senior Executive Service. Not your bowling buddy or some Navy chump you screw on weekends. *Mister*.''

Jerusha stared at Atchinson's red face. His eyes were bare slits in the fiery flesh, the corners of his mouth pulled back in the beginning of a smile. What had started as one more incident in her ongoing conflict with Jim Atchinson had ballooned up way past what either of them had bargained for.

"Mister," she said quietly. "Point taken, sir.''

Atchinson looked uncertain for a moment at her capitulation, then started to deflate. "Good, I'm glad we got that straightened out. Mister.''

"May I ask you one other thing?''

Atchinson stared at her, suspicion evident in his expression. "You can ask. I may not give it to you. What do you want?''

"You think there's any truth to that stuff about fat men

having short dicks? I was just wondering, because you always—"

"Get out," Atchison said. "I won't tolerate your insubordination. Get out."

Jerusha stood slowly, towering over him. Atchison vaulted to his feet, his face a mask of fury again, and started around his desk as though to physically force her out of his office. She moved quickly to the door, evading his grip, and slipped into the outer passageway. Atchinson paused at the door to his inner office. "You won't get away with this, Bailey. I swear to god you won't."

With what? What the hell is—man, have I ever stumbled into something I don't understand. And I'll be damned if I have the time to worry about it just now. "No rental car," she said finally. "I've got it."

She walked down the corridor to her own rabbit warren of offices and made it to her desk before the anger really hit her. The rental car wasn't the issue at all. It just happened to be there, something Atchinson could nitpick about to prove that he had the power to do so. From her first interview at NSA, she'd known he would be a problem. Known it, and figured she could work around it. There'd been people like that in the Navy and she'd made it work then.

But Atchinson was becoming more than just a problem— more like a major roadblock in her career. Like it or not, she *did* report to him on paper. And while NSA's organizational chart might not really reflect the information and power flow within the organization, Atchinson had the ability to make her life miserable in mundane ways. Like rental cars. Like bird-dogging her lunch hours, counting the minutes and whipping out the employee manual over the slightest tardiness.

She should have suspected it, she supposed. Atchinson was a company man, one who didn't like anyone who wasn't spouting the approved policy. What had started as dislike when she'd gone public over the Germany conflict had escalated into Atchinson's seemingly implacable hatred. She'd done nothing to deserve the latter, and couldn't even begin to understand where it came from.

But someone might know. Someone who'd been here at NSA longer than she had, someone who'd as much as admitted that he was capable of monitoring conversations in both Intanglio and Atchinson's offices. And someone who worked for her—at least part of the time.

Weekends only, to be exact. When they both slipped out of their civilian lives and went back to their first careers in the Navy, now as members of the same reserve unit.

Peter Carlisle, the electronic intercept wizard at NSA and star sonar technician in the Naval Reserve. A skinny, whipcord-tough man with a baby face that seemed a good ten years younger than he actually was. It was the face, she suspected, that made people open up to him. It was hard to see beyond the innocent exterior to the sharp mind behind those baby blue eyes.

Jerusha doubled-checked her safe by force of habit, making sure it was locked even though she hadn't touched it since she'd entered the office. Good security habits were just that, invariable habits. That done, she headed back down the passageway and up two floors to Pete's domain.

She stood outside the cipher-locked door and pressed the buzzer. A camera fixed in one corner of the passageway stared down at her. Its picture was transmitted inside to a security screening area.

"Yes?" a voice said from the speaker grill mounted next to the cipher lock.

"Jerusha Bailey from Ops. I'd like to see Mr. Carlisle if he's available," she answered.

Mister for Pete, but not for Terry Intanglio? Why had the title sprung so readily to her lips when she answered the security guard? Terry Intanglio—*Mister* Intanglio, she reminded herself—was Peter's boss. Why then did his first name come so readily to her lips when she invoked the director's personal power?

Atchinson might have a point, she conceded as she waited

for a response from the speaker. Some weakness in her character made her assert more familiarity with the director of NSA than was really warranted. Sure, she called him by his first name when they were discussing work, just as she called Pete by his first name. But she'd know that Atchinson generally referred to Intanglio more formally—why had she chosen to ignore that? Some petty impulse to flaunt her relationship with Atchinson's boss, put Atchinson on notice that she had a way of getting around him if she felt like using it?

She felt a twinge of embarrassment, maybe of shame. If that's what she'd been doing, then Atchinson had every right to call her on it. The approach he'd taken with her might have been a little more brutal than she'd have taken with a subordinate of her own—*maybe not*—but she'd have reacted the same way.

"Miss Bailey?" the speaker said. "Mr. Carlisle will be with you shortly."

"How long is 'shortly'?" she asked, but she heard the speaker cut off just as she started the question. Shortly could be anything from a few moments to half an hour or so. And as sensitive as everything was at NSA, Pete Carlisle's domain was so critical that there was no inner waiting room. You either belonged in there, working, or you were escorted by someone who did. Period.

Miss Bailey. There it was again, the question of courtesy and rank. She got respect from an anonymous security guard she couldn't even see, but hadn't been even that sensitive to Atchinson's own issues. She sighed, the realization dawning that maybe Atchinson wasn't always as much of an asshole as she suspected.

The cipher door clicked, buzzed, then swung out. Pete peered around the three-inch-thick reinforced steel door, eyes bright and curious behind his glasses. "To what do I owe the honor?" he asked, standing in the doorway.

"I wanted to run something by you, maybe get some background," she said. She took a step forward toward the door and was surprised to find that Pete didn't move. "This a bad time?"

Pete glanced back over his shoulder, then back at her. "I've got a few minutes." He stepped out into the passageway and led the door click shut behind him. He reached back to the knob and tried it, making sure it was securely latched. "What's on your mind?"

"It's not exactly in-the-passageway stuff," she hedged, conscious of the camera staring down at them and the speaker grill next to the door.

Pete looked frustrated. "I'm a little busy right now." He followed her gaze up to the camera, then shrugged. "Every inch of this building is monitored by someone, Jerusha. You know that."

"Except your office, right?"

"As far as I know."

"What does that mean?"

"Just what it sounds like. As far as I know, no one except my own staff monitors my office."

"Your own—You mean your people listen in on what goes on in your private office?"

He shrugged. "What did you expect? You get used to it, though."

Great, just great. Jerusha played back the conversations she'd had with Pete in his office, wondering what she'd let slip that she wouldn't have said if she'd known. Nothing particularly damning came to mind immediately. Still, she'd assumed that the one spot in the building she could be certain was unmonitored was Pete Carlisle's own office.

And Pete wasn't inviting her in right now. Not that she ever had free access on her own to his spaces, but she'd been up there often on routine matters. But now . . .

"This must be a bad time," she said, still absorbing the fact that there really was no privacy anywhere within the building. "What I wanted to talk over with you was neither urgent nor classified. It can wait. You got time for dinner or anything?" There'd always been a peculiar undercurrent of potential romance to her relationship with Peter, something neither of them had ever seemed to have the nerve to follow up on. It would have complicated matters, not only within NSA but in their Reserve unit as well.

"Not tonight," Pete said. Jerusha waited for him to elaborate on that, to suggest a backup date. When he didn't, she said, "I see. Well, some other time, then." She started back down the passageway to the elevator.

"Jerusha, wait." She turned as Pete started after her. "It's just work, that's all." He hesitated as though he were going to say more, then stayed silent.

She understood. Even indicating that his section had a particularly heavy workload right then and telling her when it might let up might prove a valuable bit of intelligence to someone.

But to whom in particular? Did he really think she was that prone to leak bits and pieces of information about NSA? No wonder there had never been more to their relationship. If he couldn't trust her to keep her mouth shut about his work schedule, was he likely to think she'd keep a personal relationship quiet?

Suddenly, even though she understood it, she was fed up with the NSA rules and regulations. Travel rules, security rules, and now even her closest friend inside the organization couldn't tell her when he'd be free to talk over Atchinson and Intanglio. And given what she now knew about his office, she sure as hell wasn't going to get into it at work. "It's okay," she said, trying to sound convincing. "Like I said—nothing urgent. We'll get around to it when you've got time." She reached out and touched him on the shoulder. "I'm going to be out of town for a few weeks, though. That *Mahan* incident and India—I'll be at the War College for a while."

And was she even allowed to say that? she wondered. As circumspect as Pete was about his schedule, maybe she shouldn't have—

Stop it. You're carrying this to ridiculous lengths. "Give me a call when you've got some time," she repeated, and punched the button to summon the elevator.

Pete looked faintly relieved at not being pressed for more. "I will. Have some lobster for me at Newport."

"I will."

Pete started back down the passageway to his section, then stopped at the door as the elevator arrived for her. "I'm not going to suddenly get orders back to active duty this time, am I? Because seriously, Jerusha, the timing would not work."

"I doubt it," she said. "I'm going as an NSA representative, not with the Reserve unit. But if anything interesting comes up, I'll give you a yell."

"Do that," he said. It sounded more like an order than she found comfortable.

BANGLADESH

Elwell's immediate superior—at least in terms of rank—Army First Lieutenant Dailey Handrick, wasn't impressed. "And you believe this might be evidence that India has nukes deployed forward, right? Based on one glove?"

"I'm certain of it, sir." Elwell kept his tone neutral and polite. It was the only way to deal with lieutenants that hadn't yet managed to puzzle out the difference between their asses and holes in the ground.

"Certain?" Handrick leaned back in his chair and clasped his hands behind his head. "Pretty strong statement, Sergeant."

"Pretty strong evidence, sir. In this weather, there's not much other reason for the troops to be carrying that sort of glove, much less wearing it enough to get it that filthy."

"One glove. That you no longer have in your possession, correct?"

Elwell contemplated the disadvantages of too much education. Handrick was a perfect example of how four years at an Ivy-league school could not be immediately cured by sixteen weeks of officer candidate school, eleven weeks of Infantry Basic, and a tour at staff HQ. It was clear that even after two years of experience to straighten him out on the reality of military service, Handrick still believed that officers ran the Army.

"I gave it to the Bengali scout, sir. His people are the ones at risk—they need to have a crack at the intelligence themselves." And judging from the expression on Khan's face, he was going to be taken a lot more seriously by his chain of command than Handrick was taking Elwell.

"We're all at risk, Sergeant. The United States has commitments in this area, you know. It's not like we're disinterested parties."

"Yes, sir." *Particularly not when it's your ass that's on the front line with the Bengalis.* Most of the time Lieutenant Handrick sat dry and cool in Incirclik, Turkey, reading the field reports Elwell sent him. But since the attack on *Mahan,* Handrick had decided that the liaison efforts with Bangladesh warranted his firsthand attention. At least long enough for a good, solid look-see and a no-notice administrative inspection.

"I'll pass the information along to our intelligence people, Sergeant. We'll see what they have to say. Of course, since you don't have the glove anymore, they're not going to be real eager to jump the gun based solely on your word. But those tanks aren't moving, are they? You yourself said that. Every indication we have here is that the Bengali-India conflict is already starting to settle down. Just a bit of nationalistic posturing intended to put the world on notice that they're still alive, I guess. Who knows why these heathens do anything?"

I know. Because I've been there, watched the faces, gotten to know the people. They fight because they have to, and because it's something that men do all over the world. The one thing you can count on is that there'll always be wars. Always. "Some of them are quite devout, sir," Elwell said quietly.

Handrick waved his hand dismissively. "Of course. In their own way." His tone of voice made it clear that in the world of the U.S. Army deployed overseas, that way didn't count for much. "Anything else, Sergeant? I could manage a couple of soldiers on special detachment to you, perhaps?"

"Nuclear intelligence specialists?"

A pause, then, "I was thinking more of administrative support. A quartermaster, perhaps."

Quartermaster. "No thanks, sir. I'm fine just as I am."

"If you're certain."

"I am."

"Well, then."

Elwell let the silence drag on a moment longer. A sharper officer would have understood that it meant that there was something very unsettled in the senior noncom's mind, an issue that the officer had misevaluated and misjudged. There would have been follow-up questions, a demand that Elwell speak his mind, and at least a promise that the officer would get back to Elwell with an intelligence estimate. In short, there would have been a little respect for Elwell's judgment instead of the continual high-handed dismissal. A good officer, even a very junior one, would have understood the value of listening to a sergeant that had spent over half of his life poking into nasty, brutal conflicts all around the world, would have at least listened.

"If there's nothing else, Sergeant?" Handrick asked, clearly not anticipating that there would be.

"Just one other thing, sir. When you brief the intelligence folks," a kind word for the hasty, slightly amused mention Elwell was certain Handrick would give his report, "would you tell them that it came from me?"

Another long silence. "That's not particularly relevant, is it, Sergeant? Those who need to know you're here already know that you're here. Those who don't have a need to know might pose a bit of a security problem. I think we'll just have to count on the intelligence section doing their job, shall we?"

"Sir." *You'll count on them, asshole. Not me.* Elwell was particularly grateful at that point that he'd put in the call to Bailey. "I'll update you if anything else happens, sir."

"Fine, fine. And, Sergeant, don't worry too much about

this. I suspect you'll be ordered out of Bangladesh within the next week. If the diplomatic efforts continue to show progress, there'll be no more need for our presence there, even in an advisory capacity. Now, this afternoon I'd like to take a look at the patrol logs for last month."

"Yes, sir. I'll be standing by for that." *But not counting on it. And if I think you're pulling a fast one to get me off scene to save your slick little butt, you're going to have a really really tough time tracking me down to order me back. Not unless you plan on getting that spiffy clean set of BDU's dirtier than they've been since OCS.*

"This afternoon, Sergeant," the lieutenant reminded him cheerily.

"Yes, sir." Elwell saluted, executed a smart about-face, and left.

Night patrols, lieutenants, nuclear weapons—only one sure Army cure for it. Elwell could hear his sleeping bag calling him as he stepped out of the lieutenant's quarters.

USS MAHAN

Lockridge no longer counted minutes and hours. Hands moving on the face of a clock, digital figures changing silently, all as meaningless now as keeping track of what movie was showing at the base theater in Norfolk. The true measure of time's passage was gallons of water inside the skin of the ship and degrees of list. An easier way to keep track of things, he'd reflected, and wondered why he'd never realized that before. Gallons and degrees counted down—a man knew when he was done when both figures reached zero. You knew when you could quit fighting.

Hours and days weren't so easy. When the numbers just kept getting bigger, who knew when the end would be? Certainly not Fireman Irving. One minute, a kid with nothing more on his mind than how fine and right it was to be the only one roaming through the more remote parts of the ship, keeping an eye on things and checking off the compartments on his list, accumulating tidy check marks in boxes. The next—well, there'd been no more next, had there? No warning, no number approaching zero that Irving had been able to look at and know what was coming.

Jack Lockridge had it easier, especially since the pain pills Doc had given him leveled out the worst of the pain, reducing agony to a vaguely comforting red fog around him that he could either notice or ignore at will. It seemed like Threlkeld was a constant presence, standing just behind him at his right elbow or popping his head into Lockridge's cabin to report the latest numbers, then returning seconds later to update him yet again. On some level, Lockridge was aware that Threlkeld was sticking to a schedule of some sort. Hourly, perhaps more often. To simplify matters, Lockridge began timing his pain medication. Three engineering reports meant it was time to pop another capsule, and the cycle started anew.

Lockridge could gauge Engineering's progress in the angle of the deck under his feet, the way the ship responded to rudder orders, the inertia of the ship as she rode the swells. The ebb and flow of pain took on the same rhythm, fading down toward zero in the hours that he watched the ship's progress. Zero on all scales meant both he and the ship would live. Perhaps not to fight again. The hole in the hull was too great, just as the scar tissue on his hand ran too deep for his hand to fully close. He would deal with all that later, when his world expanded to include those not inside *Mahan*'s hull, when he resumed counting time by an arbitrary external standard imposed on more real rhythms.

Rhythms—was there ever an end to them? It seemed to him now, detached as he was from time, that there was order in almost everything, although not readily apparent when measured against traditional scales. Take trim, for instance. Threlkeld might tell him that they were still five degrees down at the bow, but did that actually describe the degree of difficulty crossing the bridge? The way coffee roiled up against the side of his cup?

No. Nor, when he had time to think about it, did the military's measures of threat conditions make much sense, either. *Mahan* had been simply exerting a fundamental right to freedom of navigation in relatively peaceful waters. Low-threat condition. No open-water opposition. If it hadn't been evaluated so, *Mahan* would not have been sent out alone. But from the very beginning, it had seemed a low ThreatCon evolution, and there had never been any indication otherwise.

Not until the missiles had hit.

So was there any point to ever making predictions about ThreatCons and missiles and whether some fucking crazy idiot somewhere was going to lob a missile up your ass? Or were gallons and degrees the only sort of measurements you could ever really count on?

Lockridge saw Threlkeld making his way across the bridge toward him and checked the neat grease pencil checkmarks he'd made on the window near his chair. He popped another pain pill in his mouth.

BANGLADESH

Two hours after he'd lain down, Elwell came awake instantly. His hand closed around his pistol. He lay without moving for a moment, cataloguing the noises around him. Camp sounds, stiff breeze flapping at the tattered edges of his tent, the faint smell of old curry from the rude cook space that served the Bengali troops.

No immediate danger. Still, it never hurt to make sure before acknowledging that one was awake.

Billy rolled up into a sitting position on the loose-jointed canvas cot. More Bengali workmanship and built for men smaller and lighter. Elwell wasn't that tall, but the muscle packed onto his frame challenged the resilience of his adopted sleeping equipment.

Adopted. Well, stolen. If you wanted to get technical.

He reached down to the end of his rack and pulled his boots

toward him and upended them. The habit of evicting fauna
was automatic, and Bangladesh carried some nasty versions of
critters he'd seen around the world. Nasty, but tasty enough,
if you didn't think about what you were eating. How long had
it been since a quick snack on available bugs had stopped
bothering him? At least it beat MRE's most of the time.

Satisfied that his boots weren't holding any surprises, he
placed them sole-down on the small piece of plastic next to
his cot. A quick change into fresh socks—that was the first
thing any soldier learned, clean socks whenever possible, because god knew how long it'd be before you had the opportunity again—and they were well broken in and cupped his
feet like.

*—like a glove. Now, what the hell has Khan done with it,
I wonder? That damned lieutenant is going to want me to get
it to him somehow. I wonder if he really thinks that FedEx
runs out here?*

Well, he'd be seeing Khan shortly, and he'd find out then.

7

THE NAVAL WAR COLLEGE, NEWPORT, RHODE ISLAND

It never changes. Jerusha looked up at the massive interlocking grid of three-story buildings, old and new juxtaposed against the Narragansett Bay. *Like war—it stays the same. Only the faces and the names are different.*

The Naval War College in Newport, Rhode Island, was the most prestigious of all the advanced service academies. It was home to three advanced graduate studies programs including one for officers in foreign navies. Among its graduates, it numbered the most influential admirals and generals in the United States military as well as thirty-three heads of foreign navies. Every year, the heads of the five services visited to talk to the next generation of senior leaders. The War College's library rivaled any collection of military thought in the world.

The jewel in the crown was the Maritime Battle Lab. Housed in a separate building across the road from the older portions, the MBL was the most advanced think tank on military affairs in the United States, rivaled in the world only by Frunze Academy in Russia. Behind four levels of security doors, and within an intricate array of computers and the latest technology, academicians and senior military officers war-gamed their strategy for the next conflict.

Jerusha had spent a summer at the Naval War College on temporary reserve duty. It had been an exceptionally good deal.

Rare volumes from every war America had fought, as well as priceless historical documents. She'd spent hours in the library, prowling through the stacks in the basement, pulling books off the shelves at random and letting herself be absorbed into a detailed account of some insignificant battle, into the intricacies of operational analysis, of theories on the causes of war from cultures she could barely locate on the map, much less quote well. Even though the course of instruction itself had been demanding, she'd always felt that her real education had come from the library. Seeing the accounts of men who were there, reading how they planned and executed campaigns that history now judged, was far more valuable firsthand, without the interpretations and analysis of a different generation. And that was no surprise either, was it, that she liked to see the documents firsthand, draw her own conclusions about cause and effect.

It felt no different crossing the quarterdeck as an NSA analyst instead of a student. There were the same clusters of security-badged and civilian-clad students in the passageways, the coffee mess, the library. Not so long ago, she'd been one of them, frantically trying to stay current on the assigned reading, joking with the rest of them that "it was only a lot of reading if you did it" but still unable to do less than her best to keep up.

Jerusha slid into a seat near the back of the auditorium. Just in time, no thanks due to the shuttle to Newport she'd caught from the TF Greene Airport in Providence. She'd tried to rent a car, hauling out her own credit card even though she was fairly certain she wouldn't get reimbursed for it, but there were none available at any of the airport rental agencies. Rather than hunt for one in town and be inexcusably late for the first brief, she'd taken the shuttle down to Newport. Since she didn't have a reservation for the shuttle, it had taken twenty bucks to bribe her way onto the one just leaving. The ride down the two-lane highway had been cramped and uncomfortable, and the driver had wanted to drop off a gaggle of enlisted sailors at their quarters before taking her to the War College. It had taken another twenty-dollar bill to win the argument.

The auditorium itself was a testament to how seriously the War College's seminars were regarded. It was located in the central War College building, set off along with the classrooms and offices by a guard-controlled and security-badge-access key card system. The doors themselves were deceptively decorative, but met every Department of Defense requirement for access to material up to and including that classified as Top Secret. Briefings held at levels above that were conducted in a separate steel-doored security library down the passageway or in the security vault on the second deck.

The chairs were plush and comfortable. Microphones lined the rows of seats, hung in brackets between every two seats. The entire room except the stage was carpeted in deep, rich blue, and thick, classic drapes were pulled shut behind the podium. A projection system integrated into the college's central LAN ran the display system and projected information onto two massive screens that descended from the ceiling at the touch of a button.

Even so, the microphone squealed. The noise cut through the polite murmurs from the audience and elicited a chuckle from the group.

The auditorium lights were dimmed, but she could see that the majority of the seats were vacant. Most of the people were clustered in the forward rows, some sitting in clumps as though they already knew one another. About half were in uniform, the rest in civilian attire, but that didn't necessarily mean anything. Almost everyone at the War College—students, professors, and guests—wore civilian clothes.

She'd probably know some of the other attendees herself, but there was no way she was going to walk to the front of the auditorium and advertise her tardiness. Not that anything had started yet, but on time in the Navy meant fifteen minutes early. Especially when a three-star was on tap to give a welcoming speech.

Just in time. Admiral Tallidan was just reaching the steps that led from the first row of seats to the stage, his aide trailing behind him and carrying a folder. Jerusha sank back into her seat, nudged the suitcase she'd brought with her over a few inches, and paid attention.

Tallidan was a tall man, well over six feet tall judging from his size compared to the podium. Steel gray hair clipped short, features that were craggy even from this distance. He moved with the easy grace of an athlete, not even pausing to look back at his aide as he reached back for the microphone. The aide had already detached it from the podium and slipped it into his hand like a relay runner passing a baton.

Tallidan walked to the forward end of the stage and stared out at the collection of officers and civilian specialists scattered through the large auditorium. He turned to his aide, said something while covering the microphone in his hand. The aide scampered off stage. Moments later, the lights at the edge of the stage dimmed slightly.

The admiral raised the microphone. An audible click resonated in the auditorium as he thumbed the mike on. "That's better. You get those lights in your eyes, you can't tell who's still awake." He waited for the spatter of laughter to die down, then began.

"Welcome to the Naval War College. Welcome *back*, I should say. Most of you have been here at least once. For a war game, a conference, or maybe even as a student. For those of you in the Navy, you've been in Newport probably more times than you'd care to count. But if you haven't been at the War College, then you're in for a rare treat."

Tallidan gestured at the people seated in the first row of seats. "I've got more than enough experts on tap here to tell you exactly what we expect of you in the next week or so. Most of them are a hell of a lot smarter than I am about a number of things—history, treaties, why things are the way that they are in the world. So there's just one thing I want to make clear to you, one thing I want to make sure you don't forget." He shook his head, as though remembering an unpleasant experience. "You warfighters in the room will know what I'm talking about.

"The one thing that's predictable about war is that nothing's predictable." Tallidan looked down and waited while the expected chuckle spread across the auditorium. "Except the few things that are." A louder response this time, and the admiral settled in to what was clearly a briefing he'd done many times before.

"You may think I'm joking about this, but it's never been more true than it is right now. Used to be, we could at least count on having a winner and a loser. Today, the distinction is increasingly blurred. Indeed, the entire nature of warfare seems to have taken a turn back toward tribalism and nationalism. You know yourselves from your own experience." He paused and swept one hand out to encompass the entire audience. "What have you seen in your own careers in the days since Vietnam? Increasing emphasis on peacekeeping, the small, nasty conflict. Desert Storm was hardly even a contest, and who within the establishment predicted that? And Germany? Panama?"

An uneasy silence at that, shiftings and mutterings from the crowd of assembled officers and civilian agency executives. Jerusha felt her own uneasiness over the question. In the last two conflicts, nothing had been what it seemed—nothing.

What have I seen? How about a monumental testimony to the danger of downsizing? How about dead sailors because somebody somewhere didn't get the intelligence reports out fast enough? Too many times that I had the feeling nobody was taking reports from the ship on the scene seriously enough, tossing them out altogether if they didn't fit some preconceived idea of how the war was going . . .

"So what's the point?" Tallidan asked. "If there's nothing predictable about war, why are we here? Any thoughts?"

"Good question," someone called out from the back of the room. A murmur of agreement swept over the crowd.

"Use the mikes if you've got a comment, please." The admiral gazed out over the room again, inviting comment. Silence, the kind that fills a classroom when every student is hoping not to be called on.

"I'll tell you why, then," the admiral continued. "Even though we know that war is unpredictable, we also know that we can best prepare for that by considering all possible alternatives. Every major conflict since the Civil War has been war-gamed at the War College. Every single one. Every commander in chief and operational commander who heeded the lessons learned here has credited his time at the War College as the key factor that influenced his planning. As the one experience that resulted in reduced casualties, in better arrays of options, and in being prepared for the unexpected. And we do that the old-fashioned way, although today with the most modern equipment available. We take the best and the brightest, along with the most experienced, and lock them in a room and let them argue. Let them kick up crazy theories, float trial balloons, look at the intelligence from every angle. We set up the scenarios, run the game out on the computer, and then let them play the opposite side. They fight the war on paper fifty thousand times before the first troop is committed on foreign soil."

An Air Force officer stood, his microphone in his hand. "So what about Vietnam?"

"I'll show you what the War College recommended at the time. You be the judge," the admiral said. "Personally, I think we would have been out of there in two years. But remember, we're here to make recommendations, not give orders. Sometimes the War College scenarios are adopted as is, sometimes they're modified. Occasionally, as with Vietnam, they're ignored.

"At the War College, there are no school solutions. Nothing is sacred. As a result, we've learned a fair amount about warfare. With today's modern analytical techniques, including chaos theory, we're learning even more. And you're here to-day to push the boundaries back even further.''

Another officer stood, a Marine this time. "In the Corps, we don't believe in coincidence, sir. What's the bottom line on the Middle East? Is it tied in with *Mahan*? And what about Pakistan?''

"That's what you're here to tell us. The War College doesn't operate alone. We can't—we'd end up with an ivory tower solution that might or might not make real-time sense in today's forces.''

"So we're supposed to figure this out?'' the Marine asked.

The admiral shrugged. "Look around you. You've got every military service and government agency involved rep-resented here along with all the real experience you'd even want. If you can't find an answer, no one can and we might as well settle for war continuing to be unpredictable. Is that what you want?''

A chorus of no's greeted that last statement. The admiral appeared satisfied. "Good. Every generation of warfighters has met the challenge. I see no reason why you should be any different.'' He paused for a moment, then turned back to the podium as thought wanting to say more. The silence length-ened. Finally, he cleared his throat and said, "There are those among us on the faculty who think the future is even brighter than the past. With enough data, we may be able to pinpoint the causes of war even more accurately. It's a daunting task, ranging from social anthropology through statistical forecast-ing technology. I think of it as peering into the heart of man-kind to determine if we're even capable of peace. There are those who believe that with enough knowledge we can head off conflicts before they turn into world wars. No more Ko-reas, no more Vietnams. There might be some casualties tak-ing action before war begins, but nothing like the scale we've seen in history.'' He leaned forward and said, "Think of it as preemptive peace.''

No more wars? Who is he kidding? Jerusha was on her feet, grabbing for a microphone. "Sir, is that a unanimous conclu-

sion among your staff? Because I have to tell you, it sounds
pretty spurious. Not to mention ludicrous.''

The admiral squinted at her, apparently trying to make out
her identity, but the stage lights partially blinded him. "Your
name, madam?''

Jerusha swore silently. Why had she had to jump up, ask
the question that the admiral was clearly inviting? Wasn't it
enough that she was here? Any contributions she had to make
to the discussions could have been done in a less public manner.

"Jerusha Bailey, National Security Agency,'' she said re-
luctantly.

A sound ran through the audience, half murmur, half comment. She bore it silently, knowing the basic content if not the
particulars of the whispers. They might not recognize her face,
but they knew her name.

"Back on active duty again, Commander Bailey?'' the admiral asked. "I must say, that bodes ill for the peace process
in India. You have a remarkable habit of suiting back up just
in time for every conflict.''

For every chance to grab some glory was the unspoken
implication. Jerusha frowned, now more annoyed than embarrassed. "You'd have to ask the Navy about that, Admiral. I
just went where they told me to.''

"Indeed. And now they've told you to come to the War
College, have they?''

"No, sir. I'm here as a representative from NSA. As I
said.''

"Yes, of course.'' The admiral glanced off stage, as though
looking for cues from his aide "Well, I think I've taken up
enough time in the preliminaries. In your information package,
you'll find a list of working groups and your assignments
to—''

Jerusha slid back into her seat, feeling the blood rush into
her cheeks.

"Admiral, if I may?'' A new voice, one from the front row.
A massive man was standing, his back to Jerusha. He turned

to scan the auditorium, trying to locate her in the dim lights. "Miss Bailey's question?"

Jerusha immediately matched the voice and profile with a memory. Dean Arden Gromko, the head of the War-gaming Department within the War College. He'd been there for over a decade, including the time that Jerusha had spent at NWC.

"Why don't I let you answer that for me? You've got a mike? Fine, fine," the admiral said, sounding as close to flustered as Jerusha had ever heard a flag officer sound. "Please, go ahead."

Gromko finally located Jerusha in the auditorium. Dark eyes glittered beneath a short, unruly mass of gray. His cheekbones were high and flat, hinting at generations of ancestors storming the steppes.

Looking directly at her, Gromko said, "Welcome back to the War College, Miss Bailey," emphasizing her civilian title ever so slightly. For some reason, Jerusha found that oddly comforting. The title thing again, but coming from this man, she counted it as far more than a mere pleasantry.

During her year at the War College, she'd participated in seminar games with her class as well as volunteered to assist in supporting games held for outside participants. After watching her for a while, Gromko had tapped her as his unofficial aide. She'd watched two global wars and myriad regional conflicts standing next to him, listening to his analysis and suggestions as the conflicts progressed.

Brilliant. That was the only word she could think of that even started to encompass the breadth of Gromko's knowledge, his insights and surprising leaps of deduction. Jerusha had originally thought that the war-gaming scenarios were unrealistic, and the follow-up analysis too flattering to the participants.

Gromko had come to trust her enough to show her why she was wrong. He pointed out the subtleties hidden in the straightforward, the techniques of presenting choices and challenges to senior officers in a way that taught them without preaching at them. In many cases, winning the War College's game left the senior officer with the uneasy feeling that he or she'd missed something. It was a moment that Jerusha saw Gromko lived for, the dawning of doubt in an officer's eyes, what Gromko described as the beginning of wisdom.

"Better here than there," he'd said back then. And smiled, and she realized that whatever techniques he used on his war-gamers were at work on her as well. Now, watching his familiar shape backlit by the stage lights, she wondered why he'd plucked her out of the pack of junior officers back then to serve as his assistant.

"You will remember," the dean said, his voice slow, deep and measured, "that there are many viewpoints within the department. Some believe that war is a constant in the human heart and that no amount of research will ever change that. Others are convinced that more computers, more data, and certainly more of our departmental operating funds, our OP-TAR, will yield better answers. Many of us are arrayed along the spectrum between those two poles. The answer to your question must be no, there is no school solution. Nor are there any sacred cows, as you may well remember from your own time here." Gromko turned to scan the audience. "If any of you have further questions, please come see me at any time. I have several volumes of small-print reports devoted just to this subject. There are answers, Miss Bailey, answers in science. It's just that they may not be the ones that you wish to find."

Admiral Tallidan smiled his approval. "Thank you, Dean Gromko. We'll muster in thirty minutes in the Battle Lab."

Science. And how much does that tell you about the human heart? And does it tell you how much one ripped glove means? She contemplated that as she followed the rest of the herd across the street to the Maritime Battle Center.

The Battle Lab was smaller than the main auditorium, but not by much. An electronic screen dominated the forward half of the room, reaching from three feet above the ground to the ceiling two stories above. Continents were outlined in black, filled in with light washes of color so as not to obscure the tactical unit symbols.

The symbols clustered around the Persian Gulf, the eastern end of the Mediterranean, and the eastern and western seaboards of the continental United States. Another small clot was forming around Hawaii, evidence of a deploying battle group in workup operations. A few loners were scattered around the rest of the map, down south of Florida and off the coast of Mexico, U.S. Navy units on counterdrug operations.

Ground troops were similarly accounted for, although Jerusha found that reading ground symbology—with the differentiation between different types of units, command posts, major and secondary thrusts—was a skill that rusted if not used frequently. It had been years since she'd had to understand Army operations based on what they called cartooning, and while she thought she had the general idea, no doubt the nuances of the situation escaped her.

"And this is all real time?" one officer in the group asked.

Gromko nodded. "Yes. Allowing, of course, for a few milliseconds of delay as the signal is transmitted through the satellite system. We're hooked into the joint LINK, looking at the same pictures each area commander is seeing."

"Why real time?" Jerusha asked, taking in the complicated dance on the screen before her. "I thought we were doing strategic planning, not tactical?"

Gromko met her gaze, his eyes warm and friendly. "The world of planning has changed in the last few years, Miss Bailey. Blame it on whatever you like—increases in foreign computer technology transfer, expanded weapons ranges, even the proliferation of intelligence. Whatever the reason, the pace of war is far different from what it was just five years ago— even in the last year, it has increased markedly. It's no longer enough to try to project out a nation's probable movements over the next six months. By the time you've worked it out, he's already been there and gone."

"So you can't plan anymore."

"Not in the sense that we would have a decade ago. The

other major factor in planning now is weapons ranges and delivery platforms. Too many nations have submarines, too many have long-range tactical weapons. Warfare is no longer a matter of moving masses of troops and support units around on the ground, leaving huge intelligence footprints for the world to see. Today, a few trucks, perhaps a platoon of technicians, and a nation is poised to make a decisive strike. Intelligence can't always anticipate that or track it in time to make a difference.''

''But then what's the point of planning?''

''The point is that the process is still valid—it's just that the time frames are markedly truncated. The intelligence DADA loop is centimeters in circumference rather than months.''

''DADA loop?'' a civilian asked.

''Detection, Analysis, Dissemination, Action,'' Jerusha murmured, recalling the four points in the model.

''Exactly so,'' Gromko said. ''That's why we're tied directly into the battle group LINK. We have to see what's happening now, what the raw data is from the forces closest to the problem. We can't wait on traditional avenues of communication anymore. The LINK not only gives us virtually real-time symbology but also provides an ancillary means of communication with the battle force itself via the OPNOTE system. It's much faster than using standard formatted messages.''

''Sounds like you've almost joined the battle group as an adjunct staff,'' Jerusha said, impressed at what Gromko had accomplished. He was right, there had been some major changes in the way the Navy was doing business.

Gromko smiled, and she recognize the expression that indicated his pleasure that some deeper lesson was being taught. He was leading her gently on to conclusions that he hoped she would draw, waiting for her privately to make some connection while he expounded publicly on general principles. ''Exactly so,'' he repeated. ''Intelligence, strategic forces, planning functions—all merged into a single cohesive force. Within the next two years, we expect to complete coordination loops with the State Department and Commerce. With those additions, we can begin to have a truly national security policy in place rather than just a military aspect to it. Imagine it—total integration of every American agency, commission, and asset within one picture, on one data link. We'll be able to coordinate responses in a way that we've just dreamed about before.''

"Total integration," Jerusha repeated, an uneasy feeling forming in her gut.

The Soviet Union had tried integrating their entire industrial complex into the fabric of their union. The Central Committee dictated the security objectives of the Union and every factory, production facility, and school had had to follow that lead. Under the guise of establishing a cohesive national policy, the system had stifled every bit of individual initiative and innovation.

And now, with the former states of the Soviet Union making a stab at adopting American-style democracy, the War College was advocating adopting the USSR's method of developing national policy? This was a step forward?

Gromko should see the fallacy in that, if anyone should. Although his grandparents had escaped from Ukraine just after World War II, she knew he maintained a passion for the area.

Yet there was something to what he said. Sometimes the partnership with the industrial complex led to insanely inept military planning. At the behest of local contracts after their piece of the pork barrel, Congress appropriated money for projects the military neither needed nor wanted. Projects that were weapons without maintenance or repair budgets. Aircraft that minimally served the needs of all services without really doing the job for any particular one, mediocre in all roles rather than specially designed for one. Interchangeable parts for aircraft that didn't work for any service.

And now, joint data systems that would provide a tactical look—and a highly classified one, at that—to any civilian employee that happened to have the right password and could convince his or her boss that he or she had a need to know. The security concerns alone were staggering.

"The Persian Gulf—what specific implications do you see for us in that area?" Jerusha asked.

"Implications—well, we have some forecasts. As you probably suspect, we've already been at work on this. You'll find the material in your briefing package," Gromko answered. "But just as an example, you might consider a close connection between sanctions and the movement of military units on the ground. The ability to precisely tailor responses, drawing not only on the military forces in the area but on national and strategic assets as well."

"To micromanage the war," Jerusha countered.

"To avoid wasting men and weapons when a lesser effort would achieve the desired objective," Gromko corrected. "Miss Bailey, the world is moving on. Today's environment calls for officers to consider the broader picture, not just their little piece of it."

A small pocket of white skittered across the screen, moving with a jerky motion that indicated the data stream was not entirely coherent. "What's that?" Jerusha asked. Gromko turned to look. The light reflected at an angle off of his face, and she saw the white symbol reflected deep in his eyes.

8

USS *EISENHOWER*

Naval combat consisted of hours of boredom punctuated by moment of sheer terror, and nowhere was that hoary adage more true than in the Middle East. By noon, Gar was losing the battle to stay awake. After eighteen hours of watching, waiting for another attack, constantly juggling gas and fighter patrols in the air, the admiral had concluded that the immediate danger was past. He'd secured General Quarters and placed the ship in Condition Two, and settled into his chair in TFCC for the duration.

Unfortunately for Gar and his watch section, they'd stayed at GQ right through their downtime and were the first section set for Condition Two. They'd started off tired, augmented by additional watchstanders for the four-hour watch, and were now only thirty minutes away from being relieved. Condition Two—four hours in the rack, then back on watch. But four hours was four hours, and at least it'd be enough to get rid of the grainy feeling under his eyelids.

Gar could feel the fatigue gnawing at the edges of his consciousness. It was manageable as long as he had something to do. But now, three hours into a six-hour watch, with everything that he could think of to do done, it was starting to creep back up on him.

As he had so often in the past eighteen hours, he felt a flash of shame. Who was he to gripe about his hours when Lockridge was trying to keep *Mahan* afloat on the other side of India?

"Sir, the other day—that lead dog business. I've been giving it some more thought," Simmons said. "Now that we're going to take care of Iraq, somebody ought to do something about *Mahan*."

"They will. When the time's right." Gar took a sip of coffee. Was Monarelli awake? Probably so—he heard that grating monotone somewhere behind him, but it was hard to tell with his earphones on if it was the admiral humming or the ventilation system kicking in. The admiral had been intermittently dozing and bitching from the chair immediately behind him, that's as much as he was willing to say out loud.

For the most part he agreed with Simmons—the U.S. had to mount a response, and a public one at that. Diplomatic censure, trade embargoes—that wasn't going to cut it, not in anyone's mind. A U.S. warship had taken a hit and men and women had died. That required, demanded even, something more. Not only on general principles, but as evidence to the people on the front lines that they were there for a reason. It wasn't dying that pissed them off so much, it was the possibility that it wouldn't be for much.

"They *will* do something, won't they, sir?" Simmons asked. "I mean, we'll know about it after it's all over, I guess."

"I imagine so. But when and how—unless we're the ones making the strike, we'll hear about it on CNN with everyone else. Need to know—if we don't, we won't. But there'll probably be some warning signs, I would imagine. Maybe we'll get copied on the warning order." He pointed at the screen. Intell had input its latest estimate of the number of aircraft now on the ground in Iran.

"We've got enough to worry about around here without

worrying about what's happening on the other side of India,"
Monarelli said, breaking off from the grating hum for a while.

"They could tell us, though," Simmons said stubbornly.
Gar winced and waited for the humming to cut back in. "It's
not like the carrier is a security risk."

*Not unless you count the E-mail to spouses, the snail mail
that goes out, and any information that the COD crews let
slip. Or that the media hounds onboard sniff out—god knows
where they get their information, but I'd be willing to bet
they've made friends with every mess crank onboard.* The
cooks and their helpers were always the first to know anything,
no matter what the security classification.

The speaker hardwired into the area tactical circuit warbled
the distinctive tone associated with the crypto gear, then a
voice intoned the standard call-up. Gar heard the hatch to
TFCC open, heard the swearing from the other side of the
bulkhead that TFCC shared with the ship's CDC. He ignored
both and answered the call-up.

"*Eisenhower,* this is Fifth Fleet. Make preparations for immediate inchop of the Gulf." The voice was the distinctive
grumble of the admiral. "Is the admiral listening?"

"I am." Gar heard the admiral answer from behind him,
his voice confident and calm, a marked contrast to the whiny
tone he used to deliver ultimatums and threats to his staff.
"How soon do you want us there?"

"Yesterday."

"Will you settle for four hours?" the admiral answered. He
motioned to Gar, his message clear. Gar saw a pencil roll
across his console as the ship hunted for wind across the deck.
Whatever else she did before inchopping the Gulf, *Eisenhower*
would put fighters and tankers in the air.

Gar watched the updated flight schedule scroll across a
monitor mounted to the right of the tactical display and then
picked up the white phone to call CDC. Along with the fighters, they best put up some USW assets to try to solve the
unlocated submarine problem, even though no one knew what
the hell to do with them once they'd found them. Until they

determined nationality, there was no way to tell friend from
foe.

Gar had just started to dial the extension to CDC when he
saw a hand appear behind the clear plastic screen shown on
the monitor. Writing backward, an operations specialist added
two Vikings to the launch schedule. Gar replaced the telephone. CDC was monitoring the same circuit and would know
everything he knew. SCIF would give them the intelligence
update over the secure line as soon as there was time.

The noise inside TFCC increased measurably. Gar reached
up and tweaked the volume up on the speaker. A Tomcat, an
F-14, by the sound of it. Experienced carrier sailors could tell
what kind of aircraft was spooling up overhead by the way
the computer monitors rattled, and this was definitely a
Tomcat-type rattle. TFCC was located on the 03 level, called
the oh-three. Directly overhead was the flight deck. Most of
decks 01 through 03 on the port side of the ship were one
large open space to accommodate the hangar bay. The third
deck above the waterline housed most of the squadron ready
rooms, the flag spaces, and flag staff staterooms. Gar had
known aviators who were so used to the flight deck noises that
they weren't comfortable sleeping on lower, quieter decks.
The lack of noises kept them awake.

"Three minutes to set Flight Quarters—not bad," Monarelli
said, his voice almost drowned out by the roar of the aircraft.

I hope you're not taking that as a tribute to your leadership,
Moanin'. "I think they were probably not far from Pri-Fly,"
Gar said.

The admiral glanced over at him, an odd expression on his
face. "Anticipating the call. Just like you did. Yesterday, you
set General Quarters before Fifth Fleet called. Why?"

"Just a few second before. SCIF had an intell update—
launch indications from Iraq."

Monarelli studied him for a moment. "We've had launch
indications before."

Gar felt thin ice under his feet. "There was something about
the situation—I don't know, Admiral. It felt urgent all at once,

that's all I can tell you. I was just getting ready to call you when Fifth Fleet called.''

The admiral nodded. ''Okay. That's why you're TAO. If I wanted you to call me over every decision, we'd be dead sometime soon.''

Gar mumbled a word of thanks because it seemed called for, but he'd caught the undertones in Monarelli's voice. The words of support were for public consumption. All admirals hated surprises, but in Monarelli's book, surprises were irrevocably marked down as a mistake on someone else's part.

But that wasn't fair, Gar reflected, even as he wondered whether he'd done the right thing. The reason the ship *had* a flag TAO was to make those decisions instantaneously, to use those precious few seconds that might mean the difference between life and death for the ship and the air wing. And had there been any hard evidence of a threat, he had no doubt that that's what the admiral would have wanted him to do.

But situations like this, where there was no more than a warrior's instinct that something very very bad was about to happen, now those were different. Did you call the admiral first, or did you set General Quarters first and then call? So far, nothing had happened that showed that those critical seconds would have made a difference this time. He glanced up at the tactical display. In fact, nothing had happened at all.

But if you're right all the time, then you're being too cautious. It's like a surgeon—if every suspicious lump you biopsy, every appendix you take out is bad, then you're cutting it too close. There's got to be a certain percentage of false alarms or you're not aggressive enough.

Still, what would he do next time? Would the admiral's disapproval slow him down, make him question his own judgment? Endanger the ship if it turned out that he was right?

Gar reached for the receiver to tactical, had just closed his fingers around the cold plastic, when a movement on the screen caught his attention. It was accompanied by a quiet demand for attention from Simmons. ''More Iraqis launching, sir. Turning east, sir—east. They're not headed for the no-fly zone at all.''

"Iran?" Gar asked.

"Iran," the admiral said, watching the inverted symbols on the screen inch across the small-scale display that showed their entire operational area. "Iran again. General Quarters, dammit. Do I have to tell you every time?"

NAVAL WAR COLLEGE

Jerusha stared as the aircraft symbols inched across the screen. During the first few seconds, someone had resized the screen and it was now centered on the Persian Gulf. The aircraft were still well to the north of the Gulf itself and headed due east.

Behind here, the rest of the officers stared, mostly silent except for hastily whispered explanations to the civilians unfamiliar with the basic symbology and technology. There was one sharp comment, then a crisp "Shut up" from someone. Probably a Marine officer, from the tone of voice, she figured, still staring at the screen.

The symbols themselves seemed oddly mundane. There were no warning gongs, no sailors running to General Quarters, or any other indication that things were other than normal in the world depicted on the screen.

Not unless you understood that the inverted V's were hostile aircraft. Not unless you knew the region well enough to identify the probable launch location of the aircraft—and their probable destination.

Ike *is at General Quarters now. Or almost there—the carrier's probably taking a little longer unless they had good intell. What's the time delay on this picture? Can't be much more than a few seconds, if that. Not if this is the battle group's LINK picture.*

More symbology popped onto the board as the carrier launched fighter protection. The noise behind her died down as the uninitiated, whether or not they fully understood what they were seeing, picked up on the tension ratcheting up in the room from the military officers.

Jerusha balled her hands up into fists and beat out a slow rhythm on her legs. To stand there and watch, absolutely and completely incapable of having any effect whatsoever on the outcome, was frustrating to the point of panic. This was the same picture she would have seen had she been there. Her fingers ached for a weapons control panel.

USS *EISENHOWER*

"I want some answers, people. I want them now." Monarelli was shouting now, an edge in his voice. The clamor inside TFCC dropped for a moment, then started again, completely out of control, as everyone inside the small compartment tried to find someone to give orders to. "TAO, goddammit, what kind of watch section are you running? Get control of your people!"

"Pipe down, everyone," Gar said quietly over the ICS. "The admiral wants answers—who's got them? Intell?"

"Sir, admiral, I—" The lieutenant commander drew in a deep breath and tried to decide who exactly he was supposed to address. He settled on the admiral. "They're not headed for us, sir. No indication that they're doing anything other than what it looks like: a bombing run on Iran. Although given the Iraqi behavior with the last apparent bomb run, that's a low-reliability intelligence estimate."

"Thank you, Commander. I believe I can see that." The admiral's voice was deceptively quiet, ominous after his outbreak minutes earlier. "I think what I had in mind was an answer to a couple of other questions. Anyone else?"

Silence now, deep and embarrassed. The questions now were tougher. Why? Where exactly were the Iraqi fighters headed in Iran? What should the carrier do until instructions from higher authority came in?

The admiral drew in a deep breath. "That's what I

thought.'' He turned back to stare at the screen. "Until you do have answers, shut up. All of you."

Gar tapped out a few commands on his keyboard and zoomed the picture in on the fighters and their surrounding airspace. Five hundred miles to the north, inside those cockpits, Iraqi pilots and their bombardiers were running through checklists, double-checking their approach patterns, making sure they hit each point exactly on schedule.

The first enemy aircraft symbol disappeared off the screen.

"Anyone?" the admiral asked.

No one spoke.

Then the second, followed soon after by the rest of the symbols. Monarelli's hand clamped down on Gar's shoulder. "What the hell is going on with our LINK picture, TAO?"

Gar listened to the voices piped into his ears, following the discussion going on between his own operations specialist and the OS onboard the cruiser. Same questions, and answers that the admiral wasn't going to like. Not because they were the wrong answers, in the sense of being technically inaccurate. No, because they were the sort of answers that raised more questions.

Finally Gar spoke. "Admiral, there's nothing wrong with the LINK. Or with the E-2C radar or the Aegis system. We're no longer holding contact on the fighters. And SCIF says—" Gar paused for a moment, then continued, "SCIF says they've got imagery on the fighters. On the ground. They're on the ground with the last batch."

"All of them?" Clearly the admiral found that hard to swallow. "Again?"

Gar nodded. "All of them. They landed. In Iran. At a military airfield. Again."

ESCALATION

9

USS *MAHAN*

"We were talking, Commander. About *Mahan*."

Lockridge opened his eyes, tried to bring the world around him back into focus. Had he drifted off again? The painkillers—he'd stopped taking them this morning, knowing he needed a clear head for this visitor, yet it didn't seem to have made much difference. The questions about *Mahan*, about what had happened, were as irrelevant as the menu for dinner last night, yesterday's weather, as hours and minutes, as his reading glasses, as remembering to flush, as irrelevant as—

my career.

Lockridge almost laughed. That wasn't really a question now, was it? He had no career—no more than the people who'd died aboard *Mahan*.

He had been ashamed to realize that he was thinking about his own future when the fires were finally beaten back. It wasn't seemly, a character weakness of the worst sort. Forty of his sailors, the men and women who trusted him to keep them safe, were dead.

But he had. As consistently persistent as a bad case of the clap, the thoughts had come to him during the night, displacing his normal nighttime thoughts about his family.

More shame—his first thought should have been of Emily. *Not* that he would never again take a ship out past the breakwater, feel the first long, slow swell as the sea took the ship for her own, feel that motion that would become so much a part of his life that ten minutes after they'd left he would no longer even feel it.

There was so much to be ashamed of these days. The loss of *Mahan,* and the men and women onboard her, was the largest one, of course. But that crucial failing was simply too deep to be understood. He could not get his mind around it, merely scampered around the edges of it, trying to understand the dimension of the tragedy.

In twenty years of going to sea, he'd never had a sailor killed on his ship. He had gone everywhere, done everything onboard a ship—the Cold War cat-and-mouse games, drug operations, Desert Storm and Desert Shield, and repeated trips to the increasingly troubled Persian Gulf.

There'd been times when men had been injured, sometimes seriously. But they all paled in significance to this, the overwhelming and simple fact that—

I got them killed. I did it—no one else.

"Commander Lockridge. You owe me an answer."

Lockridge open his eyes and stared dully at the man sitting before him. Bulldog. To give him his full title, Vice Admiral Trent Canon. A surface warfare officer, like Lockridge, but now waiting for his fourth star instead of facing a court-martial. Bulldog was currently assigned as commander, Seventh Fleet. *Mahan* had been under his operational control when she'd been hit.

Bulldog's fleet nickname suited both his character and his appearance. Strong features, jowls, and eyes like flint perched on either side of a huge hook of a nose. Massive shoulders, at least double the width of his hips. In the face, wind and weather had carved out a pattern that only years at sea could create.

Lockridge knew this man, had trusted him once. Had even

gone so far as to regard him as a friend, although Bulldog was ten years older and four pay grades his senior.

There had been a time when he thought he might follow Bulldog's path in the Navy. Command of *Mahan,* promotion to captain, followed by another deep draft command or perhaps a fourteen-month tour commanding a cruiser-destroyer squadron, fourteen months or more as a commodore. Soon afterward, the first look from the flag promotion board. So maybe he wouldn't be a deep select, promoted to admiral ahead of his year group, but Lockridge, during more sane moments, had figured he at least had a shot at a regular promotion.

The stars—the goal of every career naval officer. Rear Admiral Lockridge—he even said the words aloud once, tasting the flavor in his mouth. Just once—any more would have been a jinx.

Flames, noise, smoke. Men dying, screaming out his name, reaching up and begging him to save them. Their lives had been in his hands.

He had killed them. Let them die, killed them—it made no more difference than if he'd shot them in the head, one by one. The end result was the same.

What did it matter what anyone else thought or said? Nothing he could say would erase that, would take back those few horrible seconds when the missiles struck the ship. What Bulldog thought of that, what the Board of Inquiry decided—indeed, what even the dead sailors would have thought—simply made no difference. They were dead, and he'd killed them.

Nor would the fact that there was nothing he could have done make any difference, either. Not to him, not to the Navy.

But it should, one small part of his mind insisted. *Everything on the ship was automated. There's no way I could have affected the targeting solution, shot the missiles any faster, or have done anything to prevent it.*

Fairness never played much of a role in affixing responsibility for disasters. It all came back to the one great constant: the commanding officer was responsible.

Bulldog knew that. Everyone knew it. So this farce of an investigation made no difference in the end.

For a moment, Lockridge wondered why Admiral Canon was here personally. Seventh Fleet encompassed a wide range of troubled areas, the entire Pacific Ocean excluding the Middle East itself, west of Hawaii. Admiral Canon had a sizable staff. If he was curious about the man—the friend—who'd lost his ship, the political thing for Canon to do would be to send someone from his staff to fly to out and talk to Lockridge. Why would he come himself?

"*Mahan.*" Bulldog's voice prompted, cutting through the haze gathering in front of Lockridge's eyes. "Jack, talk to me. Forty-two men and women are dead and you've got to answer questions. Do you understand that?"

Forty-two. They didn't tell me two more died. Lockridge turned his face away from the other man and saw the dead and dying encircling him, his years of experience and imagination filling in the horrendous wounds, the burnt flesh and charred faces, the smell of cooking bodies.

"I don't remember . . ." He did, though. Did and wouldn't talk about it, wouldn't go back into that hellishly burning compartment, Fireman Irving dead on the deck besides him, dead but still bleeding and bleeding and . . .

Lockridge closed his eyes, opened them again when the vision got even clearer. "She was—she was afloat. We were trying to set fire boundaries. That's the last I remember. Until later."

"She's still afloat. Just barely," Bulldog said. "You're under tow right now, headed for the Suez Canal. We medevac'd the dead and the seriously injured. For now, you're still in command. But if you don't start talking to me, I don't know how long that will last. Jack, come on—we've got to know what happened."

Why did it happen? There was no reason for it, no indication that India or Bangladesh was annoyed by the FON operations. And where did the missile come from? No indication that we'd been targeted, that there was any reason to be concerned. He played the events back in his head again and again, saw the tactical screen, watched the missile arrow in on them from the shore. Bulldog's voice dimmed to a dull annoying whine.

"Repairs—we're going to need repairs," Lockridge said finally when the smell of blood and the screaming became too much. "Singapore's closer than the Med."

Some part of his mind knew that the statement made little sense, made him sound as though he were truly insane. *Mahan* would never be repaired—the damage was too deep into her structure. That they were even towing her back for scrap was amazing enough. It would have been reasonable to just sink her in deep water. He tried to recover the fumble. "Salvage, I mean."

It was Bulldog's turn to be nonresponsive. "Singapore won't take you," Canon said finally. "They've got their own problems with India, and they've made it clear they're not getting involved in this one. It's either get you to Italy or tow you back across the Pacific to the U.S. Frankly, I'm happier with you closer to land. You'll be skirting along the coast—out of weapons range, but close enough for evacuation if things take a turn for the worse. Right now, our best estimate is that *Mahan* can make it to Sigonella."

"Why did it happen?" Jack felt his voice start to charge up the scale, made an effort to stay calm. "Who shot us?"

Bulldog looked away. "We don't know. Nobody's saying much beyond that, not at the State Department or in DOD. India claims you were inside territorial waters and preparing to launch Tomahawks, but they say they didn't do it. You'd expect that sort of response, of course."

"Launch—what the hell? What are they basing that on?"

"Intercepts, they said. Targeting packages being transmitted to *Mahan* from the States."

"Bullshit, and you know it. How could they know what the targeting packages were without crypto to break them? And sure, we carry Tomahawks, but all the packages are for the

Middle East. And we weren't getting a download for an update.''

Bulldog nodded. ''Everyone knows that, Jack. Everyone that matters. There's been no official reaction from the White House yet.''

''Not to the attack even?'' Jack felt back in control of himself except when he tried to move.

''No. We can't—Listen, do you know what's going on in the Middle East right now?''

''How could I? All my crypto's down. I can't even get CNN.''

Jack listened, trying to make sense of it, as Bulldog brought him up to date—the Middle East escalating, the aircraft leaving Iraq for Iran, the inchop of the carrier into the Gulf—and then felt a growing sense of outrage. When Bulldog finished, Jack said, ''So you're telling me they're not going to do anything? We're just going to pretend this never happened?''

''I'm not saying that.'' Bulldog sighed, then said, ''Not for the long term, at least. We've only got so many assets, and the Middle East's the priority right now. Once that's sorted out, we'll take up the question of *Mahan* again.''

''So what do I do?'' Jack asked.

''Keep her afloat. You've got enough people onboard for that. She's stable now. I'm bringing you over to *Lincoln* for a full debriefing, and I'm sending you an extra damage control team from *Lincoln*. We ought to have this figured out by the time you get to Sigonella.''

Bulldog glanced at him, then looked away again. Lockridge saw a flash of profound pity and sorrow.

''Two missiles hit my ship and forty people died. Forty-two. The rest of it *Lincoln* knows from the data tapes, from the LINK picture,'' Jack said.

Canon nodded. ''And now Admiral Fairchild needs to talk to you. We have to decide whether we'll need her here or whether to send her on to the Gulf. You need to tell us everything you can remember about that night, Jack. It makes a difference.''

The only difference it makes is whether you'll hang me now or later.

10

USS *EISENHOWER*

Gar was settling into the rhythm now, sleeping in two-hour stints, eating sandwiches out of paper bags, shucking off everything else except the keyboard under his fingers and the screen that covered the bulkhead in front of him. At some point people and machinery ceased to exist as individuals and existed only as part of a larger machine. The Gar-cog in the animal known as the *Eisenhower* functioned as a collection of subroutines integrated into the rest of the battle group. Allowing for human frailties and needs was simply another item on his maintenance checklist, food no more than fuel, and a daily shower the equivalent of washing down aircraft to prevent corrosion.

The heightened alertness, dragging on now into its third day, wasn't the result of a new threat. There were no new warnings and indications, no hint that some awesome combined force of Iranian and Iraqi aircraft were contemplating launching a strike against the carrier battle group. No, the deciding factor in the admiral's decision to stay at General Quarters was not what they knew—it was what they did *not* know.

Overhead imagery showed all the Iraqi aircraft on the

ground, but neither electronic intercepts nor HUMINT—intelligence talk for spies and in-country informants—could tell them why.

So they waited and watched, relying more and more on their collective experience inside the Gulf to provide them with the best interpretation of their organic intelligence data. They all remembered the Iraqi aircraft that had fled to Iran in the earliest stages of Desert Storm, the first in the now-inevitable series of forays into Middle Eastern politics. Those aircraft had not returned, and intelligence estimates now included them in their estimates of Iranian air strength rather than Iraqi. It was a lesson to many on the dangers of relying on promises made by allies within the region.

But why now? Last time, Iran had kept the aircraft. Why would Iraq risk that again, after spending billions to build up their numbers again. With no data, the battle group was forced to wait for the political forces in Washington to decide what it all meant.

Certainly, their own experience with American "allies" bore out that point. Tiny UAE and Oman, as well as Saudi Arabia, all found it convenient to call upon the military power of the United States when it appeared that their own boundaries were at risk. But at the moment that some accommodation could be reached with their neighbors, all of them proclaimed their belief in Arab unity and withdrew the concessions that had been extracted as the quid pro quo for American military intervention on their behalf. Overflight and landing rights were withdrawn without warning. Fuel for the non-nuclear ships, delivery of parts and supplies within the host country mail systems, shore leave for the sailors, even access to FFV—fresh fruits and vegetables—were all cut off. Yet, dependent upon the oil wealth of the region to fuel the American demand for power, the powers that be in Washington continually capitulated.

The rest of the world understood the situation as well. America was increasingly the subject of mocking commentary by the older nations in Europe, the ones that believed that they understood the proper application of military force. They laughed, or forced smiles in some cases, as they contemplated the world without the stability that the American forces brought to bear. With American forces forming the mainstay of the military might in the Middle East as well as the increasingly rambunctious Far East, that left scant resources to devote to Europe, should the need arise. All were fairly certain that America would protect Europe over Korea—but none were entirely convinced.

For Gar Tennant, the questions were far more simple. What movement by the forces ashore might threaten the battle group? And within the constraints of the rules of engagement, how could the battle group most effectively achieve its mission of preventing all-out war in America's oil sources? In part, the answers to both those questions depended on those who fed on the larger tactical picture, the one that encompassed the entire range of forces at the United States' disposal.

The answers were not long in coming.

NATIONAL SECURITY AGENCY

Peter Carlisle was on his third cup of coffee of the day when the intercept report turned up. His second in command, Damian Edgars, rapped lightly on the door then stepped in without waiting for an answer. "You'll want to see this." Damian handed over a formatted message, rows of incomprehensible numbers and alphanumeric designators running down one-quarter of the page.

Carlisle studied it for a moment. He'd been reading intercepts long enough to be able to see the formatted field definitions in his sleep. He looked back up at Edgars. "When did this come in? Any idea of who it was intended for?"

"Last night. No surface traffic in the area, so it might be a submarine. But look at the analysis on it—the duty officer had the same doubts about it that I do and decided to hold onto it and get a second opinion. You can see why." Edgars waited.

Carlisle ran his finger down the message then shut his eyes for a moment. Yes, he could understand why the duty officer hadn't passed it on, but he wished that the woman had called him at home last night rather than wait. The signal met some of the parameters for a new air control radar in eastern Iran, but not all of them. Not all by a long shot. With the satellite picture in the area degraded by a weather pattern trying to build into a typhoon, they couldn't even correlate imagery with the new transmission. It was probably nothing—too much was nothing these days, and the watch officer had no doubted figured it could wait.

And it could. There was no getting around that point, it could wait. It was the nature of electronic intercepts, the primary mission of NSA, that most of their data was relatively innocuous until it was integrated into the larger intelligence picture. That took time, too much time sometimes.

It was probably the hardest thing he'd had to get used to after he'd left the Navy and joined NSA. Going from being a submarine sonar technician, accustomed to thinking tactical and taking immediate action to preserve the safety of his ship, the slower tempo of intelligence operations had at first irked him, then driven him to distraction. Early on in his career, he'd had to either make peace with it or quit. He'd finally found a way of dealing with it that worked for him.

This signal, for instance. It could indicate that Iran was preparing a new airfield for additional aircraft, and perhaps that would be correlated with the Iraqi landings in Iran. They'd need imagery, both to ascertain the exact location of the Iraqi aircraft and to look for other indications of increased operational tempo. More fuel facilities, for starters. Temporary structures for maintenance facilities, an increase in the number of Iranian aircraft technicians in the area, that sort of thing. The people at NSA knew what a buildup looked like in pictures and in electronic intercepts.

About half of NSA was former military, the other half a collection of individuals that might have been accurately described by Carlisle's former shipmates as geeks. Computer and artificial intelligence specialists, mathematicians, electronics specialists, and a few geopolitics experts thrown in for leavening. The ex-military people he understood better, but he liked the civilians.

The watch officer last night, she was one of the former military. An AWACS officer, one well versed in the realms of electronic intercepts and aircraft movements. She'd used her judgment, decided not to call. Fine, he'd make sure not to blast her for it when he explained what his preference would have been. Perhaps she'd thought it wasn't important enough or reliable enough to interrupt his off-duty life.

He snorted at that thought. Like there was anything to interrupt. Jerusha's absence left a void he hadn't expected.

"So what do you think?" Carlisle asked finally, aware that Edgars was still standing there staring at him. "Valid? Reliable?"

"It's certainly valid," Edgar said, indicating that he thought the described transmission had been accurately detected and analyzed. It was what it was, not an electronic glitch. "But reliable?" He shrugged. "Probably not. On the other hand, can we afford to take the chance that it's not?"

Carlisle leaned back in his chair and sighed. That question was at the heart of intelligence work everywhere. People in the field thought that NSA ought to be able to provide concrete answers, absolute judgments and ground truth about what the enemy was up to. But it didn't work that way—not hardly often enough. The most intelligence could usually provide was a guess—an educated, well-reasoned one, but a guess none the less.

The real issue was how much information you did release as intelligence estimates. Too many false alarms, and the front line forces didn't take you seriously anymore. Too much filtering for reliability, and you missed the call. Pearl Harbor all over again, and that was one set of questions—and of consequences—that Peter Carlisle never intended to face.

"We pass it on, but with the full warning package attached," Carlisle said finally. He rubbed his hand over his face, felt the stubble of his beard in patches where he'd missed it that morning. Maybe the duty officer had been right not to call him—hell, he couldn't even get a decent shave these days. "It's all we've got on those missing aircraft, and we've got a battle group inchopping the Gulf later on today. It might not be worth anything—but it might make them breathe a little easier if they know we're on alert."

"And that might be a good thing," Edgar said.

"It might be." *And it might not be. But how the hell do you tell that from five thousand miles away?*

"I'll take care of it myself," Edgar promised. "Get it out within the next couple of minutes."

"Good. And pass the word to last night's watch officer that I want to see her when she comes back on. Make sure you put the right spin on it—nothing negative. She was on watch, she made the call. I just want to go over a few things with her about it."

"Feedback, not a public execution, right?" Edgar smiled. "Yeah, like you're known for the latter."

"Don't ruin my image with the troops, asshole."

THE NAVAL WAR COLLEGE

Jerusha stared down at the schedule of events. Her working group would be meeting in an hour to evaluate projections on another Iraq-Iran conflict. Her briefing package set as one of the assumptions that the conflict would allow time for a massive buildup in theater. She gave a snort of disgust, shuffled back through the papers to find the timetable again, then wondered just exactly what point Gromko was trying to make. His agenda would never be as straightforward as this one seemed to be.

The details in her briefing package offered no clues. Judging from the agenda included in the materials, they were expected to conclude that the United States should simply attempt to contain the conflict between Iraq and Iran, sending peace-keeping forces ashore to achieve that goal. The assumption was that the Iraq aircraft on the ground would be seized by Iran eventually, and that there was no possibility of any sort of coordinated effort between the two deadly enemies. There was no mention of Pakistan, India, or *Mahan*.

She thumbed through the indications and warnings in the intelligence appendix. No mention of the glove Elwell had reported, and no speculation on the presence of weapons of mass destruction in eastern India.

The working group had four hours to complete its evaluation. The results would be reported out at the first video conference, scheduled for that evening to coincide with a morning brief onboard *Eisenhower*.

Four hours. We get a total of four hours to work out the possibilities. Hell, we'll spend at least half of that trying to learn each other's names. Now, just what are we supposed to be able to accomplish? A rubber stamp job on whatever work the War College has already done.

Jerusha went looking for Gromko. She caught up with him waiting outside the president of the War College's door, chatting with the staff.

"I need to talk to you," she said.

Gromko looked at his watch. "It will have to wait. I'm briefing Admiral Monarelli on the last set of game results, and the entire carrier staff after that."

Jerusha held out the offending material. "This is nonsense. You're just fighting the last war again."

"I hardly think so. We've spent months on the analysis."

"And you think what's happening over there is just a repetition of what happened the last time? Iraq versus Iran, Pakistan versus India? What about *Mahan*?"

"What about her? An anomaly."

"How can you be sure?" she asked. "*Mahan* happened, then the rest of this. And Pakistan—this answer is too pat, Dean, far too simplistic. You've got to expand both the scope of the inquiry and the time allotted to do it in."

Gromko shook his head. "Impossible. And Pakistan is hardly a player here."

"We don't know that for sure yet. We have some assumptions, sure. But they're based mostly on past history between India and Pakistan. I think we're in real danger of letting our conclusions drive our analysis."

Gromko tapped the pristine white folder in his lap. It was already bound and printed. "We have an answer that everyone in the department agrees with except you. The working group will explore the problem within the parameters we've defined. I will brief the admiral, then courier the report out to *Lincoln* for delivery to *Eisenhower* via COD when they begin their turnover."

"Your scenario doesn't account for all the data."

"It considers all the relevant data."

"I don't think so." She summarized her conversation with Elwell and his report on the Nuke/bio/chem or NBC glove he'd found just outside Bangladesh's border. "That would make a difference, wouldn't it? And it's not in here."

Gromko sighed. "I said *relevant* data. I saw the field report and decided it was not important."

"The possibility that there are nuclear weapons forward deployed to the east along the Bengali-India border isn't relevant to what's happening along India's western border? And in the Middle East, in the same theater of operations? How can that not be relevant?"

Gromko held up a hand and ticked off the points on his fingers. "One, there is no physical evidence of this supposed glove. Two, it was a single report, not verified, and not supported by anything else in the intelligence picture. Three, there is no evidence of any correlation with *Mahan*. She was not hit with an NBC warhead, and there are no indications other than this glove that such weapons have been deployed. Four, it *is* too far away. The connection between Bangladesh and the Middle East is simply too tenuous. Accordingly, I assigned a low probability to the report."

"And what about *Mahan*? You're calling this all a coincidence." She stared at him, aware of how very familiar this all sounded. They'd been through the same sort of arguments when she'd worked for him, and Gromko had invariably proven to be correct.

"I do not know everything," he said, his voice a good deal gentler than she would have expected. "You have always expected too much from me. Perhaps the incident with *Mahan* was simply an anomaly. A distractor."

"A lot of people died over that distractor."

Gromko shook his head. "We deal in the dynamics at the operational art level, Miss Bailey. Not tactics. This has always been one of your weaknesses, staying too far down in the grass. Even with planning and operations merging and the shortened time line, there is still a distinction you must learn to make in your thinking."

"I'm not sure I want to understand it, Dean. Not if it means not caring about those people on *Mahan.*"

She had the sense that she was disappointing him, and was surprised to realize that bothered her. "Then leave operational art to those that understand it, my people here. Stay mired down in the details, Miss Bailey."

"But your answers are *wrong* on any level—strategic, operational, or tactical." Jerusha stopped, aware that her voice was getting louder. The people in the office were pointedly looking away from the bickering pair. "At least admit that's a possibility. Bring it up at the videoconference. Maybe the battle group commander will—"

But Gromko was already shaking his head. "We have an answer. Admiral Tallidan signed off on the initial faculty report. As validated by your Fleet working groups, that will be the analysis we report to the battle group."

"Get me in to talk to Admiral Tallidan."

"No."

"Then send me out to *Lincoln,*" she blurted out. "Someone has to courier the final report out to Admiral Fairchild after you brief Admiral Monarelli—you said so yourself." That wouldn't get her to *Mahan,* but she'd be a hell of a lot closer. *Lincoln* had been in the LINK that day and she was the closest carrier asset to Billy Elwell and *Mahan.*

Gromko turned and began walking away. "I need someone far less senior, a clerical type."

"I'll do the job, whatever it is. Just send me out there."

"The problem is *not* with *Mahan* at all. Dear God, woman, can't you see that?"

"So let me go and you can prove me wrong."

Gromko looked thoughtful for a moment, and Jerusha had the familiar feeling of being several steps behind him. What had she said that had caught his attention and made his expression conceal his thinking? "Very well," he said. He raised one hand and pointed a stubby finger at her. "But you will not attempt to subvert the War College's analysis and recommendations. I must have your word on that."

"You trust me that much?"

Gromko snorted. "Don't be insulting. I disagree with your ideas and your conclusions. You've got a good mind, when you choose to use it." He took a step closer to her. "Too good to be making these sorts of mistakes."

"Thanks for the vote of confidence."

Gromko continued, ignoring her sarcasm. "Your intellectual shortcomings aside, you've given me no reason to doubt your integrity. Your word on it, Miss Bailey. Your oath."

Jerusha debated for a moment, still slightly stunned by the backhanded compliment Gromko had just paid her. Not a compliment, perhaps—just an assessment and distinction, one of those fine hairsplittings that she'd scene him perform too many times.

There was only one place in the world she could make certain of finding out, and that was on the carrier. She'd give Gromko her word that she wouldn't attempt to disparage the War College conclusions, but if things started going to shit too fast, she might be the only one on scene with a real idea of what was happening.

Could she do it? Could she, as her mother had always said, play well with others? It would require some effort on her part, she realized, perhaps more effort than she'd counted on.

And more honor.

"My word," she said finally. "I will support the War College's conclusion and do nothing to disrupt the plan."

Gromko nodded. "Have my secretary make the arrangements."

She turned to go, then turned back just as she reached the door leading out into the passageway. "Dean? You're absolutely certain about your answer? No doubts at all?''

''Absolutely certain.''

Then why I am so sure he's wrong? Because nothing is ever certain in war, nothing. The one thing you can count on is that you will be wrong about something.

The truth would not be revealed until the moment that it was terribly and finally self-evident, and too late to do anything about it. Certainty was the only sure path to disaster.

''You'll know where to find me, then,'' she said.

''I will.''

Bailey stood in the door to the classroom and watched Gromko stalk down the ancient, battered passageway. When he rounded the corner and disappeared from view, she sighed and stepped back into the room to gather her notes and books. She picked them up, shuffling her preparation for today's planning session to the bottom of the heap, and flicked off the lights on her way out.

As she trotted down the old wooden steps and started up the steep hill to the parking lot, she swore quietly. She should have thought it out better, planned a more effective approach to Dean Gromko. But after hearing the passion in his voice as he talked about ending the war, saving lives, she'd thought he might be receptive to hearing what she had to say.

But she'd miscalculated, projected his reaction as it might have been from a friend, from another man. She'd forgotten that Gromko was never predictable, that he considered what would be thought subtle by anyone else entirely too overt. His agenda was his own, and one that he never shared overtly.

But you've been in command yourself. You know how it is, one part of her mind insisted. *You see things, know things, when you're out there alone. Just like in the North Sea. Just like in Panama.*

And what had Lockridge seen? Or had he just screwed up, let his ship get shot out from under him? It had been a submarine, had to have been. But whose sub?

Yes, she'd been in command. But not like Lockridge had. Not selected, trained, educated, and groomed for the sole task of taking on responsibility for a warship. No, when she'd been in command of *Ramage* in the English Channel, it hadn't been through the normal process.

And she'd made mistakes.

Normal process or not, you were there. And if you could make mistakes, what makes you so sure that Lockridge didn't?

It wasn't a question that she could answer, not yet. Nor was it probable that they'd ever know exactly what had transpired off the coast of Bangladesh.

Ever since the demise of the Soviet Union, the U.S. military had been stretched increasingly thin covering the medium-intensity and humanitarian conflicts that sprung up around in the world. First Korea and Germany, and most recently Panama and China. There were always wheels within wheels, with conflicts never exactly what they appeared to be. What had happened to *Mahan* was the first sign of something that NSA would have to deal with eventually, that much she was fairly certain. But of what?

Despite Gromko's arguments, despite the increasing tensions in the Middle East, she was convinced that the answers had to do with *Mahan* and what had happened off the coast of Bangladesh. Probably the only other person in the world who would agree would be Jack Lockridge himself.

And just how thrilled would he be to have her asking questions all over again about what had happened? Just real thrilled, especially when all reports indicated that he had his hands full just keeping *Mahan* afloat for the tugs.

"To hell with you, Lockridge," she said. "Something happened out there, and you're the only on that knows what. One way or another, I'm going to talk to you while I'm onboard *Lincoln*. I'm going to tell you about a man named Billy Elwell and a glove he found on the Bangladeshi border. Then you're going to tell me what it is that nobody's thought to ask you, what it is that Gromko doesn't know yet."

Jerusha went back to the MBC to gather up the unclassified material she'd stashed in the study carrel she'd been assigned.

The classified material, including the War College's final analysis and recommendations, would have to be double-wrapped and logged for transfer by MBC's classified material custodian.

The CMC was in the crypto vault. Jerusha rang the bell for admittance, then stepped back so that the camera mounted over the door could see her. A speaker on the side of the door buzzed.

"Can I help you?" a voice asked. Jerusha identified herself and explained her needs. "It'll be just a moment, if that's all right. I'm—I'm inventorying crypto and doing destruction. Could you give me just a moment?"

"Of course." Jerusha glanced down at her watch—plenty of time, and by now she ought to be used to waiting outside of security doors. For a moment, she wondered whether the interior of the crypto vault was monitored like Pete Carlisle's office was, and whether the CMC knew it if it was.

Finally, the door swung out. It was made of thick steel, with the interlocking bars that countersunk into corresponding holes in the opposite side of the door frame when it was locked. A small woman with red-rimmed eyes stood with her shoulder against it. "Come in. I just had to put some material away. Now, what exactly is it that you need?"

"Are you all right?" Jerusha asked, stepping into the vault. The woman drew back from her, as though any invasion of her personal space would be too much right now. Jerusha put one hand on the woman's shoulder. "Can I get you something?"

"No, no, I'm quite fine," the woman said, her words belying the swollen eyes. She'd done something to try to repair her makeup but tear streaks still marred her cheeks. Her voice was thick and slightly quavery. "Allergies. That's all."

Right. Allergies. To one asshole Dean, probably. Still, if you're going to cry, it's nice to have a crypto vault to hide out in.

"I'm Helen Tarkin," the woman said. "Jerusha Bailey—I've heard about you." For a moment, she seemed to emerge from whatever private misery had driven her to the vault. "It was very brave, what you did after Germany. Not many people would have had the courage to take the chances you did."

Jerusha smiled wryly. "It wasn't like I had much of a choice."

And she hadn't, not really. Not if you got down to what counted in the world. It had been a choice between saving her career at NSA and tacitly supporting America's secret involvement in the war in Europe, or telling the truth. In the end, she'd made the choice she thought she could live with.

Helen shook her head. "You didn't have to tell the truth. But you did." She looked directly at Jerusha, respect and admiration in her face. "I admire you for it. Sometimes I've thought—Well, I've nattered on long enough. Let's find your material and get you logged out."

The CMC quickly located Jerusha's private notes and the report that was her excuse for heading out to *Lincoln*. It took a couple more minutes to wrap and stamp the security classification on the interior envelopes and make copies of the transfer forms for Jerusha to carry. Finally, Helen handed Jerusha the package and gave her a standard briefing on couriering classified material.

"Good luck to you," Helen said.

"And to you," Jerusha said. She turned to go, then hesitated. Without looking back, she said, "Don't let Gromko get to you. He can be a real bastard to work with sometimes. I know."

There was a small, short intake of breath behind her, then Helen said, "Thank you. Coming from you, that means a lot to me. Perhaps—perhaps we could have coffee the next time you're in Newport?"

Jerusha turned back to face Helen and saw fresh tears standing in her eyes. "I'd like that. Let's plan on it."

Leaving the CMC to regain her composure, Jerusha stepped out onto the main display floor and took one last look at the main display screen. *Eisenhower* was still in the Persian Gulf, patrolling a fifty-mile-square box annotated in red on the screen. She looked small, almost insignificant, when reduced to mere symbology. Her escorts ships were arrayed around her, with one left outside the Gulf to serve as southern radar picket.

To the east, *Lincoln* was tracking south down the eastern coast of India, now en route to the Gulf from her previous location off the coast of Bangladesh, also surrounded by her escorts. The only single ship formation was indicated by an odd symbol virtually motionless off the coast of Bangladesh: *Mahan,* now under tow.

"What brings you in here?" the watch officer asked. He was a pleasant enough fellow, completely full of the qualities that would make him a good senior officer in the current thinking. A good team member, one who followed the rules of engagement and spun solid-sounding theories laced with pithy quotes from Sun-Tzu and Clausewitz. He would go far in today's Navy.

"Heading out to *Lincoln,*" she answered, not interested in going into the details but not wanting to be overtly rude.

He whistled softly. "Man, who did you piss off?"

"I asked to go."

"Oh." He fell silent, clearly puzzled by that. Why an officer would be willing to leave MBC for duty on a ship so far out of the action—much less request it—was apparently beyond him. "Well, good luck out there. Looks like you might need it."

"Why? What's happening?"

"Just this." He shoved a message across the desk to her. "Not good news for anyone, I bet. Peacekeeping operations in Bangladesh and Pakistan—give me a break. Best thing we could do is stand back and let them fight it out, if you ask me."

She picked the message up and read quickly. It directed *Eisenhower* to outchop the Persian Gulf and to be prepared for both evacuation operations in Pakistan and support operations ashore. *Lincoln* was ordered to stand by for short-term assistance in Bangladesh as Typhoon Thomas tracked north, then to join *Eisenhower* off the coast of Pakistan. Both carriers were directed to refer to the Sipranet, the top secret intelligence internet system, for further details.

"Bangladesh I can buy, but going ashore in Pakistan?" she said, still not believing what she'd just read. It was going fast, too fast for anyone to keep track of. "That makes no sense. *Eisenhower* just received a warning order on the Middle East, and they're going to pull her out of there? I don't believe it— not after Iraq shot down an AWACS. We can't just walk away from that, not so soon after *Mahan*."

And what did that say about the War College's analysis of the scenario? Admiral Tallidan had made the point in his welcoming brief that sometimes their recommendations were ignored. Was that what was happening now? Political agendas influencing sound military operational decisions? And why didn't Gromko tell her about it? Surely he had to know that the War College's recommendations would not be followed.

Preemptive peace. The phrase rang in Jerusha's mind.

12

USS *LINCOLN*

Before Admiral Fairchild could question Lockridge about *Mahan,* a warning order to prepare for humanitarian operations in Bangladesh settled the question of *Lincoln*'s immediate future. The latest Typhoon Thomas track projections put landfall just slightly north of Bangladesh.

Admiral Fairchild leaned back in his chair on the flag bridge, listening to the movements of the men around him. They were tired, bone tired. He could hear it in their voices, see it in the small mistakes that were starting to creep into everything from routine message traffic up to his morning briefings.

Two days to get up on station to the spot where *Mahan* had been hit, every second of it devoted to round-the-clock operations in case whoever had taken a shot at *Mahan* found it impossible to resist taking a shot at the carrier. There was still no clear answer on who shot her, but smart money was betting on India. The faction arguing that China was behind it as an attempt to destabilize the region was gaining favor, though.

All the more reason to go ashore in Bangladesh. No matter whether China or India posed the next threat to peace in the region, America would need friends in the area in order to intervene. Better to make them now than try to cobble together alliances for forward bases of operations after the next conflict started.

The months prior to the deployment had been devoted to preparing for operations in the Middle East. Charts, strike plans, replenishment and logistics plans all had to be reworked for a new theater of operations, and no one could tell him how the grueling humanitarian operations would affect *Lincoln*'s scheduled deployment to the Middle East.

Even with her covey of escorts, the aircraft carrier was vulnerable. India now possessed her own fleet of competent diesel attack submarines, and intell reports indicated that they were armed with keel-breaking torpedoes. Just one shot, positioned to nail the carrier directly underneath her keel, could break the spine of the world's most powerful warship. As a consequence, the air wing conducted continual surface surveillance operations. Even fighters and attack aircraft were moved from CAP—carrier air patrol—missions into USW roles, augmenting the continual acoustic and infrared searches mounted by the S-3B Vikings and the P-3C aircraft deployed out of Singapore, on the off chance that they'd catch sight of a diesel submarine coming up to snorkel.

If the subs were out here at all. Imagery indicated all but two were tied up pierside, but those missing two were enough to alter every detail of *Lincoln*'s plans.

Fairchild spent a fair portion of each day squelching rumors based on everything from highly classified reports to the latest speculations in tabloids. American troops fight best when there is a clearly defined enemy, preferably one that is a different skin tone. With an opponent like the Germans, the press would make caricatures of them, emphasize the Slavic features of Soviets, anything to make them different. There was nothing like a little reflexive racism to spur the American fighting spirit.

And that, the admiral reflected, as he watched a Tomcat taxiing forward to the catapult, was the essence of the problem. The swath of earth stretching from Turkey through the Middle East and eastward across Pakistan, India, and Bangladesh was a tangled knot of ancient rivalries and incompatible cultures. Nothing was ever what it seemed. Iran and Iraq, bitter enemies, yet now Iraqi aircraft were apparently forming up within Iran. Pakistan and India, continually threatening nuclear exchanges and nibbling away at each other's borders, yet united when necessary to face down the Middle East. And Bangladesh, barely capable of sustaining life while fighting off powerful India. What could a couple of aircraft carriers from a young but powerful nation do to affect wars that spanned centuries?

"Admiral, flash traffic from Seventh Fleet." The radioman's voice jolted him out of his reverie.

"Thanks." Fairchild took the message from the radioman and scanned it quickly. Nothing new, more cautions to be on alert, detailed queries on *Lincoln*'s plans for conducting strikes against India if she threatened Bangladesh. *If* strikes were authorized. *If* additional hostilities or hostile acts or intent were displayed. *If* prolonged operations were expected. *When* the weather allowed. The message concluded on an ominous note—following disaster relief operations *Lincoln* was to be prepared to support *Eisenhower* in peacekeeping operations in Pakistan.

The most pressing issue of all was the question of logistic support for the amphibious force still two days out from *Lincoln*. The gators would stay at sea, wait for the typhoon to pass, then inchop the area of operations. The amphibious ships plus escorts and replenishment ships, along with embarked assault air support, could be expected off the coast of Bangladesh after the danger from the typhoon was past. Half of the ARG would support *Lincoln;* the other half would continue enroute Pakistan to support *Eisenhower*. Fairchild grimaced, imagining the howls of protest over splitting his forces from the Marine Commander of Landing Forces or CLF.

India's the problem, the admiral decided, reading between lines and discerning the intent he saw taking shape there.

Somebody's more worried India than they are about the Iraqi aircraft in Iran—and the AWACS. I hope someone knows something I don't, because this sure as hell doesn't make sense to me.

Too complicated, too many contingencies and possibilities. Should they stay configured for peacekeeping operations or disaster relief? How close to the coast would send the message that America was prepared to act without qualifying as open aggression that would exacerbate the situation? No easy answers, and for a moment, Admiral Fairchild felt the heavy weight of his stars on his collar.

BANGLADESH

Fifty miles due west of *Lincoln,* Bengali scout Khan was finding the waiting no easier. Ever since the American ship had been shot, the forward movement of the Indian forces had ceased. The tanks waited now, poised along the border in the mud, silent. The tanks' crews were even forgoing the occasional small-arms fire the Bengalis had come to expect, defeated by the winds and spitting rain. At least the filthy weather was making their lives as difficult as those of the Bengali force.

Elwell was off on another of his incomprehensible missions, with no explanation other than a statement that he'd be back in two days. Khan hadn't asked any questions. He'd already learned how useless that was. Instead, he just drafted a soldier out of the ranks to accompany him on the pattern of patrols Elwell had set up, just as Elwell had drafted him so many weeks ago.

"What are they waiting for?" The soldier crouched down next to him asked.

Khan touched his temporary partner—really no more than a boy, if that concept had any meaning any longer in Bangladesh—on the shoulder. "They're just waiting. It's not always necessary to know what you're waiting *for* to know that waiting is necessary.''

It sounded sufficiently obscure to perhaps be thought couched in devote study of the scripture, Khan thought. He thought about it for a moment, wondering if there were some way he could express himself more clearly. A glance at the youngster's face told him it wouldn't be necessary. Somehow Khan had given the other soldier the impression that there was a plan, an anticipated sequence of events, and that someone knew what was going on. Perhaps not Khan himself, but someone just ahead of Khan in the Bengali chain of command.

And for that youngster, that was enough.

Khan found himself wishing that he could go back to those days when life had been so simple. It hadn't been so long ago—numbering perhaps even in weeks. It had begun with Elwell, and then his way of life had unraveled. The American ship, the rains, his wife—what else was there?

It hadn't even been such a big ship, not as American ships went, though it was far more massive than anything the tiny Bengali naval force possessed. How many men to run it? he wondered. A thousand, perhaps. He nodded, feeling relatively certain that it would take about that many, not knowing that he'd overestimated the crew size of *Mahan* by a factor of four.

''The tanks will have to leave soon,'' the young soldier said, his whispered voice confident. ''The rains and the wind—they will have to leave or rust.''

Khan grunted. More talk designed to reassure the speaker rather than convey any real knowledge. Let the child think what he would, Khan knew that the staying power of the Indian forces was immense. They had supply lines, technicians, weapons that the younger man could not even imagine. Khan himself would not have understood just how very powerful India was before he had done a two-year tour in Bosnia as part of the peacekeeping force there. The sheer glut of food, fuel, and ammunition alone had overwhelmed him.

No, what held India's force back was not the rain, as wretched and difficult as it made maneuvering the tanks, and certainly not the presence of Khan's unit opposing them. It was the presence of the American aircraft carrier off their coast, plainly in view hulking along the horizon. The aircraft onboard, too, coupled with the missiles carried by the smaller ships.

How long would this part of the world interest them? Khan knew what the popular opinion within the American forces was about the Bengali troops. All they saw was the poverty, the threadbare uniforms, the ancient firearms. To them, the spirit of the Bengali meant nothing, the fierce drive to remain independent and free counted for nothing against the power of India. Bangladesh was a poverty-ridden third world nation, and conjured up only pictures of starving children in their minds.

Like this one. Khan glanced over at the other soldier, and just for a second wondered just why nations had to send their children to fight wars.

USS *LINCOLN*

Sea state five. The carrier was starting to feel like a ship, the deck rolling every so slightly. The escorts increased their distances from the carrier as visibility decreased in the intermittent rain.

"That's it, then." Admiral Fairchild finished outlining his plan to his assistant chief of staff for operations. "Get Strike on it, have your people flesh out the intentions message. I want to sign it out later this evening, if possible."

"Yes, Admiral." Captain Chambers finished scribbling a note in his wheel book, then looked up. "Sir, how many options do you want on this?"

"A full range for Bangladesh, all the way from peaceful go-ashore to opposed landing. Just the one for Pakistan, Larry. *Eisenhower*'s going to be running the show there. If there is a show." The admiral paused for a moment. "And give me some strike options against India, just in case those forces at the border move in. Just in case. No one's made any suspicious moves since *Mahan,* but I want to be prepared if they do.''

''You think there's a chance we'll have to go ashore the hard way?''

The admiral shook his head. ''I don't think so. This typhoon's going to level Bangladesh. I just want to be prepared for the unexpected.''

Chambers nodded. ''Be nice for a change, Admiral.''

BANGLADESH

Khan stared down at the muck uncovered on the bottom of the ditch. Leeches oozed out of it, a twisted mass of parasites crushed to blood and pale flesh under his boots. He shivered and tugged hard on his gloves, making sure the seal with his field utilities was solid.

The water in the ditch surged hard against the far bank, driven out of its normal channel by the winds. It was almost impossible to hear without shouting at each other. Even at this close range to the Indian camp, the wind would have drowned their words.

''What are we looking for?'' The youngster's voice jerked Khan out of the reverie, brought him back to the present.

Khan pulled himself up to the edge of the ditch, braced himself against the wind and stared across the field at the Indian tank clusters. Soldiers swarmed over the vehicles, undoing the tarps that had been providing temporary shelter for the last five days, fighting the wind for control. Other groups of soldiers darted between the fuel and supply stockpiles, hastily tossing crates into the back of trucks.

A tarp broke free and sailed across the muddy field like a kite. Three soldiers gave chase for a short period of time. The wind bowled one of them over as he ran. They gave up as the tarp billowed over the edge of the trees.

''To see if they're evacuating,'' Khan said. ''If they are, it'll be hours yet. If it's even today.''

"We should leave," the other soldier insisted.

Khan shook off the groping hand that was trying to drag him back down in the ditch. One of the finer judgments a scout had to make was exactly when to pull out, the line between gathering enough information and just bringing back a preliminary report that did no one any good.

"*Sarge.*" There was real panic in the boy's voice now. "The water. The floods." He pointed down at the water climbing up the far bank.

Khan ignored him, squinting his eyes against the driving rain. Yes, packing up—but to wait it out, or to move to higher ground? He studied the loading process, the movement of the men. They probably weren't going to make a grab at Bengali territory during the typhoon. An advance party would have already deployed to scout, conducting the same operations Khan and his partner were on, but in the opposite direction. There'd been no reports of Indian scouts, but that was not conclusive. They could have been missed.

Finally Khan saw what he'd been waiting to see. The last of the boxes were being loaded onto the trucks, and the first four-wheel-drive vehicle bearing the red flag of a convoy lead wheeled into place. It circled once, as though the driver were stretching the vehicle's muscles, then came to a stop with motor still running. The other trucks formed up around it in a wedge, the heavier tanks at the pointy end facing into the wind.

Khan slid back down into the relative safety of the ditch. "Now we can go." He was screaming now to be heard over the steadily building wail of the typhoon winds.

The downpour began when they were halfway back to the camp. If India was so committed to staying on the border that they'd risk the unit during a typhoon, then there was more serious trouble brewing than just wind, rain, and floods.

USS *MAHAN*

The seas that barely rocked *Lincoln* were having a much more significant effect on the cruiser. The damage control team had managed to weld one metal plate in place over the smaller of the gaping holes, but were not confident that it would hold in typhoon-strength seas. The lighter temporary patches were even more of a problem for the ship.

"It's veered to the west, sir." There was no mistaking the worry in Mallard's voice. "On her current track, she'll pass just to the north of us."

Lockridge bent over to study the computer screen.

Downloaded pictures from the National weather service showed the massive swirl of clouds that comprised Typhoon Thomas, the deceptively clear eye in the center of it. "At least we're in the least dangerous hemisphere." The southern part of the storm, where the winds moved in the opposite direction of the storm's overall track, was the safer position to be in—if anything could be said to be safe about riding out a force 3 typhoon in a crippled, leaking ship.

Mallard nodded. "Those tugs did a good job. The distance they've covered in the last twelve hours might make all the difference."

"The engineers, too," Lockridge answered. "I think Threlkeld held that main shaft bearing together with his bare hands."

"I wouldn't doubt it. When do you want to turn into the seas, sir?"

Lockridge checked the chart laid out on the table beside them, compared their position with the updated storm position from the computer. "We'll run for another hour, maybe more. Depends on how she's riding. Then we turn into the seas. Make sure the OODs understand that, Greg. The seas are what we have to worry about more than the wind."

"Yes, sir." Lockridge caught the faintest glimmer of amusement on Mallard's face.

"Want to share that thought?"

Mallard shook his head. "Not really, sir. But I will. I'll make sure the OODs all understand, but I'm just guessing here—you'll be on the bridge all night yourself, won't you?"

Lockridge punched the OOD lightly on the shoulder. "Might surprise you, Ops. That's what night orders are for, aren't they?"

BANGLADESH

"The last truck is leaving, Sarge." The transportation services clerk shouted to make his voice heard over the wind that ripped at the clipboard in his hands. "No more after this. Orders—everyone on the truck."

"I can't go yet," Khan shouted back. "One of the Americans is still out there."

"Then he's going to stay out there. He's not our responsibility." The wind ripped the top two pages off of the clerk's clipboard. The clerk grabbed Khan by the shoulder and tried to drag him to the waiting transport truck.

Khan let the motion carry him forward as he raised his hand. His fist slammed into the clerk's gut. Khan turned and trotted off toward the tree line, not entirely sure how he would survive the winds but certain that Elwell would not have left had their positions been reversed.

The clerk struggled up from the ground, assisted by one of the transport drivers. He glanced down at the clipboard and saw that the missing pages were his personnel muster sheets. "Let's go," he shouted. "Everyone's accounted for."

USS MAHAN

Lockridge studied the relative wind direction indicated on the anaemometer on the bridge. Shifting now, due east, and increasing steadily. And the barometer was dropping noticeably. He tapped with his pencil eraser on the quartermaster's chart, then stretched and walked over to the hatch leading out to the bridge wing and studied the sea.

Harder, deeper waves now, tops spilling over into the troughs ahead and behind, spray obscuring his view. Instead of an orderly progression of strong swells, the surface of the sea was chaotic, the pattern of the waves less discernable than even ten minutes earlier.

"How's engineering holding up?" he asked without turning, knowing that the OOD was rabbit-eared in his direction.

"Leak's worse, sir, but they're keeping up" was the immediate answer. "The patch is not shifting at all, but they're standing by with additional braces just in case."

"Start turning now," Lockridge said. "Tell engineering that I want reports every fifteen seconds on the leaking."

"Lieutenant Threlkeld is standing by, sir."

"Very well. Let's go easy to starboard then, no more than five degrees of rudder. I want reports from the helm every five degrees." His eyes still on the sea itself, Lockridge listened as the conning officer gave the orders to the helm. A starboard turn would put less stress on the hole in the port side, his primary concern right now.

"Sir, my rudder is right five degrees, no new course given," the helmsman announced. "Passing one eight five degrees."

"Engineering reports no change, sir," the lee helmsman announced.

"Engineering reports a slight increase in the leak, sir," he said a few moments later. "But controllable."

Mahan groaned and complained as she responded to the rudder. Wind and rain beat against the ship, shifting toward the bow as she turned.

"Passing one nine zero degrees."

"Engineering reports no change."

The litany continued as the ship slowly swung through the compass, searching for the least dangerous combination of seas and wind, with two engineering reports for every five degrees of course change. Finally, Lockridge ordered, "Steady as she goes."

"Steady as she goes, aye, sir," the helmsman said, coun-
tering the motion of the ship by shifting the rudder. "Steady
on two seven zero" followed a few seconds later.

"Engineering?" Lockridge asked.

"Engineering reports this is a safe course, sir. The leaks are
controllable, but the CHENG recommends no further north."

Lockridge nodded. "Steady as she goes, then."

Mahan was taking the seas on her quarter bow, pitching
markedly more than she had been before, rolling and yawing
violently at the same time. The hull moaned continuously as
stressed metal fought the action of the waves. It was almost
impossible to be heard over the noise, and it reminded Lockridge of those initial minutes after the first missile hit when
he'd been deaf.

Lockridge, the OOD, and the conning officer hung by their
hands from the overhead steel bar that ran the width of the
bridge, their feet barely in contact with the deck. He watched
the inclinometer swing through its arc, marking the angle the
ship made with the sea.

*Thirty degrees. We can survive that. At least we could be-
fore we were hit.*

But who knew what fatal stress fractures were buried deep
below the waterline, metal atoms barely in contact with their
neighbors, the bonds shattered by the earlier explosions?
Would they hold?

They had to. Even with *Lincoln* riding out the storm just
twenty miles to the south, there would be no possibility of
SAR until the typhoon passed. If the ship took on water and
foundered or sank, the crew would be on their own against
the sea. A lifeboat wouldn't have a chance in these waters.

*Four hours, God. Give me four hours to get us through the
worst of it and I'll forgive you the second missile.*

But not the first one. Never the first one.

BANGLADESH

Kahn struggled against the wind battering his back, leaning backward into it so that he was walking almost reclined. Had he tried to remain upright, it would have tumbled him forward, blowing him across the field like a branch.

The full force of typhoon winds would hit soon. If he were out in the open then, he could drown as the winds drove water up his nose and down his throat. Shelter, he had to find shelter—staying behind because Elwell was missing seemed the most idiotic idea he'd ever entertained. After all, the American knew the winds and rain were coming. He was probably taking shelter at the village down the road, inside the concrete block building that would soon be housing the rest of Khan's unit.

But if he weren't, where would he be?

Khan thought he knew. While most soldiers would be reacting just like the transportation clerk, desperately trying to reach higher ground and safe shelter, Elwell would be thinking about the possibility—no, the *probability*—that the camp they'd been surveilling for the last month would be either relocating or battened down to wait out the typhoon with no patrols, tank crews locked down inside their machines and the rest of the troops evacuated to shelters. To Elwell, either alternative would be an irresistible opportunity for scouting.

How much farther ahead was the camp? A kilometer, maybe? Khan tried to wipe the rain out of his eyes, but it was useless. At least the wind was at his back now instead of blinding him. He picked out a few landmarks, larger trees that were still standing, reoriented himself, and pressed on.

Half an hour later, he could finally make out the blurred outlines of the tanks. He sank down to the ground for a moment, caught himself on his hands and knees as the wind tried to bowl him over. It surged under him, lifting him off the ground and sending him rolling across the mud. Within seconds, mud clogged his nostrils, forced its way into his mouth, sealed off his eyes. He tried to scream, found that opening his mouth simply increased the problem and cupped his hands over his nose and mouth to try to shield them.

His head slammed into something hard and consciousness faded. He felt himself falling, at first airborne then rolling down an incline. Warm, filthy water sloshed over his face. The wind abated slightly. He struggled up to his hands and knees and the wind knocked him down again. He tried to breathe, drew in the mixture of mud and water.

Finally, he puzzled it out. The ditch he and Elwell had hidden in so many time before. It was filling with storm-driven water and rain, filling almost to the edge of the ditch.

Almost, but not quite. There was still a bit of space above the water, yet below the edge of the ditch. As long as he didn't mind most of his body being underwater, he could breathe. And see.

He splashed the mud out of his eyes with the only slightly more liquid water and reoriented himself. The tanks were now due west of him, probably no more than a hundred meters away. He waited for a few moments, breathing deep, gathering his strength, then crawled out of the ditch.

He didn't even try to stand. As it was, he barely could maintain forward progress on his hands and knees. It was enough that he was moving, heading toward—what? For a moment, the reason that he was doing this escaped him. He tried to think, couldn't concentrate on moving his hands and legs at the same time, and gave it up.

The tank loomed out of the rain at him all at once, a sullen dark gray against a sky of rain and fury. He felt his way around it, almost gasped in relief as the massive bulk of it shielded him from the worst of the storm's fury. He fell back against one tread, exhausted past the point of caring about anything other than the fact that he could breathe.

A hand clamped down on his arm and dragged him farther along the body of the tank, into a more sheltered portion of the tread. Khan tried to twist away, truly frightened now. He looked up into a mud-caked face with two brilliant blue eyes peering out.

"What took you so long?" Elwell asked. "Come on, we've got work to do."

USS *MAHAN*

Lockridge got the four hours he'd prayed for, though whether from divine intervention or the superhuman efforts of Threlkeld and his crew, he couldn't be sure. Nevertheless, a deal was a deal. One missile—that's all God had left to answer for.

The worst of the winds were past now, the rain now falling straight down instead of sleeting into them sideways. They weren't completely out of danger yet, but the end was in sight.

"Chaplain," Lockridge began, "what we've been through—" He paused and waited for the words to come, the right words, but couldn't force them out. The same god that had kept *Mahan* afloat had also let her take the missiles. The contradiction warred with the gratitude he felt as he surveyed the damages still evident to the crew and the ship.

The chaplain nodded, understanding in his eyes. "I know what to do, Captain." Lockridge could only nod. He handed the mike to the chaplain and turned away from the crew so that they couldn't see his face.

The chaplain invited the crew to join him in prayer. He spoke calmly, an antidote to the adrenaline coursing through every sailor's body. His words were simple and touched Lockridge to his very core, though afterward the captain could not recall exactly what the chaplain had said. He only knew that they were the right words just then, too true to remember in calmer times.

Just before the chaplain finished, *Lincoln* began a standard call-up for *Mahan* over tactical. The OOD reached for the mike to respond, then stopped and waited for the final amen. *Lincoln* repeated the call-up.

When the chaplain said "Amen," Lockridge turned back to the bridge watchstanders, his face now calm and serene. Whatever his quarrel with the gods was, it was a private matter not to be displayed before his people. He reached for the mike, answered the call-up.

"Interrogative your status," *Lincoln*'s TAO said.

"We're fine, *Lincoln*. No casualties."

There was an incredulous pause, then the TAO said, "*Mahan*, your presence is requested onboard *Lincoln* for debrief tomorrow afternoon. *Lincoln* will provide transportation. Request you set flight quarters at thirteen hundred to receive our helo."

13

BANGLADESH

"Not pretty, is it?" Elwell asked. They were standing at the edge of the Bangladeshi camp, surveying the damage. Little remained to indicate that the area had ever been inhabited.

"It never is," Khan said.

Elwell kept silent.

"At least some good came out of it," Khan said finally. He patted his blouse pocket, barely distinguishable through the mud caking his clothing. It was starting to dry now at the edges, cracks forming at random on what had been a solid coating of filth. "If they believe us."

"This time they might." Elwell turned to face the Bengali. "Good work out there."

And that, Khan knew, was the only comment Elwell would ever make about Khan's decision to scout the Indians' camp during the typhoon. They'd sheltered in a ditch, almost drowning, when the winds reached their peak. They'd watched as three tanks tipped over, exposing their tracked underbellies to the world, turrets digging into the mud.

Then the eye had passed over. Fifteen minutes it'd given them, barely long enough to make the dash into the camp and search for anything that might have survived the torrential downpour and battering winds.

It had been Khan who'd found it. A small scrap of paper, barely one-quarter of a page out of an instruction manual, jammed into a crack in a tree by the force of the winds. It was soaked, spattered with mud that Khan rinsed off in a puddle. Seven sentences, ripped off the bottom of a page by the wind.

They'd scoured the rest of the area in the time they had left, searching for the rest of the manual, but the weather had done its work. Then, within thirty seconds of the first warning, the winds had ramped back up to typhoon strength, sending them stumbling and gasping back to the meager haven of their ditch.

Seven sentences. Enough to damn India in an international tribunal, when placed in context. The passage that sheer luck and bad weather—Allah acting in disguise, if you wish—had put in their hand was simply a warning to a weaponeer that the tactical nuclear warhead altimeter must be correctly set to ensure a proper detonation well above ground level for maximum effect.

How like India! In their arrogance, they assumed that the powerful war machinery could survive the force of nature. He wondered if they'd even bothered to evacuate the troops, or had left them sheltered in tents to face the awesome power of the monsoon.

"I will be back," Khan said. It wasn't really a request for permission to leave, but Elwell nodded anyway. "Take the time you need." Khan turned away from the ground that had housed the army camp and headed toward his village.

Khan's world was gone. There hadn't been much to it, but what little there had been had disappeared without a trace under the force of the wind and the sea. First his wife, now his land. Water pooled in the middle of his jute field, leaving the edges of his one half-acre plot exposed. The ground looked sick and unhealthy, too water-soaked to be anything more than viscous mud.

The plot where the shack had stood was still partly flooded, a line of mud halfway up the wall marking the high-water level. Next to where the house had been, on the spot where he'd planned to add the second room when he could, two bodies lay facedown in the mud. A black cloud of mosquitoes shimmered in the air above the bodies. People died and insects thrived.

His current crop was ruined. He wondered whether it was too late to try putting in another, then shook his head. It would be three weeks until the ground was dry enough not to drown any new seeds.

He felt a bit of thankfulness that they'd never had children. The coming year would be hard enough trying to survive alone. It would have been impossible with a wife and children. As much as he missed her, at least he would not have the added agony of watching her slowly waste away in the sucking poverty of Bangladesh.

And India would be back, not at all deterred by losing a few tanks to the typhoon.

He turned in a circle, looking again at the devastation around him, then picked up his pack and started back toward the camp and Elwell. The ways of governments and gods were always unknowable, and never more so than when they turned the world upside down every few years.

USS *LINCOLN*

The flight from *Mahan* in *Lincoln*'s helo took five minutes. The admiral's aide met him on the flight deck and escorted him to the flag wardroom. Cool air, possible only on a ship with as many air-conditioning plants as an aircraft carrier, was something he hadn't felt on his face in a couple of months. He let it wash over him, vaguely ashamed to appreciate it while his crew was still broiling onboard the crippled *Mahan*.

A man turned to face him from the coffeepot. He was tall and lean, his face weathered and battered. White at the temples, speckled gray through the rest of his hair, wiry strands clipped close to his head still showing a tendency to curl. He walked over to Lockridge and held out his hand. "Welcome aboard, Commander. Paul Sirtus, chief of staff. Your flight out okay?"

Lockridge heard the stiffness in the words, knew then that despite whatever Bulldog said, the fleet blamed him. He decided not to notice the slight. "A little bumpy, but at least it was short." Lockridge sat down, as the chief of staff motioned toward a chair. "Well, we're only twenty miles off the coast. There is still some nasty weather left over from the typhoon."

Silence for a moment, then Sirtus broke it with "How's *Mahan*?"—real concern in his voice now.

"Still afloat. We're making progress on shoring up the structural damage and restoring some electronics. The parts you sent out help. Let me know if you need them back." The critical electronics boards and components were part of a maintenance set, Lockridge was sure. Stripping them from its inventory put the rest of the ships in the hurt locker if they needed to troubleshoot less disastrous problems.

Sirtus waved off Lockridge's thanks. "Least we could do. You need anything else, make sure I hear about it. You're getting the cooperation you need from the rest of the ships?"

"Yes, sir."

Again the silence, less uncomfortable now than it had been a few minutes before. "I couldn't ask for anything more, Captain. Please pass on my thanks. *Mahan* was—*is*—a good ship. We'll do okay."

"Well." Sirtus shifted his gaze from Lockridge's face. "It's too soon to know what they'll eventually do with her."

Lockridge shook his head. "I'm trying not to think about it. Just keeping her seaworthy and trying to restore some basic capabilities. She rode out the typhoon better than I expected." Lockridge tried for a positive tone, but they both knew what lay in *Mahan*'s future. Knew it without seeing a formal message on it, knew it without discussion. *Mahan* was too hurt, too battered in places that couldn't be easily fixed. When she made Sigonella, she'd be headed for scrap. Decommissioning first, of course, the ceremony replete with the centuries of naval tradition that marked the death of a warship. Then towed for scrap, sold to a foreign nation as a practice target, and finally struck from the naval rolls. There wasn't even enough left of her to bother with mothballing.

"You look like you could use some coffee." Sirtus handed Lockridge a mug marked "Visitor" and took down his own coffee mug from the hook on the wall. They took their coffee back to the chief of staff's office and made small talk for a few minutes. Finally, Captain Sirtus got to the point. "The admiral's going to want to know if there's anything you can tell us that we don't already know from the LINK. Anything at all would help. Your firsthand impressions, that sort of thing."

Lockridge stared down at the gleaming, slightly oily surface of the coffee. It could only be found at sea, he thought, irrelevantly, this thick black brew with a personality all its own. Coffee ashore never matched the character of coffee at sea.

He tried to imagine how it would be to be on the other side of the desk, to be the senior officer searching for a delicate way to broach the subject. It would be, he decided, an uncomfortable thorn in their relationship until it was out in the open. Better to do it now, while he was still exhausted from traveling, and too tired to do anything except recite facts.

"She was a good ship, Captain," he said softly. "A good ship, with a good crew. Lord knows, I'd like to save someone else from going through the same thing, if I could."

Captain Sirtus seemed to thaw slightly. A trace of warmth and sympathy crossed his craggy old face. He'd been on the *Stark* mishap board, Lockridge remembered suddenly. Now, undoubtedly, the captain was wondering whether Lockridge had made the same mistakes as the *Stark*, or whether there was more to the story.

"It's a hard thing to do, Jack. In the midst of the all the turmoil, all the loss, to think of the other guys out here. To try to rise above it, and keep someone from ending up the same way. I don't care what the news media says, I think you'll find that everyone here is reserving judgment on the matter. There are too many things that can go wrong at sea, and we've all been too close to the same situation for us to be pointing fingers.''

"Thank you, Captain." Lockridge appreciated the chief of staff's attempt to reassure him that his presence was not unwelcome onboard the ship and that he might even find a few allies there.

"Run through it again for me," Captain Sirtus asked.

Where to start? With the fact that he'd woken up that night for no reason at all? With the first hits, the firefighting and the damage control? What was Sirtus asking for, and what could Lockridge possibly tell him that he hadn't already learned from the LINK or the message traffic?

The heart of the matter, of course. The why, the reason behind it all. Unfortunately, Lockridge couldn't shed any light on that. He'd been there, he'd woken up, and they'd been hit. End of story.

Lockridge set the coffee cup down on the edge of the credenza, his stomach now protesting. He was tired of dancing around the edges of *Mahan,* and trying to reason out for himself exactly why he'd been sent here. He had to agree with Captain Sirtus, that he served virtually no purpose by being onboard the carrier. "It's all in the traffic, Captain. Everything I know. So if we could just go ahead and brief the admiral, I can get back to my ship."

Captain Sirtus cleared his throat. "Change in plans. You'll be on the schedule for tomorrow's morning brief. The rest of the battle group CO's are flying in first thing. We're going to brief the humanitarian mission and *Mahan's* experience will be part of that evolution."

"Tomorrow? But—"

"Tomorrow." Captain Sirtus set his coffee cup down and stood. "Let me introduce you to the flag lieutenant. He's already picked up the keys to your stateroom, and he can get one of the troops to give you a hand with your bag. The evening meal is at eighteen hundred, but I'll have the mess cooks put something aside for you. From the looks of you, I doubt that you're going to want to make chow.''

"Isn't there any way I could brief the admiral this afternoon?''

Sirtus shook his head. ''No can do. The admiral wants the other skippers here. Besides, in a few hours it'll be getting dark. No night hops to *Mahan*.''

The flag lieutenant himself helped Lockridge with his bags, and escorted him down the passageway to a small, private stateroom on the same level. ''It's under the waist catapult, so you'll get some noise here,'' the lieutenant said. ''You'll get used to it soon enough, though, sir.''

"I've been on carriers before, so I know what to expect. The way I feel today, I doubt whether anything short of a real mishap could wake me up. Thanks for the help.'' The lieutenant looked uneasy at the mention of a mishap.

Is it going to be like this? Always dancing around the subject, afraid to use certain words around me, because of the connotations? He shook his head, cutting the thoughts off. For now, all he needed to do was sleep. He hurriedly stripped off his clothes and fell into the rack. Seconds later, he was asleep.

14

The angry howl of a Tomcat on afterburners woke Lockridge at 0600. His body was awake before his mind, as he struggled to throw off the last remnants of a dream. What was it, he thought, searching his memory for details. He'd been at sea on *Mahan*. He could almost feel the breeze, and taste the salt air that would have been, by then, just part of the background. They'd been steaming at twenty knots, heading south toward— toward what? He couldn't remember, but for some reason it seemed vitally important. He got up and splashed some cold water on his face from the washbasin in the stateroom. No matter, it had just been a dream. It wasn't a first and it surely wouldn't be the last. At least Seaman Irving had stayed out of this one. He dried his face with a barely absorbent Navy-issue white towel, and listened to the gentle murmurings around him, the sounds of a ship at sea. Sounds he thought he'd never hear again. It was different on a carrier, of course. The deck was almost unbelievably level, and he missed the gentle rocking of a smaller ship that made sleeping at sea so pleasant.

Thirty minutes later, after a shower, shave, and solid breakfast in the wardroom, Lockridge made his way into TFCC. He paused inside the watertight hatch, letting his eyes adjust to the gloom. Slowly, figures materialized out of the darkness. When his eyes had fully adjusted, he walked across the small room to stand behind the tactical action officer. The man glanced up. "Good morning, Commander. Anything we can help you with?"

Lockridge shook his head. "Just catching up. Any word from *Mahan*?"

The TAO shook his head. "No. Underway Replenishment is the order of the day."

The amphibious ships were still two hundred miles out, heading directly for the amphibious area of operations, a large rectangle laid out in dark green on the screen. An oiler had detached from the battle group and was steaming out to meet them. An under-way replenishment corridor was marked off in the ocean in orange. Overhead, two sections of fighters patrolled. An S-3B/helo combination were delousing the area where the unrep ship would rendezvous with the gators. *Mahan* continued her slow trek south.

"*Lincoln*, Hunter 732," a voice said. Hunter was the call sign for the S-3 squadron onboard *Lincoln*. "Buoy three is hot. Vector Hawkeye 608 in to localize."

Lincoln's TAO started swearing. He picked up the mike and said, "Roger, copy submarine contact in the unrep corridor. Weapons tight until otherwise directed." The TAO released the transmit switch and swore quietly.

"They knew," Lockridge said. The words were out of his mouth before he could stop them. "They knew, didn't they?"

The TAO turned to look back at him. "There's no way they could know. We just established the unrep corridor yesterday. Just sheer bad luck, that's all." The TAO stopped as his eyes adjusted to the dimmer light in the back of the compartment and he realized who he was talking to. He turned back to his screen and began coordinating a change in the unrep with the gators.

Lockridge heard someone come up behind him, and he turned to look. Admiral Fairchild looked at him, an odd expression on his face. "Interesting theory, Commander Lockridge." The admiral motioned Lockridge over to his side, slightly away from the rest of the watchstanders. "My cabin in fifteen minutes, Jack," he said quietly.

"Aye, aye, Admiral." It was time that he got over any reluctance to talk about it. With one last glance back at the tactical screen, the phrase *they knew they knew* beating out a refrain in his head, Lockridge left to retrieve his notes from his temporary stateroom.

Ten minutes later, Lockridge stood outside the admiral's cabin and took a deep breath. The sooner he got this interview over with the sooner he could get back to his ship. The gators, the unrep corridor, the operations ashore—none of it mattered. Not to him.

He waited until the precise time, then tapped lightly on the polished metal door. His knuckles left a faint smudge on the metal.

"Come in," he heard the admiral say. Lockridge pushed the door open and stepped into the admiral's outer officer.

Admiral Fairchild was staring down at a message in front of him. He didn't look up, although he said, "Grab some coffee for yourself, Jack. I'll just be a second."

Lockridge crossed the room and opened the door to the flag mess. He filled a standard Navy porcelain mug with the black brew and returned to the admiral's office. The message was still lying on the glass table in front of the admiral. "I suppose I shouldn't be doing this, Commander. But under the circumstances, I think you've got a right to know about it." The admiral slid the message across the table to Lockridge, keeping his fingers away from the paper as though to avoid contamination. "Can't say that I like it, but I see their point. You can consider your brief to my battle group canceled."

"Sir? I'm afraid I don't understand."

"Read it."

Lockridge scanned the message quickly. It was a Personal For from Seventh Fleet. Eyes only, admiral to admiral. He read it a second time, trying to tease out the meaning hidden within the stilted words. Commander Jack Lockridge was detached on temporary additional duty to the Naval War College, UFN—until further notice.

"You understand the gist of it, don't you?" the admiral asked.

"I see what it says. I can't go, though. I don't care how important they think their war game models are, it's simply not possible."

The admiral leaned back in his chair. "Normally, I'd agree with you. The idea of sending you TAD to the War College, with *Mahan* in the shape that she's in, is pretty foolish. But there's more to it than that. I got a call from Seventh Fleet, who wanted to make sure that this happened."

"Admiral Canon?" *What's Bulldog's interest in this? First flying out to* Mahan *to see me after we were hit, and now this.*

"Admiral Canon says you're to be there—one way or the other. Translation: if you refuse, not that you can, he wants me to relieve you."

"*Relieve me?*"

"And put my chief of staff in your spot. At least until a permanent replacement can be sent out." The admiral held up one hand as though to ward off Lockridge's arguments. "Some people would expect it, under the circumstances."

"It wasn't our fault—*my fault*—we were hit." Lockridge felt desperation climbing up his back. "Admiral, you saw the tapes."

The admiral nodded. "I know. And now I'm seeing this message."

"*My ship was attacked.*" Lockridge took a deep breath, tried to calm his breathing. It wouldn't help at this point, could only hurt him, to keep repeating the obvious. "Sir, I don't see any basis for this. None."

"Someone does." The admiral finally broke eye contact with Lockridge. "Jack, I'm sorry as hell. I promise you, if it comes to that, my chief of staff will take good care of your people and your ship. It shouldn't be longer than a couple of days, not if you do it the way they're suggesting. It's either go, take care of whatever it is that they want you to do, then get back out here—or get relieved, and get sent to the War College. Your call. Whatever the reason, they think they need you back there more than they need you out here."

"For war gaming."

"For planning."

Lockridge stood. "Planning, *hell*. It's too late for that. Look what planning's gotten you so far—submarines in your unrep corridor. You mean that kind of planning?"

"Sit down." Now a note of command crept into the admiral's voice. "That was a stupid thing to say. For what it's worth, I can think of no reason that they need you back there. Everything's in the message traffic, everything that they need to know. But we follow orders, Commander. We make our case, we give it our best shot, and then we follow orders. Now—which way are you going back? As CO of *Mahan* on TAD, or as a commander who's been fired?"

Lockridge sat down heavily in the chair. "I've had a chance to think this through—hell, that's all I've been doing since I was sure we were going to stay afloat—and I've got more questions than anyone else. No answers, though."

"What kind of questions?"

Lockridge shrugged. "The same ones everyone's been asking. Why? Why then? Was there any intelligence that in retrospect would have hinted at an attack on a U.S. warship? What's the U.S. going to do in response? Nothing particularly earthshaking, although I've probably been more insistent than most. My ship, my people."

"And all of those messages have gone through me? Through my people?"

"All except the first voice report. That went directly to Seventh Fleet. We were still under their OPCON then."

"What did you say during the initial voice report?" Admiral Fairchild leaned forward, a concerned look on his face.

"As best I can remember—" Lockridge stopped, flashing back to the moment. Smoke, thick and choking, charred electronics consoles, people dead and dying, the overwhelming noise. "It was a little busy right then, sir. I can't remember exactly. Just the facts, I guess. We'd been hit, were badly injured, no clue as to who did it."

"You're sure? That's all?"

"No, I'm not sure. But if I had to guess, that's what I'd bet. We didn't know anything else then, had nothing else to report. I was talking fast, trying to get the report out before we lost comms. It'll be on the tapes, I'm sure."

"Well." Admiral Fairchild leaned back in his chair. "I want to go through the whole thing again. Start from the beginning. There's an answer in here somewhere."

The admiral walked him through the sequence of events again, asking questions, sometimes off-the-wall, sometimes logical. Lockridge fought to stay dispassionate, to maintain some semblance of professionalism.

"I think that about covers it," the admiral said finally. From the tone of his voice, he was far from satisfied. "If anything else comes to mind, let me know immediately."

Lockridge recognized the comment as a dismissal. He stood, carrying his now empty coffee cup. "I will, sir. If I may ask— are you going to relieve me?"

"Not right now. I see no reason to."

"Thank you."

Lockridge left by the passageway door, then stood in the middle of the passageway with the coffee cup dangling from his fingers. What was there—there was something else, something he couldn't quite remember. He shut his eyes, tried to force it into his mind. Seventh Fleet had just come on the circuit, they were asking about—that was it. They'd called *him* just seconds before the missile hit, before *Mahan*'s sensors had even detected the incoming missile. At the time, he'd thought nothing of it, figured they'd missed something in the data link. But now—

Was that what they were getting at? Trying to see how much I remembered? But why? There are too many witnesses—everyone in Combat knows that they called us, not the other way around. Why would they try to make something of that?

"Sir?" The young Marine standing at attention outside the admiral's cabin door shot him a suspicious glance. "May I help you with something? Are you lost?"

Lockridge became aware that he was standing in the middle of the passageway, staring down at an empty coffee cup. "Lost? No, I'm—no, thanks. Just thought of something—" Lockridge stopped, aware that he sounded as though he were babbling. He turned and walked aft toward the other door to the flag mess, to drop off the coffee cup.

Lost. What is it about—lost, lost, lost. The word echoed in his mind, demanding that he associate it with some other fact, that he see what was so evident to his subconscious mind.

Lost aircraft. On impulse, he turned and walked back into the admiral's cabin without knocking. "Admiral, those Iraqi aircraft—is there any information on where they went after they landed in Iran?"

Fairchild looked up, his expression guarded. "Nothing hard, but indications are that they're staging along Iran's eastern border at the point nearest to Pakistan. At least that's what Pakistan claims, the reason they're howling for *Eisenhower*'s help. Why?"

Lockridge shook his head. "There's a reason behind all this, sir. Captain Sirtus asked me if there was anything else I could tell you about that night, and I told him there wasn't. But there must be something. Something *Mahan* saw that she wasn't supposed to. Something important enough that someone was willing to risk attacking an American warship. And now the Iraqi fighters within unrefueled range of the Iran-Pakistan border."

"That's got nothing to do with *Mahan*, Commander." The admiral's voice was cold.

"I think it does." Lockridge plowed on, not seeing the look on the admiral's face. "Iran sees that India's deployed on the Bangladesh border like they're making another grab for territory. From Iran's point of view, it'd be the perfect time to make a grab for part of Pakistan."

"I hardly think that—"

Lockridge interrupted him, talking almost to himself now, louder, his voice filling with conviction. "And we saw something onboard *Mahan* that would have given the game away. That's got to be it. Maybe they thought we had contact on the submarine that's been located, the one that's fouling your unrep area now. They *knew* where you were going to be, Admiral. *They knew.*"

"There's no connection between what happened to *Mahan*— and my unrep corridor. Pure chance that that sub happened to be there."

"Not chance. Somehow, they knew exactly where it was. It's all related in some way, and we've got to find out how. Until we do, we're going to run into more surprises. Like *Mahan*. Like the AWACS. There will be more attacks, things we can't explain. It's all connected somehow."

The admiral's face was impassive. "Sit down, Commander."

"We have to let someone know. Right away. Every hour that goes by puts us further out of position to—"

"*Sit down.*"

Lockridge stopped. The admiral was staring at him, the incredulity plain on his face. "I was ready to cut you some slack—hell, we all were. But you're over the edge now, Lockridge. Can't you hear how insane you sound? Nobody in his right mind would listen to this bullshit you're spouting. I'd be entirely justified in ordering an immediate fitness-for-duty psychological board."

"I'm sorry, Admiral. It's just that—"

"*Enough.*" The admiral picked up his telephone and punched in two numbers.

Moments later, Captain Sirtus appeared at the door. "Come on, Commander," the chief of staff said quietly. "There's a C-2 inbound as we speak. She's going to drop off her stick, refuel, then head out again. You'll be on her when she does."

An insistent electronic gong cut through the heavy silence

in the admiral's cabin. Fairchild swore quietly as he bolted out from behind his desk and headed for TFCC.

"After we secure from General Quarters," Sirtus said as he followed.

AARDVARK 603

The C-2 circled the carrier, heeling sharply in a right starboard turn. Trapped in the back, strapped in with belts crisscrossing her chest and encumbered by the floatation vest, Jerusha knew something was very wrong. The compartment lights, dim in the best of times, were out. The backward-facing passengers were lit only by the light coming in from two windows for the entire compartment. A few minutes before, the flight crewman had stood up, still safety-strapped to the overhead, and attempted to use the announcing system. The words were not audible over the roar of the turbo-prop engines. He'd tried shouting, but his words didn't reach the forward part of the compartment where Jerusha was sitting. But judging from the reactions of those nearer the tail of the aircraft, the news wasn't good.

The aircraft banked hard, descending at a steep angle at the same time. The straps cut into her chest as she hung, almost horizontal now. The aircraft pulled hard out of the descend, slowing at the same time, driving her back into her seat.

She knew what carrier approaches felt like, had been on-board a COD often enough to know that either there was an extremely incompetent or inexperienced pilot at the controls, or . . . But she'd seen both of them as she'd boarded, and neither had looked like the kind of nugget that would screw up a routine carrier landing.

So it wasn't routine. What the hell was going on?

Abruptly, the aircraft was level. There were a few seconds of miraculously smooth flight, and then the aircraft seemed to hit a roller coaster. It pitched nose up slightly, riding out the turbulence and slowing. The aircrew was strapped back into his seat, holding up one hand clenched in a fist.

This part she recognized at least. Close to the carrier, the air disturbed by the passage of the massive ship roiled and burbled. The last few seconds were always like this, erratic and vomit-inducing, particularly in the near-complete darkness. She shut her eyes and prayed.

The aircraft slammed into the deck, and for a moment she thought they hadn't made it. The engines screamed at full military power, a standard precaution. The power was needed in order to get airborne again. In case the aircraft had failed to snag one of the four arresting wires on the deck.

Then the hard pressure slamming her back against the seat as the hook caught one of the wires and jerked the COD to a standstill. She felt a moment of sheer jubilation as she always did upon landing, as though she'd just survived a near-fatal accident. Her hands were shaking.

She stayed in her seat, waiting for the aircrewman to indicate that they could disengage the restraining harnesses. Oddly enough, he was already standing, though normally the aircrew waited until the aircraft had slipped the hook off the wire and taxied to an unloading spot. He was shouting again, and as the engines spooled down, his words started to make sense.

"General Quarters—the ship's at General Quarters. You follow me real fast, no screwing around. I want you all inside the ship within ten seconds of the time we let the ramp down, you got it?" Even though the aircrew was only a petty officer third class, there was no mistaking the ring of command in his voice.

Evidently satisfied with the response, he nodded. "Okay, unstrap, but stay in your seats. As soon as they start to lower the ramp, I want everyone moving out. From the back first. If you've got gear, don't screw around. It gets in the way, it stays here." He paused, listening to the voices coming into his headset. "Ready—*now*."

The first thin line of daylight was showing at the back of the aircraft. The aircrewman shouted, "Up, up, get moving." He started to squeeze out of the gap between the deck and the rest of the fuselage as the ramp descended and disappeared from view.

Jerusha grabbed her carry-on and took her place in the aisle. Everyone was moving with smooth, non-panicked reactions. It was one of the first things you learned in the service, that panic could kill you faster than a missile.

The line moved quickly out of the COD. Jerusha followed the person in front of her, and as she stepped down onto the flight deck she saw a yellow-shirted sailor with a white vest on over his Nomex. Safety observer, leading the trail of trotting passengers like a mother duck. The aircrewman stood at the bottom of the ramp, keeping the line moving.

Jerusha trotted across the deck and entered the ship through a hatch in the island. She wedged her way into the compartment already packed with bodies. Some of the passengers were already moving into the passageway to accommodate the newcomers.

"Flight gear, hurry, please," a voice announced. Behind her a brown-shirt was holding open a burlap bag. "Cranials, goggles, life vests, in the bag."

Jerusha pulled her goggles and helmet off and held them out. Hands crowded around hers as the rest of the passengers dumped their gear in as well. There would be no orderly inventory now, not with the ship at General Quarters. Probably no more flights taking off, at least not CODs.

"All right, listen up," a voice said from the forward part of the compartment. "I'm Chief Sweeney. The ship's at General Quarters right now, so there's no time to waste. If you know where you're supposed to be, move to the left side of the compartment and check out with Petty Officer Ollinger. He'll coordinate your transit through the ship to make sure we don't break Zebra any more than we have to," he said, referring to the watertight integrity condition of the ship. Opening any watertight fitting during General Quarters required permission from Damage Control Central to ensure that the ship's watertight integrity was not compromised. "Follow the route you're given, no side trips. If you're waiting for an escort, move to the right. We'll deal with you when we have time, but there's not much chance that it will be anytime, soon, so make yourselves comfortable. Your escorts are probably at their General Quarters station right now. Any questions?''

"What about our luggage?'' a voice from behind her asked. Silence greeted the question, and someone pulled the young officer aside to explain in not-so-sotto-voce tones that no one gave a good god damn about his luggage during GQ and did he really want to go on being an asshole. The chief ignored the question.

"Why are we at GQ?'' Jerusha asked.

"Submarine contact,'' the chief said. "That's all I know. We scrambled a couple of flights of S-3s and some helos. You know where you're supposed to be, ma'am?''

"Flag spaces.''

"Okay, move on over then. The rest of you, get yourselves sorted out, please. I'll let you know when we know something else.''

The 1MC blared into life. "Time: plus five minutes. The following divisions makes muster reports to the officer of the deck,'' the voice continued, reeling off the standard countdown for General Quarters readiness. Before General Quarters was officially considered "set'' and the ship ready for battle, a complete muster of every individual onboard and a report that each division had set Zebra in its spaces was required. The 1MC, via the quarterdeck, would make reports every minute until all the reports were in.

On a smaller ship such as a destroyer, setting General Quarters with a well-trained crew would take five minutes or less. On a ship as large as the carrier, ten minutes was considered an excellent time.

Ollinger was wired into the sound-powered phone system, talking to DC Central, checking passengers off his list and handing them slips of paper with their routes hastily penciled on them. Not maps, but a series of letters and numbers that would have been cryptic to anyone that didn't understand how the decks, hatches, and cross-ship frames were numbered. Jerusha said, "Flag spaces," and he motioned her over to stand with two other passengers. Another officer joined them, then Ollinger sent them on their way.

They exchanged hasty introductions then headed down the first ladder, dogged it behind them, then down a second ladder to the O-3 level of the ship, the third deck above the waterline. They walked aft through two watertight doors and entered the blue-tiled deck area that indicated the admiral's staff work space.

"The conference room, probably," Jerusha decided. She made for that door, glanced overhead to make sure the red light indicating a briefing in progress wasn't on, and pulled the door open.

Inside the conference room were a captain and a lieutenant, working over a chart spread out in front of them. The captain glanced up. "Yes?"

"Jerusha Bailey, NSA. TAD from the War College, sir. I hope they told you to expect me."

The captain's face cleared. "They did. You're just in time. We're going over the latest set of projections, trying to decide where we want to be." The 1MC cut in again with a time hack. "Eleven minutes—not great," the captain continued. He held out his hand. "Jim Sirtus, chief of staff. Welcome aboard. You guys were just two miles out when we sounded General Quarters."

"Made for an interesting ride," she answered. She glanced back toward TFCC. "Maybe I ought to get current on the scenario before we talk. I've been traveling for the past thirty-six hours, so I'm behind. There's a sub in the area?"

Sirtus nodded. "Worse than that. National assets picked up what we think were downlink signals. This guy isn't far off, and he's getting targeting data from somewhere."

Pete's shop at NSA. Has to be. Wonder if he knows I'm out here? She pushed aside the question and asked, "Video downlink?"

"Yep. So we're looking at the chart, second-guessing DESRON on what he's doing, and trying to figure out who the target is. Hopefully, it's not us."

"I see. Mind if I take a look?" Sirtus nodded his permission, and Jerusha walked through the conference room and into the dimly lit TFCC. It was almost full, with extra people crowded into every square corner. She moved to a back corner and studied the screen at the other end of the compartment.

The scenario wasn't radically different from what it had been when she'd left Newport. *Mahan* was still trekking along, now farther behind her battle group than she'd been before, and *Eisenhower* was still in the Gulf, although moving toward the Straits in preparation for outchopping. Ground symbology marked the position of the Iraqi aircraft in Iran as well as some arcing arrows indicating that that Marines had already been working out their preferred landing zones and beachheads for both Pakistan and Bangladesh.

And how far along were those preparations? Were they really going in? Or just planning out the possibilities in case they had to? She turned to the officer standing next to her. "Is there a D-Day set yet?"

He uttered a harsh, barking sound that she assumed was a laugh. "You're asking me?"

Slightly taken aback, she said, "I just got onboard. Jerusha Bailey." She held out her hand.

He reached out automatically to shake it, then stopped just as his fingers slid around hers. That strange laugh again, then he said, "Well, well, well. Finally, somebody who knows what it's like to be a pariah."

"I beg your pardon?"

His fingers closed around hers, icy and hard. "I'm Jack Lockridge. And before you ask—yes, that Lockridge."

"My god."

"That, Commander, is about as far from current opinion as you're likely to get." Bitterness tinged his voice.

Jerusha studied him for a moment, taking in the gaunt features, the charred and crusted skin over one cheek. "I was sorry to hear about *Mahan*. More than sorry. I know what it's like."

His face softened slightly. "I guess you might at that. Anyway, what do you want to know? I can give you the admiral's thoughts and plans on what's happening and the relief operations almost verbatim."

"You don't sound too convinced."

"I'm not. But that's not my job right now. To be convinced."

The conversation was starting to get confusing, and for a moment she wondered about Lockridge's mental stability. There was an odd gleam in his eyes and an air of desperation about him. "Why don't you give me the admiral's plan, then I've got a couple of questions for you. If that's all right. I've got to get back up to speed, but I'm interested in what happened to *Mahan* as well." Gromko's face flashed in front of her, a silent reminder of her promise. The War College's position—well, she wouldn't violate her oath simply by asking questions.

"The short version—we're writing off the AWACS and *Mahan* in order to do peacekeeping operations in Pakistan and Bangladesh," Lockridge said. "The landing force commander ferried over yesterday with the details of both ground plans, and now we're working the boat channel assignments for this part of it. Just in case there are any problems with mines, we've ordered breaching shots from the States, too. If the situation goes to shit, there's not going to be time to hunt the mines down individually. One breaching line shot in will clear a channel faster."

"Mines—why would they be mining?" Jerusha asked.

He laid one finger over his lips. "*Why* isn't a popular question right now. We've got a warning order, we've got a plan. The general consumption story is that we've been requested to provide disaster assistance to Bangladesh. The typhoon pretty much leveled everything within ten miles of the coast, and that gives us a perfect reason to be there. The real purpose is to stabilize the border with India."

"But you don't buy that."

He shook his head. "It doesn't matter—but no, I don't. That

border's been in contention for centuries now, and nothing we do is going to make much difference. But again—we've got our orders. I can't figure out why we're that interested in Bangladesh right now, not with Pakistan and India. Not to mention the Middle East.''

Somebody's taking Elwell's report seriously. She debated for a moment filling Lockridge in, then decided against it. While it was tempting to reassure *Mahan*'s skipper that there'd been a reason his ship had been attacked, evidently the information was being closely held. It was somebody else's call as to when it was declassified enough to share with the man who had the most questions—and the most right to know.

"So what's your take on it?" Jerusha pressed, determined to break through his reluctance to talk about what had happened to *Mahan*. For some reason, she had the odd sensation that she and Jack Lockridge might have more in common than having ships shot up under them.

He hesitated, then dropped his voice down to a whisper. "I think we don't know enough yet."

She nodded slowly, saying nothing. "So what would you do? If you were Admiral Fairchild?"

"Probably exactly what he's doing. They make admiral, they know when they're expected to shut up and follow orders. I've already seen one real personal example of that just yesterday."

She waved aside his evasions. "You know what I mean. Tell me."

"Is that an order?"

"Do I look that stupid? Consider it, if you would, a request."

Lockridge took a deep breath. "I'd move all of our forces out of position, withdraw back to the Indian Ocean. Wait and see—give the intelligence picture time to develop. Get a reality check on what we're trying to do. I've got a good buddy on *Eisenhower*, guy I went to school with. I'd be willing to bet that he's got some damned good questions we ought to have answers to before we go in.

"Bailey, there's a reason that someone took a shot at *Mahan*. We need to know who, and we need to know why. We don't have enough firepower these days to parcel it out all around the globe. It's got to be used where it's needed, and we've got to know what's going on before we commit. It's got to make sense to someone."

Jerusha nodded. "And we don't know who that is yet." Some of her own frustration must have crept into her voice, because Lockridge moved in closer.

"I know."

"You mentioned personal experience with admiral's decision a moment ago. Something about yesterday. What was that about?" she asked, aware that she was coming perilously close to breaking her promise to Gromko.

Lockridge shook his head. "I'm sitting here on this damned bird farm when I ought to be back on my ship. The insanity of it—the admiral has orders to fly me back to the War College for some sort of planning evolution. That submarine probably screwed up the chance to get out today."

"You *want* to go back there?"

"Hell, no. But it's either that or get relieved. The sooner I get this over with, the faster I can get back to my ship." A note of real longing and frustration was evident in his voice. "You've got no idea of what it's like."

"I think I might." Jerusha flashed back to her days on *Ramage*, the captain dead, the XO gone, and the waters filthy with submarines. She'd watched too many ships die in that fight.

He looked at her again. "You might. But you'd be the only one around here."

There was a flurry of activity near the TAO console and they both turned to look. "They got him solid, Admiral," a voice said. "Active and passive. He just slipped above the layer."

"Good work," the admiral said. "Hold him—I don't want to go hunting for that hull again when we're headed for the beach."

"Admiral, the S-3 is requesting weapons free." The TAO's voice cut through the sudden silence in the compartment.

"Not yet." For a moment, Fairchild sounded uncertain. "Our orders—we don't know when. Let the aircrew know that, that they've got to be ready, but no jumping the gun. If he commits a hostile act, they know the rules. But until then, we wait."

"Until we lose another ship," Lockridge said, pitching his voice so that only Jerusha could hear him. "Or a couple of companies of Marines. Hell, I'm not sure that would even do it."

"Commander Lockridge," the admiral said.

"Right here, sir," Lockridge answered. The officers surrounding the admiral pulled back to make a path for him.

"Your flight—I'm going to permit the COD to take off in twenty minutes. Be on it."

"Aye, aye, Admiral." Lockridge turned to leave the compartment and brushed past Jerusha. She grabbed his elbow. "Hold on, I've still got questions."

He turned back to her, his face a haggard mask of pain. "I don't have any answers. All I've got is questions, too. And a ship full of people that need me back."

"But the attack on *Mahan*—just answer one question. What woke you up that night?"

Lockridge stopped. "If you knew how many times I've asked myself the same question—it doesn't matter."

"*Doesn't it?*"

A long silence. Lockridge stood motionless, two small points of color rising high on his cheeks. "For what it's worth—yes. I keep thinking that if I can just figure out what it was, I might understand everything that's happened since then. Not just *Mahan*—the rest of it as well."

"Back at the War College," Jerusha said, "They think *Mahan* was an anomaly. Don't expect anyone to listen to you—their minds are already made up. The guy you have to convince is Dr. Arden Gromko. He's head of the Maritime Battle

Lab. I tried while I was back there, but didn't do much good. Maybe he'll listen to you. Just don't make an enemy of him right off.''

That harsh laugh again, then he said, ''You think it'd be bad for my career?''

''Who are you?'' the admiral asked. Jerusha turned to face him.

''Jerusha Bailey, NSA, TAD from the War College, Admiral.'' She stepped forward to his elevated chair. ''I arrived on that last COD.''

The admiral glanced at her, then at Lockridge's retreating figure. ''I judge people by the company they keep, Miss Bailey. Make sure I don't have reason to fault you on your choices.''

Lincoln rendezvoused with the amphibious group on schedule, even after the fouled unrep corridor. The final planning conference was held onboard the carrier while the task group was still sixty miles off the coast of Bangladesh.

''It may be humanitarian operations, but that doesn't mean we don't treat it like any other movement of forces ashore,'' Fairchild said. ''For starters, I want a secure—and I mean completely secure—under-way replenishment area. Pick out an area to the south of us somewhere and send *Kentucky* down to delouse it.''

''Aye-aye, Admiral,'' the staff submarine officer answered.

''I want the whole nine yards—deception plan, everything,'' Fairchild continued. He tapped, with his pencil on the flat chart spread out of front him. ''The whole world knows about the typhoon and that we're going in. I don't want them to know exactly where or when. Besides, it'll be good practice in case Pakistan goes to shit. Especially after they fouled our unrep area.''

The intelligence officer nodded. ''I propose we send *Tarawa* north, along with several small boys. We'll turn on the simulators, have her making noises like the carrier. During flight operations, the aircraft will execute a deceptive descent to *Tarawa*, as though they were going to land on her deck. They'll do a flyby, and proceed onto the carrier at low altitude. It's not foolproof, but it should add to the perception that the gator is in fact *Lincoln*.''

''And what about *Lincoln* herself?'' the air boss asked.

''We'll move south. It won't add that much to our cycle time, and we'll try to convince India that we're headed for her soil instead of Bangladesh.''

''It won't fool them for long, but it might add a confusion factor to their decisions. That's about all we can ask for, this close to shore,'' Fairchild said.

''They've got those forces north along the border. If we can convince them to relocate south, that'll be good enough for me,'' said Marine Colonel Irish Kildin, commander of the landing force. ''Not that I'm worried about a bunch of Indians.''

Fairchild gave him a long, slow look. ''I imagined Custer said the same thing.''

That night, the weather cooperated. It was overcast, virtually unbroken, with patches of dense fog. At 0200, the task force split up. *Tarawa* cranked up to twenty-two knots, her maximum speed, and headed for her assigned area. The carrier limited her speed to that as well, in order to avoid giving away the deception.

Each covered a little more than a hundred miles before arriving at her designated area of operations. The first indications that the mission was not a success came from an S-3 surveillance flight.

''Red Rover, this is Hunter 701,'' the pilot said, irritation in his voice. ''I've got two Indian destroyers and a couple of corvettes cluttering up my operating area.''

''So do we, Hunter 701,'' the TAO onboard *Lincoln* replied.

''Hell of a deception plan,'' the pilot grumbled. ''I still have to make that flyby on *Tarawa*?''

Onboard *Lincoln*, the TAO turn to the admiral. ''Sir?''

Fairchild studied the picture forming on the blue-screen display. How had they known? And, more importantly, had it been just luck? Or had they somehow missed a surveillance flight, blown it with the period of vulnerability assessments provided by the intelligence department. The intelligence officer had assured them that they would be making their moves during the period of no overhead satellite coverage other then visual. As far as CVIC knew, the Indians had no satellite capability in this weather.

Unbidden, Lockridge's words came back to him. Fairchild was certain that the man hadn't known Fairchild was standing behind him, had just entered TFCC in response to a call from the TAO. Fairchild had stood at the hatch for a moment, staring at the tactical display that showed a submarine in *Lincoln*'s planned under-way replenishment corridor.

It had been as though Lockridge were talking to himself, stating the final conclusion to an analysis that existed only within his head. *They knew, they knew*. Hearing the certainty in *Mahan*'s skipper's voice had convinced Fairchild that sending Lockridge back to the States was the thing to do.

But now, looking at the tactical disposition that effectively blew *Lincoln*'s deception plan to shreds, Fairchild knew Lockridge had been right. India *had* known what has happening then, just as they did now. There was no other explanation. The two groups of opposing Indian ships were not scattered randomly up and down, but instead concentrated directly in the path of each of the two task units.

Could it possibly be just good luck or sound operational planning? It wouldn't have been that difficult to figure out what *Lincoln* might try to do.

But the location of the two groups was uncanny. How could they have managed to get the locations so accurate? And how had they known about the unrep corridor? Twice in as many days—no, he decided, he didn't buy it.

"They knew." The words were out of the admiral's mouth before he could stop them. "Call it off." He shook his head, still mulling over the precision of the Indians' maneuvers.

"Our cover's blown—no point in continuing to run the deception now, not after they have a visual on us. All we can do is make the pilot's job more difficult."

Lockridge's words echoed in the admiral's mind. *There will be more attacks, things we can't explain.* For the first time, the admiral started to wonder whether sending Lockridge to the War College had been the right thing to do.

15

USS *EISENHOWER*

"Too bad about your old buddy, Gar," Monarelli said as he entered TFCC. "Heard he got shitcanned off the carrier and shipped back stateside." Monarelli's face was flushed and animated.

Gar glanced up at the clock. His relief was fifteen minutes later as usual. Still, Smith probably hadn't wanted to get in the middle of the yelling in the conference room, and that had just let up a few minutes ago.

"I heard." Gar kept his expression impassive. To let on how much it'd bothered him would have been a sign of weakness.

"Was he always like that?" Monarelli asked, leaning lazily against the bulkhead. "Crackpot conspiracy theorist? I heard they were in vogue back during the Cold War. Guess some people just never—"

Gar's voice came out cold, deadly. "Jack Lockridge is a good man."

"Yeah, well. All I'm saying is that—"

"He's a friend of mine, Admiral. Even now."

An uneasy silence filled TFCC as the two watch sections

of enlisted people and junior officers turning over their respective stations tried very hard not to appear to be listening.

Monarelli finally broke the silence with a short laugh. "You want to be careful who you listen to, Tennant. Real careful."

"TFCC, this is the USW commander," a voice broke in over the USW C&R circuit. "We've got problems, TAO. I've got an S-3B hot and sweet on that diesel we think is Iranian, and he's hearing what sounds like outer doors opening and tubes flooding. I need a clarification on our rules of engagement in case he launches."

"Where's the sub?" Gar said, just as the symbol appeared on his screen. "Never mind, I've got him. Do you have a course and speed on him?"

"S-3 reports he's headed south, TAO, right to the Straits. As you can see, we're well out of his torpedo range. That's why I'm wondering about the rules of engagement."

"If we're out of range, he's not likely to be shooting torpedoes at us, is he?" Gar asked. Another of those mattering crises from the USW commander, each one less critical than the last.

"But he's not out of—Hold on, TAO. S-3's saying he's hearing something—not torpedoes, but sounds like a blast of compressed air that would go with—aw, crap. TAO, Hunter 703 is calling it mining. I say again, mining."

"Mines? Is Hunter directly overhead?"

"Sub's a little to the south, TAO. Maybe a mile."

"Weapons free. You tell Hunter 703 I want that sub dead *now*."

"Copy weapons free."

Gar listened as the DESRON relayed the instructions to the S-3 torpedo bomber aircraft, heard the acknowledgment, then asked, "How many did he get off, Hunter? How many mines?"

"Sounded like three, *Eisenhower*," the slightly garbled voice of the pilot came back. "Hold on a sec—" Gar heard muffled conversation off mike. "*Ike*, I hold contact on *three* submarines, designated Sierra five through seven. All unknown diesels, all launching mines. Could use some dippers up here, *Ike*. Just in case.''

"You got them," Gar said, bypassing the normal chain of command that would have routed all reports and orders through the DESRON. He heard the watch officer beside him following his lead, calling the air boss and passing on his orders.

Gar reached out and jammed the alarm lever into the GQ position. The electronic gongs started seconds later.

On the screen, the S-3 orbited above on position, injected a "torpedo launched" report into the LINK, then headed for the next datum. Overhead, the light *whop-whop* of an SH-60 helo with dipping sonar reverberated down to TFCC. On the grease-penciled status board in CDC, an OS was writing backward on a status board, the picture transmitted to TFCC by videocam.

Too late. We're too late. Even as the air boss announced Flight Quarters, followed shortly by a green deck, Gar knew it was hopeless. They'd kill the subs out there, in all probability, but it was too little and too late. The subs and their crews would be added to the litter on the bed of the shallow Gulf waters, cluttering the area even further, but it would do no good. They'd already accomplished their missions.

Finally, the last symbols appeared on the display screen. Mines, three arrays of them. They stretched across the Straits of Hormuz, their estimated positions provided by the S-3 as his best guess of where they were. They formed a complete line across the narrowest part of the Straits. Even the uncertainty associated with their positions would help.

Eisenhower was trapped in the Gulf.

DRAGON 721, DEPLOYED FROM USS *EISENHOWER*

A battle group is not entirely without resources for dealing with mines, and they're even better equipped for dealing with the platforms that lay them. By the time Admiral Monarelli finished his first voice report to Fifth Fleet's duty office, informing them that it appeared *Eisenhower* was trapped in the Gulf, prosecution had already begun.

The S-3B torpedo-bomber had been airborne for thirty minutes. She had four sonobuoys in the water to the carrier's starboard side, all sweet and cold, and was vectoring on to deploy a second straight line of them astern of her floating airfield.

The pilot was still jazzed up from the catapult shot, and the TACCO and enlisted crewman hyped over the possibility of hard contact on an actual target. After years of drills, practice, and theorizing, it appeared that their chance to make use of their training was fast approaching.

"Electrical sources," the tech announced. "Number three is hot and sweet." Sonobuoy number three was at the southern end of the first pattern they'd laid.

The tech rescaled the octave display in front of him, centering it on the frequency that had caught his attention.

"You got a classification?" the TACCO asked over the ICS.

"Working on it, sir. Might need to get back over that way just to make sure there's no surface traffic in the area."

"Can it wait a few minutes?" the pilot asked. "We're almost at the first drop point for the—"

"No, sir, it absolutely cannot wait." The tech stared down at the display, now breaking out in a rash of additional frequencies. "Classify this contact as a Kilo diesel submarine. Snorkel depth, course zero two zero, speed four knots."

The TACCO swore jubilantly. He entered a new fly-to point into the system as the S-3 heeled over in a hard turn. "We got us one, *Ike*," he reported over USW C&R, repeating the classification and course/speed information. "Interrogative weapons status?"

"How far is this contact from the carrier?" the DESRON watch officer asked.

"Thirty miles—maybe a little less. Looks like she's making a beeline for the carrier," the TACCO said.

"Weapons status is Red and Tight, Dragon 721, until you hear otherwise. He's not within weapon's range."

"Will be in a while, though. It'll save us a whole lot of trouble if we just—"

"Negative," the DESRON interrupted. "I've got guidance from Admiral Monarelli not to put weapons in the water unless you catch them in the act, Dragon 721. Maintain contact and a targeting solution. Unless you see a hostile act or hostile intent, you stay weapons tight."

"Sir," the tech broke in, "I think I've got a visual. A little to the left, just ahead."

"I got a snorkel mast," the pilot announced moments later. "Good eyes, Rimshot."

"Good ears, you mean," the tech muttered. He'd heard the hammering diesel engine as it had started up, before he'd even seen it on his screen.

"I've got a targeting solution," the TACCO announced. "Now let's see if we can hold this bitch if she pulls the plug on us." Maintaining acoustic contact on any submarine submerged and running on silent batteries was a problem, even more so in the shallow waters of the Gulf. Sounds rattled around unpredictably and the debris clotting the ocean floor made Madman detections unreliable.

"You think this is one of the ones that did the mining?" Rimshot asked.

The TACCO nodded. "Not that it matters. We ought to kill them all and let God sort them out."

Several thousand miles to the east, onboard *Lincoln,* the same theory was being discussed at a much higher pay grade.

16

BANGLADESH

Khan shaded his eyes against the sun and surveyed the horizon again. The amphibious ships, bow onto him now, were small spikes in the otherwise even interface between sea and sky. Smaller spatters of smoke belched up from the ocean between the ship and shore as smaller boats ferried in supplies and people. Occasionally, the air above them shimmered as the sunlight caught the fuselage of a helicopter. Two flights of equipment and personnel had already been landed on the ground, and Khan had been told that the ungainly looking craft would be ferrying more supplies and people from the ships for the next twelve hours.

He glanced overhead. The clouds were finally breaking up, the ominous, steadying aftermath of the typhoon replaced by thin frothy wisps of white. Even those remnants were giving way to clear patches, such as the one over the ship.

The multinational U.N. humanitarian relief force had set up camp at the location of his former headquarters. He'd have a relatively dry tent to sleep in while he tried to rebuild his home and the Bengali army rebuilt the military camp just outside the collection of tents and prefab buildings the UN was erecting.

He wondered, idly, if the Americans really wanted to take all of those tents and all of those supplies back to the ship when they were done. Perhaps if he were fast enough, he could appropriate one of the smaller tents for his own. He'd have to be quick, though. Doubtless every one of his countrymen likewise employed would have similar thoughts.

He stared again at the ship. Something besides the fluttering blades of the helicopter were marring the horizon. He squinted, and could barely make out two bright dots overhead the amphibious ship. Within moments, the dot solidified into arrows screaming toward the coast. Jets, then. Surely the Americans weren't worried about anyone interfering with the relief operations? India had not opposed the joint humanitarian effort and they were the only ones with any military force in the area. So why, then, were jet aircraft accompanying the helicopters?

Not as an escort. The jets quickly caught up with the inbound helicopters and passed them, screaming overhead before disappearing over the opposite horizon. Khan turned around to watch them go. His stomach rumbled again, distracting him from thoughts about the aircraft. It was a good sign, he supposed.

After starving for three days before the relief operations commenced, his stomach had stopped complaining. Now, the Meals-Ready-to-Eat that the Americans were supplying had brought his stomach back to life. It had come, in the last two days, to expect and depend on being filled at least twice a day.

He held off for a couple of minutes, savoring the sensation of being able to eat whenever he wanted to, and then dug into his backpack. He pulled out a shiny plastic bag containing the freeze dried rations. The Americans were continually complaining about the MRE's, but to Khan they were wonderful. Strange tastes—some of which, he had to admit, were not particularly palatable, but plenty of food. Even a couple of packs of matches and candy.

His wife, had she lived, would have enjoyed the candy.

The Indian tanks were another puzzling aspect of the relief operations. The ones that survived the typhoon were back, positioned in a group behind the relief camp.

Even in the best of times, Bangladesh could not have resisted an invasion, and to remind the Bengalis of it in the middle of this devastation was just like them. True, they'd provided a few truckloads of rice as well as some field kitchens for cooking it on, but so far India's assistance had been only minor compared to that of the U.S.

Like doctors. The U.S. along with the UN had set up a full medical camp within hours of arriving off the coast. India had yet to provide as much as one vial of antibiotics. He wondered—had the relief operations come before the hurricane, could his wife have been saved?

He shrugged. No use worrying about such things as aircraft and tanks, and his wife was long past any salvation in this world. He took a corner of the tough green plastic between his teeth and bit through it. If nothing else, at least today he would be fed.

"How ya doing?" a familiar voice asked, one that Khan now heard in nightmares of wind and water, the world destroyed. "Chicken and rice—good choice." Elwell crouched down beside his Bengali student. "Course, any of them taste better with the hot sauce on them."

Khan shuddered a bit at the thought of what Elwell might consider tasting good. Frankly, he was just happy to have calories—warm calories, at that, thanks to the self-contained water-activated heating pouch included with the MRE.

Elwell watched him shovel down a few bites of the gluey chicken parts and rice. "That glove. Where is it right now?"

"I don't know," Khan answered. "I gave it to the lieutenant and told him what we saw. Just as I will do with the instruction manual we found."

Elwell was silent for a moment. The chicken was congealing into a hard mass in Khan's stomach. "That is the right thing to do," Khan insisted, fighting down the nausea. "It is why we patrol, to gather intelligence."

"Yeah. Be nice if some of the officers saw it that way. I'm hoping your people are taking it more seriously than mine are." For a moment Elwell's characteristically impassive face showed a trace of irritation. It was enough to further upset Khan's stomach. "You think they are?"

Khan considered the matter. Officers were not necessarily any better than their troops, but they certainly came from a different class of people. Money and position earned them their slots in the Bengali Army, and there was no guarantee of competence. Of course, much the same could be said for many of the world's armies based on what Khan had seen in his UN tours of duty. "Perhaps."

Elwell sighed. "That's what I was afraid of. From what I can tell, my people aren't going to listen—at least the one's I'm supposed to report to—unless they see the glove themselves. They got tests they can do on it. I got some other connections, too, that lady I called the first night. I want to get her the info on this, too, but she's not answering her phone. Not like she could tell me much on an open line, anyway."

"But you told them what we saw."

"I did. Not sure how much weight that carries in some circles."

Khan considered that for a moment, taking another bite from the MRE to mask his confusion. The thought that someone somewhere was foolish enough to consider ignoring Master Sergeant Elwell was truly frightening. Khan pitied that particular officer, whoever and wherever he was. "I can ask at headquarters," Khan said. "Perhaps there is an intelligence summary report."

Elwell looked doubtful. And with good reason. Both Khan and Elwell had seen how ferociously out of date and inaccurate the indigenous intelligence reports could be. Still, under the circumstances, they might be better than what Elwell could expect to get from his own people. "You could try, I suppose. Wouldn't hurt anything."

"How can they ignore it?" Khan said, meaning the American intelligence network rather than his own. "You saw it. I did, too."

Elwell shrugged. "People see what they want to see sometimes. They don't want trouble here, not with Pakistan kicking up again. So they don't see what doesn't fit."

"But you don't believe that?"

Elwell shook his head. "I believe the Middle East is going to shit, but that's the normal state of affairs over there. We understand most of what's happening there, and we're pretty certain we can kick the shit out of any of the parties involved. They know it, we know it, so there's a lot of posturing that goes on that always stops short of actual shooting. But over here—India, Bangladesh, and Pakistan—we're not so sure of ourselves." Elwell stopped, stared off at the horizon as though seeing something entirely different from the flat Bengali flood plain. "We don't want to see a war, not anything that will involve us. Because we don't know whether or not we can win it if we have to fight it."

Khan stared at him, aghast. "But the relief mission."

Elwell waved it away. "Window dressing. Stuff like that, no country in the world would squawk about. It comes to a shoving match, everyone will be on our side. But let it heat up, let it look like we're going to start calling in some markers for support, and you'll see how fast most of them back down. Overnight, it'll go from applause to resolutions about American imperialism, that sort of thing. Happens all the time. We'll end up declaring the problem solved and pull out. You watch."

"So perhaps it is well that they do not take the glove seriously," Khan said. "At least we are eating."

"There's that. But there's only one thing that scares the world worse than getting dragged into a war they don't understand, and that's nukes. Especially nukes in the hands of people they don't understand."

"At least we eat for now," Khan said, and started to take another forkful of chicken and rice. "At least for now." He lifted the spoon to his mouth, paused, then dumped the contents back in the bag. "I believe I am no longer hungry."

Elwell nodded. "It does that to you."

The deep-throated roar of turbine engines lighting off cut through the relief camp like a buzz saw. After eighteen hours parked behind the camp, the Indian tanks were on the move again.

God knows why they didn't bug out for the typhoon, Elwell thought. A show of force? Maybe. Maybe something worse.

It had taken the Indians most of the day to get the tanks ready to move, repair tracks, refuel and rearm. Like anything with moving parts, tanks broke down as much when they weren't moving as when they were. The only difference was the nature of the casualties.

Elwell wasn't worried about losing track of them. While there was no way a man on foot could keep up with a tank, even pieces of shit like these were, the path that they carved through the muck was unmistakable. Elwell could have followed it in his sleep.

It would take a couple of hours before they were even out of sight. Today would be a typical first day en route for the Indians, moving out late, problems along the way. Hell, they'd be lucky if they made ten miles. And tomorrow probably wouldn't be a whole lot better.

But after that, maintaining a decent reconnaissance position was going to take some serious humping. A day, maybe two, but after that they'd need to get some mobile assets of their own, and those were hard to come by anywhere in Bangladesh. The problem was exacerbated by the second lieutenant at the Bengali camp, as unreasonable a junior officer as Elwell had ever come across in his own Army.

Well, there were ways to deal with officers who didn't understand priorities. Most of those methods were premised on the age-old adage: It's easier to ask forgiveness than permission.

*   *   *

An hour later, the question came up again. "Sergeant, what will we do if they turn inland?" Khan asked. Elwell was pleased to note that a couple of weeks of humping had toughened him up to the point that he wasn't even breathing hard, not even under the load that'd made him stagger three weeks ago.

"Then we've got some decisions to make. Sort of depends on where they are and what they're doing, I'd say. We got some gear, but we stay out too long and we're going to have to resupply. That, or live off the land." Khan's expression of mixed horror and distaste made it clear what he thought of that. "But mostly, it depends on what they're doing."

"The glove—Sarge, I do not think they believe you." Khan's voice made it evident that he was trying not to give offense, but that he had his doubts as well. "And if they're in India, it's going to be very difficult to convince anyone that we are simply lost."

Elwell sighed. So many problems, and none of them particularly related to the real task at hand. The real problem was finding out what those tanks intended to do with those missiles, and he damned sure hoped that Khan understood that. He ought to—after all, he was the one that would have to be living with the results.

Patience, he reminded himself. But even in his most honest moments, he could not believe that he himself had ever been quite so dense.

"Yes, I'm certain about the glove. Just like you're certain about what that scrap of paper says." By now Elwell knew that that simple statement would be enough to reassure his Bengali junior. They'd been through the detailed version of Elwell's analysis before, complete with how and why too many times. "And you're probably right that it's going to take intell some time to piece it all together." *And an act of God wouldn't hurt.* "And as to what we're doing in India—well, we'll just have to make sure that no one knows we're there."

"Here," Khan corrected.

"Here?"

"We crossed over about thirty minutes ago. I told you then."

"And then you said you had made a mistake, didn't you?"

"No."

"Didn't you?"

Khan was silent for a moment. At times, it was difficult for him to follow the train of thought that had served Elwell so well in the last almost thirty years. "Yes?" The answer was uncertain.

"Yes. We've been checking the map real often, every fifteen minutes. Making sure we're parallel to those guys but on our own side of the border. You got that?"

Khan was silent again, his face frustrated. Then a sound up ahead snapped both their heads up.

"Doesn't matter now," Elwell said. "You can hear the difference, can't you?"

Khan nodded. "They're headed back this way."

17

TRANSPACIFIC AIRLINES FLIGHT 708

At 42,000 feet, the world looked different. Even the clouds were a good 20,000 feet beneath him, he estimated, and the War College—well, the War College was more than 6,000 miles away. For the first time in the last week, he felt he could get some perspective on the problems. Just another briefing. He'd be in and out in one day.

Lockridge lifted the glass of wine, and held it toward the window. The sun, unobscured by fog, smog, and general atmosphere, hit the dark red liquid like a laser. The wine lit up, as though illuminated from inside. He turned the glass slowly, watching the liquid lap at the sides of the glass. He took a quick sip and then held the glass back up to the light. The full-bodied Beaujolais seemed to evaporate on his tongue, leaving behind an aftertaste of sunshine.

The business class section of the flight was only half-full. As an antidote to the claustrophobic COD, Lockridge had splurged recklessly, charging the upgrade from the Navy-paid-for coach ticket to his credit card. *If I'm going to be sent home in ignominy, at least I'll go in style. At least I'm not crowded knee-to-knee with somebody else. Gives me a little time alone, something I'm not likely to have a lot of later on.*

The rich taste of the wine seduced him away from his self-appointed task for the trip. Somehow, during the next sixteen hours, he had to come up with some answers.

Maybe the War College *was* the place to do it. That was what they did, wasn't it? Studied war, tried to find some answers?

But Bailey—what had she said? That they'd already made up their minds? Lockridge rubbed his eyes, felt his thoughts drift away from the entire time he'd spent on the carrier. Not something he wanted to think about unless he had to. Being a pariah wasn't all it was cracked up to be.

He shook his head, wondering for a moment if the wine had been a good idea. Yes, he decided it had. There weren't any rules against drinking on a commercial flight even if you were in uniform.

Rules. The Navy made it all simple sometimes. There were rules to cover everything from how to wear the uniform to the which calling cards to leave on different occasions. Directives on rules of engagement, manuals setting out weapons procedures, everything covered in detail and specifics.

Now if they could only get the other side to follow them, war would be a hell of a lot simpler and less dangerous.

But there were rules, weren't there? Maybe not ones you had to decide to follow, but ones that made a general sort of sense out of the chaos. Lockridge stared out at the clouds below, the surface bumpy and convoluted. Even the clouds followed rules. Chaos rules, maybe, physical laws about air temperature, humidity, and pressure gradients. The whole idea of chaos theory had come hurtling in to modern thought as a result of the weather. If a butterfly flaps its wings in Australia, does that change the weather patterns in the United States? Maybe that had been what caused the typhoon, some freaking butterfly somewhere.

Certainly he'd studied the rules of warfare during his tour at the War College between his XO and CO tours. Starting with Sun Tzu, the Chinese theorist, but there'd probably been more before him. Men who saw that it usually took a three-to-one ratio of attackers to defenders to take a position even before they'd invented the mathematics necessary to explain it. Who watched how terrain played in battle, observed the personal characteristics of the leaders who won.

What had it been—something about Bismarck. A discussion with a professor late at night over a couple of beers on Thames Street. Something about Bismarck's level of sophistication in controlling conflict. Small wars, carefully timed and managed to achieve limited strategic objectives. The professor had been frankly admiring of the German's ability and had said something about the German serving as a model for modern strategic planners. He also mentioned the work that had been done after World War I and World War II on the equations that quantified conflict between countries.

The Lancaster Equations, that was it. The name popped unbidden into his mind. And the professor, what was his name?

Lockridge kept his eyes shut and let the thoughts simmer. The Army, he recalled, had made the most use of the Lancaster Equations. It was from them that it had derived the axiom of always outnumbering defensive force by three to one. The Equations held factors that increased the required strength to five to one if the enemy was in a heavily fortified and protected area.

He vaguely recalled that Lancaster had also attempted to quantify the effects of patriotism, fear, and civilian panic on the course of warfare. Indeed, the original writings on warfare by Lancaster were almost absurdly comprehensive, using every letter in the Greek alphabet—and then some—to try to express the various factors that influenced the nation's will to win and that predicted the outcome of conflict.

The War College had to have a number of members familiar with the Equations. More than enough to form a study group, and more than enough to refine the equations. With the advent of chaos theory and the growing number of operational analysts and mathematicians and computer geeks on faculty, the War College could have progressed far beyond Lancaster's original work. He opened his eyes and stared at the wine again, watching the light glimmer in its depths. He felt a faint trickle of hope.

Maybe there were answers. Not in the microcosm, probably. Not to why at that particular time his particular ship had been attacked. But if he could just find a general reason for it, something that made sense, somehow that would make it a little easier.

The ruby liquid glimmered, like flames. Once again, he saw the fire licking its way through the lower reaches of *Mahan,* melting structural steel and human bodies in its advance.

His mind ran in familiar ruts, back through the events that night. He'd been asleep and something woke him up. He'd gotten up, gone to Engineering, then CDC. Then without warning, the attack.

Not without warning. He'd woken up, hadn't he? A premonition of some sort?

No.

Then what?

He shut his eyes, put himself back in the rack that evening, felt the blanket scratch against the side of his face, the gentle rock of the ship. Asleep, he'd been asleep, and then—

The ship. The motion. It had changed. Nothing dangerous, just a change in the angle of the ocean against her hull.

A turn, then. Not one that they would have woken him for—that was one of the first changes he'd made post-Naves, revising the night orders to allow the OOD considerable leeway in maneuvering the ship around other traffic. They had to call him if the other contact had a CPA—a closest point of approach—of less than two miles, or if the change in course put them more than five miles off of their intended track.

Yes, the ship had turned and he'd woken up. He felt a sense of relief as he discarded the notions of some supernatural warning system. There was a logical, rational explanation for it.

But not for the attack. Or was there? With the question of why he'd awoken resolved, his mind leaped on and fixed on the harder question: why had *Mahan* been attacked?

He felt a sense of despair as he considered the question. This wasn't a matter of figuring out what you knew about your own ship, your own patterns of reacting to her movement. The scale was too large, encompassing the geopolitical ambitions and personal psychology of too many nations and their leaders. No one could—

Maybe someone could. The War College. Was it possible that they could model what was happening in the world, predict where there would be trouble? Would that explain why it was so damned important that he abandon his command during the most tragic of circumstances?

He tightened his fingers around the stem of the glass. That someone might have known what danger awaited for his ship, that someone could have given him some information that might have prevented the tragedy, was almost too horrendous to believe. Fireman Irving, Greg Mallard, and others—their faces flashed before his mind.

The stem of the wineglass snapped suddenly, spilling the Beaujolais across the empty seat next to him. The end of it dug into his palm, gashing it open. He stared at the blood and the spilled wine, his mind nine thousand miles away on the burning bridge of his ship.

If there were answers, he'd find them. And he'd start with that professor who'd been interested in the War College, the one who'd bought so many beers that night. The name still escaped him, but he remembered the face. Bluff, Slavic—a Slavic name as well. Something hard and short, ending with a vowel, the kind of combination of letters that could conceivably make a word in English but never did.

It came to him then, the name, just as he was starting to drift off to sleep.

Gromko. The same name Bailey had mentioned. He'd be a good place to start.

18

NAVAL WAR COLLEGE

"There's got to be some reason for it," Lockridge concluded. He stared across the desk at his former professor, now the dean of academics. If anyone could understand what he was driving at, it would be Gromko.

"You sound very convinced, sir. Perhaps you give us too much credit." Gromko made a self-deprecating face. "As much as I'd like to believe that all answers to world peace lie within these walls, that's simply not true."

"But there are reasons for war," Lockridge said. "You told me so yourself that night we were out. I know you've been doing research into it, haven't you? You've got to help me, Dean. My ship's been hit and I want to know why."

"The State Department—"

"Is full of bullshit, and you know it. Please, Dean."

Gromko was silent for a moment. "You've obviously given this some thought. Tell me what you think was the cause."

"*Mahan* was in the wrong place at the wrong time. They think we saw something they didn't want us to see. Or maybe they needed to take us out before they made a move. The only thing I'm certain of is that it's related to what's going on in the Middle East and in Pakistan.''

"A plot? A giant conspiracy of some sort?''

Lockridge shook his head. "Not a plot— a plan. Someone's given this a lot of thought. An Indian Bismarck, if you will. Someone who understands that applying just the right amount of pressure at a critical juncture works far better than massive ground warfare.''

"I see. And they targeted *Mahan* in particular, yes?''

"Yes. It wasn't random and it wasn't an accident. They killed my people for a reason, I know that much.''

"And just how certain are you? Are you willing to take some significant risks with your career to pursue this theory?''

Lockridge gave a bitter laugh. "There's not much of it left at this point. If I can do anything to make sense of this, at least I'll quit dreaming about the dead. It's as though they visit me, demanding that I do something, that I make it right.''

"I see.'' Gromko fell silent for a moment, then said, "Excuse me for a few moments, would you? A brief meeting with a few professors. It's taken some time to coordinate our schedules and I'd hate to—''

Lockridge stood. "I'll come back after—''

Gromko waved him into his chair. "No, stay. We're meeting in Holman's office and I shall be back shortly. Have some coffee, give this some more thought. We'll continue this discussion in a few minutes.''

Gromko left, leaving Lockridge alone in his office. He shut the door behind him.

Lockridge sat for a moment, feeling drained. He hadn't meant to mention the dreams to Gromko, the constant sense that Fireman Irving was crying out to be avenged. It made him sound crazy, like a lunatic.

But Gromko understood, that much he could tell. And it was a relief to unburden himself to someone.

Lockridge stood and walked over to the bookshelves that covered one wall of the office. History, operations analysis, mathematics, sociology and anthropology—Gromko's tastes were eclectic unless you knew about his long-standing interest in the causes of war.

So why had he appeared to be so reluctant to believe that there was a deeper reasoning at work in the attack on *Mahan*? It seemed just the sort of question he'd find interesting. And that crack about plots and conspiracies—what was behind that? If anything, Lockridge felt that his position was entirely rational.

The door opened again, breaking his chain of thought. Lockridge turned to look.

Gromko and two masters at arms were standing in the door. Behind them was the War College physician who was the liaison between the college and the Newport Naval Hospital.

Gromko walked up to him and put one arm around his shoulders. "Commander—Jack—you must understand when I say I have only your best interests at heart. What you've been through would break a far lesser man. It's a testament to your strength that you've managed so far. Now, let me get you the help you need."

"What's going on?" Lockridge demanded. "Dean, I'm not crazy."

"Of course not," Gromko agreed. "Not at all. But I want you to have a complete medical evaluation immediately. Talk to some professionals, discuss these dreams and visions of yours. And this theory about *Mahan* and the conspiracy."

"*I'm not crazy.*"

Gromko was silent for a moment. "I'm afraid you don't have much choice in this matter, Commander." Jack noted that Gromko had given up the odd use of his first name. "You're going to Medical and you're going now. Chief?"

"Yes, Dean?"

"Escort Commander Lockridge to the Base Hospital. Take his gear with you. It is entirely probable that he will be going to Bethesda for further treatment. Stay with him, will you? He's a little bit disoriented and confused right now, and I want him to get the best treatment possible. Ensure that he sees Dr.

Rodin at the hospital and then assist Dr. Rodin in arranging the MedEvac for Commander Lockridge.''

The chief nodded. "Come on, Commander," he said flatly.

"And Chief? There won't be any need for Commander Lockridge to make phone calls or any other stops either. Just take him straight to Dr. Rodin, understand? I'll take care of the rest of it.'' Gromko sighed, and Lockridge thought he could see an cold amusement under the regretful facade. "It's so tragic—one more victim of the *Mahan* incident. Chief, we must do what is best for the commander now, as he would have done for us if the situations were reversed. He's a hero.''

"I understand completely, Dean," the chief said. He crossed the room and stood behind Lockridge, waiting.

NEWPORT NAVAL HOSPITAL, DEPARTMENT OF PSYCHIATRY

"Post-traumatic stress. Entirely understandable, given the loss of your ship. This has been building for months, Commander, and the cure isn't going to happen overnight.'' Dr. Tazeback paused, studying the man sitting across from him. Maybe he should wait and get Dr. Rodin's take on it. The chief petty officer accompanying the patient certainly seemed to think that was critical.

It wasn't, of course. Frank Rodin was a good psychiatrist, no doubt about it. He had been even from the beginning when he'd served his residency in Bathesda under Dr. Tazeback. Probably the War College just wanted to make sure that their prima donnas got the best of care. Lucky for them that the man who taught Rodin just happened to be here on two weeks of Reserve active duty. No point in getting Rodin in for what was a clear-cut case of post-traumatic stress.

Lockridge seemed smaller than he had when he'd first walked into the reception area. Perhaps it had been the two burly masters at arms accompanying him, creating the illusion that they had control of some sort of psychotic. It had been that escort that had prompted Tazeback to take charge of the man immediately, not waiting for Rodin.

Smaller, but not diminished or weakened, though. If anything, the effect was the opposite. It suddenly occurred to him that it was the same difference between a snake twisting across a road and one lying coiled to strike. Smaller target, more danger.

Was he making a mistake in discharging him from the hospital, he wondered. Probably not. Yet the given the vagaries of the human mind, one never knew for sure. He doubted that Commander Lockridge was likely to suffer a break with reality and become dangerous, although it was a remote possibility. Hell, it was a remote possibility for anyone wandering the outside would, free, unrestrained, and unevaluated.

But no, Lockridge's way of coping with the stress was more likely to take a different form. Marital stress, certainly—that was evident in the history, in what Lockridge didn't say as much as in what he did. Perhaps changes in job performance. Maybe an increasing obsession with details, a less flexible approach to change. Nightmares, of course, ones that would center around the disaster on the ship and the people who'd died. Guilt, shame, and a feeling of inadequacy. The lack of decent REM sleep might lead to increased distractibility and irritability, with decreasing job performance.

He wondered again at the War College's insistence that Commander Lockridge remain in the hospital for a few days. There was no real basis for holding him, since he hadn't been a danger to himself or to others. In some degree of psychological pain, perhaps, and experiencing a degree of paranoia. Still, if the hospital committed every officer who showed those characteristics, the wards would have been crammed to capacity at all times. The psychiatrist had learned the difference between paranoia and planning from another doctor who'd served in Vietnam. Often a slight degree of paranoia was the difference between survival and ambush.

"Nothing that can't be treated—and fairly effectively, too—

on an outpatient basis. I'm releasing you to full duty, Commander."

Still no response from the officer. That worried him, just a little. Concerned, he probed lightly.

"I expect you'll be glad to be released, won't you?"

Commander Lockridge looked up finally, and met his eyes. The psychologist drew in a sharp breath. From the muted demeanor and affect of his patient, he'd expected a dull, shell-shocked expression, perhaps a bit of relief. The cold rage, focused at someone or something outside the room, was something unexpected. For a moment, he reconsidered his decision to discharge his patient.

"Oh, yes," his patient said softly. "I'm looking forward to getting out."

NAVAL WAR COLLEGE

"I see. Thank you for keeping us informed, Dr. Tazeback. Commander Lockridge is a valued officer and I'm pleased to hear that we've been needlessly worried."

Tazeback held the phone away from his ear for a moment and studied it. Years of practice as a psychiatrist had given him an unusually sensitive ability to tease the meaning out of voices. He would have sworn at that moment that the man on the other end was anything but pleased.

"Post-traumatic stress reaction from the loss of his ship," the psychologist said briskly. "He needs some help, certainly, but he's in no way incapacitated."

"Of course. We were concerned, naturally, but if that is your professional judgment, that he's fit for duty, we're relieved. Are there any—restrictions, shall we say, or special conditions? In light of his mental condition?"

You bastard. Can't get him officially, so you'll sabotage his career sideways. What happened to the days when we took care of our own? "There's no mental condition, not as you mean it," he said quietly, holding back the harsh words that crowded his throat. "No reason he can't be returned to full duty, with no restrictions. Quite frankly, sir, I'd think that the Navy would be overjoyed to have someone with firsthand combat experience on the scene."

"Of course. Thank you for sharing that, Doctor."

Abruptly, the line went dead for a moment, and then the melodic buzz of a dial a tone cut in. The doctor stared at the receiver for a moment, and then replaced it gently in the cradle.

Commander Lockridge had just proved one axiom of psychology. Just because a patient was paranoid didn't mean *someone* wasn't out to get him.

NAVAL WAR COLLEGE

Dean Gromko frowned as he stabbed the call button. Moments later, his administrative assistant appeared at the door.

"Find Dr. Rodin," Gromko said. "Now."

Lockridge stormed through the anteroom and into Gromko's office without waiting to be announced. Gromko was seated on the small couch in one corner of his office, talking to another man seated across from him. They both jumped as Lockridge slammed Gromko's office door closed behind him.

"I've had enough of this," Lockridge began. "Send me back to my ship. *Now.*"

Gromko glanced over at his companion. "We're not quite done yet, Commander."

"Yes, we are. I've got nothing further to say to you." Lockridge's voice broke slightly. "I tried to make the best of it. I thought you might have answers, maybe some insight into why it happened. But you don't. You're just like all the rest of them, ready to write *Mahan* off. The only one left who gives a shit about her is me."

"All the rest of them?" the stranger asked, his voice calm and soothing. "Is there some sort of conspiracy at work?"

Lockridge turned on him. "Who the hell are you?"

The man stood, walked over to him cautiously. "Just a friend. My name is Dr. Rodin. Dr. Tazeback works for me."

"I don't have any friends here." Lockridge pointed at Gromko. "Just enemies I haven't met yet."

Rodin nodded, as though making up his mind. "That's what I thought."

Gromko walked to his door, pulled it open, and gestured to someone standing out of view. Two chief petty officers along with a solemn-looking captain stepped into the office. "Commander Lockridge will be going back to the hospital for a while. Captain Maderia, make sure he's accorded every courtesy consistent with his rank and—his condition."

The chiefs took up stations on either side of him. One reached for Lockridge's upper arm. Lockridge jerked away and tried to move clear of both of them. "What the hell's going on?"

Captain Maderia stepped forward. "Come on, Commander. It's just for a few days. You need some rest—even you can tell that."

"I don't need any rest. What I need is for all of you to fuck off and let me get back to *Mahan*." Despite his best efforts, a pleading note crept into his voice. It was all too obvious where this was headed.

"Dr. Rodin thinks otherwise," Gromko said firmly. "For now, let's just follow his advice."

19

USS *LINCOLN*

Admiral Fairchild had a strangely thoughtful streak in his makeup, one that not many of his superiors suspected existed. If they had, Fairchild doubted that his rise within the ranks of the Navy would have been as speedy, if it had happened at all.

The more senior he became, the more often he found that particular facet of his character was called into play. Young lieutenants, even commanders, could resolve most of their daily professional problems and challenges by simply falling back on the rule book. While the Navy was hardly as rule-bound as the Air Force, centuries of experience had codified into routine ways of handling most situations, even unusual ones.

This one, however, was not in the books.

Fairchild went over the facts again. The fouled unrep corridor and the failure of the deception plan had shaken him, and he was hoping some new interpretation or insight would allay his uneasiness, let him drift back into the comfortable and safe patterns of thought that the Navy taught and encouraged.

He'd sent Commander Lockridge back to the War College as he'd been requested, but had taken the added precaution of letting the dean know that he had some doubts about the man. That last outbreak in TFCC—Fairchild shook his head disapprovingly.

That might have been a mistake. But Vice Admiral Canon's description of Lockridge's drug-induced conduct immediately following the attack, coupled with Fairchild's own observations while Lockridge was onboard *Lincoln*, had convinced Fairchild that Lockridge was suffering some sort of nervous breakdown related to the loss of his ship. Understandable, of course. To lose so many members of his crew, to continually have to wonder what he could have done differently—even a fighter pilot like himself might have felt some stress and strain, much less a black shoe.

Funny, even as he'd ordered the man onto the next available COD, the admiral had found himself thinking about Lockridge's claim that there'd be more unexplained events, that India somehow knew where *Lincoln*'s unrep corridor was. Sure, they sounded like the ravings of a paranoid, conspiracies on a global scale. Yet, still, the timing issues were odd. And like it or not, Fairchild himself was bothered by the lack of understanding over the deeper issues in the theater of operations. One of the first tenets of operational planning was that the objectives of the operation had to be clearly defined and, just as importantly, achievable. Nothing in the current plans to send forces ashore in Bangladesh met those criteria. It was almost as though the vast behemoth that was the military was careening ahead out of control.

And Bailey—she was part of the problem, too, wasn't she? Why was she here, anyway? He didn't buy her story for a minute that the War College had sent her out as a courier for their report. Besides, it wasn't like anyone was paying attention to the War College's recommendations anyway, not based on the two warning orders for Pakistan and Bangladesh.

Fairchild sighed, and tossed the paper into a folder. He thought for a few more moments, toying with the yellow

sticky notes, heavy paperweights, and other memorabilia on
his desk. He picked up a chunk of rock, one with names scribbled on it. Flight school, and the names of his running group
back there. One night on the beach, boasting about the great
deeds they'd do some day, drunk on the future as much as the
beer, five of them had etched their names on this rock. Possession of it rotated between them until the day he'd been
selected for flag rank. Then it had been given to him permanently as a reminder of what they'd dreamed they'd accomplish in the Navy. It was more than just a memento, it was a
constant reminder of the fact that he was now responsible for
more than just his own career. The lives of the other men were
his to keep safe as well.

The rock—it was what he was supposed to throw when
needed. When he was tempted to throw his stars around instead of listening to his people.

Why the hell did Lockridge have to be right? No, he hadn't
gotten all the details right, but he'd gotten enough to make
Fairchild think.

It wasn't like he had to do anything, of course. He had his
orders.

But just exactly what was his responsibility right now? To
follow orders? Or to throw the rock?

Finally, he reached over to the credenza that flanked his
desk and picked up an ink pad and a large stamp. He quickly
pounded the stamp onto the red inked pad, and then onto the
top, left-hand corner of the memo Lockridge had left for him.

The stamped words blurred around the edges as the ink
wicked through the cheap paper. Fairchild stared at them, the
irrevocable step in making his suspicions concrete: TOP SE-
CRET NOFORN.

There was a soft, single tap on his stateroom door. The door
opened, and Captain Sirtis leaned his head around the corner
of the frame. "Admiral? You were looking for me?"

"Yes, COS. I'd like a secure, encrypted private line to Seventh Fleet. Patch it into my office." The admiral didn't look
up from the paper before him.

Captain Sirtis waited for one heartbeat, to give the admiral a chance to add any explanation he might think necessary. Before the delay became long enough to be noticeable to anyone besides the two, the chief of staff said, "Aye, aye, Admiral." The door shut quietly behind him.

As the admiral heard the door click shut, he wondered whether or not he should discuss his worries with the chief of staff before he talked to the admiral at Seventh Fleet. Captain Sirtis had been around the Fleet for a long time, and his broad range of experience and thoughtful judgment made him a highly prized officer.

No, this one was his call alone. If he was right, then the fewer people that knew, the better. And if he was wrong—well, it'd be his career alone that was on the line. A hard call, and one that not much in his previous experience had prepared him for.

That was why, he thought wryly, they paid him the big bucks. To make the right decision when in mattered, no matter how risky. And to be wrong only when it didn't matter at all.

The trick was in telling the difference between when it mattered and when it didn't. And, for the moment, he hoped he was wrong this time.

Sixteen hours later, Admiral Fairchild was way past hoping he was doing the right thing and into serious pleading with God. After Fairchild had briefed Seventh Fleet on the submarine in his unrep corridor and on Lockridge's prediction, Vice Admiral Canon had decided the situation warranted an immediate, unannounced visit to *Lincoln*. Even since the phone call, Fairchild had been wondering whether Canon knew something Fairchild didn't know that could only be briefed face-to-face, or whether Canon had decided the battle group commander was crazy and planned to relieve him.

"Okay, explain this to me, Cody," Canon said, settling down on the couch in the admiral's office. "The Lord knows I'll do just about anything I can to get away from flying that desk for a while, but I'll have to admit that your timing could

be better. Too much going on in the world right now for me
to be gallivanting about.''

Rear Admiral Fairchild nodded, and silently passed the senior admiral a briefing sheet on the failure of the deception plan.
He waited while Canon read it.

As commander of the Seventh Fleet, VADM Canon had
more than just the situation between the Bengalis and India
on his plate right now. North Korea was still posturing and
snarling, threatening to invade its southern neighbor. The argument between China and Japan over the Spratley Island was
reaching menacing new levels, and Malaysia had just stated
her intention to support Japan's claim in exchange for an oil
research and development contract. The standing regions conflict—between Russia and Japan over the Kyrill Islands, between North and South Vietnam over a small stretch of the
border, and between Pakistan and India—continued, their importance muted but still significant. No, COMSEVENTHFLT
was not a billet for any admiral bent on quietly improving his
or her golf game. With the Soviet threat gone, every hot spot
in the world was in Seventh Fleet's theater. Add into all that
the probability that *Eisenhower* was trapped in the Gulf until
they could be certain the Straits weren't mined, and you had
the making of a heart attack.

Admiral Canon scanned the page. RADM Fairchild saw his
eyes drift back up to the top of the page, and track slowly
back and forth across it. The senior officer finished it, sighed,
and tossed it on the coffee table.

"I see why you called. Heck of a coincidence, isn't it?"

"Seemed to be so to me, Admiral. There's just enough sub-
stance there to make me worry—especially under the circumstances. In all probability, this is just the product of an officer
overstressed by having his ship shot out from under him.
Thing like that happens, bound to make a man paranoid.''

"There's always that possibility. But the timing, Cody, the
timing! Dang it, that's not paranoia—that's fact! And Lockridge is right, we're in a heck of a spot out here. Christ, there's
an intell spot report that says there may be nuclear weapons

on the border of fucking Bangladesh. Some ground pounder claims he saw—well, never mind.'' Canon banged his fist on the arm of his chair. ''The question is, what do we do now?''

Bingo. He knows something I don't. Relief coursed through the battle group commander. He took a moment and studied Canon before answering. The last few years had aged his former classmate from the Naval Academy. Bulldog had been three years ahead of him then and was still ahead of him, sporting three stars on his collar to Fairchild's one. That gap might close next year, Fairchild suspected.

''Well, first things first,'' Canon said finally. ''Let's operate, for a moment, on the theory that Lockridge is right. If they know what we're doing, then the question is *how?* And how do we find out without letting them know that we know. What's your current readiness status out here, combat-wise?''

''CLF's planning for operations ashore appears to be going well. We don't have any major problems or shortfalls. A few planes are hangar queens by now, but that's to be suspected this far into the deployment.''

Admiral Canon nodded.

''Replenishment shouldn't be a problem from now on. I've sent *Kentucky* south to keep an unrep area sanitized for us,'' Fairchild continued. ''We're getting good support from LOGCOMM, although that could go upside down in a hurry. We're a hell of a long ways from any major resupply sources and the Bengalis are draining us dry.''

''Singapore's still ours, even if they wouldn't take *Mahan*. Sometimes I wonder how long that will last if they find a ready source of hard currency. That's the problem with these young Asian tigers—they don't seem to want to stay caged too long,'' Canon said.

''I think we're all right for the foreseeable future, though. Last time we were in, there was still a lot of support for the United States there.''

''Well, my people agree. But as I said, that could change quickly.''

''You know what the biggest problem is, and it's no surprise. This close to the coast, we're a little short on elbow room. CAP stations, good launch and recover courses—all in short supply. And the USW problem is horrendous, with the river dumping silt and fresh water into the ocean. Worse than it is in the Gulf," Fairchild said.

"Understood. What can we do about the tactical picture? You need more AWACS, something like that?"

"That would help, of course. But there's simply no cure for the time-distance problem—we're going to be too close in to have time to react. And the Air Force is leery about sending AWACS into potential hot spots after what happened in the Gulf."

"Yes, I know."

The two admirals fell silent, contemplating the *Lincoln*'s tactical dilemma. Between them, they had more than sixty years of naval experience. They'd seen all too often, from Vietnam on, the untenable tactical situations that resulted from micromanaging front-line operations. They'd also seen their predecessors and contemporaries go down in flames, either political or the permanent kind, for protesting over the same ineptness.

"I can give you a little help in the intelligence arena," Canon said. "It may not be much—remember, I mentioned a ground pounder who'd seen something ashore? He's an Army asset and he's got a SINCGAARS unit with him. I'll leave you the details on how to get in touch with him. You'll have to use the Marine's gear, and for God's sake, don't use it unless you absolutely have to. We never know exactly where he is or what he's doing, but if you blow his cover, we'll lose him."

"Thanks. Can you tell me what he found that's so important? Is it behind these warning orders?"

Canon nodded. "NBC handling gear. The intell spot report took its sweet time getting to us. Some lieutenant out in the field sat on it for a while. But that changes everything, doesn't it? The possibility of nukes."

Fairchild nodded. "I need to let the Marines know."

"Do it." Admiral Canon was silent for a moment, then said, "There's no help for it, Cody. We're both on point here, all because Lockridge's told us he thinks there's something more to this situation than we're seeing. If anything goes wrong, they'll hang us for not acting on his suspicions. But if we move off the coast, give *Lincoln* a little more sea room, and nothing happens, we're out of position to support operations ashore. Catch-22, any way you look at it, and all because some commander has got some crazy idea that there's a plan at work."

"I've got a couple of ideas," Fairchild said slowly. The plan that had been taking shape in his mind relied on that thoughtful streak he'd kept well hidden, and he had some doubts about how Seventh Fleet was going to feel about it. "First, I'd like to get Lockridge back out here. Second, I think I need to talk to Monarelli. If Lockridge is right, then the mining in the Gulf is related to what's happening over here." He held up one hand to politely forestall the disbelief in Canon's eyes. "And I think we ought to test Lockridge's theory that they knew about the unrep corridor ahead of time."

"How?"

"We give them a chance to do it again."

Canon was silent for a moment. Then he said, "It might work. If we're wrong, we're dead meat. You know that, don't you?"

Fairchild shook his head. "This can't make it any worse, and might do us a whole lot of good. And, from what I've seen of Commander Lockridge, he'd agree in a second."

"I hope so. He's not going to be real happy about coming back to *Lincoln*. After all, you're the one who didn't believe him the first time, who took him away from his ship."

Fairchild shrugged. "It's worse than that. I was pretty hard on him. I agree, getting him to trust us is going to be the toughest part, but it's not like we're going to give him a choice. He wants to get back to *Mahan,* so we've got that carrot to go along with the whip."

Canon gnawed on a ragged fingernail for a moment, then

said, "Make it happen. I want Lockridge back on this ship within the next twenty-four hours. You talk to Monarelli about what's going on. If you have any problems with anyone, at the War College or over in Fifth Fleet, you call me. I'll be in the flag guest quarters."

Twenty minutes later, Admiral Fairchild was tempted to roust Bulldog. He would have called him immediately, except that he wasn't prepared to admit that a mere lieutenant at the War College had him stymied. "What do you mean, he's not available? Listen, do you know who this is?" He glanced over at the rock sitting on his desk and shrugged. There were some times when it was better to throw stars around than rocks.

"I know who you are, sir, and I wish I could help. But Commander Lockridge simply isn't available." The voice on the other end was polite yet impenetrable.

"*Make* him available."

"I can't."

"Then put me through to someone who can." Fairchild fumed as he listened to the clicking on the phone. Idiotic junior officers—who the hell was a lieutenant commander to tell an admiral that he couldn't do something? Why, back when Fairchild had been a JO, it would have been—

"Hello? This is Dr. Gromko. Can I help you, Admiral?"

Fairchild leaned back and smiled. "Yes, you certainly can. I need to speak with Commander Lockridge immediately. Some idiot on your staff is telling me I can't."

A long pause, then, "I'm afraid that idiot was acting on my explicit orders, Admiral. I instructed him to use that response in order to save Commander Lockridge a bit of embarrassment later on."

"Embarrassment?"

"Of course, we all understand what he's been through. Or maybe we don't. The shock, the overwhelming guilt—I'm surprised he's been able to function this long under the burdens he's been carrying. His psychiatrist analogizes it to a tightly wound spring. Once you take the pressure off, it springs out of control. I'm afraid that's what happened to Lockridge—all that was holding him together was the pressure of being on *Mahan*.''

"Are you telling me he's *crazy*?" Fairchild asked incredulously. The fact that the same thought had crossed his own mind not so many days ago was ignored.

"It's not a term they use anymore, Admiral. Post-traumatic shock, I believe they're calling it, leading to a psychotic break. He started seeing conspiracies everywhere and was convinced that everyone was out to get him." Fairchild heard a deep, heartfelt sigh over the line. "Including me. I took it quite personally until the doctors explained.''

"Where is he now?" Fairchild demanded. "Regardless of his condition, I need to speak to him immediately.''

"He's in the Newport Naval Hospital, sir. On the psychiatric ward. But I'm afraid you can't speak to him. Dr. Rodin was quite clear about that. Contact with the outside world, particularly anything having to do with *Mahan*, could do irreparable damage right now. In a few weeks, perhaps, he'll be stable enough to—''

Admiral Fairchild exploded. "I don't *have* a couple of weeks. I need him *now*.''

"As I said, Admiral—quite impossible. Do you want pushing him into another psychotic break on your conscience?''

No more than Jack Lockridge would want another disaster like Mahan *on his. And quite frankly, my dear doctor, I don't care if dealing with this drives him insane. As long as it stops this before more people are killed. Lockridge is the only one who knows what's going on, and one way or another, I'm going to talk to him.*

"No, of course not," Fairchild said aloud, his voice reflecting none of his inner thoughts. "Commander Lockridge's health is the most important thing right now. When he's able to take calls, please let him know that I inquired after him, would you?''

"And your problems out there, Admiral—exactly what did you want to discuss with Commander Lockridge? Perhaps if he has a lucid moment, I could ask the doctors to—"

"No, no—no need for that," Fairchild said. "We'll deal with it."

"Of course, the War College is always available to support deployed battle groups. Surely there's something we could do to assist in whatever you wanted to ask Lockridge about."

"Merely an administrative matter. I thank you for the offer, though," Fairchild said. The hair on the back of his neck was stirring uneasily. There was something odd about Gromko's insistence, something that rang false. And the story about Lockridge's supposed breakdown—hell, it could be true. Lockridge had been acting screwy when Fairchild had shipped him off to the War College—maybe it had just gotten worse.

Screwy—but right. Was that possible? Insane yet dead right about India, Pakistan, all of it? After what had happened yesterday, Fairchild believed it was possible.

"Is it a problem with India's intentions?" Gromko pressed. "Because we do have an updated projection on the conflict in the Middle East. I assure you, Admiral, what happened to *Mahan* has no bearing on that."

"Thank you for your time," Fairchild said. He replaced the telephone handset gently in its cradle and stared at it for a moment. Then he picked it up again and punched in two numbers. "COS, we've got a problem." Fairchild paused for a moment, then added, "Set up a conference call with Admiral Monarelli onboard *Eisenhower*. Have the SEAL detachment officer stand by in the flag mess. I'll want to talk to him as soon as I'm done."

Admiral Fairchild had the secure, private call over the STU-4 route patched into his cabin. He placed the call himself, and waited patiently on the line while Monarelli's chief of staff hunted down his own admiral. Fairchild suspected that at least part of the delay was to impress him with just how busy Monarelli was. Not that that wasn't possible, Fairchild conceded. Mines in the water were enough to keep anyone away from the phone. When he finally picked up, however, there was nothing in Monarelli's voice that indicated the delay had been contrived.

They exchanged guardedly pleasant greetings, then Fairchild plunged right into a quick brief on the unrep corridor and the compromised deception plan. When he finished, he said, "I think both of those events may have implications for your situation over there."

"Cody, is there anyone else on this line?" Admiral Monarelli asked. "It's just you and me, right? No speakerphones or anything like that."

Fairchild sighed, reflecting that some things never changed.

"Just us, Alan. I've got a couple of people in the room with me. Captain Sirtus, my chief of staff, Captain Smith, my intelligence ACOS, and Miss Bailey from NSA—but they're just listening to my side of it. No one else is on the circuit."

"So what's this theory of yours?" Moanin' asked.

"Like I said, it's not my theory. It's more questions than it is answers."

"I don't have time for questions right now. You may have noticed, we have a few problems over here," Monarelli snapped.

"Admiral Canon thinks they're important questions." Fairchild paused for a moment, hoping that Alan Monarelli was still as much of an ass kisser as he'd ever been. True, Alan didn't report directly to Seventh Fleet right now. Fifth Fleet owned the Gulf and surrounding areas. But on her way back to the States, *Eisenhower* would first chop to Seventh Fleet, then on to Third Fleet as she passed Hawaii. Regardless of how serious his situation was right now, Alan would be thinking of that. Thinking of it, and considering just how miserable a pissed-off Seventh Fleet could make his life during return transit.

"You've already talked to him?" Monarelli asked finally.

"I called him. He flew out immediately. He's still onboard right now, but I've got the feeling he's going to be burning up some airspace between here and D.C." Cody held his breath for a moment.

"Guess it wouldn't hurt to listen," Monarelli said finally.

"All I'm saying is that we think that the Middle East problems could be a setup. So far, we've lost one AWACS in your area and one ship out here. And now they've got you bottled up while Iraq and Iran play games with aircraft. That strike you as the beginning of a major Middle East blowup?"

Silence from the other end, then, "Mining the Straits does."

"It might, if they were doing anything to take advantage of it," Fairchild said. "Sure, it's an act of war under international law of the sea, but they're not following up on it, are they? Seems to me that all they want is to keep you out of the game."

"But why?"

And that, Cody Fairchild reflected, was the million-dollar question. And the one that he didn't have any good answers to.

"I don't know. And that worries me. Listen, all I'm asking is that you keep an eye out for any indication that the players over there seem to know what you're doing before you do it. It may be all bullshit, but I thought you ought to at least know about the possibilities that we're kicking around. Don't let them force you into escalating the situation until we know what's going on for sure. When are the minesweepers going to get there?"

"We've already started sweeping with organic assets, but there'll be some small boys in action tomorrow, and I—Hold on." Monarelli's voice was muffled as he spoke to someone else. Then he came back on the line and said, "Cody, I appreciate what you're saying, but we've just regained contact on a sub that was inbound on the carrier earlier today. I've got pilots screaming for weapons free."

"Any chance the sub's bluffing? Trying to force you into taking the first shot?" Fairchild asked, thankful that he wasn't in Monarelli's shoes right now. He knew what his own answer would have been to that question, and Monarelli did, too.

"It's a damned dangerous bluff, if that's what it is. There's no way I can hold off on taking her out. Letting her get within weapon's range would be suicide.''

"Agreed. But just think about how this could be playing out if I'm right. They *want* us to think the war's in the Middle East when it's not, so they'll do everything they can to spook you. I'm not trying to tell you how to win your war, Alan, just suggesting an alternative explanation for some of this shit. That's all. You're on scene, you're going to have better info than I will.'' Fairchild hoped that it sounded as appeasing as he'd intended.

"All right. You've made your point.'' Fairchild could hear voices in the background, tense voices. "But you're risking an awful lot on the word of a guy whose ship is dead in the water. I've heard about Lockridge. Got a guy on my staff who went to school with him.''

"Who?'' Fairchild asked.

"Gar Tennant. You know him? He and Lockridge are asshole buddies from the Academy. Tennant got damned near insubordinate with me defending the guy.'' More voices from Monarelli's end, then, "I have to go. That sub is about to be a problem.''

Fairchild let his finger slip off the transmit button. "Miss Bailey, the name Tennant mean anything to you?''

Jerusha nodded. "Lockridge mentioned him when he was talking about a good friend he had on *Ike*.''

"That's what I thought.'' Fairchild depressed the transmit button on the handset. "Wait, Alan—one thing. Can you get this guy Tennant over to me?''

"Could, sure. But I'm not going to. He's one of my TAOs. Why do you even ask?''

"Because—'' Cody hesitated, unwilling to expose his entire plan to Monarelli. "Listen, I've got to have him. You send him to me, I'll make sure you're covered, however this turns out.''

"Are you crazy?''

"Probably. Come on, Alan. I need him worse than you do right now.'' And that, Fairchild reflected, was truly an understatement. Every bit of his plan depended on having someone Lockridge would trust, someone that he'd listen to even if he were wildly paranoid. Someone he knew outside of the Navy.

"Alan—it's dead serious. I've got to have him," Fairchild repeated, desperation leaking into his voice. "I give you my word it's for real."

The eerie, hissing silence of a secure circuit filled the room. Finally, Monarelli spoke. "You've never given me enough credit, Cody. I know what you think of me, you and your Academy buddies. You're tight, just like Lockridge and Tennant are. You cover for each other."

"That's not true," Fairchild started, then stopped. It *was* true.

"So I'm going to send Tennant over to you," Monarelli continued, as though Fairchild hadn't spoken. "You think I give a shit about how I'm going to look in this, you're wrong. What matters is that my people aren't dead at the end of it. Frankly, I think you're nuts. So prove me wrong."

The circuit went dead. *Like I just did you* was the unspoken last sentence.

Fairchild glanced around at the men and women he's assembled in his cabin. "I lied about something," he announced. "About Monarelli having better information than I do. Regardless of what he thinks is happening, I know what Lockridge thinks." Fairchild leaned across his desk and said, "I want Lockridge back on this ship within the next forty-eight hours. Hospital or not, I want him here."

"Sir, that's—well, it's something serious as hell," the SEAL officer spoke up. "Sure, I can spring him if you want, get him back here. But Christ, sir. We're going to the green table over it. I'm willing, but you have to know that."

Fairchild nodded. "I do know that. That's why I think this is better handled by someone else. A civilian, say." He pointedly did not look in Jerusha's direction.

Everyone else did. They saw a slow smile spread across her face, replaced by a look of grim determination. "Sir, I was wondering—" she began. She paused for a moment as though considering how to word a delicate request. "I've been on the ship for a while now, Admiral." She gazed around the room approvingly. "And a very fine ship it is, indeed. However, there are a couple of matters I left unresolved back at the War College. I was wondering if you might—"

"I'm not comfortable with you traveling alone, Miss Bailey," Fairchild said. "I'd prefer that you have an escort." He glanced over at the chief of staff, who shut his eyes for a moment then said, "Tennant can be here in fourteen hours. If he's hustling."

Fairchild continued, "So, in approximately fourteen hours, I'd like you to leave this ship. Commander Gar Tennant will be your escort."

The SEAL officer spoke up then. "Perhaps Miss Bailey could fill those hours with a little demonstration of some of our Special Forces capabilities? And we have some items that might be of use to her. Not that we have them officially."

Fairchild nodded. "An excellent idea, one I don't want to know any more about. And Miss Bailey? I want Lockridge on this ship without anyone outside our chain of command knowing about it. The faster the better."

"Sir, if I might make a suggestion?" Jerusha asked, Fairchild nodded. "I'm flattered that you want me to have an escort, but it's really not necessary. Newport itself is much more dangerous than this ship. Too many tourists attract muggers and thieves. That's where I'll need protection, not between here and the States. Perhaps if Commander Tennant could meet me in Newport. We'd save some time."

Fairchild beamed. "An excellent idea." He turned to his chief of staff. "Work out the details with your counterpart on Admiral Monarelli's staff. After all, I didn't say *where* I needed his TAO. And get the ship's communications officer up here, along with the Marine detachment communications officer. I've got a guy on the ground I need to talk to."

20

BANGLADESH

India's tanks proved to be far more reliable than Elwell had expected. He lost visual contact on them, although the deep ruts in the saturated ground made them easy to follow. Elwell and Khan pressed on, figuring that the convoy might break for the night and they'd catch up with them then. The sudden bug-out bothered Elwell more than he let on.

Khan had just asked whether they'd stop during the night when Elwell heard a familiar sound.

"Get down!" Elwell punctuated the order by slamming the flat of his hand into Khan's back. The Bengali stumbled forward, turned sideways as he hit the ground, then started to roll over. The normal worried expression was replaced by a mask of sheer anger. But Elwell was already airborne, hurtling toward a spot in the muck next to Khan. Khan reached for him to retaliate, but Elwell pinned him to the ground with his body lying slantwise across Khan's.

"Don't move," Elwell snapped. Khan froze, fighting the urge to hurt the American sergeant, hurt him hard, make up for all those midnight patrols, the comments and gestures that made him feel so inept. He could feel the blood singing in his veins, demanding that he move, hit, strike, hurt something. His hands trembled with the effort to resist, to lie still pinned down by the very target of his rage.

Seconds later, his anger gave way to fear. He could hear it now, the sound that had alerted Elwell. Distant but approaching fast, the odd air-beating sound multiplied many times. Helicopters, too many of them to sort out by listening to them, flooded the air with their rhythmic sounds out of phase with one another.

Khan shivered. Out in the open, too far from cover to run, they were easy targets for the airborne observers.

Cold mud landed on the back of his neck, then worked its way down his collar as though it were alive. Khan felt Elwell briskly rub another handful in Khan's hair. Understanding dawned, and Khan took over smearing the mud over the back of his body, freeing Elwell to work on himself. When they were both coated, they lay down in the mud and wiggled out small depressions underneath them, then heaped mud along their sides.

"Freeze." Elwell's voice was barely audible through his now mud-clogged ears. This time, Khan froze.

They had had maybe twenty seconds' warning. Enough time if you were Billy Elwell with some sort of unholy sense of hearing and who knew without thinking what they had to do. Had he been alone, Khan would have wasted precious time thinking, maybe even tried to run for the trees. He caught a shudder of motion at the edge of his field of vision and the first helicopter came into view. He wouldn't have made it.

Then again, if he'd been on his own, he wouldn't have *been* in India in the first place. That one cold fact salvaged a bit of his pride as mud dribbled into his eyes.

The sound was deafening now. They must be directly overhead, but Khan dared not move, as much out of fear of Elwell as of the copters themselves. The downdraft beat down on his back, the immense force of the wind generated by the rotor blades. How far overhead were they? One hundred feet, maybe a little less. He was too scared to even think about moving his head to look.

The downdraft was harder now, pounding on his back like the monsoon winds. In a strange way, thinking about it as an overhead monsoon stilled his panic. He'd survived monsoons, knew that the winds, as powerful and all-encompassing, would eventually stop.

Unless the wind blew the mud off him. He waited, certain that any second he'd feel a sleeve start to flap, giving away the fact that this seemingly innocuous field held more deadly animals than insects.

Sure enough, after what seemed to be an eternity, the wind started to decrease. The sound, too, lowered now as the helicopters moved away from them. Khan took a deep breath, gasped in lungfuls of dirty, muck-laden air. He started to disengage himself from the mud. Elwell's hand shoved him back down.

"Not yet," the American said. "They'll be back. And they'll come this way."

Khan stayed put, trying to listen for noise over the sound of his own ragged breathing.

The first explosion came two minutes later, loud even at a distance. The mud underneath him trembled, the surface reaching out to slap a fresh coat on his face. Then two more thuds, hard massive sounds designed to crack the atmosphere itself, the shock transmitted from so far away by the earth underneath him. There was the brief, spitting sound of antiair fire. Then silence.

"The camp," Elwell said quietly, his voice low as though the helicopters could hear him. "I think—yes, it sounded like the camp."

Khan said a silent prayer for the dead. The horror was already too large to feel sorrow over, not yet. There was no point when he might surely join the rest of his camp in the cycle of life before the day was over.

Khan heard it first this time, or so he thought. Elwell hadn't moved, hadn't said anything, so Khan said, "They're coming back." A grunt was his only answer.

The mud seemed less safe than it had just five minutes before. Somehow, when they'd survived the first overflight, he'd started to feel like it was a magical cloak that protected him from view. But when the ground had started trembling, reverberating in response to the attack, it was as though it had betrayed him. He might as well be naked, lying on the ground, begging to be noticed.

The helicopters sounded like they were flying more quickly now, and were upon Elwell and Khan much faster than they'd been the first time. When the downdraft hit them, it was not as strong. It was over before Khan truly had a chance to return to his earlier terror.

This time, he waited until Elwell made the first move. Then he peeled himself up from the mud. It clung to him, sucking noises protesting the separation as he pulled free. He got to his feet and turned back in the direction of the camp. Elwell caught him gently by the arm. "We can't. There's no point."

Khan jerked free. "We must. They will need us."

Elwell stared off in the direction of the camp for a moment, then said, "There's nothing we can do. Not with what we've got with us. We're better off trying to find out where those helicopters are staged. They're not like tanks. They need bases, maintenance facilities."

Khan stared at him. Had Elwell finally gone mad? Everything he knew about the American forces told him that Elwell should be running to go to the aid of the Bengali camp. He stared into Elwell's eyes, trying to decide whether he'd misjudged him or—

"India has had some nuclear capabilities for a period of time," Elwell said. "Remember the glove?"

"They wouldn't." Khan's confusion turned to true horror.

"I think they would. Small tactical nuclear weapons. They've got the technology, from the Russians and the Chinese."

"No. Not this close to India herself," Khan said. "It would be too dangerous for them."

"Khan, think. Remember what we heard. That wasn't conventional weapons, not to make us feel it this far away. And it wouldn't be too dangerous for them if they were using tactical weapons. Or, better yet—from their point of view, understand—neutron warheads. They're primarily lethal only to people and animals, and the radiation's got a short half-life."

Khan sagged. As much as he wanted to argue with Elwell, find some reason to get back to camp, it made sense. India would not hesitate to stamp out thousands, millions of lives, if they could do it without destroying the land itself. The land was theirs—not the people.

"What do we do?" Khan asked finally, still trying to understand the enormity of what Elwell was telling him. "Everyone—no, it's not possible. There must be someone left."

"Not where we were. And probably not many in the main camp. But there are people around who need to know about this, and we've got to make sure they get the information." Elwell's voice was grim. "At least, that's what I'm going to do. At this point, I figured you've got the right to make your own choices. But remember, while the half-life of those fissionables may be short, it's still damned dangerous back there."

"What if you're wrong? It might not have been nuclear."

Elwell shrugged. "Then I'm wrong and we've got some damned good intell for the people back there when we finally get back. I'm not going back, though. Not until I get someone who knows what they're talking about to tell me it's not hot."

Khan started to debate the point, but a quiet buzz from Elwell's front pocket interrupted him. Concern flashed across Elwell's face as he drew the SINCGAARS unit out and held it up to his mouth. "Station calling One Mike Foxtrot, go ahead."

USS *LINCOLN*

"One Mike Foxtrot, this is Alpha Bravo." Admiral Fairchild wondered for a moment whether the grunt on the other end would understand the nomenclature. It wasn't entirely necessary, since this was a secure circuit. "This is Admiral Fairchild onboard USS *Abraham Lincoln.* I've been given this frequency by Seventh Fleet."

"Copy all, sir. Go ahead;" a voice answered.

"I'm getting ready to put troops ashore for peacekeeping operations in Bangladesh. Anything you can tell me about the current situation there?"

There was a long silence, and for a moment Fairchild thought they'd lost contact. He looked across at the Marine communications expert, who said, "Still holding, sir. The digital circuit just doesn't have much background static on it."

"Where are you going ashore, sir?" the voice asked finally.

"The Bengali camp at," and Fairchild reeled off the grid coordinates.

"I wouldn't, sir. I'm—well, I'm not there right now, but I'd say it's just been hit with a major strike. I can't give you a damage assessment. Most of the troops bugged out for the typhoon, so the casualties may be light. But I doubt there's much camp left there."

"When?" Fairchild asked.

"Just a few minutes ago. Admiral, you've got Radiac monitors on all those ships. Are you showing any increase in values?"

"Are you telling me it might have been a *nuclear* attack?"

"It's a possibility. You want that I hold on while you check those Radiacs, sir?"

Onboard *Lincoln,* it took just a few moments for the unthinkable to sink in. Fairchild ordered the battle group to General Quarters and set condition Circle William, the damage control condition that isolated the ship from external air. He demanded immediate Radiac readings for all the ships. It took five minutes for the reports to be tallied and for the senior medical officer to assure him that there was no increase in the levels. Nevertheless, the ships activated their saltwater washdown systems, cloaking steel hulls in eerie fog to keep the deadly particles from settling onto their decks. Admiral Fairchild ordered his TAO to input the location of the attack into the LINK as a low-probability event. Finally, he returned to the SINCGAARS handset.

"One Mike Foxtrot, are you still there?"

"Standing by."

"Negative on the Radiac readings. We have no indication of an increase in radiation levels of any sort. Just to be safe, we've ordered standard precautions, and I'll have intelligence back from national assets within the next ten minutes."

"Don't mind telling you that's a relief, Admiral. Sir, with all due respect, I'm not in a secure position right now."

The Marine officer swore quietly, telling Fairchild all he needed to know. "When you get to one, I'd appreciate hearing back from you," the admiral said. He paused for a moment and willed his heartbeat to slow down. Nukes, goddammit, *nukes*. "Are you the guy that found the glove?"

Silence for a moment, then, "Yes, sir. Among other things. I'll have some more information for you later on today." The signal-received light blinked off before Fairchild could answer.

USS *EISENHOWER*

Gar stared at the symbol that had just popped up on his display. He scowled, then turned to look at Simmons. "Find out who the hell is playing with the LINK. I want a name."

Simmons was already on it, he saw, his lips moving as he spoke quietly with his counterparts in the western battle group off the coast of Bangladesh. As Gar watched, the color drained out of Simmons's face. His own breath caught in the back of his throat. "Simmons?"

Simmons ignored him for a moment, still talking on his

mike. Finally, he finished and turned to his right to face Gar. "Sir, it's—it's not a joke." He pointed at the screen, at the symbol that it had taken Gar a moment to recognize. "*Lincoln* put it in the LINK, sir. It coincides with the helicopter maneuvers that the Aegis held inbound on Bangladesh. Nuclear warheads, sir. They hit them with nukes."

"Dear Jesus." Gar felt the words slip out of his mouth, a prayer in the truest sense of the word. Had it come to this? Nuclear weapons?

But why in Bangladesh? The problems were over here, with Iran, Iraq, Pakistan, India—the real players, not the tiny squalid country carved out of India's northeastern region.

Gar's stomach contracted into a hard ball. He felt a wave of nausea rise over him, and almost physical sympathetic reaction to the cold, impersonal symbols on the screen and what they represented.

Monarelli stepped into TFCC. "Commander Tennant, I need to talk to you."

BANGLADESH

Elwell and Khan pushed on northwest, trying to stay headed in the direction that the helos had gone.

Harder than following tanks. Be nice if aircraft left big muddy tracks in the dirt. But at least it wasn't nukes. Not this time.

While the line between Bangladesh might stand out clear and bright on his charts, it wasn't so easy to tell the difference between the two on the ground. The same language, the same customs, the same dress—even the same folk stories, according to Khan. Just the impenetrable barrier of a difference in religions between them. With so much else in common, it made little sense.

But then again, neither did Northern Ireland and England, did they?

They'd gone maybe thirty klicks, moving at a pace that

would make good speed but wouldn't keep them from doing it again the next day, when they got their first break. They stopped in a small village as poverty stricken as the previous one to refill canteens from the common well. Khan struck up a conversation with an old woman selling bread next to it.

After a month in-country, Elwell knew a little of the language. He had enough vocabulary to deal with most routine military matters, but none of it was of any use in talking to civilians. Particularly not old women. He took Khan's canteen from him and filled it as he listened to the words flow back and forth.

Finally, Khan was finished. He turned to Elwell with a look of triumph on his face. "I think I may save us time. Her son, he works with the Air Force. Not on the helicopters, but on the base. She told me where it is quite precisely."

"What makes you think it's the right base?" Elwell asked. "If India was planning a major offensive, they'd have a bunch of forward bases near the border."

"If it's not the same one those helicopters came from, then it's still very very important. This woman, her son tells her about the base. About helicopters there, about what he sees."

"When was the last time she talked to him?"

"Two days ago." Khan moved closer. Elwell could smell the hot, rank scent of him. "Just before he died."

"From what?"

Khan glanced back at the old woman and pity tempered his excitement. "She doesn't know. His body was burned and he was very ill. But there was no fire, no charring of the tissue. She's very puzzled by it all. In her own way, she's a very observant woman."

Elwell shook his head. For a woman who'd just lost a kid, she didn't look all that upset. And how old was she, anyway? Any kid of hers would have to be what—forty years old, at least?

Khan drew back a bit. With steel in his voice, he said, "She's lost five sons in the last three years. She has two daughters and two sons left. The youngest is still in diapers."

"How the hell—?"

"She's forty-two years old." Khan waited for Elwell to absorb that, then added, "I am no expert, but I think I know what killed her son. India has so very many people, you see. Many of them are barely human, in the eyes of the military. They are used for the more dangerous jobs. The burns, the nausea, hair falling out."

Elwell glared at him, and Khan's newfound confidence seemed to melt away. "You do not agree?" Khan asked.

Elwell shook his head. "No. I'd say you're right about that. Radiation poisoning." He took out the SINCGAARS unit. "I know one admiral who's going to be real interested in the location of that base."

A Marine officer answered on the other end. Elwell identified himself as One Mike Foxtrot.

"Wait one." The voice that had identified itself as Admiral Fairchild came on immediately.

"What have you got for me?"

Elwell briefed the admiral on what they'd learned in the village, concluding with "If it was me, sir, I'd want a strike package ready to go for these coordinates." Elwell recited the grid coordinates, then said, "Did you get that?"

The admiral repeated the number back. "Well done, Sergeant. You need anything we can provide?"

Elwell wondered if he could convince the admiral to take Elwell's lieutenant onto his staff for a few months. Sounded like the man who wore the stars knew a little bit more than most about appreciating hard work by a mud puppy. "Sir, there is one thing—you guys got cellular phones on the ship, right?"

"We've got communications sources for anything you need."

"Good. Sir, if you can get through to her, there's somebody over at NSA who ought to know about this nuke depot."

"We can get them immediately," the voice answered.

"Not just anyone," Elwell said. "Sometimes it takes someone who knows what's what to make things happen, you know? Could you find this lady named Jerusha Bailey? Tell her about the depot. She'll make sure it doesn't get buried in channels."

The silence on the other end puzzled Elwell. Sure, it was a little out of ordinary, asking the admiral to skip normal reporting channels, but he'd figured the flag for an all right guy. Maybe he'd gotten it wrong.

"I think I can go you one better, One Mike Foxtrot. Stand by."

A few moments later, Jerusha's digitized but recognizable voice came over his speaker. "Master Sergeant Elwell? Where the hell are you? Talk fast. I've got a plane to catch."

After he'd filled her in, Jerusha said, "I'll make sure this gets to the right people. Good job, Master Sergeant. Hold on, the admiral wants to talk to you."

"Master Sergeant," the admiral's voice said, "I'd suggest you clear the area. We'll take it from here. Unless you've got somewhere else in mind, you might consider returning to the location of the UN camp. That's going to be a real safe piece of ground before long."

"Marines coming?" Elwell asked.

"Affirmative."

Elwell debated explaining to the admiral that no soldier worth his salt considered an area in the immediate vicinity of Uncle Sam's Misguided Children safe. He decided against it, but couldn't resist asking, "Admiral? You got any Army officer billets on your staff? Vacant ones, I mean."

"Not at the moment. But if you get commissioned and want one, I'll make one appear. Anytime, Master Sergeant."

"Oh, I wasn't thinking for me, sir." Elwell considered for a moment the look on a certain Army lieutenant's face if he were notified of a new assignment to the USS *Lincoln*. This time, discretion had no chance of winning out. "But I know someone who could probably use the experience."

ESCALATION

21

T. F. GREEN AIRPORT, PROVIDENCE, RHODE ISLAND

The cold wind slashed through Gar like a pickax. Coming from the hot, humid coast of India, the change in climate was almost unbearable. Not that he wasn't glad to be back in the States, even if it was on a wild goose chase.

No, a low probability mission, he corrected himself. Admirals never ordered wild goose chases.

Gar spotted a military helicopter parked at one end of the ramp as he taxied in. On impulse, he walked over to the flight services desk and asked about it. After a quick check of his identification card, the clerk gave him the name and point of contact for the aircraft. Gar smiled—not only did he know the pilot, but it was an old friend. It looked like he had just found a way to save the Navy money on a rental car.

"You sure about this?" Navy Lieutenant Fred Myers asked, shouting to be heard over the noise of the turning rotors. Gar, seated in the right-hand seat, smiled and nodded.

"Of course I am," he said, shouting in return. "Seventh Fleet said that all available resources were at my disposal.

Now, I think that would include his helicopters, too, don't you?''

Fred shook his head in a dubious way. "That part I'm okay with." He tapped the flight plan as he adjusted his restraining harness. "It's this part—I don't think that Newport Naval Training Center is going to be any too pleased to have us landing on their parade ground."

Gar laughed. "I'll take full responsibility. And if anyone bitches, we will just tell them that we were ordered to save money on rental cars."

"Can you at least tell me what this is all about?"

Gar shook his head. "Not now. But the first thing I'm supposed to do is hunt down a woman named Jerusha Bailey. Trust me—I'm from the staff, and I'm here to help you."

BRICK ALLEY PUB, NEWPORT, RHODE ISLAND

Gar stood at the door to the popular restaurant pub and scanned the crowd. Finding a cab to get him off the Navy base and into town had been the toughest part of the trip so far. Now if he could only find his contact.

Jerusha Bailey—all he had to go on was a picture taken for her security badge and a description provided by Fairchild's staff faxed to *Eisenhower*'s. Real tall and black hair. He glanced down at the photo again. And determined, if her photo was telling the truth about her.

He spotted her almost immediately, sitting by herself at a corner table. She was drinking coffee and finishing off some sort of dessert with chocolate. He walked over to her table. "Miss Bailey?" She nodded. He held out his hand. "Gar Tennant. I understand my old buddy's in trouble. How can I help?"

She smiled and Gar immediately revised his opinion of her. Determined, yes, but a hell of a looker as well. "Sit down, Commander. You're going to be interested in hearing where Jack Lockridge is right now."

She filled him in on what Admiral Fairchild had learned, and finished with "The admiral wants him back out on the carrier. So far, he's the only one who's been able to predict what's happening out there."

"Jack's a smart guy," Gar said thoughtfully. "Real smart. If I'd known he was worried about this, I would have been, too. I'd believe him before I'd believe an intelligence report. And trust me, getting *Mahan* shot out from under him didn't send him psycho. Jack's not that kind of guy."

"That's reassuring." She paused for a moment, then said, "He looked pretty rocky while he was onboard *Lincoln*."

"Just one question." Gar reached out with his fork and stabbed a bite of her chocolate cheesecake. "Why me?"

"He doesn't trust any of us right now. You, he might."

Gar shrugged. "Probably. But you've haven't yet convinced me that I ought to trust you."

"Orders from Admiral Fairchild not good enough reason?"

"Would they be for you?" Gar look up, held her gaze, and saw the answer there. "I didn't think so. So convince me."

NEWPORT NAVAL HOSPITAL

It was cool in the hospital, cool but never silent, no more than ships were ever quiet. Lockridge sat in a chair and stared at the walls, watching the way the light cut across the dingy green paint. The patterns moved left to right, slowly changing, a source of infinite variety to muse on. As he watched, he heard the small, efficient noises of the hospital work. Patient doors opening, shutting, the restless sound that wheelchairs made going down the hallway, voices and snippets of conversation, some related to the patients, more often just mindless chatter. He heard it all, and ignored it, reluctant to take his eyes off the fascinating light patterns on the wall.

A noise immediately outside his door distracted him for a moment. He felt a surge of annoyance, which abated as quickly as it had started. Nothing made a difference, not now.

It was enough that he was alone, entertained by the patterns
of the wall.

"Lockridge? Some people here to see you." The voice had
that quietly cheerful forced tone that Lockridge had come to
associate with hospital personnel. One small part of his mind
noted it, his shocking adaptation to life on the ward, and urged
him to resist. He turned away from the patterns to see a large
male orderly standing at the door. The door was opened partway, as though he really were checking to make sure that
Lockridge would behave himself. He saw the orderly turn
away for moment, then heard him say, "He's been medicated—you won't find him real responsive. But compared to
the way he was when they brought him in, that's a good
thing."

"Thank you."

Odd, now there was a voice he recognized, the first one
since he'd arrived here. And that was unusual, too, wasn't it?
Every time one of *Mahan*'s sailors had been hospitalized, an
officer visited them almost immediately. To prove that they
were taking care of you, that the ship still cared about the
sailor, and to smooth out any administrative difficulties.

For a moment, that question distracted him from the question of the identity of the voice. Why hadn't anyone been in
to see him?

"Jack?" That voice again—thank God, not cheerful. No,
this was filled with worry, at odds with the tone used by the
hospital staff. "Jack, look at me."

Lockridge made the effort, turned his head toward the door.
Two people were standing there, one of them a tall woman
with black air, piercing green eyes, an upturn nose sprinkled
with freckles. The other was—"Gar? What the hell . . . ?"

Gar walked into the room and crouched down in front of
Lockridge. "That's right, it's me. They got you drugged up
or something?"

"I guess." Lockridge felt his eyes starting to close, his attention wandering away.

"Commander Lockridge. Stay awake." The woman, her

voice familiar, too, but not in the same way that Gar's was. He opened his eyes, mildly curious. Gar's girlfriend maybe?

He felt the flush rise in his cheeks before he could summon her name to his tongue. "Jerusha?"

As soon as he said her name, the rest of his world fell into place. All at once, instead of the cool darkness, he felt the patina of drug-induced cool blocking his thoughts. He fought it off, forced his eyes to focus, and said, "What are you doing here? Gar?"

She crossed to him in two quick strides and took a seat on the bed next to him. "There's too much to explain right now," she said quietly, her voice carrying a compelling intensity. "I brought Gar along so you would know that you can trust me. They have you drugged—at least you recognize me, don't you?"

Lockridge nodded.

Jerusha took a deep breath. "You were right. Right about a lot of things. Gar and I have to get you out of here and back to the carrier. You do want to leave, don't you?" For the first time, he heard the slightest bit of uncertainty in her voice. She turned to his friend. "Gar?"

Lockridge found himself unwilling or unable to answer the question immediately. What was there for him outside? More confrontations with Dean Gromko? Public sessions of apology and expiation, explaining to every single officer in the Navy one by one how he managed to get his ship shot out from under him on freedom of navigation ops?

If he stayed, that was his future. He'd wander from command to command, justifying his actions, seeing the accusations during the day and the burnt, screaming face of Fireman Irving at night.

Why not just stay here? The cool dark surging up again, insisting that he reexamine the light patterns on the wall. If he could just follow those, predict how the pattern would change as the sun traveled across the sky, then perhaps the rest of it would make sense. *Mahan* would make sense.

"Lockridge." The voice cut through the rising fog, making

him realize how seductive the trap of staying drugged was. "Lockridge, concentrate. You're losing it. Unless you pay attention, get out of here, more people are going to die. You have to listen to me, Lockridge. You have to." Now Jerusha's voice was urgent, cutting to each layer of the darkness as she spoke. He felt the layers peel away, struggled to keep hold of them wrapped around him and keep him safe, but it was no use.

"What do you want from me? Haven't I lost enough?" His voice sounded thick and slurry to his own ears.

"I want one thing—to get you out of here. Everything else will make sense after that, I promise."

Lockridge laughed, a harsh, gargling sound. "Don't bother. No one's going to listen to me. They don't think a military guy can figure out, did you know that? We're just there as missile sponges.

"But I know what happened. And they'll keep me here forever rather than let me talk. The one thing I don't understand is why. The War College knew that something was going to happen, knows what's going on now. The Lancaster Equations work. They have to keep that secret at all costs. But why? Why didn't they tell us?"

"Is that what you think? Listen, Lockridge, we really don't have time for this. They're going to find out I'm here—they may be calling Gromko even now. There's so little time—I have to get you out of here before they find out."

"Jack, she's right," Gar said. "I've talked to her, I know what she's doing. You got to come with us, old buddy. Like right now."

The last shred of drug-induced calm vanished and the full weight of his anger came crashing back in. "You can get me out?" He hated how dull and slurred his words sounded.

Jerusha and Gar nodded.

Lockridge shoved himself up from his chair, almost toppled over with the effort. Jerusha was at his side, caught his elbow, and stared at him for moment. "Just take it easy. Where are your clothes?"

He shook his head. "I don't know. How long have I been here?"

"Three days at least. It took us that long to find out that they were holding you here." Her voice sounded almost apologetic.

Lockridge shook his head. Had he been sitting in that chair for three days? Was it possible?

Yes, it was, based on how unwieldy his legs felt. Anger surged through him, giving him strength.

"Here—put these on." Gar pulled out a set of khakis from his briefcase. And a pair of shoes. "They ought to fit well enough to get you out of here." Gar kept one hand near his elbow to steady him if he needed it.

Lockridge paused for a moment, feeling awkward and embarrassed. Then he shrugged, turned slightly away from Bailey, stripped down to his underwear and pulled the khakis on, his fingers following the familiar routine. For a moment, it reminded him of his last night on *Mahan,* when he had slid out of bed and slipped into his khakis so automatically.

"How are we going to get out?" he asked, his mind steadily getting clearer. From the little he could recall, the door to his room was locked from the outside. Locked doors barred either end of a long passageway, and a security guard was stationed at one end.

"Can you walk? Or more importantly, can you run?" Jerusha reached into her pocket and pulled out a badge and a piece of paper. "I think this will work out, but in case it doesn't, I may have to use force."

"What is that?" Lockridge asked.

"An order signed by a federal judge releasing you to my custody. I'm supposed to be take you to a federal correction facility to await trial."

"*What?*" Lockridge asked.

She shrugged. "Best I could do on short notice. It's fake, but it says you're going into protective custody. This ought to at least get us off the base."

They were standing at the door now, Gar helping to steady

him. "Pretend you're still groggy," Jerusha ordered. She
rapped sharply twice on the door.

The guard opened the door immediately. "Already done?
Did you get anything out of him?"

Jerusha shook her head. "No, he isn't talking. Too bad for
him—it could go easier on him if he would cooperate."

The guard scowled. "What you mean?"

Jerusha held out the court order. "This. I'm taking him off
your hands."

The guard shook his head, a scowl crossing his face. "I
can't let him go like this. It will have to be cleared through
Administration. Could take a couple of hours."

Jerusha stepped out into the hallway. "I'm afraid not. This
matter is a little too urgent for that."

"Listen, they told me to let you visit—I didn't hear anything about—" Jerusha's hand lashed out and caught him on
the side of the temple. He yelped, staggered, and she followed
it with a quick blow to his groin. Groaning, the guard toppled
over into the hallway.

Tennant glanced up and down the passageway, but no one
else was in sight. Jerusha whipped out a roll of duct tape from
her briefcase, and used it first to secure the guard's hands and
then plastered a piece of it across his mouth. She stood up and
looked down at her work with a dissatisfied expression on her
face. "It won't hold for long, but we just need a couple of
minutes. Come on." She grabbed the keys on his belt, un-
snapped them, and headed for the door that led to the outside.

"How do you know it will fit?" Lockridge demanded, following her automatically, Gar bringing up the rear.

She shrugged. "I don't. But it makes sense, in case of emergency, that he would have a key to the outside door. In case
of fire or something."

After trying a couple of keys, Jerusha found the one that
unlocked the door. Lockridge heard the lock click open, and
waited for a minute. Jerusha took a deep breath. She looked
out past him. "Ready? Because I think—" Lockridge reached
past her and pressed down the fire bar, opening the door. A

siren wailed, splitting the silence immediately. "—that opening this door will trigger an alarm," she finished, shouting to be heard over the noise. "Come on."

They ran down a set of metal stairs bolted to the side of the building. A large ash can located at the top indicated that the sailors were using the fire escape as a smoking area.

"My car is over there," Jerusha said, pointing to the small, sparsely occupied parking lot. She led the way to a compact rental car.

Security guards were converging on the building. Lockridge saw the base police cars approaching, red lights flashing. One veered over in their direction and stopped in front of them. A tall, burly security guard bolted from the passenger's side. "Hold it right there!"

Jerusha flashed her badge at him, hoping that he wouldn't examine it closely. "FBI. There's a disturbed man on the third floor—we just got out in time. You better hurry. He said he had a bomb." She dragged Lockridge on toward her car.

The security guard stared after them, concern evident on his face. But the threat of a bomb-wielding maniac on the third floor was too much, and he hopped back into his car and sped toward the main entrance.

The Newport Naval Hospital was located on its own separate complex from the rest of the Navy base. As they reached the gate only a few hundred yards away, the alarm was already being raised. A gate guard stepped out of the shack, raised one hand signaling Jerusha to stop, then stepped away as she flashed her badge at him.

Now they were on the twisting one-way street of downtown Newport. Jerusha floored the small car, quickly demonstrating her familiarity with the roads.

"Where we going?" Lockridge asked finally.

"T. F. Green Airport in Providence. We're taking the first flight we can get to D.C." Jerusha was out of town now, heading for the bridge that connected Newport with the mainland and the highway. As she pulled onto the road that led to the bridge, Lockridge caught a glimpse of flashing lights ahead.

Jerusha swore softly. "Damn. I didn't believe they could move that fast. They have the other bridge covered as well, I bet. The only other way off this island is by air or sea, and I don't hold out much chance of getting a helicopter out here. That leaves water—maybe the Coast Guard will be easier to avoid than the Highway Patrol."

Lockridge felt his confusion and fear growing. "Look, you're with NSA. Can't you do something?"

Jerusha was silent.

"You *are* with NSA, aren't you?" Lockridge said, his voice almost pleading. The thought had suddenly occurred to him that he had taken her word for everything so far. Maybe she wasn't with the NSA—or maybe she was a Russian spy. Or something worse. He turned to Gar for reassurance. "Isn't she?"

Gar nodded. "She's on the up and up."

"So NSA is—?" Lockridge began, his mind still clouded from the sedatives.

"This isn't exactly what I'm supposed to be doing," she said slowly. She was clearly distracted by the predicament of how to get off the island.

"So what about your backup?" Lockridge demanded, his paranoia clutching his heart.

Again, a small sound of annoyance. "There isn't any backup. Just me and Gar. Admiral Fairchild is taking on the problem of convincing the powers that be that there's something real wrong with the way we're handling Pakistan, Bangladesh, and the Middle East. Gar and I are just supposed to get you back to the ship."

"So there's no court order, no backup team, and no FBI. Just exactly what does that leave us with?" Lockridge demanded.

Jerusha gave a slight smile. "Ourselves. Just like it was off the coast of India with you and your ship."

Lockridge slumped back against his seat. The drugs he'd

fought off for the last thirty minutes were taking their toll. He felt the steady beat of them in his blood, pounding against his brain, urging him to simply relax and watch the light.

"Don't zone out," Jerusha said sharply. "This really isn't the time for it."

"Oh, and just when exactly do you suggest it is?" Lockridge asked, unable to keep the hard edge of anger out of his voice. "What if I just get out of the car here? Go back to the hospital, say you tried to kidnap me? Mind telling me exactly how that leaves me worse off than I am right now?"

Jerusha slammed on the brakes. The car slid and almost ran into a row of parked cars. She turned on him, her face a mask of fury. "It was too late for you the moment *Mahan* took that first missile," she said bluntly. "And it was too late for me the first time I started asking questions at the War College. I didn't ask for this, not any more than you did. But here we are. So the question is, what kind of person are you? Now that you know what's happening, do you stand by and let it go on? Or do you try to do something about it, try to stop it. Between the two of us, we have some convincing evidence, some areas that will make sense to other people. Alone—" She shook her head, her face doubtful. "Alone, the best either of us can hope for is an extended stay in the sort of facility you just left. So make up your mind, Commander. Which is it? For you and for those men and women who were killed on *Mahan*?"

Fireman Irving's face flashed in Lockridge's mind again. He had told him he would keep him safe when he welcomed him onto the ship. He hadn't been able to keep that promise.

"We have to do something," he said slowly, feeling more tired that he had in years. "I don't know what—but something."

Jerusha nodded, a look of relief on her face. "I was hoping you would feel that way." She put the car in gear again and started up the road. "But to do anything, we have to get off the island."

Lockridge nodded his agreement. "It will have to be by sea, then. Maybe we can rent a boat."

"No. They'll think of that." She shook her head impatiently. "Time is against us on this one. Given enough time, they can throw a ring of surveillance around the entire island and start closing in."

"You know, I think I might have an idea," Gar said slowly. "Turn right at the next light and follow the signs to the Naval Base Marina."

"Are you sure about this?" Jerusha asked as she eyed the rickety sailboat doubtfully. "It doesn't look like it will get us anywhere."

Gar clambered onboard and began casting off the mooring lines. Lockridge started helping, moving slowly but clearly understanding what he was doing. "There's only one way out of here and that's in a boat," Gar said, talking as he worked quickly, moving from stern to bow. "Even if I could get in touch with Fred, we can't very well hang around the parade field waiting for another unscheduled flight. We can't rent a boat—they'll be watching for that. Under the circumstances, I would say that we can't afford to be very picky."

"Are you sure it will float?" Jerusha asked. "It doesn't seem all that seaworthy."

The sloop was now held to the pier by only one line. Hands on his hips, Gar said, "How much do you know about sailboats?"

"Nothing."

"I went to Annapolis, where sailing is a required social grace. I checked this one out, and we should be fine. Besides, she's got a motor. Do you have a better idea?"

Jerusha sighed. "This boat have a name?"

Gar looked over at the bow. "Sure does. *Lucky Star*, she is."

"Let's hope she's well named."

22

NAVAL WAR COLLEGE

Dean Gromko yanked his electronic organizer out of his brief-case and carried it over to his desk. He thumbed it on and toggled the phone directory. He ran down the list of names until he found the one he wanted, then stabbed out the telephone number himself. Fingers drumming on the leather-covered desktop, he listened to the ringing.

"Coast Guard Station Newport, Petty Officer Armstrong, this is not a secure line," a voice answered.

"Commander Fitters, please. Dr. Gromko calling." He waited for the call to transfer, glancing up at the clock, counting off the minutes that it had been since the report of Lock-ridge's disappearance. Of all the damned idiots—what was the use of a locked psychiatric ward if it couldn't keep people contained?

And more than people. Plans, secrets, matters of the utmost national security importance. How dare the hospital endanger so many years of work by their lackadaisical approach to security? How *dare* they?

"Dean? To what do I owe the honor?" a robust, Maineaccented voice asked. "Not that you need a reason to call, of course."

Gromko forced a smile on his face, knowing that his tone of voice would reflect a far better mood than he was actually experiencing. "Jim, I'm afraid we have a problem. An embarrassing one, at that." He sketched out the details of how Lockridge had escaped from the psychiatric ward, finishing with "I could call the police barracks myself, but I don't know anyone there. Frankly, I'm very anxious to avoid a lot of unnecessary publicity over this. The damage it will do to the hospital, to Commander Lockridge's recovery—it makes us look foolish, you understand. Not only because one of our finest officers is clearly unstable, but because we can't seem to keep track of him."

"I understand." Gromko was certain Fitters did—not many officers made it to commander without understanding the importance of avoiding embarrassing one's seniors. Fitters might be Coast Guard rather than Navy, but the three-star heading up the War College could still hurt him. "Let me deal with them. We can get the roads out of Newport barricaded pretty fast. We've had some practice at that."

Another reason to call Fitters rather than work through Navy channels. As a law enforcement agency itself, the Coast Guard had excellent coordination measures with other area agencies. Tracking drug runners and smugglers required the ability to quickly and discretely control access to Newport.

"And he's a sailor, remember," Gromko said. "It's possible he'll think of leaving by boat."

Silence. Cautiously, Fitters said, "This sounds like a little more than just a wayward patient, Dean."

"Just find him, Captain." Gromko let the steel show in his voice, aware that he was ripping up whatever goodwill he'd built up with Fitters. "Admiral Williams will be most appreciative."

Blunt, too blunt. These are things hinted at, expected. Never said aloud, not in that fashion. Gromko tried to soften his tone. "And so will I, for that matter. What I feel for the man, what he's been through. You can understand that better than I could ever conceive. To lose one's ship, one's men—some could not survive it intact. That's why I thought of the sea approaches, of course. His doctors tell me it is an obsession with him.'' Gromko held his breath and waited.

"Christ, of course," Fitters said. "You're right—he's been through enough. I'll handle it, Dean. We'll bring him home safe and sound within the hour."

LUCKY STAR

Massive houses dotted the coastline, more castles than summer retreats by most people's standards. Built during the early days of America's industrialism, the structures reflected the results of too much money combined with too little taste.

"Still a while to go until sunset," Gar said. "Maybe an hour."

"Long enough," Lockridge said. "We can be ashore and then—"

"And then what?" Jerusha asked. "So we get out of Newport—we going to try hitching all the way to T. F. Green?"

Gar shook his head. "Not a problem. I've got friends in high places." He held up a cell phone. "Hold on, let me call them."

The coastline slipped by, the only noises the quiet puttering of the sailboat's outboard motor, the calls of sea gulls, and the water against the hull. Despite the situation, Jerusha found herself relaxing. It all seemed too far away, too impossibly sinister to even be believable.

"Halfway there," Lockridge said, scanning the coastline with his binoculars. "This might actually work."

COAST GUARD STATION NEWPORT

Commander Fitters put down the telephone and frowned. There was something about Gromko's story that still bothered him enough to make him reluctant to act. The whole thing, about Lockridge cracking up and obsessing about the sea—you'd think that a man who'd come so close to dying on it wouldn't want anything to do with water or boats or ships ever again. You'd know that you could get yourself killed on it after you'd seen your people die.

What had happened? Something Lockridge had done or hadn't done? It had to be one way or the other—everything is a captain's responsibility, everything. So whether or not a civilian would hold Lockridge responsible for what happened to *Mahan* didn't matter—Lockridge would hold himself accountable, and that would be all that counted.

Was that burden heavy enough to break him? If Fitters himself were in that position—He shuddered, ordered his thoughts not to go down that path. You couldn't start doubting yourself and ever take command again. You couldn't.

He picked up the telephone and called his XO's office. And then the State Police Barracks.

Fifteen minutes later, the first Coast Guard Boston whaler launched. The helicopters took a little longer.

LUCKY STAR

"We got company," Lockridge announced. "Looks to be the Coast Guard."

Gar squinted in the direction that Lockridge had his binoculars trained. "They're coming at us pretty fast." Gar picked up his cell phone and punched in a telephone number. "Stall them."

"Yeah."

"*Lucky Star,* this is the Coast Guard cutter *Melville.* Request you reduce speed to three knots and come right," a voice said over harbor common. "Please acknowledge."

"Not even waiting until they get within voice range," Lockridge muttered. He picked up the mike.

"What are you going to tell them?" Jerusha asked.

"Whatever they want to hear." Lockridge thumbed down the mike switch. "This is *Lucky Star*, Coast Guard. What seems to be the problem?"

"Routine safety inspection," the Coast Guard replied.

"Can they do that?" Gar asked. "Don't they need probable cause or something?"

Jerusha shook her head. "Nope. They can stop any U.S.-flagged vessel anywhere in the world for a safety inspection, and any vessel in territorial waters. Not a damned thing we can do about it. So what do we do?"

Gar transferred his attention back to the cell phone. "We run for it. We got a flight to catch."

COAST GUARD VESSEL *MELVILLE*

The chief petty officer in charge of *Melville* let the mike dangle for a moment. He turned to his first class. "This has got to be them. Nice day like this and they're under power instead of sailing?" He swept out one arm to indicate the rest of the vessels in Narragansett Bay. "You see any other sailboats running on power?"

"No, Chief. Sure don't. Especially not headed out to sea." The petty officer shook his head. "They're not slowing down any, either."

"What size engine you figure they got on that thing?" the chief asked.

"Forty-five, maybe. If that."

"Don't think it'll be much of a contest, then, will it?"

The petty officer shook his head. "They tell you anything about why we're supposed to detain these folks?"

The chief nodded. "One of them's an escaped mental patient. And the other two are just plain crazy."

"They armed?"

"No one said. Let's assumed that they are, just to be safe. Get everyone suited up. Have Carney tell the helo to stand down. We're not going to need him for this one."

The petty officer nodded and went off to make sure the rest of the crew was in bulletproof vests. And armed.

LUCKY STAR

Gar pointed at a bare chunk of rock protruding up from the bay. "Over there. I think that will do."

"For what?" Jerusha asked. "To surrender from? Can't we make a run for the land, maybe get away?"

Gar shook his head. "Not with this engine. They'll be on us in a heartbeat." He cocked his head and listened for a moment. "Speaking of heartbeats."

Jerusha heard it then, the distinctive *whop-whop* of a helicopter. "Dammit, even if we could run, the helo would track us."

"It's not theirs. It's ours."

They slowed to make their approach on the rock, then eased up alongside it, just as the Navy helicopter came into view. Lockridge made the boat fast while Gar led the way up to the flat concrete pad on top of the rock. He had put his cell phone away and was walking the helo in with hand signals. Finally, when it settled into a relatively stable hover over the rock, the helo tossed a horse collar connected to a winch out of the open side hatch. It paid out slowly, stopping two feet above the rock. Gar motioned to Jerusha. "Ladies first."

"No." She pointed at Lockridge. "He's the one that matters right now, not you or me. Get him on, make sure the helo knows that they have to get him away. If it gets sticky, they're to leave us here."

"I'm not—"

"You are." Jerusha grabbed him the arm and jerked him toward the horse collar. "Get on that helo or this has all been for nothing. You're the only one that the admiral wants to talk to, and by god you're going to go talk to him. So get your ass up there now."

Lockridge started to argue, then a look of determination

settled onto his face. "Okay. I'm going. But we'll wait for you."

"If there's time. There'll be less if you keep arguing."

Lockridge slipped into the harness. The helo hauled him up, then dropped the line for the next passenger. "You," Gar said. Rather than argue, she went up. Gar followed in short order.

"Hiya, Fred," he shouted as he swung into the helo's passenger compartment. "Thanks for the lift. You cleared to T. F. Green from here?"

"No, you said not to file for it," Lieutenant Myers answered. "You change your mind?"

Gar nodded. "You can get us in?"

"Sure, no problem. But you mind telling me why a Coast Guard helo's been following me for the last ten minutes?"

23

USS *LINCOLN*

Lockridge pressed his head hard against the back of the seat, preparing for the jolt. Of all the takeoffs and landings he'd had in the last twenty-four hours, this one was the most welcome. At least here he wouldn't have to stay ahead of the civilian authorities.

Getting to T. F. Green had been easier than he'd expected. The Coast Guard helo had made a few demands on them, but Myers had ignored them. They'd touched down on one of the airfields, ignoring the howls of protest from the tower. There'd been a C-2 waiting for them there. Lockridge wasn't sure exactly what strings Admiral Fairchild had pulled to get them permission to take off after that many safety violations, but he'd sure done something. He only hoped Lieutenant Myers didn't take the fall for it.

The landing came as it always did, the hard, slamming sensation as the COD slammed into the deck of the aircraft carrier. The engines spooled immediately to the full military power, filling the cabin with a deafening roar. At the same time, Lockridge felt the aircraft slow, and breathed a sign of relief. Good, they had trapped. At least they wouldn't have to go around and take another shot at the deck.

There was a hard thump against the bottom of the aircraft as the tail hook withdrew. A member of the flight crew stood up, began to motion to them to unstop. Minutes later, Lockridge followed the rest of the passengers out of the tail of the aircraft and onto the flight deck.

"Come on," someone screamed. Lockridge turned to see the yellow shirt, white shirt, a flight deck technician clad in a cranial set and goggles, looking like an insect. He motioned to the disembarking passengers. They followed him across the flight deck, into the island.

Opening a hatch, he led them inside the aircraft carrier scan, still on the flight deck level. As soon as the last passenger crowded into the compartment, someone pulled the hatch shut. The noise immediately diminished to a endurable level.

Lockridge passed his flight gear over to the waiting flight crew. As soon as he was done, an officer stepped forward from a corner of the compartment and asked, "Commander Lockridge?"

Lockridge nodded. "There are some other people with me as well," he said, scanning the crowd of thirty-some passengers to locate Gar and Jerusha.

"Collect your people and follow me," the other officer said. "Admiral Fairchild is waiting."

They followed him down one ladder, then through the corridor that led to flag country. Lockridge remembered the last time he'd been here, how he had been escorted somewhat more forcefully off *Lincoln*.

Admiral Fairchild was waiting for them in the flag conference room. He stayed seated and silent as Lockridge and his entourage entered the room. On his right was his chief of staff, and to his left his operations officer. There was a long moment of uncomfortable silence that Fairchild broke with "Welcome back, Commander Lockridge. Thank you for coming."

"Thank you, Admiral." For moment, Lockridge debated

saying more, then decided against it. It would be up to the admiral to decide whether or not to talk about his last visit to *Lincoln*. If he would prefer to just pretend it had never happened, Lockridge would go along with that. "How's *Mahan*?"

Fairchild ignored the question. "After you left, I received a warning order. We were supposed to go ashore in Bangladesh for humanitarian operations. Just before that, *Eisenhower* was ordered into the Gulf. While she was preparing for offensive operations in retaliation for the AWACS downing, a submarine evidently mined the Straits.

"Two days ago, I sent *Tarawa* north along with some small boys to simulate the carrier. We headed south. We steamed all night. By the next morning, I had every Indian warship in the inventory on my ass. So tell me, Lockridge—how did you know it wouldn't work? And for that matter, why is every unrep corridor I pick lousy with submarines?"

"*Mahan*?" Lockridge repeated.

Fairchild glared. "Answer my question first. If I'm satisfied with your explanation, you'll have the opportunity to check on *Mahan*'s condition yourself."

Lockridge took a deep breath and tried to decide where to begin. He had been over this so many times in his mind during the last twenty-four hours, trying to decide exactly what would convince Admiral Fairchild. But the more he thought about it, the crazier it sounded.

Gar spoke up. "Admiral, what happened after we got to Newport might affect your interpretation of what he's got to say. This is what happened." Gar outlined how he got into Newport, including his landing on the parade ground field.

Fairchild smiled slightly at that, and said, "I've already heard about that part of it. It's taken care of. Go on."

Gar continued with a recap of the chase across Narragansett Bay, ending with "Somebody wanted us out of the way, Admiral."

Lockridge locked gazes with Fairchild. He saw disbelief, anger, and deep concern. After a long moment, the admiral spoke. "I'll take care of Lieutenant Myers. Any other messes needing cleanup?"

Gar shook his head and stepped back to the wall. The admiral turned to Lockridge. "Now, suppose you tell me what all this is about?"

Take them through your reasoning. Let them get use to the shock of that while I fill in the details.

"Bear with me for moment while I explain." Lockridge walked to the front of the conference room and picked up a marker. He began drawing a diagram of a typical battle group communications setup, indicating the data link that provided a common picture to all ships. Then he drew another symbol above them, the one representing a satellite, and a jagged line led back to enable War College. It was a crude sketch, but he had done it partly just to buy time, to organize the thoughts racing through his mind.

He turned back to face the staff, as well as Gar and Jerusha. "All of the ships in the battle group share a common tactical picture. It's maintained a number of ways, the most common being high frequency—HF—radio circuits." He pointed to the satellite symbol on the board. "But you can also maintain link via a satellite—SATCOM—the way we were doing on *Mahan*. It's all automatic—frankly, we didn't pay much attention to it all." He fell silent for moment, as scenes of fiery carnage on *Mahan* flashed back into mind. "Maybe we should have." He shoved the ghosts aside and continued. "What if one of the one-way links wasn't a one-way link, Admiral? What if it were a concealed participating unit, one we didn't know about? They would have seen everything as it happened and been able to enter contacts into the system as well. They would have been there, Admiral, as certainly as if they been onboard *Mahan*."

Not all of it. Not the smoke, the fire. Not Fireman Irving.

Fairchild looked annoyed. "So?"

Lockridge took a deep breath. "What if it went further than that? You know the LINK can be filtered to eliminate contacts from a particular ship if there are problems with the data flow.

Or to reduce the data sent to a single participating unit, a PU. What if there is a filter on the system that prevents us from seeing everyone participating in the LINK?''

The admiral and his operations officer were aviators. They dealt with the LINK in terms of the picture it provided to their cockpit—and now, to their display in TFCC.

Lockridge thought it was possible. So did Captain Sirtus. Lockridge could see it in the older man's face.

Captain Sirtus was a surface officer, one with an Aegis background. His experience might be a few years out of date, but he knew what the LINK could do, had probably spent as many hours swearing at the system as Lockridge had. He knew the filters that were already in place on the system, the ones that eliminated contacts that the system had detected early on. The satellites, the super-secret aircraft flying at altitudes far greater than any aircraft was supposed to be able to.

"It's possible," Captain Sirtus said quietly.

"You can't be serious." Captain Smith, the intelligence officer, looked ready to explode. "Admiral, this is pointless. Commander Lockridge, the missile that took out *Mahan* was not a spurious injection into your LINK system."

Lockridge shook his head. "No, Captain, it wasn't. Our tactical picture looked just the way it was supposed to, with the exception of the ghosting fishing boats. From our point of view, it looked just the way we reported it—an unprovoked attack on an American warship."

"So, what's the point?" Captain Smith demanded. "Even supposing everything you say is possible."

Lockridge kept his eyes fixed on the admiral. "If you concede that there could be an unobserved participant in the LINK—and I think your own experts onboard will confirm that is possible, maybe even be able to find evidence of it—then it's entirely possible that there was another. India."

Smith snorted. "More nonsense. The LINK is encrypted. Just because you can intercept the transmissions doesn't mean you can use the data. You've got to have the right crypto equipment and codes."

Lockridge pointed at Jerusha. "You agree?"

Jerusha shook her head. "NSA's whole mission in life is to deal with foreign transmissions and intercepts. Even if you can't break the encyphering algorythm, you can get some excellent intelligence just from the fact that certain kinds of transmissions are associated with certain military actions." She shrugged. "I'm not giving away any secrets if I say that there are lots of ways to get foreign crypto codes and equipment. It's definitely easier than having to break the codes other ways."

"How easy is it for other nations to do the same thing?" Lockridge asked.

"Not impossible, of course. That's what espionage is all about," Jerusha answered.

"So you're claiming that we've got a security problem?" Fairchild asked. "Our LINK is compromised?"

Lockridge nodded. From the looks on their faces, they were at least willing to buy that much. The rest of it, however, would take a good deal more convincing. "And not by a foreign equivalent of NSA. We change crypto codes at least once a day. This is real-time monitoring of the system, not after-the-fact reconstruction. India's not intercepting our LINK. They're in it as a PU."

"Dear God," Jerusha said. Lockridge turned to look at her. Her face was drained of color, her eyes the only spot of color. "It couldn't be."

"What couldn't be?" Fairchild demanded.

Jerusha drew in a deep shuddering breath. "I—I'm not certain, Admiral. If it would even be possible. But maybe—there could be a way to check it if—*Mahan* might have records, maybe someone remembers—"

"*Will you stop babbling*?" Fairchild exploded.

Jerusha stood and started pacing, apparently oblivious to the staff's irritation. "It started with *Mahan,* it had to. Maybe a little earlier, but *Mahan* was the first critical juncture." She wheeled on Lockridge. "You woke up that night. Why?"

Lockridge shot her a puzzled look. "The ship turned. I'd

been trying to figure that out myself and I finally realized that's what it was. I felt the motion change and woke up."

"Why did she turn?"

Lockridge shook his head. "I don't know. By the time I figured out that's what woke me up, I was back in Newport."

Jerusha turned to the admiral. "Sir, I'd suggest you clear the room right now. Just you, me, and Commander Lockridge."

"*What?*" Sirtus and Smith asked simultaneously.

"I think your secrets are safe here, Miss Bailey. Now lay it out for me before I start regretting listening to any of you." Fairchild's voice was adamant.

"Wait—I know," Lockridge said. He could see it now, the tactical screen as it had been during those last minutes before *Mahan* was hit. His ship, India's escorts, and a few fishing vessels. He shut his eyes, forcing the picture to clear up. "There was a fishing vessel of some sort. At least that's what we were calling it. But I remember now, when I went to the bridge—after . . . after . . . ," he skipped over the words, "and I looked around us, there was no traffic. India's destroyers off to the north a little ways, not far. But no fishing boats." He stopped, then added uncertainly, "Or at least none with their lights on. Maybe they could have been there." But no, he was certain of it now. He'd been up at the highest point on the ship that he had access to and the fires had illuminated the sea for miles around *Mahan*. If there'd been unlighted fishing boats, he'd have seen them. "No, they weren't there," he said aloud, his voice reflecting his conviction.

Smith shrugged. "So what? Ghost contact, a radar anomaly. It happens all the time."

Jerusha turned back to Lockridge. "How many of them?"

"Three. And they weren't normal ghost contacts. There was a track, a history on them." Lockridge was certain of it now.

"They were in the LINK, but they didn't really exist." Jerusha paused for a minute.

Lockridge's expression was a mirror image of Bailey's. *And that was the crux of the matter, wasn't it?* he thought. *How could it be done? The motives behind it don't matter—although I think I do know what they are—the second we figure out how it was done.*

Mahan. It began with Mahan. *There was something—what was it? What?*

We were off the coast of Bangladesh, testing FON rights and beta testing the battle link. The turn woke me up. I went into Combat and . . .

Jerusha said, "The War College was in the LINK. And so were India's units."

"Let's get back to the point. How did they know about our deception operation?" Fairchild said. "And the submarines in the unrep corridor? Both times, we put it down to good staff work by the other side."

Fairchild turned to Captain Smith. "You made some joke about them being psychic, even. Remember that, Bud? And there are some other small things as well, times when India seemed to almost be able to read our minds. I won't say it unequivocally supports Miss Bailey's theory, but it certainly does worry me." The admiral stood, walked to the chart mounted on the bulkhead, and tapped a finger on the unrep corridor. "They knew it was there. They knew about our deception plan."

"Admiral, you can't really believe this LINK compromise theory." Captain Smith's face was a growing mask of outrage.

"The Naval War College knows something about what happened to *Mahan*," Lockridge said. "I think they knew *Mahan* was going to be attacked. Once it did, they had to get me back there, find out if I knew anything. When I started talking about *why* it happened, they had their pet psychiatrist lock me up."

Stunned silence filled the room. The admiral maintained a detached, neutral expression on his face. "Go on."

And now the hard part. "And I think they know what's going on with India, Pakistan, and Bangladesh. With the Middle East, too. It's all tied in together, and the War College is the only place that knows how."

"What makes you think that?" Fairchild asked.

Lockridge then detailed his conflict with Dean Gromko, neither glossing over his own failures nor trying to show himself in a more favorable light. Finally, he told the admiral about being forcibly hospitalized and medicated, and how Jerusha had rescued him.

By now, both Captain Sirtus, the chief of staff, and Captain Smith, the senior intelligence officer, were taking their cues from Admiral Fairchild. Their faces could not have been more expressionless had they been carved from granite. Still, they had not stopped him yet. Or worse, called Security and ordered him locked up.

"Why?" Fairchild asked. He moved, stretching his shoulders and shaking his head. "I've listen to all of that, and that remains the one question I have to have answered. What does anyone have to gain from keeping this sort of secret? And more importantly, how do they know? Sources in their foreign student contingent, maybe?"

"That's what's bothering me as well, Admiral," Lockridge said slowly. "Sounds like treason to me. If they knew we were in danger and they didn't say anything."

Captain Sirtus broke in now. "Commander Lockridge, I understand how you came to that conclusion, but you must understand how farfetched this all seems." He made a vague gesture with one hand, taking in the carrier battle group as well as the conference room. "I'm sure you know how hard this is for anyone to believe. And let me say, we all know how much stress you have been under. Do you have any proof of this? Anything at all?" For all the doubt in his voice, his tone was peculiarly gentle. Lockridge saw Captain Smith nod as well.

They think I'm crazy. I lost my ship, couldn't take the guilt. So now I have to find someone else to blame for it.

"I think I might have a way to test it," Lockridge said.

Admiral Fairchild watched him for moment, his indecision plain on his face. "Suppose you're right and the LINK's compromised. Why was *Mahan* shot then?"

Lockridge took a deep breath. "*Mahan* was an experiment.

Three false targets were injected into my LINK picture, a dry run. Someone saw *Mahan* turn to avoid the imaginary fishing boat and they knew it worked. The next false target was not injected into our LINK picture, Admiral. It was injected into India's system. I don't know what they saw. They're claiming we were inside the twelve-mile limit and that we were downloading targeting data. Maybe there was more—maybe their LINK showed launch indications from *Mahan* or a Tomahawk strike inbound on their location. We won't know until we get them to talk. But that wasn't an unprovoked attack on *Mahan*—it was a logical, tactical response to the picture they saw. We were attacking, and they responded. At least according to their LINK picture.

"I can't prove it yet," Lockridge said into the silence. "But it explains what happened to *Mahan*."

"Who?" Smith asked. "We're talking about treason, Commander."

"My God," Jerusha said quietly. "Of course. Gromko."

Lockridge nodded. "Gromko, and the War College. They're the ones who wanted me back there, ostensibly for planning, when by all rights I should have been with my ship. They wanted to know what I remembered about that night. When I started asking questions, they had me hospitalized and discredited." Lockridge gave a harsh laugh. "Who would believe me after that?"

"You're insane," Smith said flatly. "There's no proof."

"Not yet," Fairchild said. "I want my top LINK experts in this conference room within the next ten minutes. And I want answers to three questions." He ticked them off on his fingers. "Is this possible? And if it is, how do we verify? And how do we disable it?"

Captain Sirtus nodded, and left the room.

Twenty minutes later, Admiral Fairchild had his first answer: yes, in the opinion of the ship's LINK experts, it could be done. The rest of the answers took longer.

The group promptly adjourned to the computer room that

housed the LINK system hardware. They gathered around the
maintenance access computer, and started working. They began with a series of self-diagnostics, and then traced back
through the system looking for blind doors and taps. When no
answers were forthcoming immediately, they informed the admiral of that. He requested status reports every hour, along
with, of course, immediate notification should they detect anything.

Petty Officer Third Class Tinker Jones was a data systems
technician. Almost second class—the results of the last ad-
vancement exam had just been posted, and in thirteen weeks,
Tinker would be promoted.

Like many young man his age, Tinker had grown up with
computers. His parents—his mother, an accountant, and his
father, a programmer—had bought him his first one when he
was just three. By the age of five, he had taught himself to
read—at least, those words he needed to know to use his computer.

By age ten, Tinker had worked through almost every commercial game available on the market, and had begun invent-
ing his own. His parents, concerned about his future, finally
worked out a deal with him. One hour of school work or study
for every hour of play time—take it or leave it. Tinker agreed.
He graduated from high school at fifteen, and was promptly
accepted at the Massachusetts Institute of Technology as an
early admissions student.

Two years ago, Tinker had been eighteen years old and a
junior at MIT. While intellectually he kept up with everyone
in his class, his social progress had been far less promising.
Finally introduced to the world of beer and bars, Tinker
promptly embarked on a three-day drinking spree. The police
found him in his car, totaled along the highway. Tinker, miraculously, was unhurt.

MIT and his parents arrived at a joint decision. Despite Tinker's intellectual prowess, he lacked exposure to the real

world. A few years off from college and MIT would gladly readmit him. But for now . . .

Tinker understood. The next day, he enlisted in the Navy. Unfortunately for him, they sent him straight back to school. He completed their toughest computer courses in just under three weeks.

"What do you think, Tinker?" The leading chief petty officer in the division, Chief Andy Bell, had quickly gotten over his resentment of the young hot shot assigned to him.

"I need some time, okay?" Tinker's fingers flowed over the keys, calling up submenus and delving into the intricacies of the code. "So far, it looks all right. But there's no way to be sure." He looked up at his chief and suppressed a sigh of irritation. The Navy had taught him that much self-control. "You know how much code there is?"

Chief Bell nodded. "Anyone else, it would take weeks." The chief punched him in the shoulder and left. In his twenty-two years in the Navy, he'd learned how to deal with men like Tinker.

"Hey, Chief?"

The chief turned back to look at him. "Yes?"

"It would help if I could talk to the guy that thinks there's something there. You know how operators are—they start talking about a problem, they leave something important out. Think you can scare him up for me?"

"I think that can be arranged." Chief Bell headed up for the admiral's conference room to find out just who thought there was a problem, and what they thought Tinker ought to be looking for.

Fifteen minutes later, he found Commander Lockridge.

"So why do you think there's a problem?" Tinker asked. He was leaning back in a standard Navy computer chair, his feet up on a desk.

Chief Bell shot him a warning look. Tinker looked puzzled at first, then embarrassed. He took his feet off the table, stood up, and said, "Sir, I mean, why do you think there is a problem, sir?"

Lockridge marveled slightly at the transformation. If what Chief Bell had said about Tinker was true, then this gawky sailor was the key to solving the problem.

Briefly, he explained his theory, leaving out the tactical details. Halfway through, Tinker cut him off. Politely, though. "You're talking down to me, sir. Telling me what you think I can understand. That doesn't help either of us."

Lockridge shot a look at the chief. Chief Bell nodded. "Top Secret's the lowest clearance we hold, Commander. You don't want to know how high they go."

Lockridge nodded. Just how much of the tactical implications the young sailor would understand, he wasn't sure. After all, despite his apparent computer expertise, he was only a junior petty officer, one with only a couple of years in the Navy under his belt. How to lay out the complications, the intricacies and theories of managing data at a high level of command and control? He started over again.

Tinker sighed. "With all due respect, sir," he said, and sketched in his background. "I think I can probably handle any big words you need to use. Can we start over again? Everything, please, sir. It will make it easier for me."

Lockridge shut his eyes for a moment and reoriented himself. He had had enough experience with exceptionally brilliant sailors—hell, geniuses—in the enlisted ranks in Navy. But never one exactly like Tinker. Lockridge started over.

Thirty minutes later, slightly appalled by the degree to which he'd underestimated the man earlier, Lockridge finished. In the process of explaining what he was looking for— or what he wanted Tinker to look for—Lockridge had had to answer some surprisingly astute questions from the young man. At each one, his opinion went up one notch.

Finally, Tinker let him go. "Thanks, that helps." He turned back to his computer. Chief Bell tapped Lockridge on the shoulder and quietly led the way out.

"Is he always like that?" Lockridge asked.

Chief Bell uttered a short laugh. "He's getting better. We don't take him out in public much, but they don't come any better than Tinker, sir."

Tinker had an answer in twenty minutes. Or at least a better place to get an answer. And it wasn't in the guts of his computers. Chief Bell, by now getting rather tired of escorting people up and down the ladders, took Tinker with him to the admiral's conference room.

"If it's there, I may never find it. There's just too much code and too many places tied into the LINK." Tinker's voice was calm and certain as he spoke with the admiral.

"Is there a record of when the last modification was made to the system?" Captain Sirtus asked.

Tinker suppressed a surge of annoyance. Of course there was, on both hard copy and within the system itself. However, explaining to this captain—clearly a dinosaur—how easy it would be to alter those records would take hours.

Chief Bell broke in. "Of course there is, Captain, but it would take hours to discover if the mod records themselves have been altered."

And we'd never find it. You'd think they'd just let us do our job. Tinker left that comment unspoken and said, "From what Commander Lockridge said," he began, enjoying slightly the looks of surprise on the senior officers' faces as they listened to him speak, "this is time critical. You have to know now if the system can be compromised in order to decide what to do about *Mahan*," Tinker continued, as if having a very junior enlisted man discussing matters of high importance in the conference room was a matter of everyday routine. "I'd like to suggest, Admiral, that we approach the problem from another angle. Communications, sir. That's the fastest way to find out if something is happening."

"Go ahead, Petty Officer Jones," the admiral said. "You have my attention now." Tinker noted the slightest trace of amusement in the admiral's voice.

"Well, Admiral, as I said—I'm not certain I'll ever be able

to tell you whether or not the system is configured to report to an unknown PU. Eventually I could, of course. But that might take months, and the system would have to be completely off-line for me to make certain. But, if what Commander Lockridge is saying is true, your primary concern is whether or not the data is being passed via satellite to a location other than the ships in our battle group. Is that a correct assessment?'' Tinker waited for an answer.

''For the purposes of this discussion, yes. You may assume that is true.''

Tinker nodded. ''Then the easiest way to find out where the data is going to is to trace the communication circuitry. The satellite link—can we find out who else is receiving that broadcast? Or there might even be a separate channel assigned. Has anyone looked at the communications plan to see if every circuit is accounted for with something you know?''

A stunned silence filled the conference room. The officers fidgeted.

The admiral spoke first. ''Well?'' When no answer was forthcoming, he said, ''Thank you, Petty Officer Tinker. I appreciate your insights. Captain Sirtus, get the comm officer in here.''

''We'll be available if we can provide any other assistance,'' Chief Bell said, easing Tinker out of the conference room.

Just as they reached the door, Tinker stopped. He turned back to the admiral. ''Can you let me know if I was right, sir? When it's all over, I mean.''

Fairchild looked surprised, then said, ''You've got it. Now, get out of here before you make the rest of my officers look stupid.''

One of Tinker's strongest assets was his reflexive, near-insatiable curiosity. After accepting Chief Bell's congratulations, Tinker started back down to the computer room. He stopped partway down the second ladder, frozen in position.

''Hey, asshole. You want to get out of the way?'' A burly

enlisted man, an engineer by the looks of his clothes, stood at the top of the ladder waiting for Tinker to clear the way.

Instead of continuing down the ladder, Tinker scrambled back up it. "Sorry about that, man," he said hurriedly. "Forgot something."

"Asshole." The engineer pushed past Tinker and clattered down the ladder.

Why let the radiomen have all the fun? It was my solution— I want to see if it works. He went back up to the 0-3 deck and headed toward the comm center.

"So what do we do now?" the admiral asked the assembled officers. "I think I know what they're going to find. So do you, if you think about it." His fingers drummed impatiently on the table in front of him.

"There's an old principle of naval warfare, Admiral, one that I think applies here," Lockridge said carefully. "I've had a chance to think about this—maybe I'm way out of line here, but I have an idea."

Captain Sirtus uttered a short, barking laugh. "Since when has that stopped you?"

Fairchild ignored Captain Sirtus's comment. "Go ahead. Between you and that young computer man, I'm not sure the rest of us are needed."

"Using the enemy's strength against him," Lockridge said. "In this case, depending on whether you cast India or the Naval War College as the enemy, their strength is that they know what we're doing. They're reading our OPNOTES, watching our tracks on the LINK. They know what we're doing the second we start talking about it on the LINK or we start doing it. Or at least they think they do. Admiral, what if we can start feeding them bad information? Let them believe that they know what we're doing—then do something different."

"Disinformation? Using our own computer systems?" The admiral thought for a moment, then smiled. "I like it. Assum-

ing our young sailor's theory proves to be true, how do you
propose to do it?''

"You mentioned not needing a staff, with me and Tinker,"
Lockridge plunged on. "But that's where you're wrong. The
two of us can figure out how to do it, once we know for sure
that there is a leak. But not *what* to do—that's not *our* job.''

Lockridge stood, stretching muscles tight and painful from
the two-day dash from Newport to the carrier. How long had
it been since he slept? He couldn't remember, and that in itself
was an answer.

"Admiral, unless you need me for something, I need some
sleep.'' He gestured at Jerusha and Gar. "And I think they
probably do, too.''

"Get them some staterooms and some food. We'll call you
if we need you, Commander.''

Tinker punched in the cipher code at the comm center's door
and shoved it open after it clicked. Good thing it was the eve
watch. His only real friend onboard the carrier was on watch.

"Benny,'' he said when he found Radioman Third Class
Benjamin Thule hunched over a computer in the processing
office. "Wanna have some fun?''

Thule shoved himself back from his desk. "New game?''

Tinker shook his head. "It's not exactly a game. But if we
win, it means a whole lot more than killing all the monsters.''

All sorts of monsters in the world, though. Tinker kept that
in mind over the next several hours as he and Thule ran
through the circuits one by one. The communications plan for
a carrier is laid out in a matrix that encompasses virtually
every function a carrier might have to perform. The number
of circuits runs into the hundred.

Tinker and Thule ran validation checks on each one of
them. Some of the circuits were in use so often that there was
really no question of whether or not they were legitimate, and
it was simply a matter of verifying that the equipment that was
supposed to be in use was actually the serial number listed in
the comm plan. For the less commonly used voice circuits,

they simply called up the party on the other end, verifying that the circuit was valid. Their call sometimes elicited a grumpy complaint from a radioman on the other end, since the smaller ships simply couldn't keep all the circuits they were supposed to be monitoring up at the same time.

They then worked their way through the data circuits, listening in to the squeal and warble of bits flowing through the air, checking equipment serial numbers again.

Finally, they were done. All the data circuits tested satisfactory, and they were left with only four voice circuits they hadn't been able to test.

"How about this one?" Tinker asked, pointing to piece of crypto gear mounted in a rack. The indicator light on the front was on and flickering.

Thule checked his list. "Supposed to be a reserved link with the jarheads. Night spotter circuit ashore or something." He pointed out the entry on his comm plan. "See. Gunnery circuit."

"Voice?"

Thule shook his head. "Don't think so. That new stuff they've got, it's all digital. Even the voice transmissions just get treated like data." Thule rearranged a few switches and the hiss coming over one speaker changed pitches. "Even voice sounds like data."

Tinker listened to the ebb and flow of the warble. "Yeah, it does. Only one question—who's using the night spotter gunnery circuit right now?"

Thule frowned. "Now that you mention it . . ."

Tinker grabbed him by the arm. "Come on. We gotta find that commander."

Two hours later, after the admiral had discretely checked with every ship in his battle group to make sure no one was using the night spotter circuit, they had their answer. There was now at least some evidence to support Lockridge's supposition that there was an intruder on the LINK. Armed with that, the staff developed a plan to test the theory.

"It's a shell game. The same sort of thing the War College is working on." The operations officer's red laser pointer put down and circled an area of ocean. "First, we get out of visual range of India's ships. We watch the satellite vulnerability periods and any aircraft surveillance flights. Get all the big decks close together, then break them up again, just like we did before. Only this time, we make a few little modifications to the LINK picture. The *John Paul Jones* and the *Lincoln* will swap PUs. There will be some other changes as well. The end result should look like *Lincoln* with one FFG alone in the ocean, with the *Tarawa* heading north and the rest of the small boys prosecuting a submarine contact. We're setting up for that now—I've got S-3 in the air that should be reporting an unidentified submarine contact into the LINK in about twenty minutes."

Lockridge studied the plan, then nodded. "It'll work if we're out of visual range. What about our sub?"

"*Kentucky*'s too far south to worry about," the submarine operating authority, or SUBOPAUTH, said. "She's on a twelve-hour cycle. The only way to talk to her now would be to have her come shallow for a comm break, and that might tip someone off. As long as we stay out of her piece of ocean, it shouldn't matter."

The admiral spoke then. "Staying out of India's visual range shouldn't be a problem. They're not bird-dogging us now, for good reason. India's got the new Harpoon block, about eighty-miles range. Once they think they know where we are, they'll shoot."

"Why?" It was Jerusha, with a confused look for her face. "Why will they shoot?"

"They've got to do something while we're still at sea," a new voice said from the doorway. "Once we get ashore and dig in, they won't have a chance. Two thousand Marines, plus tanks, howitzers, and assorted other weapons of destruction are a lot easier to take out while they're all packaged up in a steel box like *Tarawa*."

"Colonel Irish Kildin, commander of the landing force,"

the Marine said after greeting the admiral. Lockridge had met him several times before. The tall Marine colonel was framed in the hatch, grinning. Just for a moment, Lockridge felt a flash of sympathy for the Indian forces on the ground. They didn't know what they were up against.

Irish strode into the conference room, halfway down the long table. "I apologize for my tardiness, Admiral. We needed to reconfigure our offload."

Fairchild waved aside Irish's explanation. "We haven't gotten to your part of the plan yet, Colonel. We're still talking about how to get you to the beach in one piece."

Irish leaned back in his chair, relaxed, yet with the stiff, almost regal bearing characteristic of every Marine Lockridge had ever known. "Good catch, Commander," he said to Lockridge. He shot Lockridge a sly, amused grin, then turned his attention back to the discussion in progress.

Twelve hours after the decision to implement the deception plan, Admiral Fairchild summoned the commanding officers at each ship and squadron to the carrier. The plan was briefed, along with the background that necessitated it. Not all of the officers involved believed either the LINK interception theory or that the deception plan would work. Fortunately, belief was not a requirement for obedience.

24

AARDVARK 623, DEPLOYED OFF USS
EISENHOWER

Lieutenant Commander Harmon Daggert studied the scope, automatically sorting out ground clutter from contacts, commercial air from military transports, and pairing assigned CAP stations with Tomcat and Hornet tracks. The E-2 Hawkeye didn't have the range and over-ground discrimination that an AWACS did, but what he saw was enough to provide an early alert to the carrier if the picture started to go to shit.

"You got that Lufthansa wide body outbound from Tehran?" Lieutenant Charlie Early asked. Seated next to Daggert, Early was handling the northern sector of their airspace. Another lieutenant kept an eye on the southern sector, while Daggert maintained the big picture. "He's a little ahead of schedule, but the IFF is right."

"Yeah, I got him. Germans. They're supposed to be so methodical, you'd think they'd take off on time. Maybe their civilians are sloppier than their military." Daggert zoomed the radar picture in to center on an enlarged presentation of the commercial air flight. So what if Iraq was shooting at military aircraft, mining the Straits, and ferrying flights of fighters over to Iran? Commercial airliners had schedules to meet. A few airlines, mostly American-flagged, had shut down Middle Eastern operations, but the rest of the world's commercial carriers went on with business as usual.

"Bad ground clutter around the area—what, a sandstorm you think?" Daggert asked. He toggled off an IFF inquiry, verified that the contact was radiating modes and codes for Lufthansa.

"Maybe." Early sounded puzzled. "Didn't see it in the Metoc briefing this morning, but it could have just come up."

"Maybe." Daggert watched the radar blip track to the east, worried by something he couldn't quite define. The shape of the contact, maybe. A little fuzzy around the edges. The speed a little over what he'd usually expect from commair, the course a little bit too—"*Crap.*" The green lozenge broke apart into four smaller blips. "Get Strike on the horn. We're going to need some more metal in the air."

The IFF modes and codes were still insisting the contacts were commercial aircraft, but the speed and course of the contacts that it had spawned made it clear that the classification was wrong. Fighters, Iraqi or Iranian, it made no difference, launching together in close formation to simulate a larger, less hostile contact.

"Headed due east," Early sang out, already vectoring the Tomcats under his control on a course designed to place the American firepower between the E-2 and the other fighters. "If they turn south, we're screwed."

"They're not turning. Still heading east." Daggert studied the scope, then expanded the range circle to include more area. "But it looks like they're going to have company. I've got twenty Pakistani fighters launching as well."

"Their fight, not ours," Early said.

"Let's hope."

USS *EISENHOWER*

Admiral Monarelli slammed his hand down on the conference table, breaking up the debate. He glared at the assembled officers. "Quite frankly, I don't give a good goddamn about what kind of games Iran and Iraq are playing right now. We've got to get out of this damned pond: If Iran and Iraq manage to stick together long enough to bomb the hell out of Pakistan, then that's where we're going to have to be. You got that?" After receiving a chorus of "yes, Admiral"'s from his staff, he continued.

"Find a way to get the Straits clear. One way or the other, I want to be in blue water tomorrow." He stood. "Come get me when you have the answer." The room was deadly silent as he left. After the door slammed shut behind him, his chief of staff turned to the assembled officers and chiefs. "Any questions?"

"Just one," the assistant chief of staff for operations said. "Just how the hell do we get out of here?"

Alone in his flag cabin, Monarelli slumped down onto his couch. All the anger that he'd vented on his staff had drained away, leaving behind a dull, sickening feeling. Maybe it hadn't been fair, putting it to them that way. For starters, with the minesweeping forces still out of area, he didn't see any options himself. Sure, the carrier had some limited minesweeping capabilities organically, iron pigs towed behind helicopters. Fine against older moored contact mines, but virtually useless against bottom-laid or acoustic mines.

He tried to convince himself that he was just challenging his staff, providing dynamic leadership, but somewhere inside he knew the truth. He was worried—hell, maybe even scared—and he'd lost his temper. Taken it out on them, vented his own frustration. That was the toughest part about this billet, one he hadn't really understood until now. The aloneness, the lack of anyone else you could turned to just to kick things around, float some trial balloons. Even back when he was a squadron skipper, he'd had other Tomcat COs to turn to. Not that any of them would have ever admitted not knowing what to do—hell, they were fighter pilots, no one expected them to do that.

But there were ways to talk things over, get some perspective, blow off steam without taking it out on the troops. Not so when you were the flag in command of a battle group. Only another admiral would understand.

He sat up. Another admiral. His last conversation with Cody Fairchild came to mind. He started to dismiss the idea—hell, Cody would laugh at him if he called.

But maybe not. He owes me—I gave him Tennant when he thought I wouldn't. And just what the hell had that all been about?

He could call to check on when Tennant was coming back, maybe start talking over this damned situation with the Paks and the rag heads. Cody'd probably have questions anyway, although from what he could see in the traffic, *Lincoln* had enough problems of her own to deal with.

The voices from the conference room carried through the bulkheads. Louder now, the men and women trying to solve the problem he'd put to them without a whole hell of a lot of optimism. It was rolling downhill now for sure.

Monarelli crossed over to his working table and punched in the access numbers for a satellite telephone line. He slid the crypto key into the slot and waited for the dial tone. He punched in Fairchild's cabin telephone number.

"Fairchild." Cody sounded harried, he could tell.

"Cody, it's Alan." Monarelli started to ask about Tennant, then to his surprise heard himself say, "Got a minute?"

"Sure." Puzzlement now, understandable given their history.

Monarelli launched into a description of his tactical situation, most of which Fairchild already knew from the message traffic and the LINK. "The thing is, I'm out of answers. You got any ideas, I'd appreciate them."

Silence echoed over the secure link, warbled and distorted by the secure line static. Finally, Fairchild said, "You remember what I was talking about before? And thanks for Tennant by the way—it's made a big difference."

"Someday you'll tell me what that's all about, okay?"

"Sooner than you think. But it might have some implications for your situation as well. Things are not quite what they seemed to be, Alan. They haven't been since *Mahan* was hit."

Monarelli felt depression settle in on him again, flushing out the momentary lift he'd felt at the possibility that Fairchild might have some suggestions. "It's fairly straightforward over here. The Straits are mined."

"How certain are you?"

"We heard them."

"What exactly did you hear?"

"Submarines flooding tubes and then a blast of compressed air. No torpedoes in the water, so it had to be mines."

"What if there weren't any mines?" Fairchild asked. "Have you actually seen one?"

Silence, then Monarelli said, "That's a hell of a reach. A dangerous assumption, too. You think maybe they shot out air slugs just to make us think they were launching mines?"

"That's exactly what I think," Fairchild said.

"Since the AWACS was downed," Monarelli said slowly, thinking his way through it, "there's not been a single attack against this battle group. Nothing I can point to as a hostile act—hell, they haven't even lit us up with fire control radar. Everything they've done since then has been hinky—weird, not the sort of harassing I'd expect under the circumstances. This mining business—they want us in here, out of the way, maybe watching these aircraft ferrying into Iran and maybe hoping we'll stay out of it because we think they'll kill each other off. Shit, Cody, you're right. They're running a scam on us—I can feel it in my bones."

There was a soft knock on his door and then his chief of staff pushed it open and walked in. "Admiral, sorry to interrupt." Monarelli started to blast him, then noticed the expression on his chief of staff's face. "Hold on Cody—what is it, COS?"

"The Pakistani fighters. They're not attacking the Iraqi and Iranian ones."

"They're letting them take control of their airspace without a fight?"

The COS shook his head. "No. They're joining on them. In formation. And they're all headed east to India."

"*What?*" A surge of vindication surged through Monarelli's body. He lifted the receiver back to his mouth. "Cody, thanks. I've got to go." He hung up the phone without waiting for an answer. "Get the carrier skipper down here. We need to talk."

The carrier CO proved to be harder to convince than his own staff, but Monarelli managed it through sheer dint of collar weight. Fifteen minutes later, *Eisenhower* had turned and was heading for the Straits, buttoned down at General Quarters. For two tense hours, the admiral's staff, the air wing, the squadrons, and ship's company held their collective breath, waiting for the explosion that many of them were certain was imminent. When *Eisenhower* cleared the area that had been "mined" without event, Monarelli commandeered the 1MC mike from his TAO. "Let's go kick some ass, *Ike*. How about it?" Even from inside TFCC, he could hear the cheers spreading throughout the carrier.

Monarelli replaced the mike and settled down into his command chair to mask the exhaustion that had just swept through him. Two hours of waiting, knowing that if the carrier took a hit, it would be his fault, relying solely on his own conviction that they'd been scammed.

He'd been right.

This time.

Now it was time to find out if he could pull it off again.

Monarelli said, "Pakistan. Take me eight miles off the coast. Get CLF over here. We need to talk about an opposed landing."

"For peacekeeping operations?" his chief of staff asked.

Monarelli smiled, a hard, gleeful expression. "I'd call it that. They might not."

*   *   *

Fifteen hours later, *Eisenhower* was in position off the coast of Pakistan. There'd been a few hostile acts along the way from a combined Iranian/Iraqi naval force, but the power of an aircraft carrier with a full complement of escorts made the issue moot. One Silkworm attack garnered the adversary three Harpoon shots from a destroyer that didn't even slow from flank speed. An Iraqi patrol boat sank immediately, as did an Iranian frigate. A third ship, a cruiser, was still fighting to stay afloat as the American force steamed by.

"Air superiority first," Monarelli said. He gazed at the men and women seated around the conference table, seeing them in an entirely different light. The last time they'd met like this, just before he'd talked to Fairchild, he'd seem them as obstructions, people who could screw things up and deprive him of that second star.

Now, they were extensions of his own will, of his determination. Extra hands, extra eyes, covering the watch stations and hours that he couldn't, working as one with unity of purpose.

Monarelli felt light, almost joyous. One star, two stars, even five—it didn't matter. Nothing mattered at all other than the fact that he'd seen through the mining ploy and gotten to Pakistan. He knew, with a conviction that he could not articulate but could pass on to his staff through his bearing, his manner of speaking, that they were going to win. It felt good, the righteous feeling of command, the sheer conviction that in this most demanding of billets he would not be found lacking.

"Strike—how long?" Monarelli asked.

"It depends, sir," the officer in charge of strike said, still not entirely comfortable with the new Admiral Monarelli. It had been Strike's habit in the past to hedge a little, build some margins of error into his time estimates in order to try to mitigate the full force of the admiral's displeasure. "If they're ready for us, if we can keep enough gas in the air and the attrition rates aren't too high, we might conceivably be able to—"

"No." Monarelli cut him off. "We don't do business that

way anymore." He leaned across the table and pinned Strike to his chair with his eyes. *"How long?"*

"If I can—"

"How long?"

Strike felt panic building. Panic mixed with something else, an odd exhilaration that surged through his heart and mind, calling him to step up to bat. It was impossible to remain cautious around this Monarelli, and Strike felt a fierce pride and joy surge through him. "Fifteen hours." Strike paused, waited for the questions about the details, about his assumptions, about all those things he knew to be true in his own experience but that he could not immediately quantify. The old Monarelli would have demanded them.

The new Monarelli simply nodded and turned to the commander of the landing force. "Cliff," he said, pronouncing the initials CLF as a first name, "how long?"

The Marine colonel had fewer bad habits to unlearn. "Four hours for the beachhead, another eight to consolidate our positions. I want to go in, not offload in stream. The floating causeways will slow us down too much."

Monarelli grinned. The Marine blinked. "Make it happen, Cliff." He turned back to the rest of the officers. "Anything else?" Silence, but this time filled with eager anticipation. Officers were seated on the edges of their chairs and the chiefs were already inching toward the door. "Good. I'll be in my cabin if you need me." He turned back to face them after he pulled the door open. "I heard something Petty Officer Simmons said to Commander Tennant a couple of months ago, and I think it's something we ought to think about. America's the lead dog in this part of the world. Let's make sure they don't forget that again."

After Monarelli was gone, the chief of staff turned to the rest of them. A broad grin spread across his face. "You heard the admiral. Let's kick some ass."

25

USS *TARAWA*

Tarawa steamed north, her normal running lights and flight deck illumination extinguished. The sky was overcast, spitting rain and making it a foul night on deck for the extra lookouts. Light strings dangled over the side, cutting brilliantly through the fog.

The officer of the deck was not entirely convinced it would work. From a distance, maybe. But there was still enough ambient light, even in the overcast, to see the outline of the massive old amphibious ship. He turned to his junior officer of the deck and said, "Hell of a disguise."

The ensign, who had reported onboard only four weeks earlier but had already realized that the lieutenant was a smart ass, simply said, "Yes, sir. We're a fishing trawler, right?"

The lieutenant nodded. "And a real convincing one we are. Everyone knows that fishing trawlers carry assault helicopters and have a flight deck."

The ensign shrugged. Up until this month, he hadn't even known the Indians had aircraft carriers.

USS *LOUIS B. PULLER*

The *Louis B. Puller,* the FFG selected to impersonate the aircraft carrier, had a different type of problem. For *Tarawa,* the challenge had been to apparently reduce the profile on the one-thousand-foot-long ship to that of a much smaller vessel. The admiral's plan called for *Puller* to show a light configuration consistent with that of an aircraft carrier. After much discussion, the small group of officers onboard the FFG decided that there was no practical way to simulate an aircraft carrier's profile—at least, not to scale. They could, however, by judicious use of their deceptive lighting, appear to be an aircraft carrier far away. Accordingly, they arranged their lights, including the floodlights on the flight deck, in exactly the same configuration as that of aircraft carrier. However, the distances between the lights were reduced to a third or a quarter of other normal values. Thus the *Puller* appeared to be an aircraft carrier on the horizon rather than a frigate at close range.

The plan also called for aircraft to execute a deceptive approach on the frigate, then proceed to return to the carrier at low altitude, hopefully avoiding India's organic surveillance radar.

BOGANDDIYA

"They're nowhere near any of our ships," the admiral onboard the Indian aircraft carrier to the south said. He studied the tactical screen, noting the two S-3B aircraft busily deploying sonobuoys in a localization pattern. "The submarine contact they're after is probably a whale. A common enough mistake, I suppose." His tone of voice made it clear that while it might be a common mistake for the American forces, any competent ASW officer should have known better.

Around the table, rectangular rather than the oval, that graced his counterparts' conference room, his staff officers laughed. Large marine mammals were the bane of any USW officer's life. The mammal's speed was consistent with a slowly patrolling submarine making two knots. More experienced eyes would notice that the contact would appear mushy rather than solid, and would check out the acoustics down that bearing, looking for biological sounds.

Contrary to the admiral's unstated contention, every one of them had made that particular mistake. Even the normally impressive British ships, during the Falklands war, had expended massive amounts of sonobuoys and ordnance on biologicals that they mistook for Argentinean diesel submarines.

"You know our orders. The Americans will not be permitted to land on Bengali soil," the admiral continued. He touched his laser point to the formation of amphibious ships steaming toward the coast.

"They've made it easier for us by having their carrier stand off at a distance," one officer pointed out. "This preoccupation with over-the-horizon command and control will be their downfall. There's only one frigate with the amphibious group. An easy target."

An Indian captain nodded. "Then let's do it now, while they are still in the throes of their own mistake." He smiled, displaying brilliant white, even teeth. "It is so much easier to win when an adversary's plans work against him, not for him." He stood, making it clear that the meeting was over. "Unless there are anymore questions . . ."

There were no questions. The other officers stood.

One lieutenant, the engineer who served as the damage control assistant, stared at the display, then glanced at their own ship course. A question sprang to mind, but he was quite junior to the rest of the officers, attending the meeting only because the chief engineer was stranded in his quarters with a racking case of diarrhea.

Surely, someone else would have thought of it. He couldn't be the only one that noticed the American aircraft carrier's current course.

According to the data, *Lincoln* was heading downwind with a steady tail wind of approximately ten knots. But according to the briefing, it was in flight operations, both launching and recovering a cycle of fighters.

The one constant that defines all air operations, in any navy in the world, is wind across deck. For both launch and recovery, aircraft carriers turn into the wind, generating twenty to thirty knots across their decks. Never a tail wind—never.

Well, there must be a small error. Either in the briefed heading, or in the data display. No ship on that course in this part of the world was launching aircraft.

The lieutenant shrugged, his mind returning to the problem his senior enlisted technician had reported two hours earlier with the main condenser. Unless they got it fixed soon, the Indian aircraft carrier would be forced to go to water hours, restricting the use of freshwater made by the ship and cutting of showers for the crew. He winced, imagining the chorus of protest he was about to hear from his troops. Not from the officers here, no. Water to the senior officers staterooms was almost invariably left on, even when the rest of the ship was on strict water hours.

He stopped at the hatch leading to the main passageway and looked back at the tactical display again. No, there had to be mistake. Someone would catch it soon.

USS *KENTUCKY*

"Captain, we've got company." Commander Beavers, the executive officer of USS *Kentucky,* stood at the entrance to his skipper's stateroom. *Kentucky* was operating south of the *Lincoln* battle group, conducting antisubmarine operations in a box of water designated for her exclusive use. After the fiasco with the last unrep corridor, *Lincoln* had decided that she wanted an unrep area that she was sure was free of submarines. Surface contacts, *Lincoln* could find herself, but the elusive diesel submarines in the area were another matter.

For the last twelve hours, *Kentucky* had been methodically searching the area for a trace of an acoustic signature a sonarman thought he'd heard the night before. Probably nothing, some odd ducting of sound from a far-off surface contact, but submariners took very little for granted. Captain Tran was lying on his back on his rack, grabbing a short nap. It was something all the officers onboard knew how to do, eke out a few precious minutes of sleep during the day. Too often, the nighttime hours—or at least, what passed for nighttime onboard the submarine—were interrupted.

It was, the XO thought, typical of the captain that there was no perceptible difference between sleep and alertness. Although his captain's eyes were closed, Beavers had no doubt that he heard every word.

"Classification?" Tran asked. There was not the slightest trace of sleepiness in his voice.

"Sonar's calling it that diesel sub we held before. A few electrical sources, that's all we're getting."

"Where is it?"

"Still long range. We were lucky to get anything at all. Around twenty thousand yards." Beavers marveled at that, even as he said the words. Just a few years ago, detecting a diesel submarine at that range would have simply been unthinkable. But the new sonar suite they'd installed on *Kentucky* during her last overhaul was magic—sheer magic. That, coupled with having the most experienced and finely tuned sets of ears around on the stacks made a difference.

The captain was moving now, no trace of sluggish in his economical movements as he rolled into a sitting position. Not a yawn, not a casual rub at his eyes—just the cold, unblinking analytical power that had taken him up through the ranks so quickly within the submarine community.

"It has to be the Indians. Nobody else around, not that I know of." Tran glanced up at his executive officer. "Of course, you never know."

And that, Beavers decided, was the crux of the problem. There were too many nations in this part of the world that owned one or two rusty old diesel submarines. Ancient American Guppy-class diesels, even older Soviet-type one-nucs, and, lately, the worrisome proliferation of new, cheap, and quiet diesels from the cash-strapped former Soviet Union.

"That seems the most reasonable conclusion," he agreed, knowing that the captain understood the implicit qualification: reasonable, but not certain.

Finally, Tran yawned, a brief movement that looked to be more reflex than any sign of human weakness. "Let's go have a look at them. Where's the battle group?"

"We're holding contact on a large deck ship of some sort just outside our box. Judging from the last LINK update, it's probably *Lincoln*."

Tran broke off in mid-yawn. "How close is the submarine to her?"

"Outside weapons range. As far as we know."

"Yeah. As far as we know. Any indication that *Lincoln*'s got the sub and is prosecuting the contact?"

"Not this contact. They've got a couple of S-3s up north working on one, but nothing down here. No sonobuoys, no S-3s overhead, nothing."

And there it was, the dilemma that submariners faced too often working in support of a battle group. Do you continue to prosecute the subsurface contact, not knowing exactly what nationality it was but figuring you could probably refine the classification if you could regain contact, or do you come shallow, take a big risk in being detected by your prey, to spit out a report to the carrier?

Kentucky was operating in support of the task force. This necessitated certain compromises in a submarine's desire to remain completely covert. *Kentucky* could not stay close enough to the surface to keep an HF wire trailed and actively participate in the LINK continuously. But the battle force had to have some way of talking to her. A compromise was reached.

Every twelve hours, *Kentucky* would come shallow, trail a antenna, and pick up a broadcast from a satellite. This was necessary because the low data rates available by using the ELF receiver, the only one that could reach them in deep water, were not sufficient to allow complicated messages to be passed.

Additionally, when *Kentucky* surfaced, she would take a quick snapshot of the LINK, update the data on her position, so she would know where the battle group ships were. It wasn't a perfect system, but it was a standard operating compromise.

Had there been an emergency, the battle force could have reached them in a number of ways. First, the admiral could have sent a message to the submarine, which would have been downloaded, depending on its priority, during the next satellite dump. Second, were the matter truly urgent, the admiral could order them to surface, if it were safe to do, and query the satellite immediately. Finally, the submarine could be reached by underwater telephone—if the acoustics permitted it—or by the ELF network.

"What's the rest of the battle group up to?" the captain asked, slipping his shoes back on. Like the rest of the crew, he was dressed in a blue jumpsuit. "And where's *Boganddiya*?

"*Tarawa*'s in the AOA with one frigate in direct support. *Boggy* is due west of *Lincoln*—she's been staying between the battle group and land," Beavers answered, stepping aside into the passageway so that the captain could leave his stateroom. Even the commanding officer's cabin was little more than a larger broom closet.

"And you're sure you know who's who?" Tran asked. "Two big decks with the same propeller configuration."

"Yes, sir. The furthest-on circles from their last LINK positions don't even overlap. We know who's who. *Lincoln*'s just turned north, probably to get in position to support *Tarawa*."

"Show me." The captain stepped into Sonar. Beavers followed. After examining the acoustic signatures, Tran left Sonar for the navigator's plotting table. "Show me the furthest on circles."

The navigator indicated two sets of concentric circles penciled in on the overlay. One set was labeled *Lincoln*, the other

Boganddiya. "Around 2330, *Lincoln* was here, Captain. The innermost circles indicate where they could be from their last positions if they were doing fifteen knots. The outermost is for thirty knots."

"Not their top speeds, but close," Tran said.

"Even at twenty knots, they'd have been a lot noisier than they are," the XO said. "And according to their acoustic signatures—intermittent, admittedly—they've both been running around twelve knots most of the night. *Lincoln* made a turn north an hour or so ago."

Tran studied the plot for a moment, then did the time-distance problem himself and remeasured the circles. No error—not that he'd expected to find one. Surface sailors rarely understood a submariner's need to check, double-check, and triple-check every system in the submarine every day. Living so far from the sunlight, surrounded by water pressure that would kill if it gained even the slightest purchase on their hull, submariners were as compulsive a bunch of men as you could find anywhere in the world. The aviators and surface sailors had it easy. If things got too bad, they could always punch out or jump overboard. There were life vests, life boats, and rescue helos.

Not so on a submarine. If a disaster inside the hull didn't kill you, the water outside would.

Nor did surface sailors necessarily understand how to be careful operating around the submarine. As a result, with paranoia borne of years of experience, the submarine community had evolved two competing philosophies of life. First, they were extremely reluctant to give up their cloak up invisibility, which meant they never wanted to tell the surface ships exactly where they were. Second, wherever they were, the submariners insisted on exclusive control over a box of water. Any shots fired inside it would be fired by the submarine who owned it, and no one else.

"Okay. There's no indication that the subsurface contact knows we're here. Fall in behind her, maintaining a large, safe interval, and run firing solutions on both the submarine and the *Boganddiya*. No engineering drills until we've cleared the area. I don't want to risk generating sound sources. Set quiet ship, and let's concentrate on the front end for now.''

USS *LINCOLN*

''I think it's working,'' Gar said. He pointed at the large-screen display. An E-2 Hawkeye was orbiting to the north, ostensibly assisting the S-3Bs prosecuting the notional submarine contacts. But even at that range, an E-2 Hawkeye's powerful radar provided a complete surveillance picture. The Indian carrier *Boganddiya* along with her escort was proceeding north at flank speed.

''Any sign of air surveillance?'' Lockridge asked.

Gar shook his head. ''Nothing. Not on the Spy-1, not on the Hawkeye. If they've got us, it's on their own radar.''

Without a visual observation, there was a good chance the plan was working. Especially if the Indians were relying on data received from the LINK contact. With the PUs reassigned to different ships, there was no way without seeing them that the Indians could tell which ships were which.

''Good. Maybe the first thing we'll hear from them is something that blows their cover.'' Lockridge winced at what that could be, thinking again *Mahan*. That was the problem with the plan—it relied on India to start the fight.

Like they hadn't already. And just what had the Mahan *disaster been—a warm-up round?* An upwelling of bitterness, the intensity of which had already become all too familiar.

But that was before—back when he had still had a future. As had forty-two other people onboard *Mahan*.

Again, the unfairness of it all ate at him. They should simply go ashore, wipe out every living thing in a twenty-square-mile box, and teach these people what it meant to shoot at an American warship. Let them experience the consequences of their action.

You're off base. You know you are. They shot your ship,

sure. But now you know who's really behind it.

But he had no proof. Nothing that he could take to his superiors outside the military chain of command that would convince them. In fact, as he and Fairchild had discussed, every single thing he said would be written off as post-traumatic stress reaction—or worse, as a guilty conscience. It would be done gently, with the excuses couched in medical language and psychiatric terms. There would be a medical board, a compassionate finding by the Navy that would let him retire immediately.

And it would continue. Had continued, for God knows how long, until they made one critical mistake: taking on *Mahan* and killing his people.

This would be the proof. With the evidence that this exercise would produce, Admiral Fairchild—a sane, credible witness and accuser—could demand a full investigation. Then they would pay. It rankled that he wouldn't be the one to make India and the War College suffer for what they'd done.

Maybe I can. Another idea occurred to him, distracting him momentarily from the tactical situation unfolding at the speed that grass grows. Yes, there might be a solution, one that would let him exact his own vengeance. As he stared at the approaching battle group, he worked out the details.

USS JOHN PAUL JONES

The destroyer had been playing the part of a much less heavily armed frigate for about six hours when trouble started.

"*Vampire!*" The word echoed through the CDC scene after the blood red inverted V with the long speed trailer flashed onto the screen. *John Paul Jones*'s TAO felt his gut clench, even though he had been expecting it. Right on time, right as they entered the optimum range for firing. He felt a momentary flash of admiration for the Indians' tactical discipline, a feeling that quickly disappeared as he contemplated the incoming missile.

"Okay, people, you know what to do," he said, making his voice as calm and reassuring as he could. "We've done this a million times, maybe more. Weapons free."

The flurry of activity around him was normal, so normal that it was almost anticlimactic. They had indeed performed the same mission too many times to count—but never against a real missile.

As bad as it is, it makes it a little easier that it's not into us. He pushed that thought aside, mildly ashamed that he had it at all.

The weapons coordinator located against the far starboard bulkhead slaved a standard missile to the incoming threat symbol. The fire control radar locked on. While the Aegis system could have shot the missile without a need for human intervention whatsoever, the captain had left the fire control system and engagement system on manual. If what the admiral said was true, far too many mistakes had been made already.

He had been tempted to insert himself in the final sequence as well, taking advantage of the requisite of command to fire the missile himself. Live missile firings were just too rare, and those that were actual engagements even more so. Still, had they been in actual combat, his TAO would've had the authority to launch missiles without the captain's direct order. In the end, he had decided to let the TAO conduct the attack.

Two seconds later, he felt that odd, vaguely menacing rumble that told him a missile was leaving the vertical launch tubes. The bright blue symbol popped into existence on the tactical display, arrowing directly for the incoming Harpoon anti-ship missile.

"*John Paul Jones,* this is *Lincoln.* Interrogative your status?" a voice on the tactical circuit asked.

JPJ's captain could recognize the voice of a flag TAO with an admiral standing behind him. He could imagine the tension inside TFCC as the staff watched helplessly while the Aegis cruiser fended off the incoming antiship missile. He shuddered at the thought, a ship with virtually no self-defense capability other than close-in weapons systems.

And, of course, the air wing. You couldn't forget the air wing.

Except for times like this.

Two more incoming Harpoons, and again the *John Paul Jones* did that which she had been built to do. Thirty seconds after the attack began, *John Paul Jones* had successfully engaged and destroyed all three missiles.

A ragged cheer rang out in CDC. *John Paul Jones*'s captain shushed them. "A little humility, if you please. Remember, we're supposed to be a frigate." The laughter that followed made it all worthwhile.

USS *LINCOLN*

"Taking a shot at what they think is *Tarawa*—is that hostile enough for you, Admiral?" Lockridge asked

Fairchild nodded. "It'll do." He tapped the TAO on the shoulder. "Pass to all forces—redesignate all units, as soon as safe and practical, to original PU's. All ships in the Indian task force are hereby declared hostile. Weapons free—and good hunting." Then Admiral Fairchild leaned back in his chair and said, "This one is for *Mahan*."

Lockridge stared at the screen, watching the battle unfold. *And the next one's for the Naval War College.*

USS *JOHN PAUL JONES*

"You heard the admiral," *JPJ*'s captain said. "Execute strike package alpha."

The ominous rumbling underfoot was continuous now, as the hatches snapped back and vertical launch tubes discharged their missiles. The ship was sealed tight, with positive pressure applied, so that none of the noxious deadly fumes could leak inside. Still, after the first two missiles, a thick fog of exhaust gases enveloped the ship. Visibility ahead was almost completely obscured, and, in anticipation of that, *JPJ* was making only five knots.

Inside Combat, the extraordinary quickly became ordinary. Harpoons were already locked onto the positions of the Indian units, and it was a simple matter to order the execution of each firing.

USS *Lake Champlain,* another Aegis cruiser, joined *JPJ* in executing the attack, adding her missiles to the circle of fire and destruction to the south. Even *Puller* was allowed to participate, firing her Harpoons from quad canisters mounted on either side. The FFG's captain had been so insistent that the admiral had almost been afraid he would want to approach to guns range.

BOGANDDIYA

Perhaps it is a blessing that so few sailors onboard any large ship know exactly what is happening in any one moment. Onboard the Indian ships, those in combat knew immediately what had happened. There was perhaps fifteen seconds for shouted accusations on competency, for angry words of blame to fly, but there was certainly not enough time for them to unravel the puzzle that had taken Lockridge a month to figure out.

Nor was there time for those belowdecks to realize that they were doomed. The ships were already at General Quarters in order to execute their own attacks, with compartments completely dogged down and all battle stations manned. Thus, there was no General Quarters alarm to warn them.

The lieutenant who'd first noticed the anomaly in the American aircraft carrier's course was an engineer. His battle station was in Main Control, and he had slipped out of his chair long enough to take another look at the main condenser. His technicians had finally isolated the problem, a leaky main seal, and drained the condenser in preparation for replacing it. It lay half-dismantled on the steel grating that served as a floor in

Engineering. Four decks below Combat, the compartment was crowded with two massive steam turbines and the associated cooling and lubricating gear. The ship's main shaft ran through the space, coupled to the turbines by massive gear reduction systems.

The first three Harpoons fired at the Indian aircraft carrier were shot down by the ship's close-in weapons system. However, at that range, the shrapnel that shredded the deck and superstructure killed most of the bridge crew and damaged both radars.

The fourth missile hit forward. It slammed into the side of the ship, penetrating three compartments before detonating. It killed the forward damage control party and severed one loop of the ship's fire-fighting system. The remaining teams scrambled to cross-connect the saltwater fire mains and to fight the fire.

The fifth missile, which had been fired by the FFG, hit amidships, skimming just inches above the main deck, clipping a 50-caliber machine gun mount before penetrating a thin steel superstructure. It punched a ragged hole almost entirely through the ship before exploding. The force gutted Combat, killing the ship's captain.

Four decks below, the lieutenant heard the first impact and knew what it meant. He made an immediate, reasoned decision—the ship was going to die, and there was no reason for his men to do so as well. Seconds later, when he heard the second impact, he knew he had done the right thing. His men were already scrambling out of the doomed compartment and heading for their lifeboats.

Their way to the weather decks was blocked by the fireball that consumed the center of the ship. They opened one hatch just enough to verify that, and scrambled back down into Engineering. Using an emergency escape hatch that connected to adjoining compartments, they tried one alternate route after another. Finally, they found a series of connecting hatches through the main shaft alley and crept through it, on hands and knees through foul water, to the aft section of the ship.

There, after unbolting a maintenance access panel not intended as an escape route, they made it to the weather decks.

Out of a crew of over 2000, only 428 men made it off the ship alive. Most of them were engineers.

USS KENTUCKY

Without warning, the ocean above erupted into explosions and the eerie groaning squeal of metal breaking up. The acoustic signature for the contact designated as *Lincoln* peppered that line of bearing with noise spike and transients, visual translations of the sounds of catastrophic damage. The main propulsion gear components showed abrupt decrease in speed then ground to a stop.

"She's hit, *Lincoln*'s hit!" Beavers said. He turned to stare at Tran, his eyes mirroring the horror he saw in his captain's face.

Tran's face was cold and alien. For just a moment, Beavers got a flash of the crushing responsibility the man bore.

"We're going to finish what they've started," Tran said. This was why submarines accompanied the battle group. Silent, and located, they could, under the worst circumstances, exact a telling vengeance.

Did the Indians even know they were here? Tran doubted it. There had been no indication that they had been detected, no sign of circling helos, no sonobuoys in the water, no targeting-mode sonar. No, he suspected they were unlocated.

As they should be. For times just like now.

His mind flashed back to *Mahan*. In an instant, he made his decision.

"*Boganddiya*—two torpedoes. Depending on what the submarine contact does in response, we'll deal with her next."

USS *LINCOLN*

Admiral Fairchild watched the pictures being fed back from the TARPS-equipped Tomcat. They were live, transmitted digitally, and displayed on TV screens inside CVIC. BDA—battle damaged assessment—instantaneously.

He saw the crew swarming over the decks, now deployed in a terribly familiar configuration. They clustered in groups of twenty to thirty along the edges of the ship, near the water line.

"Abandon ship—my God, it doesn't look that bad," Admiral Fairchild said.

In his mind, it had not been necessary to sink India's aircraft carrier. Just put her out of commission after making her show her hand. There was no way to avoid doing that without killing someone, but in the back of his mind he had decided that the casualties would be proportionate to the damage inflicted on *Mahan*.

Mahan. He turned to look at her skipper, half-afraid of what he would see on Lockridge's face.

USS *KENTUCKY*

"Tubes flooded." The sonarman's voice sounded almost mechanical, so often had they rehearsed this very evolution.

Captain Tran nodded. "Weapons free—sonar, you have permission to fire."

The noise of the first shot penetrated the steel hull of the submarine. A slight rattle, not nearly as dramatic as it should have been, given the firepower of the weapon. A second rattle, then, "Bridge, Sonar. Tubes two and four fired."

Captain Tran took three steps and pulled aside the curtain at the end of the compartment that comprised Sonar. Squiggly green lines traced their way down the waterfall display, the torpedoes hunting their quarry. The sonarmen had their hands poised over their headsets, ready to rip them off at the last moment. Even without the headset, they would probably be able to hear the impact. Or at least see it on their displays.

Captain Tran watched the torpedoes race straight for their targets, reflecting with satisfaction on the probable reaction onboard the target ships at this very moment. It served them right, the bastards. The shot that killed them would be as unexpected and deadly as the one that had hit *Mahan*.

USS *LAKE CHAMPLAIN*

''Torpedoes. *TORPEDOES.*'' Onboard *Lake Champlain,* the sonarman's first word was soft, almost unbelieving. The second was a scream that everyone in Combat heard even without headsets on.

Lake Champlain's captain turned, stunned. He heard the TAO behind him rap out an evasive maneuver order to the bridge and order the countermeasures deployed. The hard, staccato electronic beat of the collision alarm followed shortly after. The captain turned back to the TAO.

''Shut that thing off. If it's an acoustic homer, the last thing we need is more wire in the noise,'' he bellowed.

The TAO nodded and complied

Lake Champlain was now rocking hard to starboard, making a sharp turn to cut back over her own wake while quickly accelerating to flank speed. Four gas turbines were online now, and the two massive propellers beat hard against the water.

The captain grabbed one arm of his brown leather chair and steadied himself against the motion of the ship. He turned back to the large-screen display and stared, horrified, at the symbols racing toward his ship.

USS *LINCOLN*

''What the hell?'' Fairchild shouted.

Lockridge had his hands clamped over his headset as he

listened to the USWC&R circuit, his eyes wide and horrified. "*Lake Champlain* says it's not an Indian torpedo—they use a Soviet-made variant. It's one of ours. *Kentucky*—Admiral, we didn't tell her!" Lockridge shouted, straining to be heard over the voices and alarms now filling the compartment. "Admiral, what did you say?"

"*Kentucky*—my God." Only Lockridge, standing next to the admiral, could hear the quiet oath that followed. Fairchild looked at Lockridge, his face stricken. "She was too far south, not a part of the operation. She must have come up, taken our LINK positions, and figured they were real. And decided to settle the score on her own."

USS *KENTUCKY*

The two torpedoes circled in an ever-increasing spiral. There were a multitude of targets in the area, far too many for their simple brains to sort out. Still connected to *Kentucky* by a guide wire, they maintained their search patterns, waiting for the operator on the other end of that umbilical to make a decision.

The one nearest to *Lake Champlain*'s first noisemaker disregarded it immediately. It was too loud, the sound source too consistent to be a real target. American technology had advanced to the point that decoy-discrimination circuits were built into the tiny minds of each weapon. This one, the first torpedo decided, was not a target. It veered away, still in search mode.

The second torpedo, farther away, was not as certain. It broke out of its search pattern and headed for the noisemaker. Most of the other targets were too far away, and of the ones remaining this one, with its constant tonals attenuated by distance, was the most attractive. Two thousand yards away from the noise source, the second torpedo reevaluated the contact and concurred with the first torpedo. It broke off its approach, seconds before the operator could intervene, and returned to a search pattern.

Onboard *Kentucky,* the sonar operator, who had done this far too often in simulator drills, found reality much tougher than a training problem. Even with the assistance of the rest of the sonar crew, it was increasingly difficult to keep the big picture, to focus on which sonar blips were contacts and which ones were noisemakers. He had, in submarine vernacular, lost the bubble.

He diverted his attention momentarily from the second torpedo, concentrating on the first. It was the closest to a real target, and the sonarman entered a course correction, guiding it into a deadly accurate intercept. Satisfied that it would reach its target with no further intervention, he snapped the guide wire and turned his attention to the second torpedo.

USS *LAKE CHAMPLAIN*

"Now!" *Lake Champlain*'s skipper ordered.

The helmsman slammed the helm all the way over to starboard, jamming the rudder mechanism aft into the stops. The captain could hear it as it hit the stops, a hard sound that rang throughout the ship. Now if only it didn't jam there—the danger of that was the reason that hard rudder orders, those that exceeded in degree the normal maximum rudder order, were rarely used. If they lost maneuverability at this point, it was all over.

Lake Champlain cut hard to starboard, heeling violently into the water. "Starboard engine back full," the captain ordered, using the power of the shaft to further steepen the turn.

Lake Champlain canted at a twenty-two-degree angle, then slowed slightly.

"Rudder amidships," the OOD shouted. He was standing on the port bridge wing, looking back down their wake, judging the exact moment at which it would be safe to come out of the turn and return to top speed.

The reported top speed of the Aegis cruiser was thirty-two knots. They had topped that slightly during engineering trials, as well as during work-up operations. Even then, though, they had maintained all safety precautions, including watching the temperature of the oil flowing over the shaft bearings.

Each ship had a margin of safety built into it, a capacity in capability that the designers prayed would never be needed. A few more knots—the captain was counting on it now.

USS KENTUCKY

The first torpedo, which had been happily following along its target's wake, was now confused. It was approaching the intersection of two swaths of roiled water, one slightly more disturbed than the other. Still, the difference was not so great as to enable it to be certain. Internally, it debated a moment, then compared the angles of each wake to the course it had been following earlier. It reached a decision and bore to the right, heading back down *Lake Champlain*'s wake and away from the cruiser.

USS LAKE CHAMPLAIN

"It worked." *Lake Champlain*'s captain experienced a moment of triumph as he saw the small, deadly form just under the surface of the water veer away. By God, it did work. The torpedo evasion maneuvers that they'd practiced so many times, had had so many doubts about—in the end, it had worked better than any of the decoys or the Prairie Masker gear.

Now for the decision. Sonar had made clear that it was an American submarine doing the firing. A mistake, but no less deadly for being unintended.

What now? Take a shot at *Kentucky*, convince her that continuing the attack would lead to her own death? Or hope that someone, somehow got the word to her before she fired again?

They had already tried Gertrude—it had been the first thing he'd thought of. But at these speeds, the noise over the hull would mask out any communication almost completely. So there was the choice; slow down, get on Gertrude, and hope to show the submarine the error of her ways before the submarine took another shot, or simply try to evade her.

So far, running had worked. And each minute at flank speed put that much more water between his ship and the attacker. But by the time they were out of range of the submarine torpedoes, it would certainly be too far to use Gertrude.

The men and women on the ship were his responsibility—but so was the well-being of the aircraft carrier. The captain quailed inside, and reached a decision.

"Right full rudder." The words were out immediately, before he could give himself more time to think about it. Meeting the panicked gaze from the officer of the deck, he said, "You heard me. We're going back in. And we'll kill *Kentucky* if we have to, to keep the carrier safe."

USS *LINCOLN*

"Torpedo is at eight thousand yards, Admiral. It's acquired us. Or, at least I think it has—there's no way to be certain." The voice came from the USW module, which had now been patched directly into a speaker in TFCC. The limited duty officer lieutenant in charge there had had fifteen years of experience as a sonar enlisted man before being commissioned. "I'm recommending we try evasive maneuvers as well."

It won't work, Lockridge thought. The maneuvers depended on speed and maneuverability, not something a carrier was noted for.

His anger grew to the boiling point, threatening to spin out of control. It was one thing to train against enemy attack, to prepare for those moments that one hoped would never come. But when it was one's own country, and you were fighting against people just as well trained and equipped, it simply wasn't fair.

And not just the submarine. No, it wasn't *Kentucky*'s fault at all. It was the War College's—*dammit, they were supposed to train us not to get killed. Not to kill each other.*

Deception, double-cross, and treason. No matter who would finally take the blame for *Kentucky*'s attack on her own battle group, everyone in TFCC knew who was really responsible.

The Naval War College. And no matter what else happened, Lockridge intended to see that they paid for it.

The deck of the carrier was slanted, an odd and unsettling sensation. Even in the rough seas, you rarely felt the deck move, not in this massive floating office building. It was clear that the officer of the deck on the bridge—certainly accompanied by the captain of the ship by now—was going to try everything he could, including crossing his own wake.

Not that it would work. No, they had outsmarted themselves by trying to deceive the War College.

Deception—that was the key. Too much of it.

"Admiral," Lockridge said, his voice cutting through the noise and din coming out of the speakers. "There's only one way out of this. We have to correct what we created. They're working off the false LINK picture we injected. You know that submarine skipper—his cover is blown now, he thinks India's diesel submarine is in the area now. He won't stop shooting until he has to. We have to tell him the truth."

"And just what do you suggest?" Fairchild snapped. "We can't get through on Gertrude—and there's not time for anything else."

"Take *Lincoln* up to top speed and run her straight at the submarine," Lockridge said, feeling the rightness of his recommendation as he said it out loud. "Strip off the deceptive lighting—light up everything you've got on the flight deck, everything on the mast. Tell the other ships to do the same. *Kentucky* will hear us, and I have to believe that the men on her are smart enough to know what an aircraft carrier—a U.S. aircraft carrier—at top speed sounds like. We've got to give her more data so she'll realize who we are. She'll be uncertain enough to come up and look before she takes another shot—Admiral, it's our only chance. We can't kill our own sailors. Not like the War College did."

Officers do not get selected for flag rank if they have difficulty making decisions. Fairchild reached for the tactical net mike. "All stations this net, this is Alpha Alpha. Turn on every light and every active sonar you've got. And stay clear of *Lincoln.* We are approaching datum."

USS *KENTUCKY*

"*Jesus.*" *Kentucky*'s leading sonarman ripped his headphones off and moaned. But quietly—that habit that was so deeply ingrained that not even the agony pouring into his ears, amplified by his signal processing system, could force him to break it.

He moaned again, ears still ringing, as the sonarman standing behind him snatched the headset, turned the amplifier gain down, and tapped him on the shoulder. The headset was all the way on the second sonarman's head before the first moved out of the way.

The active sonar scope in front of him bore mute witness to what had happened to his shipmate. Bright noise spokes, concentric rings of sound minor lobing across the spectrum showed a surging tide of acoustic water energy being dumped into the water. The sound was evident through *Kentucky*'s hull as well—hard, ringing strokes that echoed off the submarine.

The sudden onslaught had caught the first sonarman unaware, but the second was prepared. He kept his hand poised over the amplitude controls, not trusting the automatic gain control circuits within the sonar suite.

The classification was so quick, so automatic, that no one had to think about it. The first sonarman whispered it to the captain, not even able to hear it himself over the ringing in his ears. "Those are American, Captain. SQR-89 sonar. I'm certain of it."

Tran stared, aghast. "They can't be. All of our ships are to the north. We're attacking an *Indian* aircraft carrier."

The sonarman shook his head. "No, sir." Now there was agony in his voice, and not from the blasting sounds that still rattled his brain. "The target's coming straight toward us now at flank speed. It's *American*, Captain. It's *ours*. I'd stake my life on it."

Ten minutes later, *Kentucky* hovered silently at periscope depth. After a final clearance from Sonar, the captain extended the low-light night scope up, peeking just barely above the waves, and ran it around in a complete circle. He stepped back from the periscope, leaving the scope extended and visible above the water. Every set of eyes in the control room was fixed on the TV monitor slaved to the periscope. They all knew what he had seen.

The ocean around them was ablaze with light and ships. American ships. Even from this distance, the periscope could pick out the number outlined in bright lights on the aircraft carrier's island—73. They had taken a shot at the USS *Abraham Lincoln*.

Captain Tran spun back around to Sonar. "Call off those torpedoes!"

The sonarman's key hand was already poised over the key. He flipped it clockwise in one motion, pulling the headset away from his ears as he did so. A spike of noise waves, louder than the active sonars, flashed across his sonar screen. "I got the second one—the first bit a decoy."

"Surface the ship," the captain said. He sat back against the navigator's chart table, horrified beyond imagining. "I think I'm going to have some explaining to do to the admiral."

USS LINCOLN

To the captain's surprise, Admiral Fairchild did a good deal more talking then he did asking questions. When the brief, surprisingly pleasant conversation was concluded, Tran was surprised to find himself still in command of USS *Kentucky*.

And with new orders.

26

USS *MAHAN*

India's forces were arrayed around the crippled carrier. *Bo-ganddiya* was still afloat, but probably not for much longer. The remaining Indian forces were too busy ferrying off the crew and tamping down the fires that spewed out from her flight deck to concentrate on the American ships in the area. Lockridge had finally convinced Fairchild to let him get back to his ship.

Getting back to *Mahan* was a good deal more complicated than getting to *Lincoln* had been. *Mahan*'s crew had restored enough of her engineering capability to enable her to cast off from the tug for flight quarters, but she could make barely eight knots under her own power. With the helicopter hovering astern of her, the OOD experimented with courses until he was generating acceptable wind across the deck. While helicopters were far less critical about wind over the deck than fixed-wing aircraft, they, too, had their preferences.

Finally, they made their approach. *Mahan* was still listing three degrees to port and the decision was made that it would be safer to lower Lockridge and Tinker to the deck in a horse collar rather than risk the approach.

Lockridge stood framed in the hatch, staring down at the ship. They'd worked miracles to get her in this good a shape at all in the time that had passed, and he could not help feeling a surge of pride in his remaining crew.

Evidence of the damage was still visible. Smoke scars and twisted metal blackened her deck, and the gaping hole in her port side, although patched and watertight for now, shone like a malignant tumor. No radar antennas turned, and the approach was conducted on ship-to-ship channels rather than a dedicated flight-control circuit. Among the most critical losses onboard *Mahan* were her communications gear, particularly the classified circuits, and the damage to the sensors.

"Now, sir. Hands crossed over your chest, that's fine." The flight crewman supervising his descent stood next to him, attached to the aircraft by his own safety line. "Should go just fine. Remember, they have to touch you with the grounding wire before you hit the deck, so you may be hanging around while they do that. Don't get worried about it."

Lockridge nodded. It had been years since he'd done the horse collar transfer but he remembered the routine all too well.

"Okay, just step out, sir. I've got you." Odd how reassuring the words of a very junior petty officer could be, but this was his area of expertise. Lockridge relaxed slightly and stepped off of the aircraft into thin air.

He immediately looked back up at the impossibly thin wire connecting to him to the helicopter. The helo appeared to be rotating in midair, although Lockridge knew that it was he who was turning. Then the swinging started, gently at first, his arc growing longer quickly. Nausea assaulted him, washing over him in waves. He shut his eyes and said a silent prayer that he wouldn't puke.

Something hit the wire above his head. He chanced looking down, certain that he would get sick if he saw the deck spinning under him. The flight deck crew was just removing the grounding rod from the flight deck.

The deck was spinning faster now as he swung back and

forth over it, descending on each arc. Finally, on one fly-by, a sailor caught hold of his legs. For a moment Lockridge thought the force of his swing would pull them both over the side. Then others piled on, hands clamping down onto his cotton khaki pants, some of them leaving greasy marks as they skidded across the cloth.

Finally, his feet touched the deck. He stumbled and two sailors held him upright. One stepped back, rendered a crisp salute. "Welcome back, sir. We kept her afloat for you." Four bongs sounded over the flight deck speaker. "*Mahan*—arriving."

Lockridge returned the salute. "It's good to be back, Maguire. I—" He stopped, about to apologize for having left at all, for having abandoned them to a critically injured ship. But the look in Maguire's eyes stopped him. Something—pride, perhaps. Self-satisfaction, surely.

He hadn't really left after all. Even with only a couple of months onboard, the ship was already his. His character, his way of doing business, was what had kept them afloat, made them work against the odds to restore the vestiges of combat power. He'd been here, the myth of the commanding officer, even if his body had been elsewhere. For the first time since the missile hit, he felt Fireman Irving's presence start to recede.

"The ship looks good," he said finally, and saw the nod of satisfaction from Maguire.

"She does at that, sir."

"She'll look better after we unpack a few crates." Lockridge looked up, then waved at the helo crew. Tinker was hanging in midair, waiting for the flight deck crew to ground him.

Seconds later, Tinker was on the deck. The man who'd helped him into the horse collar already had the first packing carton staged at the hatch. He waved back, motioning Lockridge off the flight deck.

"Sir, we'll take it from here," Maguire said.

"Yes, of course. There's engineering gear in there, the cards for the fire control system, and it all needs to go to—''

''Sir.'' Maguire looked faintly offended. ''We can handle it, sir.''

Lockridge felt an inescapable sense of pride. Yes, they could handle it. They'd done a fine job so far and the last thing they needed right now was his presence on the flight deck, fouling the drop area with his lack of safety gear and micromanaging the under-way replenishment. ''I can see that. Very well, I'll be on the bridge.''

Lockridge turned and walked toward the hangar. It took all his self-control to avoid doing two things: looking back and crying.

It wasn't easy, not by a long shot. *Mahan* had sustained damage in virtually every part of the ship. Some of it had been minor and quickly repaired with supplies onboard. Other injuries, like the damage done to the electronic components and to the radars, not to mention the patched gash in the ship's side, were either beyond their technical capabilities or repair-part critical. While some of the sailors could repair microcircuit cards, none of them could build them from scratch.

At least so Lockridge had thought. Walking through Combat now, seeing what miracles they'd wrought, he wasn't so sure of that.

The SPS-48 radar was up and running, although the -49 was beyond hope. The scope slaved to the -48 was fuzzy and shaky. The edges of the picture quivered uncontrollably, and there was a dead spot near the left lower side of the screen. The combat information system had no IFF capabilities, and the target acquisition and automatic firing circuitry that was the hallmark of the Aegis system was inoperative.

Still, they'd achieved miracles. The Harpoon fire control system was up, as were the close-in weapons systems. In the opinion of the chief gunner's mate, the 5"54 would be good for a couple of rounds as well, although he held out no hope that it would last long. The barrel was warped, not badly enough to prevent firing it at all but enough so that the heat generated by expending rounds would probably cause it to shatter at some point. "Give you some ranging rounds, sir, but not so sure about the fire for effect ones."

Lockridge could only stare. Even that was far beyond what he'd hoped for.

The missile fire control system was the critical item in *Mahan*'s list of casualties, and the crew had saved that part of the briefing for last. The senior missile tech onboard, a grizzled chief who might well have been in the Navy before missiles even existed, had the most impassive face Lockridge had ever seen on a sailor.

"Our capabilities are limited, Captain," Chief Armstrong began. "I guess you've heard that often enough in the last hour to know what that means on *Mahan*."

"It means someone's worked a bloody miracle, Chief, if the previous briefings are any clue." Lockridge shook his head, still stunned by what they'd accomplished.

"We'd done a lot, but we were missing a few key computer cards, sir. Those ones that you brought with you. We installed them right off and started running system tests. I can give you two functional cells, sir, that's all." Chief Armstrong's face was chagrined.

"*Two?*" Lockridge couldn't contain the grin that split his face. He felt the tears of pride crowding his eyes again, blinked a few times, then said roughly, "I think two will do just fine, Chief. Just fine."

Lockridge handed the scribbled sheet of paper to his new communications officer. "That's what we came up with. Get copies to all the watch stations, hold whatever briefings you need to. We'll get one shot at this, no more."

Tinker nodded. "This will work, sir. I'm sure of it."

The arrogance of youth and genius. Wonder what he'll be like in a few years? Probably a civilian, back at MIT. Damned shame to lose him, though. I wonder if— Lockridge cleared his throat. "Petty Officer Tinker? Anyone ever talk to you about commissioning programs?"

Tinker flushed. "No, sir. Chief Bell says I don't play well with others and that a wardroom would eat me alive."

"Ah." Lockridge considered this for a moment. "Tinker, I'm about to commit heresy, but I want you to hear this: sometimes chiefs are wrong. When we get this all sorted out, we're gonna talk."

When we get this all sorted out—and when might that be? Lockridge sat alone in his cabin, staring down at the timeline they'd worked out with the Army sergeant on the ground. One shot, and one shot only at getting this right. The plan had too many contingencies, too many things that could go wrong. For starters, it depending on the Indian Navy staying out of the way.

Now, that just might be achievable. According to what he'd been told, the Indians had circled *Mahan* and maintained a guard on her for the first few days. When it became apparent that the ship was barely afloat, and after having their offers of assistance firmly rejected, the ships finally left. Headed south, no doubt, to join the Indian carrier battle group, leaving the wrecked *Mahan* as a matter for shore-based SAR to deal with when the American ship's crew eventually gave up their fight to stay afloat.

But the crew hadn't given up. Hadn't made the call for rescue that India had expected. They'd been smart about it, kept their progress secret from the increasingly less frequent coastal patrol boats that bombarded them with offers of rescue.

As a result, *Mahan* was a derelict to the Indian Navy. There was no indication from the outside that she was at least partially functional. Radar tests had been conducted in stages, with the power to the arrays in test mode so that no signals radiated, and rotation tests of the actual masts conducted at night. There'd been no test firing of the 5"54 gun, no dry runs on the CIWS. They'd given their adversaries no reason for suspicion.

So it was at least possible that at the critical moment there would be no Indian Navy vessels in the area. At least not at that moment.

But Lockridge had no illusions that the entire evolution could be conducted without any response from the Indian coastal forces. They were too close-in to a vast number of patrol boats that could carry shoulder-mounted antiship missiles, Stingers, any variety of weapon sold on the open market. At the very most, *Mahan* might have fifteen minutes to prepare herself for the counterattack.

When we get this all sorted out . . . Well, the most optimistic outcome would be that most of his sailors were able to abandon ship before *Mahan* sank.

The crew knew it, too. He could see it in their faces, in the grim determination with which they approached every task. Tomorrow would be *Mahan*'s last mission, and they intended to make it count.

Lockridge closed his eyes again, summoning up Fireman Irving. In the last two days, the dead sailor had become less of a nightmare and more a source of inspiration. The face Lockridge saw now was the open, smiling face of the kid from Kentucky who'd just checked onboard his first ship, eager, dedicated. Overlaying that was the grim visage of a warrior after revenge.

"This one's for you, Fireman Irving. I think you'd be proud of your shipmates," Lockridge whispered. He thought he saw the fireman nod.

27

BANGLADESH

Khan was almost back at the former Bengali camp when the first missile passed overhead with an angry, sucking buzz, louder and more menacing than a mosquito. It moved quickly, the sound cycling down like a train passing by. Ten seconds later, noise and flame erupted on the horizon. The ground shook under their feet. For a moment, Khan didn't associate the two, the angry insect and explosion.

Missiles—but what kind? They had to be Indian—Bangladesh possessed no more firepower of that sort. Everything they'd had was at the forward camp and had been destroyed in the helicopter attack.

So the missile had to come from an Indian unit by process of elimination. But why were they firing on their own front lines rather than targeting the few remaining Bangladesh fuel depots or military fortifications left standing?

Another missile, landing closer this time. Kahn abandoned his questions and ran for his life.

When he got to battalion headquarters, he was surprised to see it still standing. Odd that none of the missiles had even come close to touching the ramshackle collection of tents.

Nor were the few remaining staff officers scrambling for
their lives. Instead, they stood outside the tents, cheering and
screaming. Khan stood at the edge of the clearing, gaping at
them. One of them saw him and motioned him over, including
him in the celebration.

"It's the Americans!" The jubilant officer said. "They're
taking care of the Indians—if anyone can, they can. They were
poised to attack—four battalions, just ten kilometers away."
A familiar figure stepped forward. "Welcome back, son."
Master Sergeant Elwell said. "About time you got here."

"What is happening?" Khan stuttered. "How did you—"

Elwell shrugged. "Remember what I told you about having
some friends in the area?" He pointed out toward the sea.
Khan could see the damaged American warship still on the
horizon. Smoke drifted around her hull.

"The ship?" Khan asked.

Elwell nodded. "Don't ever count an American out of the
battle until you see his grave."

USS LINCOLN

Along with the rest of the staff, Admiral Fairchild watched
the pictures being transmitted back from the unmanned aerial
vehicle—the UAV. The image was surprisingly clear and
sharp, with little instability due to the vehicle's own motion.
There had been some debate about sending in a Tomcat, but
Admiral Fairchild had pointed out that the Indians still possessed some inside—air missiles, and, under the circumstances, he suspected that they would be most eager to use
them. There was no point in wasting a costly aircraft, not to
mention the lives of aviators, when the UAV could do the
same job.

The information from Elwell at the Bengali headquarters
had been critical. Once they had established communications
and managed to convince the Bengali leaders that they were

who they said they were, the response had been over-whelmingly positive.

The Bengalis, trapped and desperate, were more than eager to provide targeting coordinates. Because of their extensive experience with United Nations peacekeeping forces, they were completely familiar with targeting protocols and report-ing when working with the United States Navy.

The Tomahawk missiles fired by *Mahan* had done the trick. Not only had the sight of missiles boiling out of the Indian Ocean convinced the Indian task force that their only chance for survival was to turn and run, but the word soon made it to the Bangladesh forces that America not only cared, but cared enough to send her very best.

The effect was devastating. The Bengalis had done a mas-terful job at providing coordinates, and missiles impacted in the center of a formation of tanks only four kilometers at that time from Bengali headquarters. From what Fairchild could see, the remaining opposition forces were in disarray.

The UAV flew over the battlefield for nearly an hour, evi-dently virtually undetectable by Indian antiair radar. Finally, when its fuel was almost exhausted, the operator onboard *Lin-coln* flew it back out to the ship and brought it to a skidding halt on the flight deck.

Bailey finally broke through the crowd of excited staff members to reach the admiral. She could see that the admiral knew what she was going to ask, if not exactly why.

"Okay, what is it?" the admiral demanded. Bailey could see the trace of victory still flushing the admiral's face, the brilliant sparkle in his eyes, the relaxed lines of his face. No, winning wasn't everything—it was the only thing.

"I need an aircraft. And some time," Bailey said, not both-ering to lead in to it easily. With the attack ashore stymied, she felt a growing urgency beating inside her brain. The War College—given enough time, they could put the correct spin on this as well. How, she didn't know, but they were masters of deception. She had to get back to the War College, keep them from destroying the evidence of what they had done.

Had to—and it had to be now. If they waited any longer, it would be useless.

Admiral Fairchild nodded, as though he had expected the request. "You know, of course, that I could take care of this," he said, in a tone of voice that indicated he did not expect Bailey to believe him but felt obliged to trot the argument out anyway. "After what I saw, I can call in some big guns. Maybe not as big as NSA, but bigger and in the political arena. There will be an investigation, indictments—you know I can do it. I can have every law enforcement agency flooding the War College within minutes."

Bailey studied him for a moment. "You can probably get it started, Admiral. But it will take time. And that's the one thing we don't have, any more than those Bengali troops did. They don't know what they're looking for, either. By the time they get the entire college shut down, Gromko and his people will have this whole thing covered up. You know I'm right."

Admiral Fairchild scowled. "You don't have much faith in me, do you?"

Again Bailey shook her head. "That's not true, Admiral. When it comes to executing a war at sea, I trust you probably more than any man I've ever met. You listen to common sense, and aren't afraid to make decisions. I would be honored to serve with you again, Admiral, under any circumstances." Bailey took a deep breath, felt the rightness of what she was about to say. "But we're both over our heads on this one. Even you, no disrespect intended, sir. Unless I get back there fast and do something about this, there won't be any evidence left. If we move now, before they have a chance to dissemble everything, we have a shot."

"What about NSA? A few phone calls, and they could have the entire complex packed with federal agents, don't you think?"

Bailey shook her head again. "Same problem we're going have, Admiral, if we go to the official way. Nobody is going to believe us at first. By the time they're convinced, it'll be too late. Don't you see?" Bailey's voice ended on a pleading note. "If we're going to stop it, if we're going to have to prove what happened to *Mahan,* we have to do it now. No chain of command, no federal officers, and no publicity. We just do it. Just like you sent me to get Lockridge out of the War College."

"Easier to ask for forgiveness than permission, is that?" the admiral asked. "How much time do you need?"

"Forty-eight hours, Admiral. Half of that the travel, the other half—well, if it's going to take longer than that, we're out of luck."

The admiral sighed. "For the sake of expediency, just assume I've made every argument you can think of."

"I'll testify to that—if it comes to it."

For a second time, the admiral surprised her. "You will do no such thing. I explicitly forbid it. If asked, you'll tell the board of inquiry exactly what happened here. You got that, lady?"

Bailey nodded, at a loss.

The admiral continued. "An S-3 will be at your disposal in approximately fifteen minutes. If you need weapons, see the SEAL team rep between now and then. I will arrange for tanking support en route to Hawaii. From there, you will have two government transportation requests waiting for you at Hickum. In return, I expect an immediate phone call via SATCOM from you the moment this matter is resolved to your satisfaction. At that time, I will quit stonewalling my own superiors and start answering questions. Forty-eight hours—no longer."

"Thank you, Admiral. I owe them—you know that."

"And now you owe me. Go on, get out of here. The phone call—don't forget it."

"Speaking of the telephone—Admiral Monarelli for you on STEL, sir." Captain Sirtus held out the telephone.

Fairchild picked up the receiver, held it to his ear for a moment, then pulled back from it with a grimace. "Alan," he said loudly, "stop shouting. I'm not deaf. Now, what's all this about?"

Fairchild listened for a few minutes, a grin spreading across his face. "Turned and ran? No kidding? About what you'd expect, isn't it? They did that during Desert Storm as well." He listened for a while longer, then hung up the telephone after a few words of congratulations. He turned to his chief of staff.

"You're not going to believe this. Moanin's air wing ran a three-nation strike force into the ground. They'd already made one bombing run on some targets in Kashmir, and Moanin' caught them launching for another one."

"No shit. Wow. Who would have thought?" Sirtus said. "No disrespect to Admiral Monarelli intended, sir."

Fairchild waved off his apology. "India had a couple of carriers in the area, but Monarelli convinced them to coordinate the retaliatory strikes."

"He's working with India's forces?" Sirtus's face grew serious. "That's a problem for us, then."

"I don't think so," Fairchild said thoughtfully. "Pakistan's a long way from Bangladesh. Different interests at stake. And India knows that in the end she's going to have to live with us in the world. A nation's policies don't always have to make sense in a larger context."

"But we're going to—"

Fairchild waved him off. "Look at it this way. We were enforcing the no-fly zone over Iraq to protect the Kurds a few years back, right? Remember what we were doing with our oh-so-great ally Turkey?"

"Looking the other way while Turkey bombed the hell out of them," Sirtus answered.

"So how's that so different from what we're doing right now, with us holding India off in Bangladesh and *Eisenhower* supporting India's retaliation against Pakistan and the Middle East?" Fairchild sighed and leaned back in his chair. "It's no different, not to me. We're getting no guidance out of D.C. because they can't figure it out themselves. They're controlling us by negation, waiting for us to flush things out so the State Department can step in and pick up the pieces. But first there've got to *be* pieces to pick up. So we're on our own. And unless I hear otherwise, my plans haven't changed." The admiral's face was grim. "They owe us for *Mahan,* even if it was the War College's fault. And they're going to pay."

28

THE NAVAL WAR COLLEGE

Bailey slept. Shortly after the excitement of the catapult launch from the aircraft carrier, she found her eyes drifting shut. The drone of the aircraft's engines, the gentle rocking in the air, and the silence of her companions all combined with her exhaustion. Before the carrier was even out of view, Bailey fell asleep.

She woke up four hours later to the pilot's voice crackling over the interior communications system. They spent thirty terrifying minutes—terrifying at least to the non-aviators—sucking fuel from a KC-135 Air Force refueler before returning to the course that would take them to Hawaii. The pilot woke her again thirty minutes out from Hickum, his peeved voice indicating more clearly than his words how much he appreciated spending the entire nine hours talking to himself. Still, the prospect of a two-day layover in Hawaii did much to alleviate the ill will.

They were cleared to land immediately. A Navy lieutenant was waiting for her in the passenger terminal, holding a cardboard signed with the word *Lincoln* emblazoned on it. Bailey spared a second to admire Admiral Fairchild's discretion.

There was at least a good chance that the name Bailey was persona non grata at every military base around.

The lieutenant asked no questions. She handed Bailey two Government Transportation Requests and said she would take her to the airport. Bailey glanced at the flights—she had only one hour before she would be en route the mainland. Precious little time to plan anything.

On the other hand, precious little time for the War College to interfere. Unless they had already—

"And your identification, ma'am." The lieutenant driving the car passed her a manila folder containing a military identification card. There was not a trace of curiosity in her voice.

Bailey examined the tickets again. How Admiral Fairchild had managed to pull this off on short notice—well, that was a story she would have to hear. Maybe when she made that phone call. At any rate, she had a new name, one that matched the name on her airline tickets. Jerusha tucked them into her jacket pocket.

The lieutenant pulled up to the front door of the terminal and started to hop out and open the door for her. Bailey forestalled her with a gesture. "Thank you—for everything. Someday, maybe I can return the favor."

The lieutenant shook her head. "Not unless I joined the Navy, ma'am. I don't need to know."

Bailey took another look at the woman's uniform and revised her opinion of Admiral Fairchild upward.

It felt odd to have thirty minutes left to kill. Jerusha went to the gate, obtained her seating assignment, then wandered around the terminal until she found a Starbucks coffee stand.

Finally, boarding for her flight was announced. Bailey proceeded past the gate attendant, handed over her ticket, and felt slightly surreal as the flight attendant said "Welcome aboard, Ms. Smith."

Jerusha had an aisle seat. She could feel the caffeine starting to kick in, her mind racing now, going over the possibilities. Eight hours back to the mainland, another six to New York.

From there, she would rent a car, drive the rest of the way rather than risk the T.F. Green Airport.

If the admiral's preparations were any indication, she might have some problems getting back to the base. He had gone to the length of obtaining fake ID for her. Did he know something, had he heard something since she'd left the carrier?

No, probably not. The S-3 was equipped with secure communications. If the admiral had needed to get word to her, he could have. Just routine paranoia, then. Again, Bailey wondered how he had managed to pull it off.

The rental car—she would have to use her own credit cards for that, and her own name was on her driver's license. She checked the package again, wondering for a second whether Admiral Fairchild had been able to pull that off as well. But evidently the admiral figured if she could get that close, she was on her own.

She needed a plan. Whatever she was looking for had to be in the battle lab or in Gromko's office there. She had access to most of the building—at least she did if they hadn't purged her from the data base—but the most highly classified areas had retinal scanners and keypads at them.

Was there anyone she could trust? Not outside of NSA, and even there the revelation that even Pete's office was monitored bothered her. There was no doubt that Atchinson would do anything he could to stop her, just on general principles. Any professors? No, there was no telling who was involved. Same thing for her fellow war-gamers. Even if there'd been one she thought she could trust, would she want to put them at risk as well? More than that, jeopardize their chances for success by making a mistake?

It had all gone bad from the start, from the very first day that she'd walked into Gromko's office. Something nibbled at the back of her mind. The dean's office—what was it?

Secretary. That was it. The dean's secretary, Helen something. The one who had sympathized with her, the one who had covered up for her. But she was Gromko's secretary. If anyone would be loyal to the dean, it ought to be Helen, right?

Wrong. The longer she thought about it, the more sense it made. The secretary's words of kindness, even in the face of the dean's disapproval. Granted, she had not said them in front him—but then, Jerusha wouldn't have expected her to take that chance.

Besides, Gromko clearly abused her. Jerusha had seen it in the way he talked to her, treating her as though she were a piece of furniture. Yet she had been there her entire working adult life, had seen deans come and go. If there was anyone who knew where the skeletons were at the War College, Jerusha thought it might be her.

Twenty-six hours after she'd left *Lincoln*, she was in a rental car approaching the Jamestown Bridge, fighting off the bone-deep weariness that the naps on the sequence of flights had done little to dispel.

Jerusha paused before she headed over the bridge. So far, there had been no sign of pursuit. But now she was approaching the lion's den. She remembered that the helicopter chase and Gar's rescue. What were the chances that the War College was on alert even now?

She eased back onto the road and started over the bridge. From the high point on the bridge, nothing ahead looked suspicious. Then again, she couldn't see that much at night.

Finally, she crossed the last bridge into Newport. The town was still awake, teaming with summer visitors. Drunken students and yuppies wandered the near-dark New England streets, staggering down the sidewalks and yelling. It would be easy to get lost in the throng, pass as a tourist, and find somewhere to sleep. For a moment, her weariness threatened to overwhelm her.

But then again, her odds of breaking into the War College might be better at night. There would be no one around to give the alert, except for some particularly overachieving students. No one to notice a rental car, to supplement whatever security measures were already in place. Perhaps she should take the break-in route after all, try something on her own before trying to find Helen.

No, she had a plan. Best stick to it. With a sigh, she turned off on the side road that led to Helen's house, trying to remember the details.

Helen's house stood far back of the road, screened from the traffic and tourists by a thick hedge. The driveway, however, was not gated, and Bailey pulled the rental car into it.

The house was small but immaculately maintained. The lights were off, the curtains drawn. Only Helen's Toyota parked next to the side entrance made it clear that it was occupied.

She turned off the engine, got out of the car, and walked up to the door. She took a deep breath, then knocked.

After a few minutes, Helen opened the front door clad in her bathrobe. With her hair down, mussed around her face, she looked years younger than she did in the office. With a start, Jerusha realized that she was not much older than she was herself.

Helen looked astonished to see her, and then scared.

"Don't worry," Jerusha said quickly. "I'm sorry to bother you, but it's urgent. I don't know what they told you at the school, but whatever it was, it wasn't true. But I need your help—there is no one else I can ask." She motioned back toward the car. "All I ask is that you let me tell you what happened. Please, I won't hurt you. If it were so important—"

Helen held up one hand to forestall her comments. She stared out at the rental car, then squinted back at her. "You're in a lot of trouble, but I guess you know that. And I didn't believe everything I heard at the College, not at all. I never have, you know." She squinted up at Jerusha, her eyes unexpectedly friendly behind the glasses. "Come on in—oh, before you do, pull the car back around house. No point in taking any chances, is there?"

For the first time since she'd left the carrier, Jerusha felt optimistic.

*   *   *

An hour later, Helen nodded her head gravely. Contrary to what Bailey had expected, the secretary had had no problems believing the story that sounded incredible even to Admiral Fairchild. To the contrary, she appeared relieved.

"It explains a lot," she said finally. "No, nothing specific— and I never would have been daring enough to try to find out. But you hear things." A small, wistful smile on her face. "The deans—most of them, before, have been nice men. Absent-minded, certainly. They forget things. Of course, they have so much on their minds. One can't really expect them to . . ." Her face closed off, and Jerusha wondered how many small courtesies forgotten and unintentional slights she had endured during the past decades. "What I mean is, you forgive them a certain amount. Because of who they are, what they have accomplished in their lives. And for the War College. They're always so smart—brilliant, really."

"But Dean Gromko was different?" Jerusha probe gently.

Helen nodded. "For one thing, he used the secure telephone much more than the others. I was in and out of the vault every day, checking out the crypto key for him. Lots of secure telephone calls, and not always in English."

"But most of the deans speak a second language, don't they?" Bailey asked. "Dean Gromko more than others, I guess."

"Of course, I know that, Commander." There was gentle reproof in her voice. "But one becomes accustomed to the rhythms of running the dean's office, the way things are done. It is the academic background, I believe, that makes their habits so similar. But not Dean Gromko's."

"So these telephone calls—they weren't normal, is that it?" Jerusha asked. "What else?"

Helen flushed gently. "There was the matter of . . . of . . . inappropriate relationships. You know."

From the look on her face, Bailey could guess what inappropriate relationships met. "With the students?" she asked.

Helen shook her head. "No. With the faculty. I could hear them in his office."

Now, that was interesting. And Gromko had chosen Maderia to show Jerusha around, hadn't he? Maderia had made a point of staying in touch with her.

And what had Maderia said about the battle lab? That it was the wave of the future—a place for a dress rehearsal of the future. That was it—and her primary duty, in addition to teaching classes, was as part of the battle lab.

So maybe part of her duties was keeping an eye on Jerusha Bailey. Not that they were worried Jerusha would stumble onto their secrets—no, they thought they were too good for that. It was the disaster with *Mahan*—had they planned it the way it happened? Or had it gone too far, got to of control? She debated for a minute, then decided that the only thing that had gone wrong with *Mahan* was that there were survivors.

That must have been what really worried them—how much did Lockridge remember? What did he see? Did they slip up somewhere, make a mistake that he might remember? No wonder they were so eager to get Jack back to the War College. Not so that he could help other officers keep from making my mistakes—so they could keep him from exposing theirs.

"I wish I could do something else to help," Helen said finally. "It's going to be over, you know. I can't continue working there—not with what I know now." She gave a nervous laugh, then said, "Perhaps I can take sick leave for a while. He will see it in my face, you know. I've never been very good at hiding things."

Bailey leaned closer to her. "I think you underestimate yourself. I suspect you're very, very good at hiding what you don't want other people to see." That earned her a shy, slightly startled look from Helen, gratifying in and of itself. "But there is something you can do to help. And you're probably the only one. We have to put a stop to this, you know we do. But if we give them time, they will find a way to cover it up. No one knows that better than you."

"Oh, no. I couldn't," Helen began. "You're not going to—"

Twenty minutes later, Jerusha had her convinced. Jerusha explained how the people in India and Bangladesh had suffered, the children left homeless, the pitiful tin shacks ruined. Jerusha talked about *Mahan,* the agony Lockridge had suffered over the attack, and finally—Fireman Irving. Haltingly at first, and then with the words overwhelming her, Jerusha told her Lockridge's story about the young sailor's last hours. By the time she finished, Jerusha was fighting back tears and Helen was openly sobbing.

Jerusha promised Helen complete immunity, the witness protection plan, and her cooperation if Helen decided to write a book, the latter conditions dependant completely on the matter being unclassified. That, Jerusha knew, was a long shot.

They would take Helen's car, since it had a base sticker. Even given the lax security at the main gates, it was better not to take chances.

Nineteen minutes later, they pulled up in front of the Battle Lab. Helen parked her car in the visitors lot, made some half-hearted last-minute protests, then led them to the front entrance. "It is very secure, you know," she explained. "But, as I said—completely automated. The alarms are monitored at the OOD desk at the War College, but there is no separate security staff. If we can get past the scanners inside, and no one else is here, we should be fine."

"Only two other cars in the parking lot," Jerusha noted.

Helen nodded, then said, "The first floor is underground parking. The entrance is back behind those bushes. Maybe twenty parking spaces—all for professors, of course. None for support staff like myself. These are probably for the janitorial staff, and they'll never say a word."

"Can we get into the parking area?" Jerusha asked. "Be nice to know how many people are inside."

"We don't have time. The longer we spend around here, the more likely it is that things will go wrong. Let's just get in and get it over with. I'll try the retinal scanner. Here goes nothing.''

She walked to the front entrance and up to the retinal scanner. She bent over, placed her right eye against it, and waited for moment. A red light over the door flashed green and she pulled in the handle. She motioned Jerusha inside ahead of her. Helen had said that there might be acoustic monitors outside of the building, and they should not talk unnecessarily once they were around the building.

Jerusha followed her into the building, moving quickly. They had agreed that they would go immediately to Gromko's office. Helen had the key to it.

Another retinal scanner protected the door to the office spaces. Helen handled that one, too, then clicked out a quick pattern on the cipher lock. She shoved the door open. She stepped inside then motioned to Jerusha to follow her.

29

THE NAVAL WAR COLLEGE

"What are we looking for?" Helen asked.

"I don't know." Jerusha felt her frustration building. Now that they were in Gromko's office, she had no idea.

And that had been a real bright move on his part. What did you expect to find, a wall chart detailing the attack on Mahan? *A DayRunner notebook, with a notation on the To Do page: Sink USS* Mahan? "I'll know it when I see it."

"What makes you think it'll be in his office at all?" Helen asked. "It could be locked up in the vault—that's where it should be if it's classified above just secret."

"No, it won't be where anyone else can get to it. The Battle Lab does plenty of projects that are legit. It's Gromko, a few others—the key decision makers, the ones he can trust. And his former students from India." That much Jerusha was certain about. Gromko trusted no one—no one that he thought was capable of playing this game on his level. People like Helen Tarkin didn't count in his world.

"The safes are all locked," Jerusha noted, twisting the black knob set into the top drawer. She sighed, rummaged through the few papers left out on Gromko's desk. "All routine administrative stuff, nothing of interest here. So what now?''

Helen was fidgeting next to the doorway. ''I don't know—one of them might be the same combination as his safe in the office. We could try it.''

Bailey stared at her for a moment, chagrined. Just as she'd been damning Gromko for not recognizing Helen's importance in the scheme of things, she'd made the same mistake herself. ''Go ahead, Miss Davis.''

Helen stepped around Jerusha and approached the smaller safe set behind Gromko's desk, ignoring the larger, three-door one against the wall. ''It's just that—well, you know that they're absentminded. You tell them and tell them about security, but it doesn't seem to sink in. They use the same combinations all the time—too much trouble, too many great thoughts crowding their minds to remember a couple of extra numbers, I suppose.'' Her thin, pale fingers were manipulating the numbered dial deftly. ''I've seen him open his office safe before—it might take me a few tries.''

She'd just started to spin the dials clockwise for the second time when they heard a door creak open out in the hallway and the sounds of voices. Jerusha shot over to Helen, clamped her hand over the woman's mouth, and pulled her down on the floor behind the desk.

The voices moved down the hallway, approaching them. Most of them continued on. There was a soft scuffling outside Gromko's office, then the hard click of the cipher numbers being punched, the quick rhythm of someone so familiar with them that it was a sequence of finger movements rather than individual numbers. The door lock clicked, then the door pushed open. The light came on.

Jerusha stood up.

''Dr. Gromko,'' she said, her voice calm and steady.

There was a pause that stretched on too long. Finally, Gromko said, ''We don't allow guns in these spaces, Miss Bailey. You know that. What are you doing in my office?''

''You know what I'm doing here. Why don't you explain

everything to me so I can quit searching your office?''

''Why don't you explain first what you're you're looking for?'' Gromko glanced at the weapon in her hands. ''And put that down. Immediately.''

''I think I'll keep it, thank you. And yes, perhaps you could help. I need the file on *Mahan*.''

''The details of our conclusions on the *Mahan* incident are available on the web page now. I don't know why you think that you needed to—''

''Not the public story. The real one.''

To his credit, Gromko didn't pretend ignorance. Instead, he smiled. ''Ah, I shall win my bet. I thought you would eventually figure it out.''

His confirmation chilled Jerusha more than any file or document could have. ''Thanks for the vote of confidence. So what was all that crap about promising to support the War College's position?''

''Hardly crap, as you put it.'' Gromko frowned. ''Though if that's what you thought it was, I am disappointed. You did keep your word, did you not?''

Jerusha nodded. She'd trod perilously close to the edge of it, but she felt that she hadn't broken her promise. ''In ways you can't imagine. So tell me, why *Mahan*? What was it that you were worried that Lockridge had seen that night? The fishing boats?

''He was *supposed* to see the fishing boats. You have to understand, *Mahan* was the end of years of research. It was, of course, my idea. The concept of the flashpoint in conflict, that one event needed to spark war, was mine.''

''Who's paying you, Doctor? India? Or the Middle East?''

It was Gromko's turn to look puzzled. ''Pardon?''

''You'll have to come up with a better answer before your trial. *Mahan*. You knew the Indians would attack, correct? How much lead time was there? Enough to warn *Mahan*?''

''Why would we have done that?'' Gromko asked, genuine puzzlement in his voice.

Cold rage ran through Jerusha's body. She clamped her

hands down on her weapon to still the tremors. "I guess you're the kind of spy that stays bought, then. I'm asking you again—*how long did you know?*"

Gromko threw back his head and laughed. Jerusha stared incredulously. When he finally stopped, he said, "I'm afraid I counted my money before all bets were in. So close and so wrong."

He took a step closer to her. "But very close. Closer than anyone has gotten before. That's why I let you go to the carrier, Jerusha. To see how far that agile mind of yours would take you. I had your word on it, and I trusted that. Sooner or later, your doubts would bring you back here."

"Stay where you are," Jerusha ordered. She resisted the impulse to glance behind her and make sure that Helen was still hidden.

Gromko waved one hand grandly. "Your tour in purgatory is over. Come back to us, Jerusha. Take your place on my team."

What did he mean, so close and so wrong? There's something here I'm not getting—everything is off-key. And why is he so confident?

"I'm no traitor."

"Neither are we." Gromko sighed heavily, then gestured at the couch along the wall. "May I?"

"Go ahead."

After he'd settled onto the cusions, Gromko studied her for a moment. "Define the the term *traitor*."

"From now on, the dictionary will have your picture next to the word," she said. For a moment, she thought again about Helen, still crouched behind the desk.

"Not at all," Gromko said, his voice mild. "Patriot, perhaps."

"You're not from India and I don't see how Ukraine's involved."

"Oh, come on, Jerusha. Surely I taught you better than that. You think I would take money to betray the United States?"

Gromko chuckled. "Look at the bigger picture. What has all this proved?"

"That the LINK is vulnerable to intrusions. That you sold crypto secrets and material to a foreign government and set *Mahan* up to be attacked."

Gromko shook his head. "Not at all. What this proved was that the flashpoint for war is considerably lower than I originally thought. It's a good thing we ran the experiment—a lack of hard data could have led to terrible miscalculations."

"Miscalcula—You didn't," she said, horror dawning on her face. "You had India take a shot at *Mahan* just to test one of your theories?"

"That's it," he said, his voice evincing nothing more that his customary self-satisfaction. "Worked well, don't you think? The data we retrieved was well worth the price we paid. With the Lancaster Equations refined by actual experimentation, the War College will truly hold the keys to peace in the world." He leaned forward on the couch. "That was the problem with the original formulas, of course. They were developed after World War I and refined after every major conflict. *After,* Jerusha. There were no controls, no measures of success, no controlled variables. They did the best that they could with what they had, but their resources don't begin to compare with what we've got today. And in the years to come, we'll have even more resources."

He stood and walked slowly toward her. "Join us, Jerusha. Be part of the first real revolution in military affairs. With knowledge comes power, and I am going to make the United States the most powerful nation that has every existed."

"What would it involve?" Jerusha asked, feigning a glimmer of interest. "Your team, I mean."

"More than you ever dreamed of. As I said, you are so close and so wrong. I'm willing to overlook that flaw in your reasoning, given what you've accomplished so far." Gromko edged forward. Jerusha slid her finger inside the trigger guard.

"It sounds tempting," she said. To her horror, it did. "You've defined the variables that allow you to predict war—

minor conflicts of other types, too, I would suspect. And you're asking me to join you in refining them.''

Gromko shook his head. ''Still trapped by your own concepts of fair play. War is never fair. It is the one constant in humanity and yet you seem to think that fair play enters into it. The American preoccupation with justice would have been her downfall in the next century.''

Another step forward. ''We don't predict war, Jerusha. We don't analyze the variables and find ways to stop it. That would be as dangerous as welding a lid on a boiling pot.

''We set the back fires, activate the safety valves that blow off the pressure harmlessly and prevent greater loss of life. In short, my dear—we don't predict wars.

''We start them.''

30

Jerusha's horror threatened to overwhelm her. Gromko's pride in what he'd done, Lockridge's tortured nightmares of Fireman Irving—her mind reeled, trying to reconcile the two images. "You bastard. You unspeakable bastard."

Gromko darted forward, far too quick for the large man that he was. His hand reached out for the gun, closed around the barrel, and started to jerk it from her grasp.

Jerusha fired.

Inside the small, secure office, the noise was deafening. In the echoes of the aftermath, she heard Helen scream.

The force of the impact slammed Gromko back against the door. He hung there for a moment, a look of profound shock on his face, his lips moving silently, then moaned and slumped to the deck. Blood welled up impossibly fast from his shattered chest, turning his white shirt almost black and spilling onto the carpet in front of him.

Gromko kept his eyes fixed on her for a moment, then his eyes went blank. He toppled sideways onto the carpet.

"Are you okay?" Jerusha asked, turning and walking back to the desk. "Helen?"

The secretary was pale and crying, verging on hysteria.
"No, I can't believe it. It didn't—how could he—you shot
him." She looked up at Jerusha, her eyes flooded with tears.

"I had to. He grabbed the gun. You heard, though. You
heard everything."

There were shouts and the sound of people running outside
the office. Jerusha pulled Helen up gently from the floor. "I'm
sorry I got you involved in this."

Helen shook her head. "I heard everything. The dean, the
War College—he's dead, isn't he?"

"He is. But it's not over. We have to straighten this out,
find out what else is happening before it's over."

"I heard everything," Helen said. "Everything." She took
a deep breath and seemed to reach for some inner source of
strength. "I'm not sorry you shot him, Commander. In a way,
it was kinder than what would have happened to him if he'd
lived."

"It was a kinder way to die than he gave those sailors on
Mahan," Jerusha said, her voice hard. "He had choices. They
didn't."

"I only have one question, Commander." Helen looked
away. "What if I hadn't been behind the desk? He offered to
make you part of it. Would you have said yes?"

Jerusha shook her head. "No. When I kill, I stop wars. Not
start them."

She looked up at the clock, did the mental subtraction, and
nodded.

Like Lockridge is doing right now.

31

USS *MAHAN*

Lockridge watched the minute hand click over to the twelve. It was time for *Mahan*'s last fight. A brawl more than the integrated and computerized war he'd trained for, but a fight nonetheless.

He and the TAO were standing behind the one working radar console, a mass of cannibalized parts and dangling wires. If anything, the picture had degraded slightly over the last twelve hours. The screen now flickered dark occasionally, and the few track identifications that the operator had entered by sheer reflex showed no indication of staying slaved to any particular radar blip.

"How long have we been up?" Lockridge asked, more to give the TAO something to focus on than anything else.

"Twenty seconds. It's working, sir, from what we can tell. The lookouts have two fishing vessels." The TAO pointed to two blips on the screen. "The bearing's off by twenty degrees, but it looks to be a constant error. We can correct for it manually."

"Very well."

It shouldn't take them long. They have electronic intercept systems, they'll understand what an SPS-48 detection means coming right after a land attack. Thirty knots at least—a couple of minutes, no longer, even if they're in port right now.

"Sir, I have them. I think." The operations specialist pointed out a cluster of small radar contacts on his screen. "About twenty-five knots, I made it." He cocked his head and listened to the headset. "Lookout's got them, too. A cruiser and a destroyer flying India's flag, just coming up over the horizon. Three smaller patrol boats with them. They're all at flank speed, bearing constant, range decreasing."

Lockridge turned to Chief Armstrong. "You ready?" The chief grunted an assent. "All right, ladies and gentleman. Let's show these bastards the error of their ways. TAO, you have weapons free."

"Weapons free, aye, sir." The lieutenant's voice was steady, unnaturally so. Lockridge could only imagine the effort that it took. "Chief, designate targets—oh, hell, no track numbers. Call them skunk one through five. Take tracks one through five inclusive with Harpoon."

Chief Armstrong, seated partway across the compartment in front of the Harpoon console, repeated back the order. He stood immediately behind the sailor actually operating the fire control panel.

"*Vampire*—correction, multiple vampires. Incoming missiles!" the radar operator shouted. "Sir, coming off those patrol boats."

"CIWS is in full auto," the TAO said, reaching out to touch the fire control key on his console as though for confirmation.

"Three miles."

"Three miles—acknowledged."

"First Harpoon away."

The quiet voices echoed the litany of the drills they'd practiced so many times. Order, confirmation repeated back, reports of firing—all flowed smoothly, as though they were operating with a full crew manning all consoles instead of a few technicians crouched over half-assembled gear.

Mahan shuddered more violently than she ever had during

practice live-fire exercises, the tensile strength of her hull stressed almost to breaking. Lockridge listened to the sick groans and squeals of metal parting from hasty weld, the hard explosive snap of damage-control spars giving way.

"Flooding at frame eighty-three. Repair two responding."

Lockridge acknowledged the report without looking at the woman manning the sound-powered phones. "Five minutes, no longer. After that, they clear out from below the water-line." He'd been tempted to leave the damage control lockers unmanned completely, not wanting to risk one more life in this suicide mission, but the crew had resisted to the point of mutiny. They'd gone through too much to save *Mahan,* and they weren't willing to let her die without at least trying to resurrect her one more time. In the end, Lockridge had capitulated, but insisted on volunteers only. It didn't surprise him when every last sailor volunteered.

"CIWS tracking—engaging," the TAO reported. A hard buzz-saw whine cut through the compartment and the automatic Vulcan Phalanx identified the incoming target as meeting missile parameters and spewed out a stream of depleted uranium pellets at it. Seconds later, the CIWS on the other side of the ship kicked in, stuttered, then fell silent.

"Got one!" the TAO shouted. The ship's hull rang as debris from the missile peppered it. "And a second one."

That left two more inbound.

The starboard Phalanx cut out then, leaving an eerie silence in its wake.

The Harpoons. Please, dear Lord.

Seconds now before they knew. The crews onboard the patrol boats would be shouldering a second set of Stingers, locking onto *Mahan* at this very second. It made his skin crawl to think of them sighting his ship in the crosshairs, placing fingers inside the trigger guards, and then—

"Get everyone out of here," Lockridge ordered. "Be ready. I want the lifeboats in the water as soon as—"

The nightmare began again. Fire, flames, and the noises that wiped out everything in the world. The starboard bulkhead

disintegrated, spraying shrapnel across the compartment. The
screams again, the darkness alleviated only by light streaming
in through the holes, so unnatural and bright.

"Sir?" a voice said. Lockridge felt someone tug on his
sleeve. "Sir, we have to get out of here. Are you ready?"

"*No*. The Harpoons. I have to wait."

"They were all good shots, sir. Every one of them. You got
all of them, sir. Thank you. Come on, now. Let's go."

The words brought Lockridge an odd sense of peace.
"You're certain?" *How could he know from inside Combat?
The radar picture was gone with the first shot. How can he—?*

Lockridge turned to face the voice and stared into the smiling, unmarked face of Fireman Irving.

32

NAVAL WAR COLLEGE

Jerusha tugged open the steel door that led into her spaces at NSA. The analysts and clerical workers gathered around the coffeepot fell silent, their last words seeming to echo in the space.

"Welcome back, Jerusha," one said, breaking the spell. A chorus of greetings followed, the words tumbling over her to hold back the silence.

"Thank you. It's good to be back." And it was, she realized, as she stared at them. Even Atchinson—something in his face told her that they'd come to a turning point in their relationship, and that it had less to do with Intanglio than it had to do with the last conversation they'd had before she left. He'd even shown up for the memorial service held at the Pentagon for the men and women killed on *Mahan,* and Jerusha had seen him try to comfort one of the sailors that had survived.

She glanced at her friends, her coworkers. Even Pete had left his lair on the upper level to come down and greet her. She started toward them, then changed her mind and walked up to Atchinson. "Good morning, sir." She held out her hand.

Atchinson paused for a moment. "Welcome back, Miss
Bailey. Good work." The tension bled out of the atmosphere.

"Thank you, sir."

"Don't overdo it. One sir a day is enough."

The trip back to the States, the shock of learning Jack Lockridge had been killed on *Mahan,* and the business of wrapping
up the operation at the War College had delayed her return to
NSA. During those last days, the extent and true nature of the
War College's operations had shocked the nation and rocked
the defense establishment to its core. Ugly surprise upon ugly
surprise, the roots to so many of the minor regional conflicts
planted firmly in the files in Gromko's office. And the Middle
East—even in her worst moments, she had not dreamed how
truly evil Gromko had been. So many casualties, so much
waste.

There'd been too many surprises, but finding out that Atchinson might even possess a sense of humor hadn't been one
she'd expected.

She accepted a cup of coffee and a donut from Pete and
was just starting to fill him in when Atchinson tapped her on
the shoulder. "By the way, the rental car. I approved it."

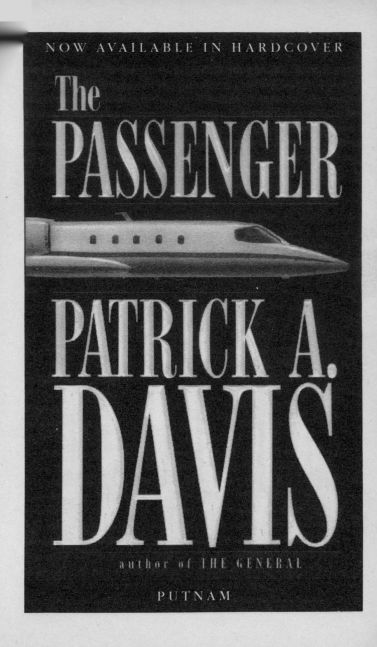

NOW AVAILABLE IN HARDCOVER

GROUND

BONNIE RAMTHUN

A NOVEL

ZERO

PUTNAM